THE
PERFECT
LIE

Also by Jo Spain

INSPECTOR TOM REYNOLDS MYSTERIES

With Our Blessing
Beneath the Surface
Sleeping Beauties
The Darkest Place
The Boy Who Fell
After the Fire

STANDALONE NOVELS

The Confession
Dirty Little Secrets
Six Wicked Reasons

THE PERFECT LIE

JO SPAIN

Quercus

First published in Great Britain in 2021 by

Quercus Editions Ltd
Carmelite House
50 Victoria Embankment
London EC4Y 0DZ

An Hachette UK company

A CIP catalogue record for this book is available
from the British Library

HB ISBN 978 1 52940 724 2
TPB ISBN 978 1 52940 723 5

This book is a work of fiction. Names, characters,
businesses, organizations, places and events are
either the product of the author's imagination
or used fictitiously. Any resemblance to
actual persons, living or dead, events or
locales is entirely coincidental.

10 9 8 7 6 5 4 3 2 1

Pr   .A.

Pap   rests

For all my friends and family across the sea

PART I

The Lie

Erin

THEN

JULY 2019

The day your life changes can begin in the most ordinary way.

Danny's arm is draped across my body and I wake to the feel of him stirring.

His hand cups my face. I sense he's actually been awake a while; that he might, in fact, have been watching me.

'You had a nightmare,' he says.

I crawl into the space of his body and inhale him.

I had a nightmare, again.

I never have to pretend with Danny.

My husband knows my history, all the things that haunt me.

The bad dreams are frequent, even after all this time. The feeling of being suffocated, of screaming but no sound coming out. The feeling that there's nobody there to help.

Danny, too, has seen evil. I guess it's what drew me to him.

My parents might struggle to forgive me for emigrating to this side of the pond but I made a decent dent in hostilities when I married a cop.

Danny kisses away the residue of the dream and then we make love, slowly, at his insistence.

He's intense, quiet; there's meaning in all his movements and his eyes never leave mine. Danny's had a lot on his mind recently. Work, long hours, late nights. There's ongoing trouble in his job but we don't talk about it. Our promise to each other is to keep his work and our home life separate. But I've barely seen him these last few weeks and last night we exchanged only a few words. I guess both of us are due a reminder that it's us against the world, even if the world keeps intruding.

When we're done, he rests up on one arm and tickles my nose with his. His forehead is damp; his eyelashes long enough to make any woman jealous.

I laugh – a giddy release.

'Hey!' he says.

'I'm laughing with you, not at you, Detective,' I say.

'Mm-hm. How do you want your eggs?' He jumps up, an athlete's recovery time, asking for my breakfast order but, I can tell, already distracted by the day ahead.

'From a chicken,' I say.

'Duck, you sucker,' he shoots back. Then, hesitantly, 'Sorry.'

'For not giving me an orgasm?'

He smiles, but his eyes don't play ball. Danny is drowning. He needs time off; I know he does.

'For having to leave you,' he says. 'I love you.'

'The bed's not the same without you, but I'll forgive you if you get the coffee going.'

Danny heads for the kitchen and I lie there, listening to him tinkering with the temperamental coffee pot, then padding towards the bathroom down the hall. I hear the sound of the shower being turned on. It needs a full three minutes before it reaches any temperature above freezing.

The bedroom is already awash with sunlight, even though it's barely 7 a.m. I ordered the drapes online and their blackout ability was oversold. It bothers Danny more than me; he's a light, restless sleeper. I love waking to sun, I love waking to rain. Let it all in. Be happy to be alive.

It feels like a good day. Hell, I might go on that run I keep threatening. On the beach, before the tourists hit. Then I'll read through some manuscript submissions and check in with the office – the joy of working from home and making my own hours. When we first moved here, I commuted daily to the city and the publishing house I work for. Three hours a day on a train to and from paradise. I'd planned to go freelance but my boss offered option C and I've never looked back.

I force myself to sit up and search the floor for clothing, find Danny's T-shirt and a pair of leggings.

In the large, open-plan area that comprises the main living space of our top-floor apartment in Newport, Suffolk County, I'm faced with the detritus of last night's takeout. White cartons and plates congealed with chow mein and egg fried rice. I glance at the sink, already overflowing with crockery, and then at our faulty dishwasher and sigh.

Part of the lease's selling point was all mod cons included.

I turn the dial on our old-fashioned radio to listen to the local morning news programme, then make a start.

What our apartment lacks in efficiency, it makes up for in location. Our pretty white-painted building, with its black Georgian-esque ornamental window shutters, has an unimpeded view of Bellport Bay, right over to Fire Island. We're a minute's walk from the beach, its miles of grassy dunes and white sand; two minutes away from McNally's, our regular bar; and we've a host of restaurants and stores at our disposal.

This town is a picture-perfect diorama of a Long Island seaside port and our apartment is slap bang in the middle of it.

I open the floor-to-ceiling French windows to admit some of the already hot summer's day and let the salty sea air hit my lungs.

The news programme is hosting a panel discussion and I listen as a contributor, who's also running for office, gets stuck into Newport PD. They discuss the latest hot controversy – the failure of the local PD to deal with an increase in drug dealing, a problem that's spilled over from Nassau County. The locals in these parts get quite agitated about tourism-impacting headlines and this issue is definitely a vote-getter. Another of the panellists is shrieking about ineptitude and corruption in law enforcement when I turn off the radio.

Danny works in homicide, not drugs, so the latest furore doesn't have direct relevance for him. But attacks such as these put a dent in the morale of every police department. It's hard enough doing an often thankless, frequently dangerous job on low pay without enduring unfounded and ignorant accusations about competence.

I've done a decent surface clean by the time the coffee is in the cups and the shower has stopped running. I wonder if I can talk

Danny out of a quick scrambled eggs and into stopping by the new diner on Maple Street before he leaves for work. We can discuss the long-awaited weekend we have planned. Danny has vowed to take next Saturday through Monday off. We're going to drive up to Hartford, stay somewhere quaint, eat and drink our way through New England.

And then: a cop's knock on the door. Quelle surprise.

They have a special sound, those fists the police learn to make.

I mutter under my breath. It's not even 7.15 on a Tuesday morning and already Danny's being summoned for work. Bang goes the dream of us sharing pancakes.

Another rap on the door, seconds after the first.

Fuckity fuck, I'm coming.

I can hand over my detective husband for the rest of the week, I remind myself, because then he's all mine for a good seventy-two hours.

I ignore my inner warning system, reminding me of all the other times in the last two years when I forgot I was with a cop and made plans.

I open the door and see Ben Mitchell, Danny's partner, standing there.

Danny told me that when they were first paired, back in homicide in Manhattan, the boys on the force used to hum 'Ebony and Ivory' every time the two of them entered the office together. Ben's blond and his skin is practically translucent. Danny is as black as night. There wasn't a whole lot of woke thinking behind that one.

The two men work well together, but Ben and I don't. I got the sense, early, that he didn't like me. I think it's down to the fact that Danny used to follow Ben around like a little puppy. In fact, Ben's the reason Danny works and lives in Suffolk County. Then I came along and inserted myself in the middle of the bromance.

There are two other uniformed officers in our hallway and Ben has a look on his face that tells me, for the love of all that is holy, something big has happened and the forthcoming weekend is now a non-runner.

I never learn.

Behind me, Danny enters the living space and I know he's seen Ben's face too. He's probably already planning how to make it up to me.

'Erin,' Ben says, his voice grave, 'I'm afraid I have bad news.'

The day your life changes can begin in the most ordinary way.

I've experienced it once before. Just like this, the knock on the door.

I wait for it, my stomach tight, the battle response of a war-weary soldier.

Who's dead?

Ben's expression changes – his attention is drawn over my shoulder, to Danny.

I turn, thinking Danny has caught Ben's tone, recognises it, and is probably readying himself to comfort me. I might be far from my family, but he'll get me to them, ASAP. He'll take care of everything.

But Danny's not looking at me.

He's staring at Ben, utter defeat on his face.

Then my husband walks to the French windows and out on to the small balcony.

I watch him, confused.

He turns, I catch his eye.

Danny doesn't look like Danny at all.

His expression is indescribable. A mixture of pain and apology. He opens his mouth as if to say something, but instead, just swallows. He looks away, like just the sight of me is causing him pain.

He lifts one leg over the balcony.

What the fuck are you doing, I think, but am too confused to say.

Then he raises the other leg so he's sitting on the iron grille.

He uses his hands to push himself off.

He's gone.

Sudden movement at the door as Ben and the others rush into our apartment.

I'm paralysed.

Four floors down, there's a thud.

That's my husband's body.

It's all over in seconds.

Erin

Now

December 2020

Somebody has tried to make the bowels of Suffolk County Court seasonal. A mini Christmas tree looped with cheap tinsel scents the guards' office with pine and a small portable radio is dialled to a station that's playing festive tunes on loop.

Feliz Navidad.

It's incongruously cheery.

I think of Christmas three years ago, the first in our then new apartment. Danny and I had only been married a couple of weeks. I'd picked up a plug-in, artificial, cheap white tree in a thrift store, just to tick a box. I wasn't a fan of the season. I'd fallen out of love with it back in Ireland, right about the time the world had reminded me there's no Santa Claus, no magic, no innocence at all.

Danny, though, was the Christmas fairy incarnate. Six feet of rugged hunk who liked nothing more than watching *Home Alone* while munching on candy canes.

I heard him before I saw him, outside our front door, struggling to get his key in the lock, cursing as he tried to turn it just the right way, jiggling and pushing it at the same time. That door, he was fond of saying, expects you to whisper to it like a lover before it'll open up.

He'd dragged in a six-foot Fraser fir and laughed at the look of surprise mingled with horror on my face.

'We don't have enough decorations,' I'd said. 'And how the hell did you get that thing in the lift?'

'I took the stairs,' he'd replied.

Then he'd wrapped his arms around me.

'She'd want you to enjoy our first Christmas here,' he'd whispered in my ear.

That Christmas, Danny reminded me there was no guilt in living.

He made cinnamon toast, along with eggs, his expert culinary turn, and handed me a beautifully wrapped box. He'd bought me a green cashmere scarf from Barney's, one that would suit my black hair and emerald eyes perfectly. By eleven, we'd had a whole bottle of champagne. Lunch in McNally's with its owner and our friend, Bud, an experience made edible by our inebriation. A heady mix of seasonal cocktails back in the apartment, then some fooling around on the rug beneath the Fraser, during which we discovered exactly what people mean when they say those pine needles get everywhere.

All happy memories.

They make me wince.

Karla arrives and sits down beside me, a billow of ridiculously shiny black hair and expensive material she wouldn't usually wear, smelling of red apples and cold air.

'The blouse looks good on you,' she says, teasing a button closed and tucking my hair behind my ear. Convent girl; that's the look she's going for. She visited yesterday to drop off a new outfit, told me to scrub up so I look like I actually give a fuck about living. She also tried to press a holy medal into my hand but I refused to take it. She can pray to the God she believes in. I'm trusting to the justice system. I'm not sure which one of us is more deluded.

When I first walked into Karla Delgado's office in Patchogue, I had no idea how things would end up. But, within an hour of meeting her, I knew that if I was ever in a corner she was somebody I'd want on my side. At thirty-five, she's only three years older than I, but she's the person I've come to depend on.

I can't lean on my family.

They expect what we got before.

Justice.

They don't understand what it's like over here. They don't understand how flawed the system is.

'Are you ready?' Karla asks.

'No,' I answer, honestly.

She watches me for a moment, knows that I'll stand and walk into court when I'm told.

I've been saying no for the last seventeen months while still putting one foot in front of the other.

She leaves, tells me she'll see me in there.

When I enter the courtroom, I'm taken aback by its size.

It's small – tiny – with wood panelling on the walls, church-like pews, a witness box, the judge's bench, the defence and prosecution tables.

Out of the corner of my eye, I spot some of Danny's former colleagues to the rear of the court. I recognise them, even in civvies. Colleagues and friends, allegedly.

One of them glances in my direction and the others follow his gaze.

The look on their faces.

I turn my head away, heat in my cheeks.

Everybody here wants the truth.

Not all of us agree on what that means.

There's a flutter of activity.

The sheriff appears, announcing Judge James C. Palmer. A native of Sag Harbor, Karla tells me. Yale law and renowned prosecutor in his day. Experienced, conservative, but fair.

Karla crooks her arm under mine to help me stand.

It's time.

I'm about to be tried for murdering my husband.

Erin

THEN

When I first met Danny, in the summer of 2017, I was on a night out with a mission to find a New York firefighter for my sister, Tanya.

She'd flown over for a long weekend and after ticking the tourism boxes with an open-top green-line bus tour and burgers in the Empire diner, we'd headed to a bar in Tribeca where my co-workers assured me all the hot emergency responders hung out.

'Does it have to be a firefighter?' I asked Tanya. 'Will you settle for a Navy Seal, or, I don't know, a meter maid? Is it just the uniform?'

Tanya slammed her tequila and surveyed the room.

'My ass is on fire and I need somebody to—'

'Thank you, that will do.' I cut her off.

I ordered two more tequilas, wincing at the thought of what the night was doing to my credit card. I'd moved quickly up the ranks of the publishing house I worked in but I was at least a year off becoming a senior editor and my junior salary just about covered my rent and a basic social life.

Tanya had already gone to mingle by the time the drinks were served, and by mingle, I mean Captain Ahab leaving port to hunt Moby Dick. She returned with two men, one whose name I barely caught before she had her tongue down his throat (our mother used to warn us kissing could get you pregnant and with Tanya, you could see why). The other, Danny, was meant for me, even if I hadn't asked for him.

'FDNY?' I asked, taking in his wide shoulders and strong arms.

'Nope.'

'NYPD?'

'Close.'

I frowned.

'Newport PD,' he said.

I snorted my drink.

'You're a hick.'

He watched me, quietly.

'I'm from the city. Served NYPD up until a few months ago. Nothing wrong with wanting a quieter life.'

'Yet, you're drinking here. Get sick of the moonshine out in the sticks?'

He laughed.

'Danny Ryan,' he said, holding his hand out.

'You're kidding,' I said.

His face filled with amusement.

'What's wrong with my name?'

'Your name is more Irish than mine and I'm named after the country. You're not really called Danny Ryan?'

'You think I can't be from Ireland because I'm black?'

I blushed.

'Relax, Irish.' He smiled. 'I'm not going to cite you for hate crimes.'

I laughed nervously, hoping he was joking. It was something I was still trying to get my head around, living over here. Wit and sarcasm is carved into our DNA back home but most of the Americans I worked with were straighter than the Stanford Linear Accelerator.

'Might have to arrest your sister and her date for lewd behaviour in a public place, though,' he said, a smile on his lips as he sipped his Sam Adams.

'Isn't he a cop, too?' I asked.

'He's a court clerk, I think,' he answered.

A room full of public service men and my sister had inadvertently stumbled upon the only other civilian apart from the bar staff.

'I've no idea where Ryan comes from,' Danny said. 'But maybe we're cousins?'

I watched his face closely. Okay, there was humour there. Humour, and total fuck-me eyes.

'How long are you staying, anyway?' he asked.

'I live here,' I said. 'My sister's the tourist.'

And with that, the most glorious grin broke out on his beautiful face.

'Well, then,' he said.

'Well, then,' I replied.

'No thinking,' he said. 'Your favourite movie ever.'

'A Fistful of Dynamite. Do I pass?'

'Duck, you sucker.'

'You're a fan?'

'James Coburn doing a dodgy Irish accent, Rod Steiger in any-thing, Sergio directing and Ennio Morricone scoring. It's the best film of all time.'

The next morning, Tanya had to get her own hangover pain relief drugs from Walgreens.

Six months later, we got hitched.

Marry in haste, my mother always said, repent at leisure.

When I wake in the back of the stationary ambulance, the para-medic tells me I've been out cold for thirty minutes, but my head feels so fuzzy, he could have told me thirty days. I try to talk but my tongue is too large for my mouth and I can taste something metallic. I blink, realising that I've been given something. The pinch on the front of my hand confirms it. A cannula is taped there and the paramedic holds me gently, but firmly, as I lift my head and try to see what else has been done to me.

Where's Danny?

And even as the thought enters my consciousness, the heat drains from my body and I see it all over again: his eyes as he looked at me one last time, his leg swinging over the balcony.

Him jumping, me falling.

It was a nightmare, wasn't it?

Then Ben is standing at the ambulance doorway and I know it happened, because otherwise Danny would be in here with me, holding my hand.

'What . . .' I croak.

'Is she okay?' he asks the man tending to me.

'Small bump on her head from the fall; I've given her a mild sedative so she's probably a bit groggy, but fine.'

'Is Danny okay?' My voice is small between them.

Silence. The paramedic looks away. A barely perceptible shake of Ben's head.

'Is he . . . ?'

I can't even finish the sentence. All I can think of is the verge of concrete that separates our building from the landscaped gardens that surround it.

'I need to see him,' I say, hauling myself into a sitting position, my limbs so limp and heavy I can imagine this is what paralysis feels like.

'You can't see him,' Ben says, which infuriates me just enough to send adrenaline shooting down my legs and get me standing.

'I want to see his face!'

'You can't,' Ben says.

Doesn't matter. I'm fighting. I try to get out of the ambulance, screaming blue murder, sobbing, as the paramedic and Ben restrain me.

He's only thirty-three. Danny is only thirty-three.

He cannot be dead. You can't just . . . die.

'I have to see him!' I yell. 'I want to be with my husband! I want to see his face!'

'Four floors, Erin,' Ben cries and there's enough emotion in his voice to bring me to a halt. 'You don't want to see him. You . . .'

His voice trails off. My head is swimming, filled with a whooshing sound that makes him sound much further away.

'You wouldn't recognise him,' Ben says.

They don't bring me to hospital. I refuse to go.

But they won't let me back into our apartment, either.

I have nothing with me. No phone, no purse, no keys.

No husband.

No answers.

The woman who leases the apartment directly beneath ours comes to wait with me beside the emergency vehicles. She gives me a pair of flip-flops, because I've nothing on my feet. She also brings coffee but I can't taste the sugary sips she makes me take.

Other neighbours hang back, but they're all out, standing by the cultivated shrubbery, hands to their mouths, shock written all over their faces. Even our creepy neighbour from across the hall, the one who watches everything but barely says hello.

Most of the apartment residents knew Danny. They liked having a detective in one of the units – it made everybody feel safer.

Around us, life continues as normal. Bells ring out in St. Catherine's Church, the tip of its spire visible beyond the adjacent park. The small road that leads to the dunes is already filled with cars parked up: family vehicles, their owners on the beach with dogs and Frisbees, barbecues and sun cream.

Yellow tape flickers by the pink hydrangeas at the side of our building.

Four of them have come down now with boxes. I recognise them – they're Danny's files. I guess they have to remove remnants of his work from the apartment, now he's removed himself from the apartment. They have other things, too. His laptop. His phone. His gun.

His gun was in the safe in our bedroom.

He could have used his gun.

He didn't have to do it in front of me.

I'm resisting, with every fibre of my being, the urge to run at that yellow tape, to dive under it and get to my husband. To lie beside him and hold his hand while all this is happening. To curve myself into his shape and tell him I'm here, that I won't leave him, even if he left me.

It's only abject fear of what I'll see that's keeping me rooted to this spot.

Ben said he landed face down.

I never see my husband dead.

I'll regret this decision for years to come. Forever.

Instead of moving, I keep asking why over and over. What possessed him? Was he possessed?

It's hard to analyse anything when the same horrific scene keeps replaying itself in my head and I'm trying not to scream, not to collapse, not to sob.

Ben walks towards me. The neighbour from downstairs slips away as I take the bag Ben hands me and rummage for my phone, which he's put inside.

The screen is blank. No missed calls, no texts, but then, what was I expecting?

Sure, my world has just imploded, but nobody knows yet.

How could they? I'm the one who has to tell them.

'I don't understand,' I say to Ben.

His face is a mask of professionalism and I want to smack it, to shake some feeling into him. He was there, he watched his partner jump to his death. How is he so calm?

'Are you sure you don't want to go to the hospital?' he asks. 'They can give you something.'

'I don't need anything!' I sob.

'You might, later, to help you sleep. You can go back in, in a while. Unless you'd rather stay somewhere else.'

'What's wrong with you?' I say. 'Did you not just see that? What the hell just happened? You're his partner! Why did he do that?'

'You tell me,' Ben says, and his tone is angry. He turns away so I hardly catch his next sentence. 'You're his wife.'

I drop my bag, phone and all, and grab his arm, my fingers digging into the flesh underneath his jacket sleeve.

'What does that mean? You think I knew he was going to do that?'

'I . . . no. Of course not.'

Ben removes my hand, gently, his face contrite. I think this might be the first time Ben has ever touched me. I've known him almost two years and we've rarely gone beyond spiky small talk.

'It's nobody's fault,' he says. 'When people do these things . . .'

'People?' I echo. He's slipping back into work mode. Giving me the line.

Danny wasn't people. He was my husband. He was a respected detective. He was Ben's friend.

Ben starts to walk away.

A sudden, cold knot of fear tightens in my stomach.

'What was it?'

He stops.

'What?'

'You came to my door this morning. You said you had bad news.'

Ben hesitates.

'It was nothing,' he says. 'Nothing at all.'

I'm thrown.

'Ben, please, when can I see him?'

Ben shakes his head.

'There's going to be an autopsy,' he says.

I can't stay in the apartment that night. Nor in the building, despite my downstairs neighbour practically bending over backwards in her efforts to take care of me.

I need to be on my own.

I am on my own.

Danny isn't just my husband. He's my best friend. He's my only immediate family in America.

Was.

Sure, I have a circle. My work colleagues are all good folk; and all live in Manhattan.

Danny's family is American, but there's nobody close by. He'd been raised in New York but when his mother became a widow she used her husband's pension pay-out to fulfil her lifelong dream of moving back south where she'd come from, but this time to Florida. Danny's younger brother Mike serves in the military and is rarely on US soil.

Danny used to say the force was our family but I never felt that. I wasn't a police wife – I had my own life, my own job. I wasn't into the whole rotating barbecues on the weekend, watching other people's kids play softball, organising trips to Martha's Vineyard together.

In the back of my head, though, I always thought if something happened to him they'd step up.

The female officer who drove me over here is from Danny's precinct. I recognised her, I've seen her plenty of times. But she barely said two words to me in the patrol car.

This place I've made my home feels so very strange to me, right now.

I'm traumatised. I know this. Possibly in shock.

Maybe I should have gone to the hospital.

But I'm not ill. I'm just trying to get my head around the notion that I could witness something so utterly horrific and be expected to keep going. To breathe, stay standing, put one foot in front of the other.

Danny was just seventeen when the Towers fell. His uncle was a serving officer at the time and went down to Ground Zero; he'd helped people. When Danny decided to join the force, Ellis had sat with him and told him that no matter how much physical training Danny undertook, what the job really required was mental preparation.

'You will see things,' Ellis had said. 'And then you'll go home and have dinner and make small-talk and watch movies and act normal. Then you'll be normal.'

Act normal.

Ellis' advice plays in my mind when I check into the ridiculously expensive hotel in Patchogue, because it's the only one that has a room free and I'm lucky to get it. Tourism season.

And I try not to think about driving past this hotel last month and Danny saying he might treat me to a stay here on my birthday.

My birthday is not until August.

Did he know then what he was going to do?

The room is a large double; there are chocolates shaped like roses encased in pink gauze on each pillow, a complimentary fruit basket and mineral water, a large flat screen that welcomes me by name when I open the door.

I sit down on the floor at the foot of the bed and start to dial.

And when I've choked out the words that shatter Danny's family and send my own loved ones into yet another spiral of distress, I crawl into the double bed, still wearing my dead husband's T-shirt.

I close my eyes and I see his face.

I see the look on his face.

It wasn't just apology. Or regret.

Danny looked guilty as he walked to that window.

What did my husband have to be guilty about?

Harvard

December 2016

There had been a point the previous evening, possibly around 10 p.m. but certainly before midnight, when Ally should have confiscated the several unopened kegs at the dorm hangout and put them aside for the next one.

That point had come and gone. Instead, Ally had been the one who'd tapped the penultimate keg and organised a new drinking game, one she'd felt honour-bound to pioneer.

At least she'd had the sense to confiscate the phones first.

Ally had one simple rule for the dorm parties she organised: there was to be no fear of social media shaming to limit the fun.

The role of a proctor at Harvard University involved several, very serious responsibilities.

Guiding the students through academic life; making sure they followed the code of conduct; assisting in college living; mentoring; and of course, an element of being the disciplinarian.

The male proctors had it worse. The jocks didn't take too well to having their independence tempered rather than extended at university. With the girls, it was generally just a battle to keep them safe and focused on studies.

Being a proctor could be hard work, especially when most of the people who got the job were juggling further study themselves. But it also entailed making sure students had fun and Ally's MO was the dorm party. In fact, Ally's student social events had become so legendary, the biggest problem was limiting how many guests the girls could have over. Canaday Hall was not the prettiest dorm at Harvard (the red-bricked, functional-looking building was affectionately termed 'The Projects' by some) but under Ally and several other proctors' guidance, it had become the most popular among the fresher babies.

The popularity came with cons, though. Organising the students' social life left Ally with very little time for her own. Her boyfriend had a proper grown-up, full-time job and it meant that their relationship, which had felt like it was going somewhere good, was currently under strain. She'd missed two calls from him last night alone.

And then there were the hangovers.

That December morning, Ally was paying hard for the wildly imaginative drinking games of the previous evening. The early hours call from Professor Shipton, assistant lecturer of English 42, British Literature from 600 to 1600, didn't help.

'Ms Summers, I thought your phone was going to ring out,' the English professor drawled, as Ally rubbed her eyes and tried to discern if the excruciating banging in her head was alcohol-related or the side-effect of a particularly nasty brain tumour.

'Sorry, Professor Shipton, I was in the shower,' Ally croaked, trying desperately to sound like she was already up and at 'em.

'At 8.30 a.m.? I would have assumed you'd be in the library by now. How *is* the PhD going?'

Ally's jaw clenched. She'd never had Ship, as the students called him, when she'd taken English as a concentration, but he still made a point of inquiring after her doctorate each time they spoke, in what could only be described as an incredulous tone. Her supervising faculty advisor had recommended that Ally ignore him. Professor Aiken reckoned Professor Shipton was envious of Ally's dissertation choice: 'Nothing New Under the Sun: Crime Literature – Boundary-Stretching or Theme-Limited?'

Ally wasn't sure if Ship was indeed jealous or just plain old dismissive of any doctoral student who chose to specialise in crime fiction. She strongly suspected he considered the genre barely a notch above chick lit.

'I'd a late one last night,' Ally replied. 'Didn't put the books down until a few hours ago.'

She felt the silent rebuke on the other end of the phone and reacted with disproportionate indignation.

Ship had no way of knowing Ally was lying.

'Indeed. I can only imagine the stress generated by reading whodunnits late into the night. In any case, the point of my call. Lauren Gregory is one of yours, isn't she?'

Ally frowned. She sat up in bed and placed her forehead against the windowpane, the freezing glass instantly distracting her from her irritation and her headache.

Outside, the snow in the courtyard was at least a foot deeper than yesterday and entirely unspoiled. The joy of a snow fight in a pristine new fall had diminished now that they were ten days into an early freeze. Ally was used to the harsh Cambridge winters but even she'd been taken aback by the sudden onslaught of sub-zero temperatures in early December, after such a mild autumn.

'Lauren's one of mine,' she answered Ship and it came with a flash of memory.

Lauren hadn't been at the dorm party last night.

'What's the problem?' Ally said.

'I was hoping you could tell me. She's been missing lectures.'

'Since when?'

'All week. I've checked with her other professors. Is she unwell? My office has had no communication.'

Ally pinched the bridge of her nose and tried to quell her unease.

'I'll get back to you, Professor,' she said.

'Please do. Lauren isn't somebody I've had to worry about but missing three classes in a row this close to exams is worrisome.'

Now, Ally remembered asking Lauren's roommate about her absence the previous night. Megan had said something about study. Ally took it at face value, even though she knew the two girls weren't particularly close and Megan was unlikely to actually know or care what her roommate was up to.

Ally had, in fact, been planning to suggest a move after Christmas.

It was quite common for freshers to swap roommates after the first few months had passed. The college tried its best to pair compatible students but it didn't always work out. Once people settled in and stopped trying to impress each other, either genuine friendships flourished or strains became apparent. And Megan and Lauren were chalk and cheese.

Within five minutes of ending the call with Professor Shipton, Ally was dressed and making her way towards entryway E and Lauren's room. Canaday Hall worked in such a way that each entranceway – A, B, C, etc. – was separate and there were no internal corridors. It was convenient for fire safety management but, more importantly, it allowed for quiet space when one dorm was having a party and the others weren't. It did mean, however, having to brave the freezing temperatures outside just to move around the building.

Ally passed students bundled up in thick winter coats, scarves and hats, as she trudged through the snow. Some of them had already walked across half of campus to get to Annenberg Hall, the dining room that sat, happily for Ally and her students, adjacent to the Canaday dorms.

Inside the stairwell, Ally had to unwrap quickly to adjust to the central heating. She pulled her phone from her pocket as she took the stairs and dialled her boyfriend, only to get his voicemail.

'Hi, babe, it's me. Sorry I missed you last night. I know that's happening a lot. It's reading week coming up, let's plan something nice. Love you.'

There. She'd make it up to him next week. She really was madly in love with him. They'd been together three years now and it felt like more could be on the cards. She had to remember to make a little time for them both in all this madness of study and work.

By the time Ally arrived at Lauren and Megan's room, her face was red from the cold and her blonde hair damp from the icy wind outside.

Megan was in bed, facing the wall, happily ignoring the 8.45 a.m. bells ringing out from Memorial Church.

'Megan, where's Lauren?' Ally asked, noting the perfectly made-up bed on the other side of the room.

The room was so tiny, the girls could hold hands while they

slept – if they so chose – yet Lauren and Megan had managed to cram two desks and multiple free-standing clothing rails into the small space. The room was jam-packed; barely any of the white brick walls was visible.

Megan grunted.

'What?' Ally said. 'I can't hear you. Where's Lauren? Did she sleep here last night?'

'I don't know!' Megan shrilled. 'I don't know where she is. Breakfast or . . .' Something, something.

Ally shook her head unhappily. Out in the corridor, she began the process of reassembling her various layers.

Ally tried to not have favourites. It was her job to be there for all her ten students. But she preferred Lauren to Megan, for sure.

Lauren was far more determined than Megan to make something of her time in education. Megan had applied to Harvard because it was expected of her and every generation of her family before her had done the same, right back to the university's foundation.

Lauren didn't go to as many parties and she studied hard, but she was engaging and funny, too. She and Ally had once spent two very pleasant hours discussing exactly what Rory Gilmore had been thinking when she'd chosen Yale over Harvard. Ally had never met anybody before who liked *Gilmore Girls* as much as she did.

Ally recalled there was a boyfriend, too, though Lauren was cagey on the subject.

Ally entered Annenberg Hall just as the snow began to fall again.

The scene inside was warm and welcoming. Hundreds of students were gathered at tables beneath the great hammer beam trusses and stencilled ceiling and the lights that dotted the walnut-panelled walls were already aglow, an attempt to see off the morning gloom.

She spotted a gaggle of her students, heads bent low over plates of large novelty waffles stamped with the university crest, all of them hugging cups of coffee like their lives depended on it.

'Morning, ladies,' Ally said, arriving beside them. 'Have any of you seen Lauren Gregory?'

Half-hearted shakes all round.

'Maybe she's in the library?' One of the girls shrugged.

'She's not,' another clarified. 'I just came from there. The pipes have frozen and they're not letting students in until they get the heating going.'

Ally started to walk away, but one of the boys at the next table grabbed her arm. She recognised him; he interned at *The Crimson*, the university's newspaper, where Ally herself had been an editor during her final year.

'Lauren, babe with long, curly brown hair?' he asked.

Ally bristled but nodded.

'You've seen her?'

'She was down at the Porch.'

'In this weather?'

The boy shrugged.

Ally shook her head in frustration.

Donning her knitted hat once more, Ally went back outside. It was 9 a.m., she'd yet to have her own breakfast, she needed to get some work done today and here she was, roaming around campus trying to find a student who hadn't caused her an iota of trouble so far.

It was going to be one of those days.

Ally spotted Lauren from a distance, perched on the snow-covered steps of Memorial Church, also known as the Porch, her arms wrapped around herself.

Lauren was dressed for the weather – a giant grey wrap coat and matching beanie – but no amount of warm clothing allowed for sitting around outside in these temperatures.

Still, at least she was safe. Ally had had an awful feeling after Ship's call – and then when she'd seen Lauren's empty bed – that the girl might be in trouble; that she could have, in fact, gone missing and nobody had known. And Ally was self-aware enough to admit that she'd been worried about how that would reflect on her, first and foremost.

'Lauren, what on earth are you doing?' Ally called on approach. She tried to keep the irritation from her voice, but it seeped in anyway. Hell, it was cold, and Ally was hungry, hungover and pissed off.

Lauren didn't even glance up.

Ally was beside her now, looking down at the top of the other girl's hat, the curls covering either side of her face. Lauren's hair was wet; God knew how long she'd been sitting there.

'Where have you been for the last few days?'

'The city.'

'Oh. Okay. I wish you'd told me you were going to miss class.' A pause. 'Why are you sitting here?'

'I'm waiting for the church to open.'

Ally narrowed her eyes. There was something off about Lauren, something not quite right in her tone.

'It's not open today,' Ally said. 'The choir's practising for the Christmas carol service.'

Lauren's whole body seemed to sigh.

Ally shuffled from foot to foot. The bitter cold was starting to bite her toes, despite the fact she was wearing two pairs of socks and her boots were fur-lined.

'Hey, how about we get indoors?' Ally said.

No reply.

Ally swallowed her frustration and hunkered down until she was level with Lauren.

'What's going on, sweetie?'

Ally realised, in that moment, that she had never seen Lauren Gregory look miserable, or upset, or stressed.

All of which she looked now.

Ally also realised that, in all her twenty-five years, she had never seen anybody she knew beaten up, either.

'What on earth?' Ally gasped, staring at Lauren's swollen lip and black eye. 'What happened?'

Lauren blinked and looked down again.

Her next words were so low, Ally had to strain to hear them.

And when she realised what had been said, Ally's heart sank.

'It was my fault.'

Erin

THEN

My sister manages to defy all laws of time, space, gravity and last-minute ticket queues to arrive on Long Island a mere thirty-six hours after Danny's death.

I'll learn later that my father organised this. He got straight on the phone to an old colleague in the Department of Foreign Affairs and they got the Irish embassy over here involved, then the airline. It's the first of many acts of kindness that will be performed for me, without me realising the effort behind them.

Things you should know about the Kennedy girls:

We were all born with the same blue-black hair, green eyes and pale skin. Similar looks, very different personalities.

Tanya first, then me.

Niamh . . . Niamh was our baby sister.

When Niamh was a tot, she used to crawl into my bed at night because I was the warmest, apparently. I would hold her in my arms, her hot baby breath on my cheek until my mother came and lifted Niamh back into her cot.

When I want to, and even when I don't, I can still recall the tickle of Niamh's eyelashes on my neck.

When I open my hotel room door, groggy and disoriented, I'm expecting to see a chambermaid in the corridor. I woke for a short period earlier then made myself return to a sleep I didn't need. I know some people dealing with a tragedy can barely close their eyes. I can't be awake. When I'm awake, it's real. When I'm asleep . . .

I wish I could just keep sleeping.

The room hasn't been cleaned and the Do Not Disturb sign is probably causing consternation to the housekeeping staff.

But it's Tanya standing in the hallway and even though she's pretty much just off a plane, she looks like a supermodel, as always. Her hair is in a slick high ponytail, her dress is effortlessly chic, and she's wearing designer heels. When I travel, I go in leggings and hoodies.

She wraps her arms around me. We stay like that for what feels like an age.

The last time we hugged with this sort of desperation was in Dublin airport five years ago, just before I got on the flight to move here. The time before that is still too hard to think about.

'How long are you checked in for?' Tanya asks, slipping straight into organisational mode.

'I don't know,' I say, squinting as I try to remember my exchange with the man at the desk yesterday. 'I think I paid for two nights?'

'Do you want to stay longer?'

If I say yes, she'll march down to the foyer, demand an unlimited stay at a discounted rate and Lord help the poor fool who tells her this is peak season.

'No,' I say. 'I need to go back to our apartment tomorrow. Danny's mother will be coming up and . . .'

'She's not staying in your apartment,' Tanya says.

'She's not?'

'Erin, sweetheart, there is no way on earth you are playing host to your mother-in-law in the same apartment where Danny . . .' she trails off, painfully. 'I'm going to be taking care of you there, if you choose to go back. This place is close enough, isn't it? I'll go downstairs and sort out a room for Gloria.'

I'm about to protest but don't bother. Tanya's right. I can't be the one making coffee and sandwiches for Danny's mother. I can't let her sleep in our bed while I take the couch, looking at that window. And I can't even think about cleaning the apartment when I haven't showered or even brushed my teeth in a day and a half.

Tanya drags in a large suitcase. Then she pours me a double measure of Jack Daniel's from the mini-bar, herself a single of vodka and is opening a Coke mixer when I say:

'Tanya, where's Mam and Dad?'

She hesitates over the tumblers.

'You know they never fly.'

It's like a gut punch.

'Not even for this?'

She shrugs.

'They, of all people . . .' I say.

Tanya inhales deeply.

'You know what they're like.'

Yeah. I do. And I'd already guessed how they'd feel about the manner of Danny's death. Up until recent times, the Catholic Church wouldn't allow a suicide victim to be buried in consecrated ground.

My parents didn't rail against the Almighty after what happened to Niamh; they grew even closer to God.

Which is interesting, because it strikes me now that God might be on an extended vacation when it comes to us Kennedy girls.

'To Danny,' Tanya says, raising her drink. I look at the golden brown liquid she's handed me, tip my glass to hers, and have the first sip in my mouth by the time she adds, 'the selfish asshole'.

I splutter the whiskey and Coke all over myself.

'Well,' she says. 'Isn't he? Who does that to the person they love? Why not get in your car and drive off the side of a cliff so it'll look like an accident, or fill your pockets with rocks and walk into the sea or go into the woods and put a gun in your mouth . . . I don't know. To make you watch like that, Erin? That was fucking heartless.'

With every blink, I see Danny, one leg over the balcony, then the other . . . a heartbeat when he met my eyes and knew what he was about to do.

If I had run to him, if I'd screamed stop – would it have made any difference?

Later, Tanya orders everything on the room service menu in an attempt to make me eat, from sliders and tater tots to sundaes and caramel waffles. I force down a small bread roll, practically at knifepoint. She gives up on food eventually; gets back to business.

'Was he depressed?' she asks.

'No,' I say.

'Well, maybe he couldn't tell y—'

'He wasn't depressed,' I snap, hating how defensive I sound.

'Weren't there any signs?' Tanya says.

Here we are. The signs question. The one I'm already tormenting myself with.

'No. I don't know. He was – he'd been working really hard lately. He was . . . stressed. A little moody. There's trouble in his job. But we were looking forward to stuff. I mean, this weekend we were going away. We were excited about it.'

Weren't we? Or was it just me?

Everything has a question mark after it now.

'I don't get it,' Tanya persists. 'There must have been something in the lead-up. You don't just . . .'

She stops talking.

'I guess you never know what's going on in somebody else's head,' she says.

I fall silent.

There were no signs.

But yesterday morning, when Danny started to nuzzle my neck and then we made love . . .

Danny was a night bird. I preferred the morning.

I'd be fast asleep some nights and he'd wake me up, teasing, chancing his arm.

Yesterday morning, it felt different.

All along, he must have been thinking, this is the last time. As he moved inside me and when he cupped the back of my neck with his hand, every second was a countdown to the moment he'd never be with me again.

I swallow, the pain so dense there's a haze in front of my eyes.

'So, funeral directors,' Tanya says and it's like a bomb going off.

'I can't,' I say. I get off the bed and head in the direction of the
en suite but Tanya gets there first and fills the doorframe. She'd have
made a great linebacker.

'I hate that this has happened to you,' she says, barring my way.
'I hate that you've barely had time to breathe and that now I'm
here, talking to you about funerals. But this is something you need
to do, Erin. Even after Niamh,' an intake of breath, 'even when
Niamh died, it was our folks who had to sort it all out. Nobody
does it for you.'

I stare at the floor.

'It could be a while before Danny's body is released.'

'Why?' Tanya asks.

'They're doing an autopsy.'

'For what? It's obvious how he died, isn't it?'

'I don't know!' I shout, but Tanya doesn't flinch, she doesn't
move at all.

'Well, you need to find out when you'll get his body back. You're
his wife, you should be told everything. Don't they have – fuck it,
what do they call them here – family liaison officers?'

'I don't know,' I say. 'Tan, seriously, I'm glad you're here but
I can't think through all this right now. I can't. Please. I just . . . I
just need to pee.'

I close the door and sit on the toilet, my elbows on my knees
and don't even bother to listen to the whispered conversation she's
having outside on the phone.

The way Tanya phrased it – they have to give back Danny's body
– it's such an odd concept, that his body is mine in death. I certainly
got no say in how it was handled in life.

Where, how, do I start to deal with all this?

There are so many unanswered questions in my head and Tanya is just poking at the obvious ones.

Why are they doing a post-mortem on my husband's body?

Why was Ben at our door yesterday morning?

Somebody needs to give me some fucking answers.

The municipal building that houses the ninth precinct headquarters is an anonymous, white affair, only distinguishable by its flags and the police crest mounted on the exterior wall.

I convince Tanya to wait downstairs, to let me do this on my own.

The building is almost empty at this hour, but there are still some admin staff, a couple of detectives hanging about, a strange atmosphere hanging even heavier.

Nobody maintains eye contact with me when I enter. Nobody approaches to offer their condolences.

It's like they're embarrassed.

A cop killed is understandable, it seems. A cop killing himself is shameful.

The force is family, my ass.

I find Ben Mitchell in the office he and Danny once shared.

Ben's shirtsleeves are rolled up, there's a styrofoam cup of coffee on his desk and he's peering at pages from an open box in front of him.

It's one of the boxes that left my home yesterday morning.

I don't speak for a moment. I'm transfixed by the items on Danny's desk.

There's my husband's computer – the floating symbol on the screen indicating it's merely sleeping.

Beside it, a framed picture of the two of us on a trip to Cape Cod. A good day. He wouldn't let me order anything but fried clams and key lime pie and we got drunk on Moscow Mules.

The only other feature is a novelty calendar filled with photos of unlikely pin-up heroes – pizza delivery guys and matronly traffic wardens. A piss-take on the usual calendar-girl spreads.

'Erin?'

Ben says my name as a question.

I enter the office and close the door, take a seat at Danny's desk.

'I'm not sure you should be—'

He trails off.

'Can I get you a coffee?' he asks.

There's more than coffee in his cup. His eyes are red, his cheeks blotchy. Any sign of colour on his pasty face is a telltale.

'No,' I say.

'Christina asked after you.'

Christina, his picture-perfect wife. Messaging through her husband, who didn't even know he'd be seeing me tonight. Not a call, not a text. I stare at Ben, not even acknowledging it.

'Okay,' he says. 'What can I do for you?'

'Don't give me the Detective Ben Mitchell treatment for a start.'

Ben's shoulders fall slack. He rakes his fingers through strands of blond hair, blinks, sighs heavily.

'How about you talk to me like I'm newly widowed and my husband was your partner and best friend,' I say.

'It's not as easy as that.'

'Bullshit.' I lean across the desk. 'The officer who drove me to the hotel yesterday barely spoke to me. Nobody from the department has phoned since it happened. Not a peep from Captain Sullivan.

I walk in here tonight, it's like I'm Bruce Willis and you're Haley Joel Osment.'

'The circumstances around Danny's death are just – not regular,' Ben says.

'Right.' I push the chair back. My husband's chair. I'm sitting in it. He never will again. The circumstances are pretty goddamn irregular, for sure.

'Ben, what the hell is going on? Fine, I didn't play mom-and-pop. I didn't come to your Sunday lunches with creamed corn and cheesecakes. We didn't do foursomes out on sailboats and all that crap, but I watched my husband jump to his death yesterday and nobody is talking to me, nobody is telling me anything, nobody will even look at me!'

I've started shouting and my eyes are watering. The things I promised myself I wouldn't do when the Uber pulled up outside.

The red drains from Ben's face.

I take a deep breath; angrily rub my eyes dry.

'Why is there an autopsy?' I ask. 'Why did you take his work files and Ben, just what were you doing at my apartment yesterday morning?'

Ben looks over to the closed office door.

There are only a handful of people outside, but I can still see his eyes scanning the open-plan office, checking who's there and who's not.

'Danny was— Shit, Erin, don't put me in this position.'

'Don't put you in this position?'

I turn Danny's novelty calendar around.

'Look at it,' I say. 'Saturday, Sunday and Monday, what does it say?'

42

He reads. Blinks, rapidly.

'Hartford,' he says.

'The road trip we'd planned,' I say. 'This weekend.'

I turn the calendar back towards me. Flick it to August. My birthday. Ringed in red biro.

Those things were coming. They were happening. He was expecting them.

'Why did my husband kill himself?'

I ask myself, as well as Ben.

His answer is pitched so low, if there were any other noise in this office, I don't think I'd hear it.

'Danny was the subject of an ongoing internal investigation,' he says.

I gawp at him, my brain trying to catch up with his words.

'What?' I ask. 'For what?'

He sighs.

'I'm not allowed to tell you.'

Erin

Now

Before I married Danny, I told him I couldn't take his name.

I figured I'd put it out there, just in case he got funny about it and it proved an early warning sign.

'Oh,' he said, surprised, maybe a little hurt but smart enough to hide it. 'Well, I guess it's outdated to expect women to take their husbands' names.'

'Well, unless your surname was something cool like, I don't know, Elba or Clooney or Pitt.'

'Hang on, are you just naming other men you want to sleep with?'

'Yes.'

'Why don't you want to be Erin Ryan?' he asked. 'I'm not pushing, just asking.'

I sighed.

'That's why, Danny. *Erin Ryan*. You might as well draw a leprechaun on my forehead and sell tours.'

'Kennedy is pretty darn Irish,' he said. 'But, you should keep it.'
'Yeah?'

'Yeah. People will think you're connected. A Kennedy on Long Island? Think of the parties we'll get invited to.'

Funny because, right now, I'd like to be called Erin Ryan. I'd like that name heard, while I'm being tried for my husband's murder.

Karla has prepared me well.

'Opening arguments are brutal,' she said. 'Vicious. They will assassinate your character, your personal life, every action you've ever undertaken or even considered undertaking. They will sell you to the jury as the devil incarnate and you will sit there for the whole thing, not a single flicker of anger in your eyes, no furrowing of brows, no curling of lips. You will not even listen to what they're saying, okay? Stay blank. Stay detached. Look at me. Look at the judge. Look at the floor. Do not, I repeat, do not make eye contact with the jury when the prosecutor is painting you as the sort to eat your own young and capable of murdering with a glance.'

'And what will you do?' I asked, when I'd finally got my breath back.

'I will do my job. And I am exceptionally good at my job.'

We drew the short straw when Prosecutor Roberts was assigned to my case. Karla has already warned me but it isn't until I see him in action that I realise his smile is probably as damaging to me as all the evidence the police say they have.

He's suave. Handsome, like Daniel-Craig-playing-James-Bond handsome. Not pretty, but confident. Charming. He inflects his speech with blue-collar humour, but a worldly person will hear the hint of a drawl that says this man has never known anything but money. And that's attractive in itself. Roberts has manicured fingernails and the casually tousled hair that is only achieved at the hands of a professional, but he's classy enough not to overplay how wealthy he is.

I swallow as he simpers to the jury. Two minutes in and they're already lapping it up. Jurors five and six, women in their thirties without wedding bands, look like they're ready to hand over possession of their ovaries, gift-wrapped and tied up with neat pink bows.

'Ms Kennedy's attorney will tell you that the evidence the police have against the accused is circumstantial,' he says, his hands planted on the wooden rail to the front of the jury box, his posture friendly and conspiratorial.

'But let me tell you this. Murderers are often – not always, but often – very clever people. Now, I'm not saying the good officers of the law aren't just as clever, but every now and again, our law enforcement agencies encounter a criminal who is not only smart, but devious and strategic, too. It happened with Maud Parker, who was tried right over in Manhattan—'

Karla is out of her seat like her ass has been burned.

'Objection, Your Honour,' she blurts. 'This is outrageous.'

Judge Palmer sighs heavily. He's a big man. I don't just mean tall: this man is long and broad; he expands in every direction. Even his hair is big.

'Objecting during opening arguments, Counsellor?' he says, peering over the rims of his spectacles. 'That's novel.'

'Mr Roberts is referencing an infamous case in which the accused was found guilty, Your Honour. It's biased and it's also misleading, as the prosecutors in that instance had a weight of actual evidence against the defendant.'

Prosecutor Roberts does his best to look equally outraged but I can see he's burying a smirk as he glances over at Karla.

It's a game. It's all a big game.

'I'm pretty sure the prosecutor *is* biased against your client, Ms Delgado, and that it's in his job description at the DA's office,' Judge Palmer says. 'But the jury, as you've selected them, are twelve good men and women who are certainly objective. Mr Roberts, watch yourself. Counsellor Delgado, please, sit down.'

I can tell by Karla's body language she's bothered by the dismissal. She told me previously that when judges overrule or sustain an objection, even when they instruct a jury to ignore something an attorney or witness has said, there is nothing that can alter the fact that juries are human beings; when they hear something – it sticks. In this instance, I'm guessing, what they heard is that I'm as guilty as the infamous killer Maud Parker.

I tune out the rest of his opening argument as best I can.

I'm not listening as Prosecutor Roberts describes my refusal to take my husband's name, like that's something that speaks to guilt.

Nor as he talks about that night five months ago when my life fell apart – again.

I glance sideways, over my shoulder.

I know who's sitting behind me, but I'm wondering who's sitting on the other side of the courtroom, in the seats behind the prosecutor's table.

Then I see them.

My husband's family. My in-laws.

It's like a wedding, really. The two families divided on either side.

Are you with the bride or the groom?

I'm with the groom. Very definitely. And I'd like to see the bride spend the rest of her natural-born life in jail.

I make eye contact with his mother for one second and in that moment, I can feel such heat rush through me, it's like I'm on fire.

She *hates* me.

Karla nudges me discreetly and I whip my face forward.

Just in time to hear Prosecutor Roberts say:

'But perhaps this fantastical plan of revenge all started the night Erin Kennedy found out her husband, Daniel Ryan, was being investigated by Newport PD.'

Erin

THEN

One of the things I loved about Danny was the way he spoke about his mother.

I have plenty of friends who can't stand their mothers-in-law – sometimes because the woman in question is a total bitch, other times because of the very connection the husband has to his mom.

It never bothered me that Danny worshipped Gloria. Clichéd as it sounds, it meant my husband had been reared a gentleman, one who appreciated women.

It helped that Gloria was very fond of me and I of her.

Danny's mother was no-nonsense, no bullshit, a woman after my own heart. She had worked hard her whole life to escape the poverty she had been born into and when she married Elijah Ryan from Yonkers, she married for love. Certainly not wealth, because Elijah had figured himself for a writer and every job he took was just a means of earning a few dollars until he wrote the next Great American Novel.

I'd seen some of Elijah's writing. It was the anniversary of Danny's father's death and we'd driven down to Florida to spend it with Gloria. While unpacking some of the old boxes his mother had left taped up, Danny found a volume of poems his father had been working on before his death. Danny presented me with the book, an unspoken but hopeful look in his eyes, the sort I get from people all the time when they desperately want to see something published but would never put me in the position of asking outright.

Gloria took the book from my hands the second Danny left the kitchen.

'Sweetie, don't you think for one second you got to read that godforsaken trash just because my baby is making goo-goo eyes at you and don't have the sense he was born with.'

Gloria tossed the book on the counter and returned to squirting cream on to the tinned peaches she'd opened for dessert.

She paused, looked out the kitchen window at the palm trees swaying in the garden and the gentle bay beyond.

'Your eyes shine like the pebbles on the shore, washed up in a sea of frothy passion.'

I swallowed.

'That was one of his best lines,' Gloria said, and we both burst out laughing.

When she arrives at the hotel in Patchogue, I'm shocked by her appearance. Gloria has never been stereotypically attractive but she's always had a fresh-faced, youthful warmth to her – a dimpled smile, like her son's, that can light up a room, and a strategic sense of style that means she always looks classy, even when wearing her cleaning overalls.

But today she looks old. Tired. Beaten.

I've had a shower, under Tanya's instruction, and am wearing a clean T-shirt and skirt. I look positively glowing compared to Gloria.

We say nothing, just hold each other for the longest time.

'Mike?' I ask, when I pull back.

'Hasn't left Syria yet,' she says. 'They're organising compassionate leave. It's a mess over there. Sure ain't helped that they're sending our boys in then pulling them out, like they're toy soldiers and the world is a sandbox in the President's backyard.'

Even in grief, Gloria has no problem taking a dig at US foreign policy. She'd nearly had a heart attack when Mike announced he was signing up. Gloria's own father had been drafted for Vietnam and was shot dead by a VC sniper during the Tet Offensive, just two weeks after he touched down.

'Gloria,' I say, glancing around the crowded lobby.

'I'm allowed to get mad,' Gloria says. 'If anything happens to him now, after . . .'

Gloria trails off.

'How about we get a little fresh air?' she says, changing tack. 'I've breathed nothing but plane and automobile fumes since I woke.'

Gloria doesn't need a walk. She's taken one look at me and decided that I'm the one who needs to be brought down to the ocean, the one who needs to breathe.

I nod, and let her guide me outside, her arm tucked under mine like I'm escorting her.

Gloria and I stroll along the marina, not talking, pretending to people-watch the lunch crowd sitting outside cafés and bars. Glasses clink, the smell of scampi and fries fills the air and bells ring in the wind on the harbour.

We stop at a vendor and Gloria buys a soft pretzel and a Coke.

'If you're hungry we can get something proper,' I say.

She presses the paper bag into my hand, the dough's warmth seeping through to my hands.

'I'm not hungry,' she says.

She makes me eat every bite.

The salt of the pretzel and the sugar of the Coke do their job and I feel more human than I either want or deserve.

Gloria's steps are laboured by the time we reach the harbour. We're not walking fast but she's in her sixties and has spent a lifetime in backbreaking, physical work and on top of that, has just sustained the biggest shock of her life. I nod at a bench and we sit down, both looking out at the water, where the sun's rays glisten white and blinding and the gulls swoop low on the water.

'I'm so sorry, Gloria,' I say, and the tears start again.

'Lord, what do you have to be sorry for?' she says.

'I didn't see it coming,' I say.

'I didn't see it coming,' Gloria says, quietly. 'This is not your fault, Erin. Don't you ever, ever think that.'

'But I lived with him,' I say. Her willingness to absolve me of blame is not a relief. It's devastating. I should have been able to save Danny. For her, as well as for me. She deserved that.

'I saw him every day, I slept beside him every night,' I say. 'How could I not have known there was something so terrible in his head that he wanted to . . . ?'

Gloria squeezes my shoulder and at the same time closes her eyes. When she opens them, she has that determined look on her face she wears so well. That's when I know she's not coping better than I am. She's just acting better.

'When Danny started high school,' Gloria says, 'the whole year, all he talked about was this summer camp all his new friends planned to attend. He was a popular kid – good at football, basketball; any sport, he could turn his hand to it. And he had that grin. Lord, that smile. He didn't need to try to fit in but he liked to, and he'd got into his head that the summer break was the best way to make solid all those new friendships. Everyone was going – you can imagine what he was like, haranguing me day and night.'

'He never let up when he wanted something.'

'That was my boy. Of course, I couldn't afford to send him to that damned camp but I never once told him that,' Gloria said. 'He didn't ask for a lot, neither of them did, and it was my job to provide for them when the requests did come in. We'll see, I kept saying, and everyone knows not getting an outright no is as good as a yes. Then, some time around spring break, he just stopped asking. He had a new goal. Told me he was getting a job when school was out – fourteen years of age and already he'd landed work cleaning cars in our local filling station. His new plan was he wanted to work the summer months and start saving up for a car. Figured two years was enough to build up a healthy bank balance and he'd be driving by sixteen.'

'Maybe he knew, deep down, there wasn't enough money for camp?' I say.

'He knew that when he started asking,' Gloria says. 'But there's always hope. No, Mike told me. Those two boys heard their dad and me arguing over a job Elijah had lost. I got upset. I can't even remember what the job was – I think he was a building supervisor and somebody complained that he was always too busy with his pen and paper to let anyone in the front door.'

'Your eyes are like pebbles,' I say.

Gloria gives a short yelp of a laugh, then her face grows serious again.

'Danny had no interest in cars, honey,' she says. 'He hated the garage, hated his summer job. I know this because the following year he got a job packing groceries and the following, when he did turn sixteen, he spent his money on a camping trip. Not a car.'

'He didn't say anything to you because he wanted to protect you,' I say. 'This is different.'

'It's not,' Gloria says. 'If you didn't see that there was anything wrong with Danny, it's because he didn't want you to. It's exactly the same. Danny was good at taking care of other people's feelings.'

'Up until he wasn't,' I snap, then immediately turn to her, contrite. 'I'm sorry. I don't mean to . . .'

'Erin, I've gone through the seven stages and some I didn't even know existed just since we sat down.'

I nod, look back out at the water, take a breath.

'His partner told me Danny was being investigated.'

Gloria inhales, sharply.

'For what?'

'That's what I asked, but he wouldn't tell me. After . . . after it happened, they took his files from our apartment and they . . . they all seem off with me. Nobody from the station has called or sent a card or – whatever the etiquette is, I'm pretty sure it's missing. Did he tell you anything?'

I look at her. Danny confided in Gloria, I know he did. He talked to his mother every week, long phone chats when he was driving to work or walking on the beach. I'd overheard him on those calls, talking something or nothing.

Gloria stares out at a boat that's come into view. A schooner, its sails billowing in the open sea breeze. Fresh haul on board, striped bass and shark, probably.

'I knew something was wrong,' Gloria says. 'He seemed . . . not himself. Depressed.'

'He wasn't depressed,' I say, just as I did to Tanya.

'I think he was,' Gloria says, softly.

'I know what it looks like,' I say. 'With Niamh—' I choke, then compose myself. 'Sorry. I know depression, Gloria. Danny had stuff on his mind but he was absolutely fine. He was—'

I stop. Even as I say it, it sounds so stupid. Of course, Danny wasn't fine.

His mother takes my hand.

'Erin,' she says, 'you can't judge everybody else by your own experience of the world. What you felt after Niamh, what your family went through, that was your own, personal response. And you could be open with it. People expected it. Danny dealt with his problems differently. As do we all. Just because he got out of bed every day and smiled and made plans, that didn't mean he wasn't hurting inside. I know my child was hurting. I could hear it in his voice. I just wish I'd done something to fix it. But when your baby ain't a baby no more . . . it's hard, Erin.'

I can't bear this. I can't bear the idea that not only has everything I know been taken away from me, but that everything I thought I knew is starting to evaporate along with it.

'How could you know if I didn't?' I say.

'I know, because his father was exactly the same,' Gloria says. 'Elijah was never happy. And everybody thought he was. My God, at his funeral, they lined up to tell me he was the most joyous person they all knew. The man stressed himself to a heart attack. Erin—'

She hesitates.

'Can you consider that, maybe, just maybe, Danny protected you from the worst of it because he knew you needed to be protected? Because you'd dealt with enough already?'

I stare at Gloria.

Then I stand and walk away, wait by the rail at the dock.

I hear her approach and together, silently, we start to walk back to the hotel.

I'm too angry to say anything.

This is what suicide does, I think. Makes everybody left behind question everything and everyone.

'Danny knew I was strong,' I say, after a while, and even I know I'm trying to convince myself. 'He knew I was strong enough to cope with him being dead. Otherwise, he never would have killed himself.'

Gloria purses her lips.

But if I'm right, it begs the question.

If Danny thought I was strong enough to cope with his death – was there something in his life that he thought I couldn't live with?

Harvard

December 2016

Reading week, and the respite it offered.

Ally had planned to spend her students' pre-exams study week catching up on her own doctorate work and making time for her boyfriend. Her plans were now out the window, but that didn't matter. What mattered was that at least Lauren Gregory was back on campus.

Three days had passed since Ally had found Lauren sitting on the steps of Memorial Church.

When she'd finally coaxed Lauren back to her dorm, she'd spent the first couple of hours trying to warm the girl up.

Then, when she was happy Lauren wasn't going to be struck down with hypothermia, she tried to get her to open up about what had happened.

Nothing. Lauren refused to talk.

In the days that followed, the bruises had grown uglier, the silence worse still.

From the little Ally had gathered, whatever had happened to Lauren had occurred on the first night that she had been down in Manhattan. She'd stayed up there for days after, afraid to come back to her dorm, terrified of telling anybody.

Megan had only been able to feign the slightest degree of sisterhood solidarity before disappearing, Ally suspected, to one of the boys' rooms.

Now, en route to Lauren's room, Ally was still deliberating whether she should inform somebody more senior that Lauren was obviously in distress.

The only thing that had prevented Ally from doing so until now was Lauren's absolute insistence that Ally tell nobody.

I'll be fine, it's my business, Lauren kept repeating.

For the first time as proctor, Ally felt well and truly out of her depth. Sure, she was older than her charges and she knew the college inside out. She also knew that there was help to be had, if Lauren wanted to talk. But she couldn't force Lauren to open up. Nobody could. The fact the event had taken place off-campus also meant the university wasn't entirely responsible for dealing with it.

Unless Lauren had gone to Manhattan with another student . . .

As of yet, Ally didn't know if Lauren had been attacked by a man or a woman. She didn't know if she'd been robbed by a stranger, or if she'd fallen out with her boyfriend. She didn't know if Lauren was still at risk, or indeed if other women were at risk. And Ally also didn't know if it had just been a beating, or something more, though the fact Lauren hadn't been to Planned Parenthood or any medical facility at least meant rape was probably unlikely.

She'd honoured Lauren's request for privacy but it was taking its toll.

Ally paused at the door to Lauren's room, which was firmly shut.

From inside, she could hear the sound of soft, desperate crying.

Ally's stomach knotted. Lauren sounded utterly heartbroken.

It gave Ally pause for thought.

Whoever had hurt Lauren had left her emotionally as well as physically marked.

To Ally's mind, this was the first clue that it could have been somebody close to the girl who inflicted the harm.

Maybe her boyfriend?

Ally had never met the guy, even prior to the assault. It wasn't unusual for boys from hometowns to stay home, but Lauren was practically a local girl – she'd grown up close to Cambridge. If Lauren had confided in her boyfriend, surely he'd be here by now? Unless he was staying away . . .

When she entered the room, Lauren stopped crying, but she didn't look at Ally.

Ally took up position on Megan's bed and placed coffee and a paper bag of bagels on the windowsill.

'I'll go to the library today,' Lauren said, as though that was what mattered.

'Don't worry about that,' Ally said.

'I don't want to fall behind.'

'Lauren, whatever happened, I think it's important you don't carry on like it was nothing. It's obviously got to you. You've barely left this room in days.'

Lauren bit her lip.

Ally sighed, heavily. She couldn't let this go on.

'I'm not . . . I'm not an expert on this sort of thing,' Ally said.

'But I had a friend back home who, well, she was in a relationship and he was . . .'

Ally trailed off. She didn't know if it was even the same thing. Her friend's boyfriend had been a little controlling, weirdly possessive at times. But he'd never been physically violent.

'Where's home?' Lauren asked.

Ally was thrown.

'Um, Providence. Rhode Island. You ever been?'

Lauren shook her head.

'Well, there are forty-eight other states you should try first. I'm kidding. It's lovely. It's just also where my folks live.'

Ally paused.

'Do you have a boyfriend?' Lauren asked.

Ally nodded. 'You'll have seen him here a couple of times. He hasn't been up much lately, though. He works.'

'He's older than you, isn't he?'

'A little. What about your—'

'Do you love him?'

'I – yes.'

Ally stopped. Lauren's face had clouded with such distress, Ally's words stuck in her throat.

'Oh, God,' Ally said. 'Please, Lauren. Tell me what happened.'

She reached out to take the other girl's hand. It was deathly cold.

'Whatever it was,' Ally said, 'it wasn't your fault.'

'My mother, my brother . . . I don't want them seeing me like this. I'm meant to go home for Christmas. And if my father hears . . .'

'They'll want to help—'

'I don't want them to see me!'

Ally grimaced.

'You'll be able to go home. The swelling will go down. You'll look fine by next week.'

Lauren stared out the window. Some yells from below were followed by a bounce of a packed snowball against the wall near the glass pane, making both girls jump.

'He's older than me,' Lauren said.

'Who?' Ally asked, momentarily distracted by the ruckus outside.

'My . . . boyfriend. You asked.'

Ally nodded at the marks on Lauren's face.

'Did he do this? If he hit you, Lauren, you have to leave him. You know what they say. They never do it just once.'

'If I tell you what happened, will you promise not to hate me?'

Ally swallowed.

'How could I possibly . . . Lauren, I told you, you're not responsible for this. You can't *make* anybody hurt you.'

'And we can't tell anybody. *I* can't tell anybody. I swore.'

Ally nodded, making a promise she knew would be impossible to keep.

Then she listened, dumbstruck, as Lauren told her everything she'd gone through.

Ally hung her head, ashamed.

She was Lauren's proctor. She was meant to look out for her.

How the hell had this happened?

'I'm sorry, Lauren,' Ally said. 'But you cannot keep this to yourself. You just can't. I know you're frightened. I get it. But we have to tell somebody.'

'I swore I wouldn't.'

'It doesn't matter!'

Ally fell quiet as Lauren started to cry. She watched helplessly as the other girl wrapped her arms around herself, her body creasing with pain.

'Who would I tell?' Lauren murmured.

And suddenly, Ally didn't feel as useless. God, it was so obvious.

She knew exactly to whom Lauren could take this.

The other girl was watching her now.

Ally was so sure of the solution, so confident, that for the first time, Lauren looked hopeful.

Erin

Then

It's important that I go into the apartment on my own.

To her credit, Tanya understands.

She's letting me get away with a lot today. Including not digging as to why, when Gloria and I returned to the hotel, I couldn't get out of there fast enough.

By chance, the cab drops us in the space right beside Danny's car in the parking lot beside my building.

I suppose Danny's car is my car now.

Tanya tells me she'll sort the driver and follow me up in twenty. I nod, distracted.

A quick glance into Danny's car tells me it's already been searched and emptied by his colleagues. It's never that tidy.

I don't walk around to the main entrance. Instead, I hop the low, white-picket fencing to the left of our building and walk through the gardens, then let myself into the internal stairway. I don't want to risk the elevator. Whatever about meeting one of our neighbours in passing, I can't be stuck with one in a confined space for aeons of awkward silence.

Eight short flights of stairs. All of these apartment blocks were built with a maximum of four floors. Newport wanted to ensure the town served accommodation needs but didn't have its low sky-line ruined by anything that looked remotely high-rise.

High enough, as it turns out.

I pause at the final flight, then take the steps before I can talk myself out of it. At the top I open the door into the hallway.

It's utterly mind-blowing to me that everything about this corridor can look so unchanged.

The palm tree pot plant beside our door is thriving. The carpet is still that rusty shade of brown, plush at the edges, more thread-worn in the middle. The walls are the same cream, dotted as always with commercial black-and-white photographs of the bay.

I slip my key into the front door and jiggle it, like this is any other day.

Then I walk inside.

I don't mean to look over at the window immediately, so, of course, that's the first thing I look at.

And sink to my knees.

The pain in my stomach is so intense, I feel like I'm about to vomit and loosen my bowels at the same time. I lean forward, the hand on the parquet floor propping me up, the other clutched to my mouth as I swallow bile. When I can breathe, when the floor is no longer a blur: I look up at the window again.

If Danny had had to open the window himself, would it have taken a bit longer? Long enough to stop him?

I sit back on my calves and look around.

The apartment feels different. All our things have been moved, touched, examined and then put back better than we'd left them.

A thought hits me. I clamber to my feet, rush to the bathroom.

Danny had just finished his shower. Had he left something here? A message? A sign?

I almost expect to see a note written in steam on the shower door.

I'm losing my fucking mind.

A minute later, my head is resting against the porcelain sink as I clutch Danny's razor, the bristles still caught in it.

He shaved. He shaved before he killed himself.

Later that afternoon, I set about finding an attorney.

I have to figure out if I can break the lease on my apartment before I can move. I wouldn't be able to take on a new place if I had to pay off the remaining six months contracted on my existing one. Not on one wage.

And with that in mind, I also need to work out where I stand when it comes to Danny's pension; if he'll even be entitled to a pension if he was under investigation, as Ben claims.

I've even begun to wonder whether – in this delightfully litigious land – I should sue the Newport County Police Department.

If what Ben said is right – if Danny was under a cloud at work – then I'm entitled to know if his job contributed to the stress he so obviously broke under.

Don't get me wrong, it's not money I'm after. It's vindication. Maybe if his employer has to take responsibility for ruining his life then I won't feel so responsible for not saving it.

Problem is, I don't know any attorneys over here bar the libel lawyers we use in publishing.

I phone an author of mine, David Fox, who lives and works in the city and, to my knowledge, has connections with everyone, everywhere.

'Erin,' he says, his voice so filled with compassion it almost makes me cry. 'We all got the call. What can I do?'

'I can't talk about it,' I say, knowing that will cover it for him, that he's sensible enough to not push and probably relieved, too. 'But I need a lawyer. Out here, preferably. Somebody who knows how to deal with police.'

He says nothing for a moment, while he thinks.

'I know somebody. Pitbull. I'd follow her into the trenches. I helped her out a while back. I don't have her address but she moved out there some years back.'

'If I've a name I'll find her,' I say.

He tells me and repeats his offer of assistance with whatever I need.

I hang up before I start to cry.

I leave Tanya with Gloria at the hotel, then I walk around Patchogue for what feels like hours trying to find David's contact on Google Maps. That's my strategy, for what it is. I don't seem to be able to do anything the way I normally would. Sensibly. I'm not even wearing my Skechers. I'm wearing cheap sandals and the blisters are fucking killing me.

Karla Delgado has a picture of herself in the window. That's how attorneys sell themselves around here. She's smiling, arms crossed, wearing a sharply cut grey business suit and expensive white blouse.

Friendly, but a tigress, that's what the photographer was probably directing when he took that shot.

Karla, though, has a look in her eye I'm familiar with.

Just take the goddamn picture so I can get back to work.

I've been that soldier.

I almost smile. I stand back some more on the sidewalk, look the office up and down. Two floors, clean, light grey blinds in the windows, small but professional.

Inside, a woman in a pair of denim shorts and a check shirt tied at her midriff, dark hair tied up in a messy bun, is on her hands and knees sorting paper into piles on the floor.

She looks like the woman in the picture; probably a sister or cousin, employed as a secretary.

'I'm looking for Karla?' I say.

'You found her,' the woman says, sitting back on her hunkers.

I blink.

She smiles.

'I brush up real nice for court,' she says, seeing my doubtful expression. She stands, rubs her hands on her shorts, offers me one to shake.

'It's after six?' she says.

'Oh, God!' I slap my palm against my forehead. She must have closed up for the day. 'I'm sorry. I'll go.'

She studies me, reads something I don't think I'm even trying to project.

'No. Something brought you in my door. And not just to distract me from case prep.'

She glances upwards and I groan, inwardly. I can see now the crucifix hanging around her neck.

I start to question David's recommendation but I feel too awkward to excuse myself. Politeness. I've known people to actually die from it. My grandma was too polite to intrude on her doctor about the lump on her breast that was the size of a small planet.

He has enough to be doing, I can't be bothering him.

'I . . . David Fox recommended you. I'm his editor. At Phoenix Publishing, I mean.'

A ghost of a smile on her lips.

'Any friend of David's is a friend of mine.'

I open and close my mouth, unsure of how to go about telling her what I must.

'Coffee?' Karla says.

I've had nothing since the pretzel this morning. I'm operating on adrenaline and denial.

'Please.'

'Let's go.'

She holds open the door for me and, confused, I walk back out on to the street.

Karla lets the door close behind her, doesn't bother to lock it, and we stroll a couple of yards to the open-air seating area of the café next door.

'Why have a coffee machine when you can practically knock on the wall and have somebody fix you a double espresso?' she says.

We take a seat at one of the few empty tables. It's early evening but still balmy, and the café is full of people meeting up after work. I'm just starting to worry it will take a while for us to get served when Karla yells so loudly I almost fall out of my seat.

'Boy!'

A middle-aged man who has a beard as long as my hair and a

surfer's tan looks over from one of the other tables, where he's taking an order.

'What?' he snaps.

Karla waits until he comes over to us, his expression sour enough to turn milk.

She flicks casually through the menu then looks up at him.

'Grande, iced, sugar-free vanilla latte with soy milk.'

She looks expectantly at me.

'Um – Americano?'

I see him write two Americanos on his pad before he leaves.

I haven't seen this level of hostility in service since my last stop-over flight in London, when I innocently wandered into an allegedly renowned cocktail lounge and ordered a still water.

I, unconsciously, inch my chair further away from the table and from Karla.

'I bailed him out of county a few months ago,' she explains, noting my discomfort. 'He'd gotten liquored-up and was yelling racial slurs at the clerk. Spic, being one of them. Pendejo.'

'You still drink coffee here.'

'You think I'm going to walk a block just because that a-hole can't keep a civil tongue in his head?' She shakes her head. 'So, David. Just a professional relationship?'

'I'm sorry?'

'Not a girlfriend?'

'Isn't he married?'

'Aren't they all? I guess he is one of the good guys, though.'

I nod.

'He helped me out of a nasty one,' she says, but adds no more detail. 'He suggested you talk to me, huh? What do you need?'

She pauses to study me.

'Home purchase, will, or dispute with the inland revenue?'

'I . . .'

'Bankruptcy? Divorce?'

'Eh . . .'

'I'm running out of options.'

'I thought you were criminal law? Your sign . . .'

'Ah, hell. You committed a crime?'

I shake my head.

'Praise Papa for that. I do specialise in criminal law, but this is a quiet town. I get people coming to me for all sorts. And I've worked all sorts. Started in a big litigation firm in the city before I moved down here. Sue me, sue you, sue fucking everyone. You heard of them?'

I don't know what to make of this woman.

She watches me again for a moment or two and then her features grow sombre.

'Okay,' she says. 'Why are you looking for a criminal defence lawyer if you haven't committed a crime?'

'I'm not sure what I'm looking for,' I say. 'I, um, just need some legal advice. My husband, he's . . . he was a police detective.'

Something flashes over Karla's face. Something like panic.

'He's dead,' I say.

'Oh. For a moment I thought you were going to say he was beating you or stalking you and I was about to ring David and read him the riot act. I might owe him some big favours but those cases are motherfuckers, as well he knows.'

She sits back, taps her lips with her finger, thinking.

'I'm sorry for your loss,' she says, then hesitates. 'Your accent. You Irish?'

I nod.

'I presume your husband was American?'

I nod.

'So, you're here legally, anyway.'

I suspect we could keep going this way, continue to play twenty questions until Karla establishes exactly what kind of guidance I need, so, as soon as Boy has returned with our coffees, I cut to the chase.

I tell her that Danny killed himself two days ago, that I need advice on my apartment lease, help with his will, guidance on his pension and then I drop the bomb about him being investigated for what, I don't know, because his partner Ben won't say and nobody else has been in touch to tell me anything.

Her mouth forms an O and her coffee remains untouched.

'This all happened in the last two days?' she asks.

'Yeah.'

She places her hand over mine. I swallow.

Then she nods, and when I look at her, her demeanour is professional and urgent.

'The police who were at your apartment when you came to in the ambulance,' she says. 'They were all guys you knew?'

Her question is out of left field. I furrow my brow as I try to remember. Ben was there, obviously. Some other officers I'd seen at the station.

'There may have been a couple I didn't recognise.'

'Uniforms or plain clothes?'

'Eh, plain.'

'And they took all of Danny's possessions from the apartment?'

'Well, his files and stuff. Not his clothes or anything personal.'

'But, his personal computer and his phone?'

I nod. That was a blow. Danny had lots of pictures of us on his laptop. He was diligent about uploading.

'Did you give them permission to take those things?' she asks.

I shake my head.

I'm puzzled and yet, I have a sinking feeling I know where this is going.

I was in shock. I've got to give myself a break.

But, oh my God, I'm so stupid.

Why didn't this occur to me?

'Did they have a warrant to take things from your apartment without your permission?' she says.

'They were Danny's things. I thought, because he was a detective . . .'

'You don't know exactly what they took or why they took them, Erin. The police – they only remove items from a person's home when they consider it to be a crime scene. Suicide is not a crime. Even if he was being investigated at work, they had no right to take his possessions without clearing that with you.'

Silence.

Karla takes a deep, troubled breath.

'I'm going to talk to his precinct. They like to shut down stuff like this quick so it's important we let them know early you have legal representation. I'll see what I can get out of them but I also want you to go through your place and try to find anything Danny might have left that gives you a clue as to what was going on at work. They took his files and so on, but did he have a diary, or an iPad, or anything that could help? Look through everything.'

'I don't know—'

'Just promise me you'll look.'

I acquiesce with a nod.

'Good,' she says. 'We're going to figure all this out, okay?'

I stare into my coffee.

I think about how Danny's workmates have treated me.

I think about what Karla's saying.

It's getting harder to breathe. I can feel a lump in my throat and a burning sensation at the back of my eyes.

Not here, I don't want to cry here, in public, with a woman I've just met.

'Oh, honey,' she says.

'It's just . . .'

The tears come.

'I've nobody here,' I sob. 'I mean, I've friends, and my sister has come over and Danny's mom is up from Florida, but I've nobody who lives here with me. I've no family. They know I'm on my own – his workmates. They know and they're treating me like a leper. This is my home but it doesn't feel like home any more. I've nobody . . . I've no—'

I can't even talk. I'm choking on sobs and hiccups and the people in our immediate vicinity are staring, alarmed at my meltdown.

'I understand,' Karla says, gripping my upper arms like I'm drowning and she needs to keep me afloat. Funny that. 'Erin, do you hear me? I understand. I know what it's like to feel alone here. I know what it's like when you don't have anybody. Look at me.'

I compose myself enough to meet her eyes, which are filled with such empathy, I know she's telling the truth. She gets what it means to feel like an outsider. Far from home. She gets it.

'It's only when bad stuff happens we realise that making a life away from your family is actually pretty tough,' she says. 'But there are a lot of us in the same boat, chica. You just need to ask and somebody will be there for you.'

And in that moment, a silent bond is forged.

Somebody had once been there for Karla.

And Karla, a woman I've only intended to hire to help me with some legal issues, has just committed to be there for me.

I owe David Fox a drink.

Urgent, not-so-quiet whispering outside my bedroom door.

Tanya's on the phone again. To my parents, if her side of the exchange is anything to go by.

'This is her home, Ma, where the fuck else is she going to stay? She can't stay in that hotel permanently. You should see their rack rate. Jesus.'

A pause.

'I know every time she walks in she sees that window, but what can she do? No, nobody has offered to put her up. Well – there's a barman she's friends with, he suggested . . . Bud something. No, I didn't think a bar would be a good idea, either.'

I lie in bed, staring up at the ceiling.

I remember Danny lying on top of me, remember how it felt with his arms around me.

How could we be that close and I still didn't know?

It doesn't matter where I am.

I'll always be thinking of Danny.

Gloria's words are still running through my head.

Danny had his share of darkness. You do not work as a detective in

New York, even out here in our lovely Newport, and not encounter situations that mark you. Danny had come home from work on many occasions and just walked straight to the fridge, taken out a beer and slugged half of it before he could even say hello.

The thing with Danny, though, was that he preferred to carry that work burden alone. He could be dealing with the worst case of his life and he'd still let me moan about some minor stress I had in work that week – a bullish agent looking for a bigger advance for her client's book; a book we'd paid big money for dying on its feet in the stores.

I knew he had more worries than I did but I told myself my job was a distraction for him, a way for him to switch off.

I should have been asking him about his work.

I should have been worrying about those times he went quiet.

I should have told him I was there, if he ever did want to talk.

Tanya opens the bedroom door, gingerly.

'Can't sleep?' she asks me.

'Tanya,' I say, sitting up. 'Am I self-centred?'

'Where's this coming from?'

Tanya sits on the edge of the bed. I see now how tired she looks – she must be jet-lagged after yesterday but she hasn't complained once.

'Something Gloria said,' I say. 'She implied Danny might have protected me from whatever he was feeling because of what happened to Niamh.'

Tanya sighs.

'Sweetheart, what happened with Niamh was horrendous. If Danny was trying to protect you because of it, that says more about him than you. It says he was a good guy, which I think you know.'

'But if he was actually, properly depressed and he should have been confiding in me – what sort of a wife does that make me? It's meant to go two ways, isn't it?'

Tanya looks at me, pityingly.

'I'm going to make you a hot drink and then, honey, I think you might need to take a tablet. You need your sleep.'

I sigh.

When she leaves, I look around the room, Karla Delgado's words playing in my head.

Before I know it, I'm making my way through Danny's drawers.

Tanya returns, sees the mess I've made on the floor and bed as a result of pulling out his belongings, and tries to disguise the sheer panic on her face.

She places a peppermint tea on the bedside locker and kneels on the rug beside me.

'What are you looking for?' she asks.

'I don't know,' I say. 'Anything. Anything that seems strange or not right. Something that could give me a clue.'

She picks up a bundle of small cards, held together with elastic, which I've taken from among Danny's boxers. Danny used to collect them in restaurants and bars as keepsakes.

Tanya flicks through them as I search. I barely notice as she stops on one.

'Who's your GP, or whatever you call them over here? Physician?'

'We don't have a specific one. Danny had one in the city, Dr Symon, but we just used the medical centre here.'

'Who's Dr Leslie Klein, MD, MPH?'

I frown.

'It might have been somebody he encountered through work,' I say.

Tanya hands me the card.

Leslie Klein is no ordinary doctor. She's a practising psychiatrist. And on the back, in Danny's writing: Friday/3 p.m.

I stare at it, then reach for my mobile as Tanya watches, still concerned.

Karla told me to ring her if I find anything – any time, day or night.

I'd explained to her that I could afford to pay her hourly rate for looking into Danny's pension and things like that but I wasn't sure I had the means to have her on the end of a phone line.

She'd dismissed any talk of money as irrelevant until I pointed out it was very bloody relevant to me.

'I owe David Fox.' She'd shrugged. 'He practically saved my career, even if it wasn't a career I ultimately wanted. And if you come via him, then you're the favour I'm repaying. We can work out a fee and we stick to that – regardless of when you call.'

That had made me marginally more comfortable, slightly more so when she pressed the point.

'Seriously, Erin,' she'd said. 'I'm not going to BS you. You're ticking all my boxes. You're a friend of a friend. You've come to me with the most interesting case I've had in a long time. I've had an . . . ha, let's say interesting relationship with police departments. And you're a sister from another mister. I'm supposed to be behind the wall and you're probably supposed to be building it, but we're both immigrants, huh?'

At that, I'd actually laughed.

Karla answers on the second ring.

'I think I might have something,' I tell her. 'He has a card here for a psychiatrist. It says Friday, 3 p.m. That's tomorrow. What should I do?'

Karla answers after a few seconds.

'Did you have any plans for tomorrow?' she asks.

Dr Leslie Klein's office is over in North Bellport, down a quiet side street populated with other discreet professionals, if the tiny name plaques and quaint gated entrances are anything to go by.

Her secretary frowns at me. Even in a place frequented by people seeking psychiatric help, the appearance of a white Irish woman claiming admission to an appointment made for a black American man stands out.

The secretary buzzes through to the doctor, mumbles something incoherent, and within moments, Leslie Klein appears in the pastel-appointed waiting room.

Dr Klein is graceful and elegant. She's wearing loose linen trousers and a silk pashmina. Her greying hair is swept into a French chignon and her glasses hang around her neck on a gold chain.

'I'm sorry – and you are?' she asks me.

'Erin Kennedy,' I say.

The tiny lines on her forehead – which, incidentally, is smoother than mine, despite the fact she's got twenty years on me – furrow.

'I'm sorry, I've no appointments free at the moment, Erin,' she says.

'You do,' I say. 'I think you were due to see my husband. He's not coming.'

She takes this without too much reaction. Client confidentiality probably means she shouldn't even acknowledge the fact she's expecting Danny.

But now I know. I can see it in her face, the way she looks at me: with familiarity.

And the fact the waiting room is empty.

Danny was coming to see this woman.

Not just this Friday at three.

Every Friday at three.

It was a standing appointment.

The sudden realisation hits me like a brick and I don't even know how I know.

'He's not coming because he's dead,' I add.

To this, she reacts. Her eyes widen, her lips twitch.

'I'm very sorry to hear that,' she says. 'So very sorry.'

I watch her. Something is bothering me but I can't put my finger on what.

'Please, come in,' she says.

She stands aside, ushers me into her office, away from the secretary, who is good enough at her job to pretend she's not listening but can't hide the fact her typing has slowed.

The office is straight out of the modern psychiatric handbook of furnishings. No oppressive mahogany desks in here. The pastel theme continues, through to the soft beige couch that faces her deep, plush armchair.

How many times did my husband stretch out his long legs on this couch?

The wide windows face on to tranquil woodland that lies on the other side of the lane. There's no traffic noise. It's peaceful. Just the rustle of leaves through the open window, the tinkle of a wind chime, the hint of incense in the air.

She sits, but I stay standing.

'Thank you so much for coming to tell me,' she says. 'When did it happen?'

'Tuesday,' I say.

'How are you coping?'

I open my mouth. Close my mouth.

'It's good to get on with things,' she says. 'To let people know, to look after his affairs. But you must remember to take time for yourself. To process it all.'

'Don't you want to know what happened?' I butt in.

'If you want to tell me.'

'He killed himself,' I say.

There it is again. Her eyes, flickering with something.

'I really am so sorry,' she says.

'Are you?' I ask.

She nods.

Hesitates.

'How did you find out he was seeing me?'

'I found your card.'

'Ah.'

'I didn't know before.'

Nothing. No 'Didn't you?'

No surprise at all.

Leslie Klein knew my husband hadn't told me of his visits.

I swallow a sob – where do they keep coming from? – and stare out the window.

How much does she know about me? About our marriage? About Danny?

'I think, Erin, you might have come here for answers about Danny. But I'm afraid—'

'He was a patient of yours, then?'

A pause.

'He was.'

'For how long?'

A split second, a moment where she considers saying 'I'm not at liberty to say', but seems to change her mind.

'A while,' she says.

My reaction is physical. I clutch my chest.

Years?

Did it start before or after he met me?

'I can't discuss my sessions with Danny with you,' she says. 'I think you know that.'

'I don't know anything,' I say, staring at the white rug beneath my feet. My voice doesn't sound like it belongs to me and she sounds like she's in another room – like there are two people having a conversation back where normality ended and the surreal began.

'Was he . . . did he have a diagnosis?' I whisper.

'I can't—'

A catch in her throat.

'There were things going on in his work,' I say. 'Did he tell you he was under investigation? Did he tell you anything about that?'

She flinches.

'I've heard the news,' she says. 'The Newport PD are under pressure.'

'No, that's something else,' I say. 'That's the drugs stuff. That had nothing to do with Danny. I was hoping if he was seeing you, you'd know something.'

I stare at her, desperate.

Please, please, tell me something, I will her. Anything.

She looks away.

'Erin, you should know he loved you very much—'

Nope.

Can't do it. I can't listen to platitudes.

I rush from the room, out past the secretary, through the front door and out into the lane.

I stand against a railing, scented jasmine tickling the back of my neck and the back of my throat as I take in deep gulps of air.

And I realise what it is that bugged me so much about Dr Leslie Klein.

When I told her Danny was dead – when I revealed how he died – she wasn't surprised.

She'd been expecting it.

His psychiatrist knew he was a suicide risk.

I didn't even know he had a psychiatrist.

Erin

Now

Karla's opening argument for my defence, I felt, was ridiculously brief.

The police have no real evidence and I'm obviously innocent.

That pretty much sums it up.

Afterwards, we argued, and I asked her was she planning on using a fill-in-the-blanks strategy for my entire case. To which she replied that I read too much fiction and not all court cases contain *To Kill a Mockingbird* soliloquies. Then we both told each other to fuck off, hugged, and prepared for the first witness for the prosecution.

Dr Leslie Klein was not happy about being summoned by the other side. She'd told me as much, even though we weren't supposed to be in contact with each other in the run up to her testimony.

For a start, being called as a witness goes against her professional ethics. Leslie doesn't like to reveal anything about her clients, living or dead. Secondly, she's on my side.

That's what I tell myself as she slowly, inadvertently, hangs me.

Prosecutor Roberts keeps flashing those pearly whites at everybody in the court. The jury. The judge. The public on the benches. Leslie. He has the room in the palm of his hand, if the relaxed stance of most of these people is anything to go by. The only tense person here is me.

Leslie's contribution starts off okay.

'Dr Klein, when you first met the defendant, can you tell us a little about the state of her mental health at that time?' This is Prosecutor Roberts' opening gambit.

'No.'

'Excuse me?'

'When I first met Erin, she called to my office to inform me that Danny Ryan was dead. We spent, at most, ten minutes together. That is not enough time to make an informed opinion about a person's mental health.'

Leslie inclines her head slightly, like she's right now evaluating the prosecutor, after less than ten minutes in his company.

He's undaunted.

'But you can tell us that Erin Kennedy had previously been in the dark about her husband's sessions with you?' he says.

'Objection.' Karla doesn't even look up. 'Leading.'

'Sustained.' Judge Palmer doesn't look up, either. This is a case to decide my future and everybody seems to be more interested in reading the material on the desks in front of them.

'My apologies,' the prosecutor says. 'Perhaps you'll elaborate on the reason for the defendant's visit?'

'Of course. She came to inform me her husband was dead.'

'Did you tell her how long you'd been treating Danny?'

'In a manner. I confirmed I'd treated her husband for a period, but not the specific length of time.'

'Did you discuss anything more?'

'No.'

'Did you meet again?'

'Yes.'

'Why?'

'Erin and I became . . . friends.'

'Friends. Not doctor and patient?'

'No.'

How we both regretted that. Leslie could have refused to give evidence if I'd been her patient. They might have tried to compel her but the State is funny about things like that. Probably because half the judges and prosecutors have shrinks of their own.

'But Danny was your patient.'

'Yes.'

'And, as a friend, did you subsequently tell Erin for exactly how long Danny had been your patient?'

'Yes.'

'When did you start treating Danny Ryan?'

'Autumn 2017.'

'A couple of months after he met Erin Kennedy?'

Leslie pauses.

'Yes.'

There's an intake of breath in the court.

'And did you tell the defendant why you were treating her husband?'

'I never spoke about the exact content of Danny's sessions.'

That's a clever massaging of the truth. Sure, Leslie never told me exactly what had been said. She just hinted at the overall theme.

'How did Erin Kennedy take the news her husband had sought

psychiatric help subsequent to meeting her?' Prosecutor Roberts asks.

Now, people are giggling.

'Objection. Calls to speculation.' Karla looks up this time, but only momentarily. It's a warning shot across Roberts' bow. *I might be busy reading here, but I'm still watching you.*

'Sustained. Keep it straight, Counsellor.'

Prosecutor Roberts flashes the Daniel Craig grin and holds out his hands like he's an errant schoolboy. He turns back to Leslie.

'I'm just trying to get at the defendant's state of mind as far back as seventeen months ago.' He shrugs. 'By your recollection, what did the defendant say when you told her you had been treating Danny Ryan for the full eighteen months of their marriage? Her exact words, please.'

A pause. Leslie's voice when she answers is tight and full of apology directed my way.

'She said if he wasn't dead already, she would, um, fucking kill him.'

It's a real shame she couldn't have massaged the truth out of that one.

Oh, Danny. Back then, there were so many things I had still to learn about you.

Harvard

December 2016

The first moment Ally realised something was very, very wrong, was when she returned to campus.

Lauren had done everything Ally had asked of her. She'd shown the type of courage that Ally hadn't even fully realised was required. It was only when she'd seen Lauren physically shaking with fear when Ally asked her to tell her story that Ally understood her own remove from what had happened; the ease with which she'd been able to tell Lauren to *do the right thing, to go to the professionals, to record the facts*.

Afterwards, Lauren had been very quiet.

But it was done, at least, and now Ally could start to take care of her.

Ally had popped out to the doughnut store off-campus, the one Lauren said she liked, and picked up a box of every sort, along with two strong coffees.

She was on her way towards Canaday when she saw the door to Dorm E, Lauren's dorm, open.

Ally's boyfriend emerged.

Ally stood still in the snow, her breath forming hot white clouds in the early afternoon air.

He stopped, too, like a deer that's suddenly realised it's caught in somebody's crosshairs.

He looked over at Ally.

They were only yards apart.

The students, usually ever-present, were either in class or avoiding the cold.

They were alone.

They could hear each other without moving any closer.

'What are you doing here?' Ally said. 'Is it follow-up? I thought Lauren reported everything?'

'Ally, I . . .'

He looked back at the door through which he'd just emerged.

'I'm sorry,' he said. 'When you said . . . I thought I could help. I didn't know who was involved or what . . .'

He stopped. His face said it all.

Ally glanced up, her attention drawn by movement.

Lauren was at her window, looking out.

Distraught.

Ally's boyfriend stayed where he was, silent.

'Wait . . .' Ally said. 'You know him?'

He started to shake his head, but then he looked down at the ground.

'It's complicated,' he said.

Tears sprung into Ally's eyes as she put two and two together and came up with five.

She dropped the box of doughnuts and the tray of coffee on

to the snow. The box bounced open; sugar-frosted confectionary spilled out on to the ground.

She ran towards the dorm.

Her boyfriend tried to grab her arm but she pushed him away with such force he almost toppled over.

He didn't try to follow.

Upstairs Ally hammered on Lauren's door, but Lauren wouldn't open it.

'Please,' Ally gasped, her heart racing, 'Lauren, let me in.'

Then, weakly, a response:

'You made me say what happened. You said he would help.'

Ally sank to her knees in the corridor and placed her head against the shut door.

She would make her boyfriend explain himself, Ally thought.

She stood up and, with effort, made herself go back downstairs.

When she opened the door to the outside world, he was already gone.

Erin

THEN

McNally's is an authentic Irish bar for anybody who's never actually been to Ireland.

Its owner, Bud 'McNally' Johnson, claims he has not-so-distant old country lineage on both his maternal and paternal side, but local legend has it his people arrived on a certain Mayflower and were among the first to issue a polite fuck-you to the English during a little known tax dispute involving tea. He's related to one of the old families of Long Island – the Gold Coast mansion owners, the families too wealthy to ever reveal just how wealthy they are. He has the look of money about him; an unnatural mop of hair for his age (almost seventy), all-year-round tan, shiny white teeth.

But Bud, apparently, also had a drink problem in his younger days, and ended up a little disinherited and a lot familiar with bars.

Makes total sense he'd open one.

Danny and I loved happy hour in McNally's on a Friday night.

I'd never realised he was coming to meet me direct from his sessions with his psychiatrist.

When I land there, after being in Dr Leslie Klein's office myself, most people are sitting outside enjoying the early evening's blue skies and lingering, glorious sunshine.

Inside is pretty empty, except for a guy down the far end of the counter who looks too well off to be here but probably knows the owner.

I climb on a high stool, tuck my trainers under the foot rail, and try to mentally summon the right cocktail that will obliterate the last few days. From the speakers, Hozier sings 'Take Me to Church'.

At my behest, Tanya has kept Gloria company today. She's taken her to get her hair done, Gloria as unwilling as I imagine I'd be, and they're still out shopping for a tie to bury Danny in. I know what suit he'd like – the grey one he got married in – but he's lost the tie he wore that day and I can't focus on little details like which one to replace it with. Not when I can't face burying him.

Bud places a pint of Smithwick's red ale in front of me.

'Sorry for your troubles,' he says.

'Bud, the only people who drink Smithwick's are men older than my father.'

'No, I think you've got that wrong, sweetheart.'

But he duly fetches me a Sam Adams.

I keep my head down, indicating I don't want and can't handle company, though I know Bud is hovering.

I take out my phone, see the trillion missed calls, messages and emails, and put it back in my handbag.

A lot of my recent communications are from work. I don't need to read them to know what they say.

We're so sorry. Don't worry about anything. We're here if you need us. A deluge of sympathy that, to acknowledge, would break me.

Bud is back with a plate of what he deems comfort food. Bacon, cabbage and potatoes. Except Bud's interpretation is crispy turkey bacon, slaw and a mountain of fries.

When I leave, unsteady on my feet, he tells me the drinks and the food I never ordered are on him.

He's a darling and I am going to cry if I stay here and the rest of the regulars come in and start being nice to me.

I take what some might call the circuitous walk home, an hour-long diversion along the beach, thanking my lucky stars for nightfall and how it clears the tourists.

When I first moved here, I enjoyed the presence of the summer people, as the Long Islanders call them. It made me feel like I was still connected to civilisation, all those other accents and faces.

Danny, at the time, had been living on a beachfront up in Montauk, the end of the world. He'd been renting with a couple of other guys so it hadn't been an option for me to move in. He suggested we find somewhere further along the beach, just before it tipped into the ocean. I politely and firmly put my foot down.

'I did not move to New York to live in the ass-end of nowhere,' I told him. 'I had my pick of places at home to do that.'

Newport has five thousand citizens. Our nearest proper-size town, Patchogue, has twelve and a half thousand.

Danny considered this a happy compromise. I considered the summer influx of non-locals to be the only time the place was worth living in.

That soon changed.

I'd even begun to dream of those houses up in Montauk, the large ocean-fronts, only American beach grass and seaside goldenrod between your deck and the clear blue sea.

I take my sandals off and walk barefoot through the sand.

I never did get that run in on Tuesday. I snort. All I'd had to worry about that morning was my weight. Something nobody had warned me about when I moved to the States: the food and portion sizes. I've gained at least three pounds a year, every year, since I moved over.

Danny could eat and drink whatever he liked; he never put on a pound or seemed to suffer the ill-effects of alcohol or a Chinese takeout binge.

Danny was the healthiest person I knew. The sort who lived into their nineties.

Unless they were shot in the line of duty.

Things I used to stress over having a cop for a husband, number 579.

The list of my concerns was long, and still, Danny taking his own life never made it on.

I turn and walk to the edge of the ocean; gaze over at Fire Island. I can see the early haze of bonfires being lit on the horizon. Night revellers, with cases of beer in ice and hampers of rye sandwiches filled with pastrami and pickles. Just the thought of their normality and the absence of any for me almost floors me.

Is there anything I can do to stop this aching, nightmarish pain, this feeling that I'm being hit repeatedly by a freight train every waking hour?

Answers. If I had the answers.

I saw the way my husband looked at Ben Mitchell the morning he came to our home.

It was like . . . like Danny had been betrayed.

When I turn to leave, I know instantly somebody is watching me.

I look along the beach. In the distance, some walkers, the odd jogger.

I scan the dunes.

It's only a rustle but I see the back of somebody, walking away.

A man. Dark hair.

Before I can dwell on it any longer, I give myself a shake.

Shadows, I tell myself.

I take my phone out as I walk, text Ben.

If you cared for Danny at all, it reads, tell me why he was being investigated.

Ben says he'll call by after his shift. I clarify that I will meet him in the small residential park beside our building.

I'm not having him in our apartment.

I don't need somebody like, say, my husband's psychiatrist, to explain the concept of triggers to me. It's tough enough being at home. Having Danny's partner, the co-witness to his suicide, back at my door would be too much.

I sit on a bench just inside the park, which is well lit by the Olde Worlde lamps I used to mock when I moved here but ended up finding delightful.

'This place is more English than England,' I told Danny, every time I spotted one.

'We're all just counting the days until the new season of *The Crown*.' He'd laughed.

The air is fragranced with the bark of red maples and cedars and the ever-present smell of the sea. The grass is warm on the parts of my feet exposed in my sandals, but I can feel the creep of the dew. It's silent, bar the repetitive whistle of a mockingbird seeking a mate.

I close my eyes, only opening them when I hear the sound of footsteps.

I turn and see Ben coming in the gate.

I stand.

'Let's walk,' I say.

I've never really liked Ben, but whatever I'm feeling now, it's new. Being around him makes me feel uneasy.

It's the way he struggles to meet my eye. How, when he does, it's like he's looking through me, not at me.

We fall into step beside each other.

'Danny was seeing a psychiatrist,' I say.

Ben says nothing.

For fuck's sake.

'You knew.'

'I was his partner.'

'Me too.'

Ben sighs.

'We spent our working day together. I had to account for him going missing on Friday afternoons.'

'Any other afternoons I should know of? Did he have a rich widow on the go on Tuesdays? Gamblers Anonymous on a Thursday?'

'Don't,' Ben says.

We've walked back towards my building.

Without meaning to, I make towards the side of it, and the area beneath my apartment.

Too late, he realises.

'Erin,' he says, but I'm a good ten yards ahead of him now and it's dawned on me that I still haven't seen where my husband died.

The police tape is gone.

The blood has been washed from the pavement.

I stare at the ground where I imagine he lay but it's useless. It doesn't look like anything happened here and yet, I'm a breath away from where Danny took his last.

'What was he being investigated for?' I asked.

If I didn't know better, I'd say Ben is more freaked out being at this spot than I am.

'Erin, can't you just let him rest?' he says.

'No,' I say. 'I need to know.'

'Fuck, you should just remember him as he was!'

I take a step back at the ferocity in Ben's voice.

He's immediately contrite. He looks away, and in the light thrown across us by the building's exterior lamps, I can see a film of tears sheen his eyes.

'I don't want to remember him,' I whisper. 'Remembering him means he's gone. Ben, I'm begging you. I feel like . . . like I'm suspended right now. Like time has stopped. You can't just tell me something like that and not explain yourself. Why was Danny being investigated? What was on his mind when he did what he did?'

'You know there's no closure for this,' he says but I can hear the give in his voice. 'No matter what I tell you, it will never give you what you need. He's never coming back.'

I wait.

'You remember that case Danny led last year,' Ben says, reluctantly. 'The guy who was accused of killing that young woman in Babylon?'

I frown, recall the details. An eighteen-year-old girl had been found strangled to death, her body hidden in bush grass out near Fosters Creek. A local black man had been charged with her death. It had happened only a couple of months after we'd got married. Danny had been the detective who solved it, though he told me privately he didn't deserve the plaudits that were heaped on him. Dwayne Miller was a crackhead who'd harassed the girl for money outside a well-known bar and several people had seen the interaction. When she'd opened her purse and given him ten dollars, he'd spotted a few fifties in there. He'd followed her, waited until they were on a quiet road, tried to grab the bag and then things got ugly when she fought back. The police found the bag five hundred yards away from her body, everything but the cash still inside.

Open and shut.

'The All-Sides group have taken on Dwayne Miller's case,' Ben says.

I swallow.

The All-Sides group was set up by a man who'd received twenty-five years for small-time dealing because he'd broken the three-strike rule. The man had educated himself in prison – and came to realise the fact he had an addict for a mom, had been beaten and abused in several of his foster homes and had never received so much as a how-you-doing from the State, should have been factored in after his first strike and preventative action taken then.

Danny was always very fair when it came to understanding the rationale behind why some people crossed the line. He got, as much as anybody raised with money problems, how easy it was to be suckered by life, to make the wrong choices and end up in a bad place.

But once somebody had committed a criminal act, Danny always said there was a difference between a reason and an excuse. Dwayne Miller had had a hard life. But that didn't mean he was entitled to ruin somebody else's.

'And?' I prompt.

'All-Sides only take on cases they think they can win,' Ben says. 'There were questions asked at the time of Miller's trial.'

'Questions asked by who and of whom?'

'We, eh, had no forensic evidence on Miller. The DA was a little concerned about the confession that Danny had procured. It was taken when the assisting officer had stepped out of the room. I wasn't there at the time. It was felt . . .'

He trailed off.

'Say it.'

'It was felt that Danny might have got a bit too caught up in the case. That he knew Miller did it and made the parts fit the whole.'

No.

Danny would never press for a conviction against somebody if he thought they were innocent. Even if . . . even if the case reminded me of something close to him.

'Maybe it was, I don't know . . .' Ben hesitates. 'Maybe it was playing on his mind when he did it.'

'This is . . .' I can't find the right words. 'Is that all? I can understand him being upset by that but it's not enough to make him kill himself. No way. Did he talk to you about it? Did you reassure him it would all be fine? That they'd find nothing?'

Ben swallows. I study him, and my heart sinks.

'I saw the way he looked at you that morning, Ben. It was like you'd let him down. You didn't . . . tell me you backed him up? He was your partner!'

'It was complicated, Erin—'

Ben hangs his head.

I pace, my head full of thoughts I can't quieten. It's still not enough. Even if Ben didn't have his back . . .

I turn and face Ben.

'What are you not telling me?' I say.

'I—'

'Ben? What else was he being investigated for?'

In the silence, I can hear the strains of music coming from one of the open windows in the apartments above. Billy Joel's 'Piano Man'.

And as the seconds between my question and Ben's answer stretch, my own heartbeat grows louder and my mouth drier.

'Seriously, Erin,' he says. 'Don't ask a question you don't want to hear the answer to.'

I take a step back. Then anger picks up where the shock has left off.

'What is that supposed to mean? Christ, Ben, Danny mightn't have been perfect but he certainly wasn't a corrupt detective.'

'Erin, do you really think Danny did everything by the book? You, of all people?'

I baulk.

I know Danny wasn't a cardboard-cut-out cop.

It's knowledge that weighs heavily on me.

Harvard

December 2016

Ally had borrowed the car from a junior in her old house of Winthrop. He was the son of a neighbour in Providence and Ally had been his go-to since he'd arrived in Harvard two and a half years ago. The forced friendship had worked out exceptionally well because Marky-Mark, as he was affectionately known, came with his own wheels, which he seemed completely incapable of staying sober enough to drive. Whenever Ally needed the car, it was always available, albeit with a smell of weed inside that would make a state trooper high were she to lower the window for a licence check.

The temperature had warmed in the last twenty-four hours, and the snow had stopped twenty-four hours before that, which meant Ally was now negotiating the roads of Cambridge in pure slush.

The wipers were barely clearing the rain that beat down on the windscreen and every couple of minutes, the grey muck and ice that was caught in the wheels of the vehicles ahead splashed on to the windows, making driving visibility poor.

That and the fact Ally kept crying, the tears blurring everything in front of her that wasn't already covered by rain and sleet and slush.

She pulled up outside the diner on Massachusetts Avenue.

She had told Lauren Gregory that she, Ally, could be trusted. That Lauren should listen to her. That Ally wouldn't let her down and she'd get Lauren all the help she needed.

She'd steeled Lauren for the fight ahead of her – her fight, not Ally's – and she sent her off to tell her story, even when Lauren didn't want to talk.

So Lauren had. She'd faced her fears, encouraged by Ally. Lauren had done everything she was supposed to do.

And now she was too scared to do anything, because she couldn't even trust Ally, or the people Ally referred her to, could she?

Everybody, it seemed, had let Lauren down.

Inside the diner, by the window, Ally could see Lauren sitting on a stool. The top of her head was obscured by the red-chequered blind pulled halfway down, and her body was positioned behind the neon sign that declared the restaurant open, but Ally knew those curls, and recognised the small hands and chipped nail varnish clasped around the large milkshake.

Lauren had agreed to meet her here. She didn't want Ally in her dorm.

Didn't want anybody seeing them together.

Ally dried her eyes roughly and turned off the car's ignition.

In two days Lauren's exams started, her first big test of fresher year. Lauren was smart. Up until all this had happened, she'd been studying and excelling.

No matter what happened, Ally could not let Lauren crash out of this term without sitting those exams. She had enough knowledge to scrape a pass and that was all that was needed. Then Lauren could go home for Christmas, remind herself she had people who really cared for her and when they returned in January, Ally would get Lauren a counsellor.

The rest of it, Ally's own problems, she'd deal with.

Because she'd also been let down by somebody she trusted. Badly.

Right on cue, her phone rang.

She eyed her boyfriend's caller ID for a moment or so, then knocked off the call.

Three years – three years believing in somebody, thinking they had the same moral compass as you, and it turned out she hadn't known him at all.

It took less than thirty seconds to run from the sidewalk into the diner and less than half that for Ally to get completely soaked.

She pulled off her parka inside the door then stood on the welcome mat and drip-dried for a few seconds, the smell of burgers and coffee filling her nostrils.

With more reluctance than she cared to admit to, she joined Lauren at the window counter.

'Lauren, I don't know what to say,' Ally said, which was the truth. She'd thought about it the whole way over here. How could she even begin to apologise?

'We have to stop talking about this,' Lauren said.

She twirled her straw in the milkshake which, up close, Ally could see was just for show. Lauren hadn't taken even a sip.

A waitress arrived with a pot of coffee and a clean cup.

'Can I get you something, sweetie?' she asked Ally. The waitress was already pouring before Ally had finished shaking her head.

Ally waited until the waitress left before she spoke again.

'I'd no idea, Lauren,' she said. 'I thought . . . I thought he was one of the good ones.'

Lauren shrugged.

'People will say it's my fault.'

'Nobody . . .'

The look Lauren gave Ally was withering.

'Some people might think that,' Ally said, lamely. 'But they're assholes. And there *are* lots of good cops.'

'Really?' Lauren snorted. 'That black student the cops in South Boston were caught on camera punching in the gut – all he'd done was stand there with his hands out waiting to be cuffed. He's an honours student. Last week, some cop fired five warning shots into a man's back in LA. You tell me where I can find a good cop. Go on, tell me.'

She was giving up. Ally could see it in the slump of her shoulders, the quiet, resigned tone of her voice.

'This is my fault, if it's anybody's,' Ally said. 'I'm meant to protect you. I had no idea what he was capable of . . .'

'Forget it. It's over.'

'If you want to talk to somebody like an attorney or—'

'Stop!' Lauren's voice was low but ferocious.

Ally met Lauren's eye.

'Haven't you done enough?' Lauren said, her face incredulous. 'Don't you know how dangerous this is? There are good cops? Are you that naïve?'

Ally gulped.

She had seven years on Lauren. A lifetime of experience at this age. Apparently.

But everything was upside down. Ally didn't know who to talk to, who to trust or how this could happen in a world that up until now had seemed like a safe place.

Lauren sounded very much like the adult.

'I won't let that man hurt you again,' Ally said, weakly.

'You can't promise that,' Lauren said. 'You've no idea what he knows about me, what he knows about my family. Or what he could find out about you. I've broken my word now. If we don't just make this go away, he'll come after me. And you.'

Ally hung her head. She stared into the dark surface of her untouched coffee, then at the rain pelting down on the car she'd parked outside.

'What will you do?'

'I'll sit my exams. I'll go home. Celebrate Christmas. Then come back and pretend it never happened.'

'Can you do that? It doesn't sound healthy. I think, if nothing else, you should speak to—'

'I'm not speaking to anybody else, Ally. It's over. I'm going to forget it ever happened and you should, too. Promise me. Promise me you'll forget it.'

Ally's mouth fell open.

How could she make such a promise?

How could she not?

Her first real task as proctor and she'd failed miserably.

'I won't tell anybody,' she said, almost choking on what she hoped wasn't a lie.

Lauren studied her for a few moments, then looked away.

'How will you get home for Christmas?' Ally asked.

'My brother's collecting me.'

Ally nodded, slowly.

She didn't believe Lauren could get through Christmas at home without breaking down and telling her family everything. And once it was out in the open, the weight would be lifted from Ally's shoulders. Lauren's family would know how to handle this. Even if Ally hadn't.

'What about you?' Lauren asked.

Ally tensed.

'I was supposed to be spending it with my boyfriend,' she said.

She glanced quickly at Lauren's side profile. It gave nothing away.

'I won't be now. Obviously.'

Lauren nodded, one curt dip of the head.

'Obviously,' she repeated.

They both fell silent for a few moments.

'It was just sex,' Lauren said.

'What?'

'That's all. Just . . . bad sex. I shouldn't have made anything of it. Everyone can make mistakes.'

Ally flinched.

In the reflection in the window, she could see the tears in Lauren's eyes.

Erin

THEN

Karla's Chevy pulls up outside my building the afternoon after I talk to Ben. We'd agreed to meet over the weekend. Karla is insistent she's going to help me, practically pro bono, and I've a couple of texts from David telling me to let her. But she's also pragmatic and aware that she's got other cases, the ones actually paying her bills. To shoehorn me in, she needs to do it out of hours.

She's asked if we can talk while she drives because she needs to drop something off to a client on the east end of the island.

Tanya and I are having Gloria over to the apartment for dinner later so I tell Karla she can drop me by the farmers' market in Westhampton and I'll make my own way back.

'Nonsense,' she says. 'I'll drop you home.'

She puts the car in drive.

'And you can fill me in on what you found out from the psychiatrist,' she says.

'And from his partner.' I sigh.

She glances sideways at me.

'And thanks, by the way,' I say. 'Again. It meant a lot, what you said to me on Thursday. That we . . . that people like us can find each other. I'm not – I mean I'm not a total loner or anything. You're not meeting me at my best. This week has just, I don't know . . . I feel like I've lost my footing in the world.'

'You're grieving, chica. But you've done the right thing. You've reached out and asked for help. And even if I didn't owe David, I'd have helped. The second you walked into my office I knew we were going to be spending a lot of time together. My mama always said I get a good read from a person. It helps in the job I do, to know who the good ones are. Hold up, what is this motherfucker at? This ain't the Sunday school run!'

Karla honks at the car dawdling in front of us and pulls around it at speed.

I grab the passenger door handle and hang on. She drives like she talks – fast.

'Do you only represent good guys?' I say, catching my breath.

'Hell no. A pay cheque is a pay cheque. But I like to know who to fight harder for. No skin off my nose if some dick ends up in county.' A pause. 'Unless he's my coffee dick.'

She's deadly serious.

'How did you and David meet?' I ask. 'I'm guessing it was when David was a journalist?'

David had worked as an investigative reporter before he'd ever written books, something which helped no end with his research skills, even as a fiction bestseller.

She smiles thinly.

'I had a bit of a rep for busting corrupt officials in the city, including police. I fed David for his articles, he fed me tidbits for my cases. Above board, nice and professional. Then I took on an individual in the Mayor's office and some powerful people were not happy. I came in for a lot of flak. Sustained flak. David had something on that person, which I won't be repeating, and he handed me a file. I brandished it in a very significant boardroom and the pressure was dropped. He got me out of a very tight spot. Information is everything, Erin.'

She flicks on the radio for the hourly news and we listen for a few minutes. The news anchor tells us Long Island house prices are rising; the next story reveals the clean-up for last June's storm is costing more than expected. This segues into a segment on the incompetence of the authorities on the Island and the increasing threat to tourism from the headlines being made by local crim-inality. Just last week, the reporter tells us, the gang believed to have moved its drugs business to Suffolk County was involved in a feud hit with a rival gang over in Nassau County. Not one person has been arrested yet and questions are being asked about whether the local police are failing because they're not up to it, or because they're not inclined to go after the gang leaders.

It's a not-so-subtle allegation of corruption.

Karla knocks off the news before the weather.

'Sounds like Newport PD has its fair share of problems,' she says. 'So, the psychiatrist and Danny's partner. Ben Mitchell, isn't it? What has he told you and do you trust him?'

I fill her in on the very little I learned from Dr Klein, then what Ben told me about the accusations against Danny.

'I don't like Ben,' I conclude. 'But that doesn't mean I don't trust him. He was Danny's friend. But, it turns out there was plenty I didn't know about Danny.'

'Well, let's look at the facts,' Karla says. 'You've been told Danny was under investigation for his handling of a confession, but we've yet to see concrete, official proof from the ninth precinct about the veracity of that claim. And even if he was under investigation, you don't know if he was guilty, but you do know he was keeping it from you. That could be because he was innocent and he didn't want you involved in something that he could deal with.'

'But then there's Dr Klein,' I say. 'Why wouldn't he tell me about her?'

Karla chews the inside of her lip. Her dark hair is tied back in a ponytail and I notice now she's wearing leisurewear – and yet, when I got into the car, none of that occurred to me because Karla has an absolute air of competence about her. I've never seen this woman in a suit and yet I know full well she's a capable attorney.

I mouth a silent curse as we sharply overtake another two cars in the face of oncoming traffic.

'I don't know about that one,' she says. 'But men are funny beasts. Especially when it comes to talking about what's in those tiny brains of theirs.'

'Are you married?' I ask her.

'I enjoy one-night stands too much,' she says, plainly.

I blink. Fair enough.

'Let me keep trying to get some answers out of his boss, Captain Sullivan,' Karla says. 'I contacted the department yesterday and met a brick wall. But they have to speak to me eventually.'

Karla drops me off at Westhampton and tells me she'll be back in an hour, then travels on to meet her client.

I walk around the open-air market and something happens. I realise I need this normality. Freshly cut flowers and fruit and vegetables scent the air. Trestle tables are stacked with displays of honey jars and oysters on beds of ice. It's soothing. It's familiar.

Maybe the body just can't sustain grief, shock and active denial without a thirty-minute break every now and then.

I ask the woman at the oyster shack to put an order together for me and I move over to the flowers. I want to spoil Gloria and Tanya, considering how little attention I've given either of them since they both arrived.

I'm drawn to the vibrant blue hydrangeas, the signature flower of the Hamptons.

As I smell them, I'm assaulted by a memory. An afternoon on our lawn at home, Tanya making daisy chains, Niamh and I helping our mother snip hydrangeas for our grandmother.

The shock of being hit with old grief, when I'm struggling to cope with my present grief, is so alarming I drop my wicker basket.

Its contents – ripe plum tomatoes and courgettes with their flowers still attached – jump, but the basket lands the right side up. Two of the tomatoes split and one clears the edge and splats on the ground.

I bend over but before I can retrieve the basket, somebody is handing it to me.

I stand up quickly, not making eye contact, just wanting to thank the stranger and move on, away from this mortifying situation.

But he still has a grip on the basket handle and I'm forced to look up.

It's a man, around my age, good-looking, dark-haired, dressed in the sort of clothes that are a kind of uniform in these parts. Light designer pants and polo shirt, a Patek Phillipe on his wrist. Oozing wealth in that cultured, refined way. His mouth is pleasant, a hint of the cheeky grin that might usually reside there, but right now he looks serious and concerned.

He feels familiar to me, but I can't quite place him.

'Are you okay?' he asks, and his voice is deep but soft, a touch of New York but university-cultivated.

I nod, still trying to figure out where I know him from.

'You look like you've seen a ghost,' he says. 'Can you talk? Does your face feel funny?'

'What?'

He stares at me, studying my features in a way that's far too intimate.

'Um – thanks?' I say, and try to leave.

'I had to check,' he says, apologetically. 'I'm doing that thing. F-A-S-T?'

He spells out the letters. I still don't know what he's talking about.

'You dropped your basket and then you didn't say anything. The signs of a stroke, you know? Face drooping. Arm weakness. Speech trouble.'

'Oh,' I say. Then, 'What's the T?'

'Time to call an ambulance.'

'Are you a doctor?'

Now he's embarrassed.

'Just a concerned citizen who spends too much time getting first aid advice and other life tips on Twitter.'

I smile politely and turn to leave again. It hits me, then, where I know him from.

'You were in McNally's in Newport. Yesterday.'

He looks startled for a moment, then nods.

'Well, um, you're clearly okay,' he says.

Now he's the one eager to get away.

I turn and am about to make my way back to the oyster stand when it occurs to me.

I pivot, but I can't see the stranger any more. I walk in the direction he went, towards the section where the bottles from the local vineyards are on display. We don't have many wineries on the South Shore of Long Island but on the North Shore, all along the Long Island Sound and the North Fork, the landscape is dotted with them. I've barely drunk wine from outside Long Island since I moved here.

I spot the stranger a few yards ahead and now I notice – he doesn't have a basket. He has nothing in his arms and he's not stopping at any of the sections. He's just walking back to the car park outside.

'Hey,' I call.

He keeps walking, then he stops and there's a split second before he turns around.

I don't know why, but I can sense immediately he's put that smile on. That, seconds ago, his expression was not happy.

'There's no need to thank me,' he says, jokingly. 'I save lives here regularly.'

'I saw you in McNally's yesterday,' I say.

A twitch in his jaw.

'I think we've established that,' he answers.

'Did you follow me out to the beach after I left? Was that you I saw in the dunes?'

It's fleeting but it's there. The giveaway.

'Are you following me?' I ask.

He frowns. He's considering lying, I guess.

'My husband is a police detective,' I say.

And then there's no sign of deception in his features. Just . . .
pity.

'I know,' he says.

I step back.

That, I was not expecting.

'I'm sorry,' he says, full of contrition.

'You are following me!' I say.

'No. Not like that.'

I've moved a good few yards away from him.

'Are you police?' I ask.

'I'm Cal,' he says.

I scan my memories. Danny had no friends or workmates called
Cal and, even if he had . . .

'Why are you stalking me?' I say.

His face flushes and he shakes his head, adamantly.

'It's not what it looks like,' he says.

'I don't know any Cals.'

'My full name is Caleb J. Hawley. You can look me up. I knew
your husband in a, um, in a personal capacity.'

'So why not come up to me and say that?'

'I didn't want to intrude.'

'You are intruding! You're following me around the place.'

'I was in McNally's first yesterday. You came in.'

'But you knew who I was,' I say. 'And today?'

'Today was . . .'

I narrow my eyes.

'I guess I've been trying to summon the courage to approach
you,' he says, weakly.

I don't buy it.

'You know Danny is dead.'

'Yes.'

'You should know I still have plenty of friends in the police department,' I say. 'Whoever you are, you're acting like a weirdo and I don't like it. Stop following me.'

'I'm sorry. I'm not trying to scare you.'

'How do you know my husband?'

He purses his lips.

'Listen,' he says, 'I'm sorry. I've gone about this all wrong. I should leave you alone.'

'Obviously. But I'm entitled to know what you're playing at.'

A hesitation.

'There are things . . . your husband was involved in. I can't talk about it.'

My hands, already trembling, start to shake.

'And you don't,' he says.

'I don't what?' I ask, confused.

'You don't have friends in the police department.'

I feel like I've been slapped.

'What did you say?'

'Just, take care of yourself, Erin,' he says, then he spins on his heel and walks hurriedly towards the car park.

He knows my name. How does he know my name?

Erin

Now

Bud knows how the legal system works over here. Tanya does not.

Karla manages to get them a pass to see me in my holding cell prior to today's hearing. Because of the media attention on the trial and the fact I'm an Irish citizen, everything about my care in advance of and during the trial is being handled with kid gloves.

Tanya has visited me in jail already but she's struggling to get her head around the fact that I'm still incarcerated, that I'm not out on bail.

'It's not like at home,' I tell her, for the fiftieth time. 'It's a murder charge, Tanya. I have an Irish passport. They think I'll flee the jurisdiction. Bail is hard enough to get in any case. I was always going to be denied.'

'You know, with Niamh—' she starts to say.

I cut her off.

'I can't talk about Niamh,' I say.

I talk *to* Niamh, all the time.

Tanya looks around the cell and sniffs. She looks entirely out of place in her Chanel skirt suit, whereas I blend in. I belong here.

This cell is old-fashioned – there are actual jail bars; a narrow, hard mattress; one small chair; a sink and a latrine. My cell in the detention centre isn't much different, except instead of a grille, I have a metal door with a small viewing hatch.

At night, when I come back from court, I walk the few feet of my cell, back and forth, until my legs feel like I've done something with them.

It's six steps from the window to the door.

Six steps. Six seconds. Then I turn and do it again.

I've made friends with the walls in my cell. At least when I'm in there I'm away from the other inmates. We're a strange collection of young and old, extremely violent and not so bad. There are some gang members – girls as young as nineteen in a few cases. A lot of black and Latino women, though not as many as make up the statistics in the male prisons. A couple of women are here for murdering their husbands. Both claim self-defence. I suspect one of them is telling the truth.

The common denominator is that almost everyone here is poor. Except me.

During the day, when they bring us out for yard time, I see them watching me, hear them whispering.

I'm a novelty. An inmate accused of murder and somebody who's not afraid to take on the cops. I might look like a good girl, easy pickings, but they don't quite know what to make of me and the fact I'm the centre of such fuss causes even more confusion. The Irish embassy representative is on to the prison authorities regularly.

Until I'm found guilty in a US court of law, nobody wants me to come to any harm.

So, I've my own cell. I've monitored exercise time, supervised interaction in the canteen and other communal areas. It isn't jail as I ever imagined it. There's no forced camaraderie, not even the threat of bullying. Yet.

They give me books, which you'd think I'd find solace in, given what I used to do for a living – but these days I find I can't read more than a few sentences without losing my concentration.

There's nobody to talk to.

The guards are cold. Aloof.

The system has stripped them and me of humanity.

I'm absolutely isolated.

It's funny, how few words you use in a day when you talk to nobody in any meaningful way.

Depressing, really.

I welcome this trial – just to hear normal people, to be around people who don't look at you like you're dirt. Or at least, not all of them.

'Well, it won't be for long,' Tanya says. 'We're getting you out of here.'

If sheer love and willpower could make that happen, I'd be a free woman.

'He had us all fooled,' Bud says. 'But those people in that court won't be fooled.'

'Oh, Bud,' I say, shaking my head, sadly. 'It's not like luck has been on my side lately, is it?'

Bud takes a deep breath. He looks old in this light – ha, like I can judge – but I can see all the red lines on his face, the tiny broken capillaries that have lived there from way back when he used to drink too hard.

'Who are they calling next?' Bud asks, trying to ease the tension.

'Danny's boss,' I say. 'Sully.'

'Hmm,' Bud says. 'Let him explain his way out of this, eh?'

Let him, indeed.

It's fourteen days until Christmas. My family and the embassy managed to pull enough strings to ensure my trial date was set early and I didn't have to wait the usual year to two years. Still, I suppose I'm going to be spending Christmas in jail.

Before they leave, Bud comes across and whispers something to me, so Tanya won't hear.

'We're going to fix this,' he says. 'Like we promised. He'll be punished for what he did to you. And for what he did to that poor girl.'

I wish Bud was right.

'I've heard rumours of a car,' Bud adds, quieter again.

'What car?' I say, frowning.

'A car on the road outside your apartment that night. Later, after it happened. A dark sedan, windows blacked out. No licence plate. No CCTV on that stretch but I know all the store owners. A guy further up the street, his CCTV is angled up your way. I'm looking into it.'

My stomach knots.

I've a feeling I know who owns that car and why it was there.

Erin

THEN

When Karla picks me up from the farmers' market I tell her immediately about the strange encounter with the man calling himself Cal Hawley.

'Hawley,' she muses. 'The name seems familiar. I've got a family thing this afternoon but I can look into it.'

'No, Karla, you're doing enough for me. I have a pal, our barman, as it happens. He knows everything about everyone, I'll call him later.'

'Okay, let me know what you find out. I don't like the idea of this guy approaching you out of nowhere, but at least he had the good sense to do it in a public place.'

'But he didn't approach me, really,' I say. 'I just realised he was following me and confronted him. What he said about Danny's colleagues – I think he knows what's going on, Karla. I think he knows Danny was under investigation.'

Karla falls quiet.

'And still could be, Erin,' she says. 'This Cal guy could be Internal Affairs. He might want to know what you know, although it would be unusual. In my experience, Danny's department would be happy for this, whatever it is, to just go away. But that might not be the case here. Which means you have to be careful who you talk to.'

'He seemed too . . . preppy to be IA,' I say, but then, what do I know?

I fall silent as she drives me home. All of this might be a distraction from Danny's death but ultimately, it's too much for me and I think Karla senses that.

Outside my building, she says something before I get out of the car.

'I wasn't kidding, Erin. Call me if anything happens. I've dealt with a lot of cops.' She purses her lips until they form a tight line. 'I know Danny was one, and it sounds like he was a good one, but Erin – when they're bad, they're really bad.'

I nod, obedient and a little speechless.

Inside, I hail the lift and stand there with my head resting against the wall.

My brain feels like it's going to explode.

I get into the elevator and try to rearrange my face to show I'm coping, knowing that Gloria will already be upstairs.

When I open my front door, Danny is standing in the apartment, over at the window, looking out at the bay.

It's not Danny, of course.

It's his younger brother Mike, but my heart still stops beating.

For just a moment.

The brothers have the same height and build; they even look

alike. There's only a couple of years between them. But the simi-
larities end at superficial appearance.

'Mike was always going to end up in the army,' Danny told me
once.

'How come?' I asked.

'He's a crazy motherfucker,' Danny said.

By the time I met Mike, he'd grown up a little compared to his
wilder days. He was twenty-nine at our wedding and looked ten
years older. There's a lot to be said for discipline on base and being
shit-scared nearly every day of your working life.

Gloria sees me standing at the door in that split second it takes
Mike to turn around and my heart to find a rhythm again, and she
rushes over. She's guessed what's going through my mind.

'Mike got his leave,' she says, taking the bags from my hands.

He stares out the window for another few seconds then crosses
the room and puts his arms around me.

'No words,' he says, when he lets go.

I sigh. There really aren't.

Tanya is simultaneously hosting and hanging back.

Gloria won't sit down. Instead, she moves around the room,
touching things.

She doesn't know it, but the apartment looks different to how
it did a few days ago. Tanya found a Macy's this morning and now
the chairs are adorned with throws and cushions even I don't recognise. There are Diptyque candles lined up along the kitchen island.
A large vase of fresh flowers sits in front of the French windows,
almost covering the exit.

The apartment looks like it would have had I lived alone and not
with a man who thought cushions were something that got in the

way of being comfortable and fragrant candles were an expensive substitute for a good room spray.

I want to tell Gloria that Danny's hands never brushed off that throw, that he never stood on that rug. But there's no point. If she thinks she's walking in his footsteps, let her.

'Take anything you want,' I say to Gloria.

She shakes her head.

'It's all yours,' she says. 'I had Danny's childhood. You had the man.'

I'll make sure before she leaves tonight she has something belonging to Danny. A T-shirt, something that still smells of him. Not the one I've been wearing every night since Tuesday.

Mike is still standing but he's not going around touching inanimate objects Danny might have last been in contact with.

He's having an almost allergic reaction to being in the apartment.

I glance over at Tanya, who sees my discreet glance at Mike and nods.

We've always been more or less able to read each other's minds.

'ETA on dinner is about thirty minutes if you fancy some fresh air, Mike,' she says.

'I'll show you the neighbourhood,' I say.

Gloria nods approvingly, already distracted by Danny's slim bookshelf with his beloved, well-thumbed Bill Bryson books.

Minutes after I've arrived home, I'm back out on the street, Danny's brother by my side.

'I'm gonna hope that by "show me the neighbourhood", you mean a local bar,' he says.

I smile.

Danny told me that when he was younger, Mike would get

buzzed on cheap liquor and do all kinds of dumb-ass things. But, as he got older, Mike used drink more as a crutch. It was something the family kept an eye on, making sure Mike never tipped from infrequent morose drinker to full-time maudlin drunk.

Mike, Danny used to say, gets a bit depressed.

Yet, it's Mike standing here now.

Five minutes later we're in McNally's. Bud is hosting a large party out back so I don't get a chance to ask him about Cal Hawley, not that I would with Mike here anyway. If I tell Mike strange men are approaching me and acting all weird, I can only imagine how he'd react.

'Two whiskey sours,' I tell the bar waitress.

'Whiskey,' Mike says, pulling out a bar stool for me before taking his own. 'You know I've been drinking weak-as-piss beer all this tour, right?'

'Do they even have bars in Syria?'

Mike almost grins. We're both trying so hard.

'We socialise on base,' he says. 'And import everything.'

'I bet it's like Hooters on Saturday nights.'

'Yeah. Except, instead of women, we have camels.'

Mike makes it sound jokey but there's an undertone. I can tell, just sitting beside Mike, that he's seen things he isn't going to be sharing with anyone else.

'Why did he do it, Sis?' Mike says. He's called me Sis since Danny and I got engaged, which has always made me feel warm inside, coming from a family of all girls.

I shrug. Just because this is a new person asking me why doesn't mean I suddenly have the answers.

'Turns out he was seeing a shrink,' I say.

Mike frowns.

'Because of the job?'

'I don't know.'

I pick up my drink, sip it, let the bitter aroma go up my nose and make my eyes water so there's a reason for my tears.

'You know he never loved anybody the way he loved you,' Mike says.

'I'd hate to be somebody he didn't love.'

Mike shakes his head.

'I mean it,' he says. 'Even his ex didn't come close to you.'

'Well, that's hardly saying much considering he'd no serious girlfriends before me,' I say to Mike. 'And at least his casual flings got dumped in person. I got the message from beyond the grave.'

Mike looks at me strangely. He signals our waitress, two more whiskey sours. When he lifts his arm to get her attention, I see a tattoo on the underside.

'Army ink?' I ask.

'You get bored.'

'Yeah, I'd say it's real dull out there.'

'I'm being shipped somewhere else,' he says. 'I wanted a memory. Trump is pulling us. You know, people hate this guy but, technically, he's engaged in fewer wars than Obama.'

Mike likes to drop what I call opinion bombs. Some things don't change.

Suffolk County flipped from Democrat in the last election and Danny said he was toying with the idea of moving.

My thoughts, led by whiskey, turn to what Ben told me last night.

'Mike, did Danny ever—' Hell, how do I phrase this? 'Do you

think being a cop changed Danny over time? Like, he got less . . . himself?'

There's that funny look again.

'Huh?' Mike says.

I screw up my mouth, try to find the right words, which is pretty tough when I don't even believe what I'm asking.

'He was under investigation. They say there were concerns about how he handled a suspect. His partner, Ben, he implied Danny was suspected of forcing a confession. I guess . . . by beating up the guy or something. And Ben thinks that might have been playing on his mind when he, you know.'

'My brother didn't kill himself because of an allegation that he had a run-in with a suspect,' Mike says. It's exactly the reaction I had with Ben. 'No way. Even if he had, he'd hold his hands up and say, fuck it, yeah, I crossed a line.'

'The guy in question got life in Woodburn for murder,' I say, playing devil's advocate. 'But . . . I think there might be more. Stuff they're not telling me.'

'We need to find out what, then.'

'Mike, I have a lawyer helping me.'

'He's my brother.'

'I know. He was my husband. Let me deal with this, okay?'

'Nah. I gotta do this.'

'Mike – if you go in there, boots first, I'll never find out anything. And it will get back to your CO and you'll be hauled over hot stones. I'll get to the bottom of this. I loved him. You trust me, don't you?'

He hesitates, then nods, then we both stare into our respective glasses.

I feel a heavy hand on my back. Mike's.

'Danny wasn't perfect,' he says. 'And we all have secrets.'

'I know that.'

We both cry a little, then – me, with the art of somebody who's been crying on and off solid for days; Mike, with the shock of somebody wondering what the wet stuff is that's leaking out of his eyes.

'We should go back up and pretend to eat dinner,' I say, feeling heartsore for all the effort Tanya is making to ensure I eat.

'Your sister is a good woman,' Mike says. 'I guess she's gonna go home soon?'

'I suppose.'

I don't want to think about it. I can't imagine being on my own in the apartment and, according to Karla, it could take a few weeks to ease me out of my lease without penalty.

'You're gonna miss her,' Mike says. 'Just so you know, my tour will be up soon, after I relocate. You know I got itchy feet but I can come over here, take care of you for a while. If you need it. I'm not intruding; I just want you to know the offer is there.'

I try to keep my face placid. I'm taken aback, trying to figure out if Mike has some old-fashioned notion that he's supposed to step into the role of replacement husband on behalf of his brother, who choked on his end of the deal.

Mike reads my face and if I'm not mistaken, that's a smile.

'It's not that,' he says. 'You know, Erin, the military is tough for people like me.'

'A black man?' I frown. I'm pretty sure the US military is floor-to-rafters black men.

'Jeez, woman. You only see colour?'

Mike picks up his drink, takes a sip, watches me over it.

Oh.

I suppose, yeah, now I think about it. Mike has never had a steady girlfriend.

This is his polite way of telling me he's not going to be Danny's stand-in. I feel like an idiot now.

He stands, offers me his hand to get down off my stool.

'Ma'am.'

We open the door to an evening shower. We stand under the bar's porch, wait for it to pass. I can tell there's something on Mike's mind by his stance. His shoulders are hunched and his expression shows he's deep in thought.

'What?' I say.

'It's nothing.'

'It's something.'

Mike chews on it some more. I watch and wait.

'You said Danny never had a serious girlfriend.'

'And?' I say.

'He was seeing a girl for a long time before you got together. Steady, like.'

I swallow, my heart gives a little flutter.

Danny and I weren't jealous types. We spoke about former partners, even one-night stands.

I'd been burned by a few guys. Danny said there'd never been anybody close enough to leave him in any pain.

'He never told me.'

Mike shrugs.

'What was her name?' I ask.

'You know what, I can't even remember. You're right, it probably wasn't serious.'

Mike is lying.

We look at each other for a few seconds. He blinks first.

Now Mike, too, realises that Danny wasn't always truthful with me.

And Mike, like me, is probably wondering why.

Later, when Danny's family have left, I sit cross-legged on my bed. My laptop is on the bedspread, pillows propped up behind me.

I start with Danny's Facebook page, and thank the gods I'm able to guess his password.

My name and birthday.

I have a Facebook page, too, but I rarely use it. Danny admired my disregard for it, even while he was a little addicted to it himself. Whatever we were doing, he'd stop, take a picture of the two of us and post it. I'd mock: 'Because if you don't share it, it never happened, right?' He'd ignore me. The odd time I did go in to look at posts, it was mainly because I'd received a notification that Danny Ryan had added a picture of me. Then I'd have to get out quick before I got completely obsessed with correcting his grammar and spelling.

It's you with a Y and an O, Danny.

It's duck off with an F, Erin.

So, I'm not overly familiar with Danny's activity on Facebook, which is why, instead of checking out his friends, I spend the next half hour in floods of tears because every other post he's put up is of the two of us and you have never seen a couple who looked more in love.

Tanya comes in, sits beside me, and rests her head on my shoulder.

I blow my nose with a tissue from the box that has magically taken up residence on my night locker.

'Don't believe the life you see on Facebook, huh?' I say.

'I believe that,' she says, pointing at a picture of Danny and me on a sailboat in Oyster Bay, arms wrapped around each other, the sun reflecting on our sunglasses, sea spray in our hair.

I click my tongue, angry with myself for getting distracted.

Then I go into his friends list.

'Who are you looking for?' Tanya asks.

'Danny's ex,' I say.

I can feel, even if I can't see, Tanya's frown. She fiddles with the belt on her silk dressing gown, then takes a deep breath before launching in.

'I'm sure you're Facebook friends with your exes,' she says.

'I'm not.'

'It doesn't mean anything,' Tanya says. 'Lots of people are. What's so special about this one, anyway?'

'I didn't know she existed. Danny claimed he had no serious girlfriends before me.'

Tanya faces me.

'You know that is what's known as a lie of convenience, right?'

I ignore her.

'What's her name?' Tanya asks.

'I don't know.'

A sigh from my sister.

'I don't see the relevance of this.'

I shrug.

'Maybe this girl dumped him and he just wanted to move on,' Tanya says. 'Honestly, Erin, you can't be getting into this online stalking thing. Your head is playing tricks on you.'

I ignore her and open a search bar in Google, where I type in Dwayne Miller's name. A few articles come up and I scan the ones that mention the All-Sides Project. The reference to why they're looking at it is opaque, just a line about a mishandling of protocol by local police detectives.

'Who's he?' Tanya asks.

Only minutes have passed but I've forgotten she's there.

'Tanya, could you make me a cup of tea?' I ask.

She narrows her eyes.

'The real stuff.'

That has her.

'Proper cuppa coming up,' Tanya says, and bounces off the bed.

As soon as she's occupied, I check Danny's friends list for the man I met today. Cal Hawley.

He's not there.

I Google him, Caleb J. Hawley, and get multiple hits straight away.

Resident of East Hampton. One of the most salubrious addresses on Long Island. Trust me, everywhere out here is pretty damn nice, but as you travel east, well, let's just say any notion that there's no such thing as 'class' in America goes out the window.

There are a few pictures of Cal, as he calls himself. Winning a local yachting regatta. Attending a charitable golf tournament. Giving an angry quote about the building of apartments in Montauk. They take their sea views seriously out here. Then an article where he's praised for fundraising for an anti-drugs charity.

I can see on the internet what Caleb J. Hawley gets up to and how he feels about new builds and drugs.

But I can't really tell who he is. There's no information on his job or his family background. He clearly comes from money, but not the celebrity kind, and he keeps a relatively low profile.

I grab my phone and dial a number.

Bud answers the bar phone. I can hear the crowd of regulars in the background.

'Bud, it's Erin Kennedy.'

'Erin? Staff said you were in earlier. Sorry I missed you. You leave something here?'

'Eh, no. Can I ask you something?'

'Anything you need, sweetheart.' I hear a muffled shout – Bud is telling his regulars to be quiet, his hand placed over the phone so he doesn't deafen me.

'Bud, you heard of the Hawley family, East Hampton?'

The thing about the old families on Long Island is that they all know each other.

They know the nouveau-riche families too, as they like to call them, but the old families are an incestuous bunch and every one of them is a repository of information on the rest. This is why I've called Bud instead of wasting my time trying to further Google my way through Cal's back story.

'Sure I do, sweetheart. Wall Street and other diversions. Great-granddaddy Hawley lost big in '29 but clung on by his fingernails. Granddad Hawley invested heavily in military in '39, they clawed some of it back. Lost out, but not too badly, Black Monday '87. Daddy Hawley steadied the ship with computer investments. And they're still on the up. Family home in East Hampton, smaller mansion getaway up on the Gold Coast, penthouse on Park Avenue, apartments across Europe. They keep private, no celeb scandals in the gossip pages – if you're lining up husband number two, you probably couldn't do better.'

I can't help but smile. Thank you, Bud, for speaking to me like I'm a normal human being.

'Anything else I can help you with?'

'No, that's it.'

'You call if you need me.'

He's gone.

I stare at the picture of Cal Hawley.

How, in the name of God, does he know my husband?

I dial Karla next.

She answers the phone breathlessly, like she's climbed three flights to get to it.

'Erin,' she pants. 'What's up?'

'I'm sorry for calling so late,' I say. 'Actually, for calling at all. It's just you said . . . Are you busy?'

'Not really.'

I hear muffled talking; she's placed her hand over the receiver. I'm mortified. She's with somebody and I've disturbed her in the middle of it. And even distorted, it sounds awfully like she's having to apologise to somebody for diminishing whatever was just going down to not important.

'I'll be quick,' I say. 'This Cal Hawley guy, he's from a really wealthy family out here. I can't figure out how he'd have encountered Danny at all. I'm wondering if I should try to meet him?'

'Not on your own, you won't. Let's give it a few days and see what happens. I tried ringing Danny's department again this afternoon and I've sent a few more emails, including to his union. Still nothing.'

There's a pause for a moment.

'Sometimes, Erin, not hearing something is hearing something,' Karla says.

'I'm sorry?'

'Are you a fan of CSI?'

'The TV show?'

'Sure.'

I wonder if Karla is drunk. It is a Saturday night, after all.

'You know how cops triangulate cell phones to establish a suspect's whereabouts?'

'Eh, yeah?'

'But if you're clever, you realise that leaving your phone on pings your location. Now, for the police, a phone turned off is almost more telling than one left on. Because who turns their cell phones off, huh?'

'Karla—'

'My point is – an attorney comes knocking on the door of a precinct to ask about a dead cop, and why his possessions were removed from his residence without a warrant, and nobody will say anything. That silence worries me. It speaks very loudly.'

I bite my lip.

For some reason, I'm suddenly very conscious of having this conversation over the phone.

'Chica,' Karla says.

Whatever she's about to say next is drowned out by a woman shouting at her.

'Is that another woman? Are you fucking kidding me?'

Not even bothering to cover the phone this time, Karla roars:

'¡No me chingues! Vete a la chingada.'

My eyes widen. I don't speak Spanish but I can recognise the intonation of a fuck you in any language.

'Sorry.' She's back. 'What I was going to say is, this Ben guy – if you think there's even a hope you can get him to talk, you should lean on him. It's like I said: In my experience, when a department shuts down like this, they shut down. There's only one thing cops dislike more than internal investigations and that's people knowing about them. Danny is dead. His department is probably hoping this just goes away now. Ben might feel some personal loyalty.'

I close my eyes.

Part of me wants it all to go away.

But I have to keep asking questions.

'Erin,' Karla says, 'Ben has told you that Danny was under investigation, but did he actually answer you when you asked why he came to your home that morning?'

I frown.

'I . . . um, no. He didn't. Not exactly.'

'I'm interested to know what he was doing there with two other police officers.'

The knot in my stomach tightens.

In my shock at learning that Danny was being investigated and his partner had somehow abandoned him, I hadn't pressed Ben on that.

But I think I can guess where she's going with this.

Harvard

January 2017

Despite imagining she would do nothing else but stress about Lauren's situation, Ally found herself distracted over Christmas vacation. She'd stayed on campus for much of it, helping out with exams, grabbing hours in the library when she could, organising some socials and soirées for visiting guests. Her favourite professors liked to connect their best students with alumni from the university, and over the festive season, plenty of them descended.

Ally found herself occupied most of the time but never so busy that thoughts of Lauren were very far from her mind.

She'd welcomed the week-long trip home to Providence, just to get out of Cambridge and leave her worries behind for a few days. Home wasn't exactly fun – her mother had been fine with Ally attending Harvard, proud even, but she'd expected her daughter to get a job once she'd got her degree. She didn't understand that a PhD would open up the world for Ally. In her mind, Ally had become an eternal student, one who'd never leave Harvard, who'd never make enough money to take care of her once blue-collar, now slightly better off middle-class parents.

Her father didn't care what Ally was doing because her father didn't care much about anything that didn't come in a glass bottle or wasn't playing sport under Friday night lights.

By the time she returned to campus on New Year's Day, Ally felt good about her plan to help Lauren, a feeling only marginally diluted by the eight unopened emails from her boyfriend.

She'd blocked him from her phone but she hadn't thought to block his email address.

There they were. Apology after apology.

She skimmed them, one by one.

They all said the same thing.

You don't understand. It wasn't like you think it was. Talk to me, Ally. There are two sides.

Except there weren't.

Lauren Gregory was eighteen.

There wasn't a second side to what had happened to her, whatever Lauren chose to try and tell herself; whatever Ally's boyfriend claimed.

Ally deleted every email, then grabbed her coat and bag and went to meet Professor Müller, her own former proctor, over at The Heights Bar in Smith's campus centre.

Ally had cemented her friendship with Lucy Müller, now a law lecturer in the college, at around the time Ally was moving into one of the twelve undergrad houses for her sophomore year. Lucy had taken her aside and chastised her for being too polite with the absolute bitch with whom Ally had shared a room through freshman year, and who was now destined for the same house as Ally.

'I don't want to cause any trouble,' Ally had said.

'I figured,' Lucy had replied. 'But Ally, you can always come to me with problems and I will sort them out, discreetly.'

True to her word, Lucy had ensured the troublesome roommate was not placed in the same house as Ally. Ally didn't know how Lucy had managed it, but she'd quietly registered in the back of her head that if she was ever stuck, Lucy Müller was the person to go to.

And Ally had gone to her again, two years later, during the worst time of her life. Lucy had come to her aid, even though she had no longer been her proctor. It was her job, Lucy said, to never stop looking out for her students.

They'd been friends ever since.

Lucy had ordered a bottle of Californian Chardonnay before Ally arrived and the two women toasted in the new year, before making small talk about Ally's doctorate. When they ran dry on that, Lucy proffered some tidbits of scandal from within the faculty.

By the end of the first glass, and possibly before they'd even started it, Lucy realised Ally had something on her mind.

'What's up?' she asked, peering over the glasses perched on the end of her nose. 'It sounds like you're on top of your dissertation but you know you can always ask for an extension. Aiken is a good supervisor. She's fair.'

'I'm a bit behind because of . . . stuff, but it's not that,' Ally said.

'A student, then. Drugs, pregnancy or inability to cope?'

Ally sighed, heavily.

'I have one; she got into trouble,' she said. 'Not her fault. But I advised her to take the guy on, and it, uh, let's just say, it didn't go well. Lucy, you ever think you know somebody?'

'The great advantage of growing old is discovering how little you know about everything and everyone and learning to live with your own limitations. In the words of the wise *Game of Thrones* writers, you know nothing.'

Ally smiled sadly. How very true.

'I want to help her,' Ally said. 'She needs to talk to somebody. I don't mean legally, just . . . mentally. She plans to bury the whole episode but I really worry if she does, it will eat away at her.'

'Her or you?'

Ally met Lucy's eye.

'Both.'

'Just be careful,' Lucy cautioned. 'Sometimes what you think is right for other people is a projection of your own response. Or a remedy for your guilt. Do you feel guilty?'

Ally picked up the bottle of wine.

'Damn right I do.'

She left The Heights a little tipsy, parting ways with Lucy at the Charles Sumner statue. She had the name and number of an able and trustworthy counsellor in her phone to pass on to Lauren, who would be back in her dorm in a couple of days.

Ally had just reached Harvard Hall when she heard her name called.

Professor Shipton strode towards her, the thin wisps of hair that usually covered his balding pate flapping about in the icy wind.

'Happy New Year,' he said breathlessly, once he'd arrived beside her.

'And to you,' she replied.

'I was hoping to catch you. I've been marking the Christmas exams.'

'Today?'

He looked at her blankly.

'Over Christmas,' he said. 'I expect my students to be punctual and I aim to be no less tardy.'

'English 42 being so up to date and all.'

Ship stared at her. He wasn't used to anybody being smart with him. Ally wasn't used to having such a loose tongue, but she had an awful feeling she knew what was coming.

'Lauren Gregory,' Ship said.

'Don't tell me she failed. She was at every exam. I walked her there myself.'

'I noticed. Not a good sign, is it, when the proctor has to physically force a student to turn up?'

Ally sighed, loudly, rudely. The professor looked further taken aback.

'Perhaps we should talk when you are less inebriated, Ms Summers.'

Ally wanted to snap that it was 9 p.m. on New Year's Day and all she'd had was two, albeit large, glasses of wine, but this time she held her tongue. It was more important she found out how Lauren had done in her exams.

'My apologies, Professor,' she said. 'I'm tired. Long day catching up. How did Lauren get on?'

'Well, she's scraped passes but barely. I expected much more from her. Whatever's going on, you need to get your house in order.'

A pass. Ally would take that. Most people would have missed the entire exam period if they'd endured what Lauren had.

'I'll bear that in mind,' Ally said, already walking away.

She hurried through the Yard and was rounding Thayer Hall when her phone buzzed in her pocket with a text.

She pulled off her gloves and took out the phone, expecting it to be from Lucy, checking Ally had got home safe.

It wasn't. The text was from an unknown number and contained two lines.

We're watching you. It's lonely out here, isn't it?

Ally pulled up abruptly, her heart beating. She immediately did a 360-degree turn, her eyes darting back towards the dark Yard, dotted with ancient trees, then at the buildings around her. Who was watching her? From where?

She couldn't see anybody.

It was a joke, she thought. Somebody randomly texting people and just happening to message a woman on her own on a lonely college campus.

She'd barely time to register those thoughts when the phone beeped again.

Stop interfering with Lauren Gregory.

Then again.

Do his lecturers know that Marky Mark sells weed in his house?

Then again.

Does anybody other than Lucy Müller know about the abortion you had when you were twenty-one?

Ally dropped the phone.

Her breath came in short, fast bursts.

Realising she might need it, she bent down and grabbed the phone so roughly that her fingers scraped on the gravel beneath the layer of snow on the path.

Then she ran, as fast as she could, until she reached her room.

Erin

THEN

Sunday.

I should have been enjoying a long weekend in Connecticut with Danny.

We'd have stopped for lunch somewhere on the drive up. I'd have had clam chowder, my New England fave. My recent motto, which I repeated to Danny often: if it swims, it slims. He'd have pointed out that chowder is made with cream and that I'm too perfect to worry about what I eat. I'd have pointed out he was the one who got me hooked on it.

I'd have ordered sugar cream pie for dessert.

We'd have blared Joe Cocker in the car and pulled up at a beach on my instructions to walk off my calorie-laden lunch.

Then we'd have checked into a New England old-fashioned lodge.

I'd have brought three books – only an amateur travels with one – and read none of them, even though one was a submission and

I'd put it on my Kindle so Danny would mistake it for a pleasure read and couldn't accuse me of working.

And we'd have spent Sunday morning in bed.

None of that is happening.

Danny is lying on a slab in the morgue and I'm standing on the porch of Ben Mitchell's Dutch-colonial revival, ringing his bell at 9 a.m.

His wife Christina answers, her red hair in a tidy ponytail, her face make-up-free and fresh.

I say nothing for a moment, just stare at her, trying to read her expression, which is running through a gamut of emotions.

'Erin,' she says, and I can tell in how she utters my name that whatever policy Ben has decided to adopt towards me doesn't come with her full endorsement.

And yet, we're not friends, Christina and I.

I've nothing against her, on a personal level. We just don't have a lot in common. I work, she's chosen to be a stay-at-home mom. I'd never judge a woman on her choices, but I feel that I'm judged. A lot of the spouses – men and women – of detectives end up as full-time homemakers. Partly because the job demands so much of its employees. If there are kids involved, it's the non-cop expected to do all the legwork and that's easier when another job isn't being juggled, too.

I can hear children in the back of the house, fighting over something that sounds like Road Blocks and who's on what level.

Danny and I didn't have kids, hence the two professions operating in harmony. We'd talked about it. Both of us liked the idea of children but we always managed to come up with reasons for putting it off. I didn't want to leave my job; he knew he'd never be able to cut down his hours and he couldn't hack desk work. We wanted to buy our own place. We wanted to travel more. It wasn't the right time.

But I digress. The real reason Christina and I aren't friends is less to do with her domesticity and more to do with the fact her husband and I never warmed to each other.

'I'm so sorry,' Christina says. 'I've been meaning to call . . .' She can't finish because there really is no excuse that's going to cover this one.

'I think everyone meant to,' I say, pointedly. 'Is Ben home?'

I know he's home. His Lexus LC is in the drive.

I've never understood how the hell Ben managed to buy such an expensive car when he and Christina already had a high-end SUV for ferrying the kids. He earns what Danny did and we are so far from Lexus-buying territory. Danny's Honda Accord is parked right outside. Danny explained it away by saying that cars were Ben's passion and that he and Christina, thanks to their three children, didn't go out much or travel.

I was pretty sure they had college funds and health plans to worry about, but I didn't say anything. I knew the rules. You don't fall out with your husband over his friends.

'Would you like to come in?' Christina says. 'I've a pot of coffee on and I can warm up some eggs. Please, you're very welcome. Always, Erin.'

I am not playing happy families with the Mitchells.

'No, I'd rather stay here,' I say. 'Could you get him for me?'

'Um. Okay.'

Christina hesitates.

She wants to hug me. I can tell.

I fold my arms across my body, protectively and defensively.

I needed a hug the day Danny died, or maybe that night I spent on my own in the hotel up in Patchogue.

Where the hell were you then, Christina?

She disappears inside.

I look up and down the street.

The houses are all large by normal standards, modest by Long Island's. Two floors, a basement, gambrel roofs with curved eaves, huge gardens and perfect hedges. You get a lot of that round here, especially in the village of Bellport, Ben's neighbourhood.

First, the kids are quietened, then there's some urgent, hushed whispering, and finally, Ben appears at the door.

'Erin,' he says.

'What did he do?' I say. I hold up my hand to forestall any interruption. 'Do not BS me, Ben. I've had enough. This is something bigger than Danny roughing up a suspect in custody or you wouldn't all be acting like I've the bubonic plague. I'm his wife. I deserve to know.'

Ben lets me make my little speech. Then he looks over his shoulder and walks out on to the porch, closing the door behind him. He cocks his head towards my car.

'You don't give up, do you?' he says.

'I'm not leaving,' I say.

'I'm not asking you to. Just, not here.'

Ben is in a T-shirt and shorts, bare feet. Maybe he was going to do a bit of gardening today. Rake the leaves from the pond out back. Prepare some burgers for the barbecue.

We walk down the lawn.

'You drive here alone?' he asks.

I nod.

'You're going to need somebody to drive you home.'

'Ben, you think with the amount of shit I've been though this week I can't drive ten minutes from here to Newport?'

'I'll get my running shoes; I can get a cab back.'

'I don't need you to fucking drive me! Ben, what is going on? Why were you at my home that morning with two officers in tow?'

He stares up at the morning sun, his eyes narrowed and blinking in the light. He's so pale, he's almost translucent.

'When they started to look at Danny over the Dwayne Miller case, they found more.'

'What?'

His face contorts.

'You've heard we've been having some problems with drugs across Suffolk County? The allegations that the dealers are operating with impunity?'

I nod and shake my head at the same time.

'Everybody's heard about it, Ben. But Danny didn't do narcotics cases.'

'These guys don't just need narcotics officers in their pockets, Erin. You think nobody gets hurt in their game? You think homicide cops aren't useful to them?'

'What are you saying?' My voice is quivering.

'Look, there's real trouble on the job. There are too few arrests being made in certain precincts, like in Newport, and the allegations have spilled out of drugs into other departments. It was . . . well, it was claimed that a few homicide investigations had come up unnecessarily short. There was one, a few months ago, Danny handled it alone. I was on leave. He had a chief suspect in – and he let him go. Didn't see the guy for it.'

'You seem to be conveniently absent from a lot of these incidents, considering you were his partner,' I snap.

Ben's jaw clenches.

'You assume I was the one letting him down, Erin,' he says. 'And that's fine. But you might want to consider the idea that Danny was pushing me, and everybody else, away. He shouldn't have continued questioning Dwayne Miller on his own that time – that had nothing to do with me. And he could have filled me in on that murder case he handled when I was off, but he kept dismissing it.'

'Why?'

'I've asked myself the same question. In the end, I was happy to presume it was because Danny's instinct was right. Afterwards, I was told it was widely believed the guy worked for the gangs and had performed a punishment hit. The dogs on the street knew he was guilty.'

'And, what? Danny just let him off? Didn't pursue it? You know Danny was a good detective.'

'Yeah. That's the problem, Erin. I did. And the bosses did, too. That's why his failure to close that case rang alarm bells. Top brass had been directed to look through the ranks, to see if there were any dirty cops at work. Danny had already come to their attention with the Miller case. Then . . .'

He closes his eyes – he can't even look at me when he says:

'They found proof Danny was up to something.'

'Up to what?'

'They found out he was taking bribes. Erin, when I came to your door that morning, I was there to arrest him.'

'No,' I say, and every fibre of my body repels it. 'Bribes from who?'

'From criminals. Drug gangs.'

'No. Never. Danny was anti-narcotics. He would never—'

'I'm telling you the truth.'

'And I'm telling you no!' I cry.

Ben looks back up at his house, his face filled with fear, and then back at me.

'Stop it,' he hisses. 'Stop!'

'Not until you tell me the truth. I knew Danny.'

'Erin,' Ben whispers. 'You didn't—'

He stops.

Danny and Ben became friends when they met in the academy. Thirteen years, that's how long they knew each other.

And I can see now, on Ben's face, thirteen years' worth of secrets. A whole life beyond me.

'What was Danny capable of?' I ask.

Ben shakes his head.

Erin

Now

Danny's old boss is on the stand. Captain Sullivan.

I always liked Sully, as Danny and the others used to call him. He turned sixty last year but he's the sort who seems like he's always had an old soul – he's quiet, takes a while before he replies to anything. I admire that. He considers things, doesn't just jump to conclusions. He was a good boss, hung back, no micro-managing, just made sure his team did their job right.

I felt sorry for him when the Newport PD came under such strain just over seventeen months ago.

Until I realised how happy he was to go along with my life being destroyed.

Today, he's appearing for the other side.

But we're ready for him.

'Captain Sullivan,' Karla says, circling her prey. 'You met Erin Kennedy over three years ago, didn't you?'

'I did.'

Sully touches his ear, discreetly. He has a hearing aid. I know it, the jurors probably don't. It kind of looks like he's sending a baseball signal to someone at the back of the court.

'You were Danny Ryan's immediate superior, weren't you?'

'Yes, I was.'

'You attended their wedding.'

'I did. Though I had my concerns.'

'Excuse me?'

'It seemed a rather rushed affair. The wedding.'

I clench my jaw and I can see the tension in Karla's stance. That one has backfired.

She moves on quickly.

'In all the time you knew Erin Kennedy, up until the night in question five months ago, did you ever see any sign of her having violent tendencies?'

Sully hesitates.

'No. I did not.'

'Erin has no criminal record at all, let alone one of previous violence?'

'No. But she did experience a deep trauma seventeen months ago and sometimes that can trigger a change of personality.'

'I'm sorry, Captain, do you have psychiatric training?'

'No, ma'am. I've just seen it all, is all.'

'I've seen plenty, too, Captain. But I try to refrain from making assessments pertaining to a person's character if I'm not qualified to do so – especially in a court of law.'

Sully inclines his head. Point taken.

Judge Palmer sighs.

The artificial heat in the courtroom is getting to us all. I have a banging headache that started this morning somewhere in the back of my cranium and has now expanded to squeeze out all functioning synapses. I could only manage an apple from the breakfast tray and I think hunger is compounding the pain.

'You mention the trauma of seventeen months ago,' Karla says. 'Can you tell me, after Danny Ryan jumped from his apartment window in front of his wife and several of your officers, did you or anybody in your department offer or suggest counselling for Erin Kennedy?'

'That would not be our responsibility,' he says.

'Really? The wife of a long-serving, respected detective is not your responsibility? I thought you guys took care of each other's families when a serving spouse passed?'

Roberts stands up.

'Objection.'

'To what?' Judge Palmer says. 'And why are you standing?'

Roberts blushes a little and sits down.

'These don't sound like questions, Your Honour. Ms Delgado is just casting aspersions.'

'Are you asking an actual question, Ms Delgado?' Judge Palmer says.

'I am, Your Honour. Captain Sullivan, did you contact Erin Kennedy after what she'd witnessed – when Danny Ryan jumped from that apartment window?'

'No.'

'No?'

'That's what I said.'

'Why not?'

'Detective Ryan was the subject of an internal investigation within my department. The situation was . . . unusual.'

'But Erin Kennedy was not under investigation for anything?'

'No.'

'No.' Karla turns and looks at the jury. Her next question is still to Sully, but her eyes are on them.

'When Erin Kennedy learned that an arrest warrant had been issued for Danny Ryan the morning he jumped from their apartment, at that point did anybody from your department contact her in an official capacity?'

'No.' Sully is tight-lipped. Angry.

Like the rest of them, he reckons I should never have been told moves had been made to arrest Danny.

It's just like Karla said at the time. When Danny was declared dead, the department's troubles were meant to go with him.

'So,' Karla says, 'Erin Kennedy experienced trauma and not one member of your department, which her husband had to her knowledge been serving faithfully, contacted her or offered any explanation or reassurance? There was no chaplain sent out? No liaison officer?'

'As I say, the situation was unusual.'

'Yes or no, please.'

Silence.

'No.'

'I think that's rather abominable treatment,' Karla says, staring Sully straight in the eye. 'I guess my client could never have expected anything other than to be treated abominably this time around, either.'

'Objection!'

'Sustained. Ms Delgado, questions and answers, please. Save your pronouncements for closing.'

'Yes, Your Honour. Captain Sullivan, on that night five months ago, did my client deny that she had been in the company of her husband?'

'No.'

'Was she expecting to see her husband that night?'

'She said she wasn't but I think she knew he was coming.'

'Just the facts, please. Did she state that she had been forced to defend herself?'

'Yes.'

'Did she show signs of having being attacked?'

'Yes.'

'Isn't it the case that, before she was arrested, she consistently attempted to get to the truth about what had happened to Danny Ryan? That, on the night she was arrested five months ago, she told you everything she suspected?'

'She lied, like most people suspected of murder lie.'

'Had you ever known Erin to lie before that night?'

Captain Sullivan shakes his head.

'No,' he says. 'But I didn't speak to her after Detective Ryan jumped. I didn't speak to her again until just before she was arrested five months ago. And I can tell you that there is compelling evidence to show she lied about how she reacted to the attack that night. She lied about killing her husband. And she's still lying about the whereabouts of his body.'

I can barely follow what comes next.

My head is spinning.

When Karla sits down, minutes later, she studies my face with concern.

The heat, the exchange, my headache – I just want to lie down.

'Are you okay?' she whispers, her mouth close to my ear. 'You look like you're about to faint.'

I shake my head. I'm fine, I indicate.

I keep sitting upright, my chin tilted, my face pale but placid. Nothing to hide, nothing to fear, nothing to be ashamed of. As instructed by Karla.

If only she knew.

Erin

THEN

The medical examiner's office in Suffolk County is an 85,000-square-foot facility located in Hauppauge in the North County Complex just off Veterans Memorial Highway. I know this because after I drive home from Ben Mitchell's house that Sunday, I Google Suffolk County Morgue, wondering why I haven't done this already, and tell Tanya that's where I'm going.

Tanya takes one look at my face and we're out the door.

The first person I see in the medical examiner's officer is a young security guard who was probably reckoning on a quiet day, it being a Sunday and all.

I am so distraught when we arrive that he thinks I'm there to report a death.

What I actually want to do is resurrect a body and find out just what the fuck is going on.

'I need to see my husband,' I say. The security guard looks to Tanya, the calmer of the two of us.

'I'm afraid the office is not open to the public on the weekend, ma'am,' he says. Then, in Tanya's direction: 'Her husband?'

'He died earlier in the week,' Tanya says.

'I want to see him!' I bark.

I need to see the man I loved and married.

Beating confessions out of people and taking bribes to turn a blind eye to gang executions? No way. I know they're lying. I need Danny back. I need him to fight this with me, this . . . rewriting of his legacy. I can't do it on my own.

The security guard, young but sufficiently mature to know a near mental breakdown when he spots one, puts his radio to his mouth and summons somebody from inside.

Another man appears from upstairs and tells me he's from the coroner's office and asks who I'm there to identify. The question has only left his mouth before he realises I'm not there with the police, that I've rocked up on my own, and within seconds he's throwing dagger looks at the security guard for involving him in the madness.

'Danny Ryan,' I say. 'I want to ID Daniel Ryan.'

The man's features tighten when he hears the name.

'I'm sorry,' he says. 'We've already had an ID on Daniel Ryan.'

'You know who I'm talking about?'

'I helped perform the autopsy.'

There's a seat behind me. I don't know if it was always there or if the security guard or Tanya placed it behind me.

'What did you find in the autopsy?' I ask, tentatively.

The man from the coroner's office seems to have found his compassion button.

'There'll be a full post-mortem report issued,' he says. 'But, you are aware of the nature of your husband's death. It was a high energy impact – he sustained massive internal bleeding and broke his neck in the fall.'

I have to swallow back the bile that comes flooding into my mouth.

His neck. His beautiful neck. I'd kissed that neck minutes before he died.

'I have instructions to say there is no need for any further identification.'

I lean forward in the seat and a groan sounds from somewhere, quite possibly from me.

I'm struggling to breathe. I take in deep gulps; no air reaches my lungs. Spots appear in front of my eyes.

Then there's a paper bag over my mouth and nose and I can smell baloney. The security guard's lunch.

There's a hand on my shoulder and the man from the coroner's office is looking down at me.

'If it is any consolation, we're releasing his body for the funeral,' he says.

I swallow. The oxygen is back. The room has stopped spinning.

I feel weak and realise I've just had my first panic attack.

'We can bury him?' I whimper.

Tanya wraps her arms around me, places her forehead against the side of my head.

'Yes,' the man says.

For a moment, I'm just flooded with relief and I can't even explain why.

'We're advising a closed casket,' he says, then walks away.

I went to a funeral of a serving officer with Danny once.

The cops from Danny's precinct turned out in full dress uniform.

The dead man's partner and his boss made a speech.

A firing party let off rounds over the coffin, which was draped in the Stars and Stripes, and there was a folding ceremony at the end, with the flag presented to his widow.

A last call was placed over the police radio for the man to sign off his shift.

Danny's ceremony is in a small crematorium twenty minutes from our apartment.

Danny wasn't religious, but Gloria insists we have a priest say a few words.

In attendance is my sister, Danny's family, my boss and some of my fellow editors and publishing contacts, along with a few of Danny's old friends, pre-police academy.

Bud is there, along with a couple of his regular patrons who we knew in passing. Karla and David Fox, also. They'd make a handsome couple – David and his shock of Clooney-like grey hair, Karla and her dark, good looks – except I've guessed Karla is not that way inclined.

Dr Leslie Klein stands at the back, her head bowed.

And behind her – the mysterious Cal Hawley.

Not one of Danny's colleagues show their faces.

The men and women who would declare themselves willing to take a bullet for one another – the officers who shared drinks and weddings and christenings and birthdays and graduations with Danny – not one of them has the decency to mark his death.

I know what they're all thinking. If Danny killed himself, it meant he couldn't defend himself, because who wouldn't want to defend themselves after being accused of being a dirty cop?

That's not what I'm thinking. I'm thinking they practically walked him off that ledge with their false accusations. The anger is coming off me in waves and everyone close to me knows enough to only offer silent support.

Christina sent a large bunch of flowers this morning, allegedly from her and Ben.

We've chosen two songs, one to accompany the start of the ceremony and the other for the part where Danny's coffin is sent into the crematorium. 'Amazing Grace' at the beginning and 'Down to the River to Pray' at the end. The atmosphere in the small chapel is tense. We're all just trying to get through this.

I watch my husband's coffin disappear behind the curtains.

I can't believe Danny is in there. I watch the closed casket slide away and I keep telling myself it's empty.

I still haven't seen him dead. How can he be dead? Especially when I have so much to say to him. I'm at my husband's funeral and I can't believe he's gone. I have no empirical, factual visual to work off. All of my being is railing against the truth.

The medical examiner's officer sent over a small bag containing Danny's wedding ring and his watch.

The face of the watch is cracked and right now it's in the pocket of my dress. I blink back mascara tears as I run my fingers over the strap.

I bought him that watch and the first time he wore it was when he took me to watch his team play the Dallas Cowboys. It was a first for me, too, going to an American football game. Danny had a season ticket for the New York Giants, handed down by his father, and his father before that – he couldn't begin to understand how I'd been living in the States for so long and not been to a match.

I enjoyed the hot dogs and giant plastic pitchers of beer, the vibrant colour and the cheers and camaraderie of the crowd, but the game itself almost sent me into a coma. I kept grabbing his arm and looking at the watch, then yelling over the spectators that the whole thing was taking too long.

They keep stopping, I'd said. Stop, start, stop, start. What is the point?

Name a better sport, he'd laughed.

Fly-fishing, I'd replied.

Look! he'd yelped. Look at Eli Manning!

We'd bickered all night, then made love because Danny liked it when we talked sports, even if I was disagreeing with him.

After the service, a few people come over to offer condolences. I stand under flowering dogwood trees, the summer sun making me itch in my black dress, and I make an effort to thank them.

Bud has organised sandwiches and drinks back in the bar. I won't be going but I appreciate the sentiment. Tanya will be my proxy.

My parents phoned this morning.

I wouldn't speak to them.

Fuck their fear of flying and yes, their inability to deal with any more grief after Niamh.

I'm their daughter, too.

I still haven't told anybody the full details of what Danny was accused of, which at least would have cleared up for Danny's family why there are no police at the funeral. They have the bare bones – that Danny was under investigation at work – but not that he was on the verge of being arrested for corruption.

And now Gloria is making a beeline for me.

'I can't,' I say to Tanya.

I'm doing everything I can to protect that woman.

I know they're lying about Danny. But I also know mud sticks and I don't want his mother catching even a hint of the smear campaign they're running against her son.

Tanya takes one look at my face and runs interference.

'Gloria,' Tanya says. 'You know Mr Bud Johnson? He's organised the refreshments for after.'

'But I want to talk to Erin,' I hear, as Gloria is led off.

I stare at the ground, my eyes brimming.

'I just need to go home,' I whisper, to nobody in particular.

Mike is standing beside me now.

'Whatever is going on, you knew my brother,' he says. 'He loved you, Erin, and he loved his family. Don't let his memory be destroyed. Promise me.'

'I promise,' I choke out.

I stand at the car, waiting while Tanya and Mike deal with everyone else.

I spot another car outside the crematorium, parked up the road.

It catches my eye because it's a Lexus.

Part of me wants to go up there and smash Ben Mitchell's face in.

The other part of me can't move.

A smell fills my nose; something familiar, expensive.

I turn and see Cal Hawley, of the East Hampton Hawleys.

'I just wanted to offer my condolences,' he says, then realises I'm not even looking at him.

He follows my gaze, sees the car I'm staring at.

'Don't believe him,' he whispers, urgently.

'What?'

I turn and stare at him.

'Don't believe Danny's partner. He's a liar.'

'I – what?'

'You buried your husband today,' he says. 'He was a good man. You should know that.'

His face is so open and honest, his words what I so desperately need to hear, I almost grab him, this man who's basically a stranger.

'How do you know?' I say.

I can see the muscles twitching in his clenched jaw, his hesitation.

'Please,' I say. 'You were in there. They didn't send even one representative. What do I tell his family? His friends? I need to know why his colleagues are doing this!'

Cal's eyes meet mine. Whatever battle he's having within himself, decency has won. Who can deny such a request from a grieving widow?

'Danny was involved in something,' he says. 'Didn't he tell you what he was doing?'

I throw up my hands, frustrated.

'Danny never talked about work!' I say. 'What have you got to do with all this?'

'You know who I am,' he says. 'Danny said you were an intelligent woman; I'm betting you've already asked the right people about me.'

His voice is gentle, his face so very kind. But he looks . . . frightened. He's reassuring me, but this man is shit-scared and he doesn't look like somebody who scares easy.

'Why would they lie?' I ask.

Cal stares back at the Lexus, his eyes narrowed.

Then he reaches into his pocket and gives me a card. It's just his name – a calling card of the wealthy – but on the back he's scrawled a number.

'Not here,' he says. 'Meet me. Where we're not being watched by him.'

Harvard

May 2017

Professor Aiken had been incredibly kind about the whole thing. Ally was deemed to be making academic progress so the extension was pushed through without too much begging on her side.

The irony wasn't lost on Ally. She'd spent the whole of last Christmas worrying about Lauren Gregory's ability to keep up with coursework and it'd only taken one bump for Ally and she'd fallen apart.

She'd handed in her notice as proctor and was just serving out the term in Canaday. Then she'd have the whole summer to catch up on work. She hoped. If she could just get her head down.

That was the problem, though.

Ally spent far too much time fretting. She was still trying to work out how someone could have uncovered her most private, darkest secret and whether or not they were prepared to leave her alone, now she'd been warned.

That the anonymous messenger knew about Marky Mark

wasn't a surprise. Nor did it bother Ally. He might be an old neighbour, but he *was* dealing in his college house and it wasn't Ally's problem.

However, Ally had told nobody bar Lucy Müller, who'd got her the Planned Family appointment, about the fateful one-night stand that had resulted in her unwanted pregnancy at the tender age of twenty-one.

Not even her ex-boyfriend, over whom her heart was still breaking.

So how the hell had somebody found out? Did they have access to her medical records? To Lucy?

Ally was so distracted walking through the Patio at Dudley House that she almost didn't notice Lauren sitting at one of the tables, a book in front of her.

The only telltale sign Lauren wasn't just a regular student studying on a summer's day was the fact that her book was placed face down, untouched.

Ally had overheard Megan speculating that Lauren was out a lot these days and wondering who the mysterious boyfriend was.

Ally paused, made to walk on, then paused again.

Lauren had taken the counsellor's number that Ally had given her, but Ally knew she hadn't followed up and gone to meet the professional.

Ally had considered herself brave to even try to convince Lauren to do anything after the texts that New Year's night, but a feeling of being duty-bound had won out. After all, it was Ally's fault that Lauren was in the position she was in now.

But when Lauren had said she didn't want any help, Ally had only too gladly backed off.

And then watched from the sidelines as Lauren struggled through the next few months.

If she was seeing that bastard again, Lauren was in big trouble.

At that moment, Lauren glanced up and caught Ally staring at her.

Ally felt the muscles in her legs twitch, urging her to walk towards Lauren.

But she couldn't.

She smiled a weak hello, then turned and walked away.

She'd regret that, for a very long time.

Erin

THEN

Days pass before Karla can get some time free to come with me to meet Cal Hawley. She's agreed she'll hang back – she just wants to be there in case this guy is yet another man screwing with me.

My lawyer is the only person I've confided in about the extent of the accusations against Danny. I tell myself I need some sort of release valve but, also, I'm conscious that with her I have client confidentiality. That, and the fact she didn't know Danny but she does know what corrupt cops look like, has made her invaluable.

In the two weeks since my husband died, I've lost a sum total of ten pounds. I have grey hair spotted among my brown tresses. My skin is pale, my nails are bitten to the quick, and I have a great big ugly cold sore at the side of my lip.

Gloria has returned to Florida, heartbroken.

Mike's compassionate leave ended yesterday and he flew back to Syria, where he'll await orders for his next deployment.

Tanya is flying out tomorrow and neither of us are happy about it. But, she has a job and a life back in Ireland and she cannot continue to babysit me – even if, as head of HR in her company, she has amassed quite a lot of annual leave sorting out other people's lives.

We've spent the last couple of days fighting because she wants me to come home with her.

You've nobody here, she tells me.

I might not have anybody. But I have something.

I have my mission to find out what was happening to Danny.

Karla and I drive to the place Cal has suggested – an inn in Center Moriches – and find him waiting at a table on the decking underneath the trestle awning outside. He's wearing a pastel polo shirt and tan slacks, expensive sunglasses perched on his head.

He should come across as all prep school and good college and Daddy's money. There's something, however, in Cal Hawley's face that tells me he's a lot smarter than his family background ever needed him to be and possibly a lot more generous, too.

Karla discreetly takes a seat a few tables away.

Let's not scare the horses, she said on the way out.

The inn is the kind of place tourists don't find, the sort of joint that looks simple from the front but is packed with locals in the know and a menu that makes your eyes and wallet water before you've finished reading the entrée section.

I've never been here. Danny and I ate all over Long Island but we did it on a budget. We'd become experts at finding the best diners and gastropubs – or taverns, as they like to style themselves here.

The waitress arrives.

'Drinks to start?' she asks. 'Can I suggest a glass of Sparkling Pointe? It's a North Fork vineyard and they use the champagne method.'

I nod, dumbly. I hope she'll be this helpful when it comes to picking food because, given I don't plan to eat it, I'm not sure I care what's on the plate.

'Is this place your local?' I ask Cal.

'I've been here a few times,' he says. 'Your lawyer seems to know it, too.'

He nods in Karla's direction, but doesn't smile.

'She's just keeping an eye out for me,' I say. 'I trust her.'

He shrugs.

I look around. I can see the creek beyond the pitch pines and we're surrounded by woodland on all other sides. It's one of the things I love about Long Island. On the one hand, the landscape is one long coastal, sandy paradise. But then there are these little parts that are so green and rich, they remind me of home.

In any case, this inn is secluded and private and I understand now why Cal suggested it.

The waitress returns with our drinks and when I take a sip, I feel my shoulders relax.

It's somehow easier being in the company of a stranger. I don't have to even bother to pretend I'm coping because he's only ever known me in this state of grief.

'Why were you watching me?' I ask first.

He exhales; a long, remorseful sound.

'I felt somebody should be keeping an eye,' he said. 'I didn't know you'd found an attorney. I thought you might be a bit lost. But none of this is your fault. You should know that.'

'Do you know what they're saying about Danny?'

'Not exactly. But I can guess. I spoke to Danny, a while before he died.'

'You spoke to him?'

Cal nods.

'How did you two know each other?'

Cal stares out at the creek.

'Danny knew they would come after him,' he said, dodging my question. 'I'm going to hazard a guess that they were throwing dirt at him?'

My jaw drops.

'Evidence he'd tampered with or a case he'd fudged?' Cal continues. 'I read that the All-Sides Project have taken on a case in Newport. Probably one of Danny's, right? And if the Project took it, somebody on the inside must have committed to giving evidence against Danny. The All-Sides crew don't just act on the statements of convicted felons; they need to corroborate the claims.'

I nod.

'Danny and I talked about what would happen,' Cal says.

'Why wasn't he talking to me?'

Cal's eyes flicker sideways. He can't explain to me why my husband lied by omission.

'I don't believe what they're saying about him,' I say. 'And yet, I cannot for the life of me figure out why anybody would set Danny up. He was well-liked. He was respected. They've said he . . .'

I look around. The outside tables are sparsely populated. The midday sun is bright and temperatures are high. People have opted to eat indoors, where the air con is on full flow. Karla is sipping a tall iced coffee and pretending to be entirely focused on her phone.

'His partner claims Danny was taking bribes,' I whisper. 'From drug dealers.'

Cal shakes his head.

'Erin, I know you don't know me but I am telling you, from the little I knew of Danny, he was anti-drugs. Hell, I met him, a few months ago, at an anti-drugs fundraiser. There is no way . . .'

'It doesn't make sense to me either.'

Cal raises a hand to his jaw and rubs it, his face thoughtful.

'He was being set up, Erin, believe me.'

'I want to. I do. But you need to tell me what you know.'

Cal stares at the table, his neck turning red.

'Your husband was trying to expose the truth about something. He was the only one who could, and now he's gone . . . You should at least have the peace of knowing that.'

This man is nobody to me. I never met him before last week.

And yet, I know, immediately, that he's telling the truth.

Maybe there's a part of me that needs it too badly, but there's something in his demeanour that tells me to trust him far more than I trust Ben Mitchell. I cling to his words, like the life raft they are.

And yet, there's still that niggling knowledge underneath, that awful grain of doubt that I can't square away.

'If Danny was being set up and had done nothing wrong,' I say, 'then why did he kill himself? You know they'll have been saying he did that because he was guilty and couldn't face it.'

'People kill themselves for all sorts of stupid reasons,' Cal says. 'But imagine what it does to your head to know people you thought were your friends are willing to believe the worst about you? To frame you, even? That would break most people, Erin.'

'But what was he looking at that could have put him on the wrong side of his own friends?' I ask, desperately. 'And how do you know about it?'

Cal's features tense.

'He . . . he was helping somebody.'

I frown.

'You?' I ask. 'Was he helping you?'

Cal glances over at Karla. If he trusts me, I'm not sure he trusts her. But then he looks back at me and sighs.

'He was helping Lauren,' he whispers.

'Lauren? Lauren who? Who is she to you?'

'My sister,' he says. 'He was trying to get justice for Lauren.'

Erin

Now

I've lived in the apartment across from Mr Novak for years but I never really got to know him beyond occasional polite hellos, holiday greetings and are-you-also-having-trouble-with-your-pipes type exchanges.

Danny and I used to joke about him, back when I thought Danny and I felt the same about everything and everyone.

God, how little I knew my husband.

We'd judged Mr Novak's character and found him wanting. He lives alone, he has a little turn of the eye so you're never quite sure where he's looking, and he speaks out of the side of his mouth. None of that should matter. What does matter is that there's something about Mr Novak that most women can instinctively sense. He's the kind of man you imagine has a telescope in his apartment and it ain't trained at the sky.

'Were you surprised that Erin Kennedy chose to remain in her apartment after Danny Ryan jumped from the window?' Prosecutor Roberts asks him now.

'Absolutely,' Mr Novak replies. 'I don't think *I* could continue living in a place after that happened.'

I hate that they get to do this. Question and assign opinions to decisions I made, on the basis of other people's base conclusions about me.

Of course I wanted to move out of the apartment. Karla had even secured an early lease exit for me – the management company had actually been quite humane about the whole thing in the end. But when it came to it, I wasn't able to leave. The apartment held too many good memories and not all of them had been erased by the bad.

Now – I'd take a flamethrower to it.

'Five months ago,' Prosecutor Roberts continues. 'What did you hear taking place in Erin Kennedy's apartment?'

'I heard a fight between a woman and a man.'

'Your statement says you saw a man enter the apartment building, earlier in the evening?'

'Yes.'

'Could you describe him?'

'I didn't see him very well, I'm afraid. It was dark and I was looking out the window. I saw somebody approach our complex and then the elevator came up to our floor and I heard Erin's door open and close.'

'Can you describe anything about this man?'

'He was tall; big build. Maybe six foot? Wearing a black hoodie and a cap.'

'Was it this black hoodie?'

Prosecutor Roberts holds up a hoodie in an evidence bag. It was taken from my apartment. Because of the colour of the fabric, you can't see that the hoodie is stained with blood.

'Could be. I can't say for sure.'

Mr Novak is being the textbook witness. Not committing to anything he can't stand over.

'Would you have recognised the man if it was Erin Kennedy's husband?'

'I don't know. Not from that distance and not in the dark. I didn't know her that well and I barely knew him at all. But yes, it could have been him.'

'Would you have been surprised to see her husband there?'

'Yes.'

'Yet, you saw a man who may have resembled her husband enter your apartment complex?'

'Yes.'

'So, you believe this man entered Erin Kennedy's apartment and shortly afterwards you heard an argument take place?'

'I do and I did.'

'Even though their front door was closed and your front door was closed and a hallway lay between?'

'Well, our apartments aren't the most soundproof builds in the county,' Mr Novak answers. 'But they were yelling pretty loud. However, in addition to that, I opened my door.'

'You opened your door?'

'Yes, and I stood in the hallway.'

'Why did you do that?'

'Well, the argument sounded heated and I considered knocking to make sure everybody was okay.'

'Did you hear any of what was being said in the course of the argument?'

'No. Just voices.'

'How did the voices sound?'

'The woman sounded angry. The man – I guess you'd say he was defensive. It sounded like every fight between a man and a woman, ever.'

There are titters in the courtroom, mainly from men.

'But you didn't knock on the door of the apartment across the hall?' Prosecutor Roberts says.

'No. I'm ashamed to say I didn't. I was reared to let people sort out their own differences. I wish now that I'd intervened.'

I have to swallow a snort at the notion of Mr Novak coming to the rescue.

'Did the fight sound like it got physical at any point?' Prosecutor Roberts asks. 'Did you hear anything being thrown, items smashing, anything that sounded like the argument you were listening to had gone beyond a verbal altercation and become violent?'

'Yes, sir. I heard several banging noises and the sound of crashing furniture.'

'Thank you. Now, how long did this fight last, Mr Novak?'

'I can't be exact. I was busying myself in my apartment, trying to keep my nose out. I think it started some time after 10.15 p.m. and it ended just before 10.45 p.m.'

'And then what happened?'

'I heard the door of her apartment open and slam shut, then the elevator being summoned. I went to my window and looked out and I saw Erin Kennedy fleeing the scene.'

'Objection!' Karla almost jumps out of her seat. 'Fleeing the scene? What kind of language is that?'

The judge turns to Mr Novak, his eyebrows slightly raised. It's Mr Novak's first slip-up.

'The defendant's counsel finds your choice of words inappropriate, Mr Novak, and I myself find it a little colourful. You were an English teacher before you retired, right?'

'Yes, Your Honour.'

'In that case, you'll understand what I mean when I ask you to please resist the urge to embellish your responses with leading language.'

Mr Novak blushes.

'Yes, Your Honour.'

'You saw Erin Kennedy leaving your building,' Prosecutor Roberts says. 'You are positive it was her?'

'Yes.'

'But you said it was dark and you *couldn't* categorically identify the man who entered the building.'

Prosecutor Roberts is being clever. He's taking away the sting of Karla's questions before she can ask them.

'The man had a hoodie *and* a cap,' Mr Novak says. 'Like he didn't want to be recognised. Erin Kennedy was hat-less and she turned and looked up at the apartment as she left.'

'You were looking out the window.'

'Yes, I was.'

'So, you saw her face?'

'Yes. And her hair. She has very distinctive hair. Long, brown.'

My skin is crawling.

'And what else did you notice about her?'

'She was running. She only paused to look back up.'

'Anything else?'

'She looked beat up.'

'Beat up?'

Prosecutor Roberts pauses for effect.

'Yes. Her cheek and lip were swollen.'

'Was there any blood visible?'

'She had something smeared on her face and across her chest area over her . . . vest thing. It could have been blood. It certainly looked like blood.'

'Did her own wounds appear to be bleeding?'

'Objection!' Karla's intervention this time drips with dismissiveness. She meets the judge's eye, looks at him like he too knows full well the line has been crossed.

'Can we clarify Mr Novak's medical expertise before we allow him to make medical pronouncements about my client, as seen from the window of a fourth-floor apartment while she was in the grounds below?'

'I don't need you to make a statement, Counsellor,' Judge Palmer says. 'Sustained. Rephrase, Counsellor.'

Prosecutor Roberts has to think about this one.

'Mr Novak,' he says, 'you saw what appeared to be injuries on the defendant's face. How bad did those injuries look to you? Was, for example, blood spurting from her lip?'

'Not that I could see.'

'Thank you. So the blood could have been somebody else's. Did you see the man leave the apartment?'

'No.'

'Did you hear a single sound from within her apartment after Erin Kennedy left?'

'I did not. I went to bed shortly after Erin left.'

'Weren't you concerned?'

'Yes, very. But she was out of the apartment so I wasn't concerned for her any more.'

Karla tenses beside me. She's heard something she likes. There's a flicker of something on Prosecutor Roberts' face and it might be annoyance. He's heard it, too. He moves on, swiftly.

'Do you have any further recollections from that evening?'

'No, sir. Like I said, I went to bed. I was woken in the early hours of the morning by the police. That's all I remember.'

'You're a deep sleeper?'

'Yes.'

'I believe the police had to knock on your door for quite some time before they roused you. So, Erin Kennedy could have returned to her apartment and you wouldn't have heard?'

'That's correct, sir.'

'Thank you, Mr Novak. No further questions.'

Karla takes a sip of water before she stands.

'Mr Novak, I'm Erin Kennedy's attorney. It's nice to meet you.'

'I know who you are. Nice to meet you, too.'

'You've seen me before, haven't you?'

Mr Novak looks uncertain.

But, you know, he's sworn on the Bible.

'Yes.'

'Where?'

A pause.

'Entering our apartment building.'

'Right. I haven't seen you, however, until today. Do you keep a keen eye on people who come and go from your apartment building?'

'I do.'

Mr Novak says it like he's proud.

He's trying to come across as a good citizen and, yes, his observations make him sound like he'd make a decent witness.

But to the twelve good men and women, this statement makes him seem exactly as Karla wants him perceived – a peeping Tom.

It's her first missile.

'On the night in question, you claim to have heard a fight between a man and a woman.'

'I *did* hear a fight.'

'You believe this fight took place between Erin Kennedy and her husband.'

'I don't know for sure if it was her husband.'

'No. But you did answer that you believe you saw the man who entered her apartment – even if you didn't see him clearly enough?'

'Yes.'

'You couldn't identify him but you could give a physical description, of sorts. You spoke to his height and build. Tall and good build, that's what you said, yes?'

'I did.'

'I see.'

Karla comes back to our table and reads from her notes. There's nothing there – she stopped writing when Mr Novak was talking; all that's on the page is circular doodles.

'When Prosecutor Roberts asked you if you heard anything else from Erin Kennedy's apartment after she left, you said no, correct?'

'Correct.'

'Then he asked you if you were concerned, and what did you answer?'

'I said I was very concerned.'

Karla raises an eyebrow.

'You said that you were concerned but,' Karla looks back down at the doodles page, 'you *weren't concerned about Erin any more*, because she'd left the apartment.'

'Um. Yes. But I was still concerned after she'd left.'

Mr Novak blinks a few times. He senses, like everybody else in the court, that he's walked into a trap.

'Objection.' Prosecutor Roberts doesn't sound convinced. 'Is there a question here to move us along? Ms Delgado is just reading back the witness's answers.'

'I'm aware of that,' Judge Palmer says. 'Overruled, but this had better be going somewhere, Counsellor.'

He knows it is. We all do.

'What were you concerned about, if you were no longer concerned about Erin Kennedy?' Karla asks.

'I was, um, concerned about the man in the apartment.'

'Why?'

'Why? Because everything had gone quiet.'

'Why would you be concerned if everything had gone quiet?'

A slight sheen of sweat has broken out on Mr Novak's forehead. It's not from the heat in the courtroom. After yesterday's heating debacle, the maintenance team have got the radiators under control and it's a few degrees cooler than the sub-Saharan temperatures of yesterday.

'I suppose I was concerned about his welfare.'

Karla frowns.

So do several jury members.

Prosecutor Roberts is busy scribbling something.

Even the judge has turned to face Mr Novak.

'You described this man as being tall and of good build. You saw Erin Kennedy running from her apartment with injuries to her face. When she looked back up at the apartment – what was the expression on her face? Did she look frightened? Nervous? Happy?'

'Objection, Your Honour.' Prosecutor Roberts sounds wary. 'If the defence objected to my witness's testimony about possible blood on Erin Kennedy's person because it was seen from a height, she can't now seek his opinion of her client's *expression* from that height!'

'I'm going to allow it, Mr Roberts, because you introduced Mr Novak's testimony on the injuries to the defendant's face first.'

Mr Novak looks at the judge and then back at the man who called him as witness and we can all see the panic behind his eyes.

'I don't remember her expression.'

'You don't remember it? You said you saw her face when she looked up at the apartment. You remember the injuries on her face. You remember seeing something smeared on her chest. You remember a lot about that night but not her expression?'

'It was fleeting.'

He seems pleased with himself. Fleeting is a good word.

'Was she fleetingly smiling? Or laughing?'

'I . . .'

'Was she crying?'

'No.'

'Did she look scared?'

'I don't remember.'

'Did she look anxious?'

'Objection! Badgering the witness, Your Honour.'

'Sustained. Ms Delgado, asked and answered. Move along, please.'

Karla nods.

She looks back at the table, considers something, then turns back to the still flustered Mr Novak.

'Were you looking at my client through your binoculars when she ran from the apartment?'

'Yes.'

Silence. Then a gasp.

Mr Novak looks like he wants to swallow his own tongue.

Prosecutor Roberts stares at his table, unable to look up.

I'd joked to Karla that Mr Novak probably had a telescope.

The prosecution obviously knew about those binoculars, too, but they left that detail out. Deliberately.

Karla doesn't let the minor victory go to her head.

'What height would you guess Erin Kennedy is, Mr Novak?' she says.

'I don't know.'

'You guessed the man who entered her apartment was six foot. What height would you reckon Erin Kennedy at?'

Mr Novak glares at her, then me.

'Five four, I'd estimate.'

'That's exactly her height. She's not a big build, is she?'

I try not to shiver as everybody in the court stares at me.

'No.'

'No. She's average build for a woman. She weighs approximately one hundred and thirty-five pounds. You saw, that night, a woman of average to small build running from your apartment with injuries to her face and you tell us that you were concerned for the man you believed was still in her apartment. What did you think had happened to him? Why were you worried about him?'

'Well – it was quiet. She could have hit him with something.'

'That was your conclusion?'

Mr Novak opens and closes his mouth.

'You didn't phone the police,' Karla says.

'People have domestics.'

'Is it the case,' Karla continues, 'that maybe you were only concerned for yourself that night, Mr Novak? A man, tall, strong, had just come into your apartment building and beaten up a woman. Were you worried that he might come to your door? Were you worried he'd start trashing the apartment and maybe bring his destruction out into your shared hall space? Or were you thinking perhaps you should have intervened before that woman was attacked and you were concerned what people would say about you?'

'No,' Mr Novak says, and his voice is firmer than I expected.

'No?'

'No. I wasn't thinking any of those things. I was thinking Erin Kennedy looked like she was running from something. She knew I was across the hall. She knows some of our neighbours downstairs. If she'd needed help, she could have come to any of us, but she ran out of the building, out of her own apartment, and my gut told me she was running from something.'

'From someone,' Karla corrects.

'No. From some*thing*.'

Karla doesn't react but I can see she's not happy.

She thought she'd broken Mr Novak. But he's had a resurgence.

Now I see why the prosecution used him as a witness.

He might be a sleazy, dirty old man.

But he's right and he knows he's right.

Erin

THEN

The night before Tanya returns to Ireland is tough.

She's still here but it's the knowledge she'll be gone and I'll be alone in the apartment tomorrow that I'm struggling with.

After discussing on the drive home with Karla what Cal Hawley said, I put it out of my mind for the evening. He hasn't told me much. After he clarified that Lauren was his stepsister, Cal clammed up. All he'd tell me was that Danny was trying to get justice for her but when I pressed for information on what had happened to his sister to begin with, Cal claimed the ins and outs weren't important – what matters is that Danny was going against his own colleagues.

I'd pressed him to meet me again and, reluctantly, he'd agreed.

'Tomorrow?' I'd asked him, hopefully.

He hesitated some more but eventually acquiesced. Then I remembered I'd have to bring Tanya to the airport and he said he'd something on that evening, and it looked like it wouldn't happen.

'I, um, guess I could be your chauffeur tomorrow?' he suggested.
I snapped it up.

Why not have a strange man – who's just told me my husband
was framed because he was essentially running a covert investigation
– drive my sister and me to JFK?

There's nothing normal about this situation, anyway.

Karla is intrigued. She's still received nothing from the ninth
precinct about this alleged arrest warrant or the investigation Danny
was under, despite Ben's claims. We know there has to be some
truth in what I've been told – otherwise his colleagues would have
been at his funeral – but I want to know how bad it is; how much
proof they have.

Karla has, however, got access to his will and is in the process of
getting access to his bank account so at least we can start to look for
all this alleged money Danny was in receipt of in the form of bribes.

I mean, it had to have been sizeable if they were planning to
arrest him, right?

And I'd certainly seen no sign of it.

'I'll call you tomorrow,' she tells me. 'When the banks open, I'll
get straight on, see what I can learn from Danny's account.'

Not for the first time, I realise I'm now utterly dependent on
these strangers who have entered my life.

Tanya and I walk the village's main thoroughfare, then turn back
towards the beach. Bunting is strung across the street between the
bars and shop fronts. Newport is gearing up for its annual village
family day, a colourful festival for the local community, businesses and kids. Last year, Danny – as a representative of the first
responders – volunteered to paint kids' faces. His artwork looked

like a drunk grandfather had applied make-up while sitting on a bouncy ball.

'You won't be asked back next year,' I'd chided.

'Next year, I'll be at the beer stall enjoying myself like you,' he'd said.

Tanya and I get hot dogs and beers to take down to the beach.

'What will you do?' Tanya asks, picking up our conversation about whether I'd return to Ireland.

'Go back to work.' I shrug.

We sit down on white sand at the foot of the dunes and watch the waves crashing on to the shorefront.

'You want to move back to Manhattan?' Tanya asks. 'You know you shouldn't run away, right?'

I grimace.

'You're the one telling me to go back to Dublin,' I say. 'And this isn't like Niamh.'

Our parents left her room exactly the way it was on that last day.

They'll never move because our house was the last place Niamh lived.

I, on the other hand, couldn't wait to get away from that house, from all the streets and fields where my sister had last walked and breathed. Home, for me, was heartbreak.

We finish our hot dogs, every bite of mine a dry lump I have to wash down with sips of beer.

'You're not having doubts about Danny, are you?' Tanya asks.

She's misread my silence on the issue over the last couple of days.

I'm not doubting Danny. I'm just trying to get to the bottom of everything.

But I am overwhelmed.

I shake my head and gaze down at my toes in the sand.

'I think his job has treated his memory, and me, terribly. But I guess . . . I guess I'm learning things about him. It's awful, knowing he had secrets from me, whatever the rationale behind it.'

Tanya falls quiet for a few moments. Then:

'If I died in the morning and you found out I'd kept some stuff from you – would it make you love me any less?'

I look at my sister. Her hair is tied back into a ponytail but some strands have escaped and are whipping against her cheeks, which are rosy from the beer. Her eyes are bright, her lips set in a perfect pout of determination. Beautiful on the inside and out.

'No,' I say.

What I don't add is that I've known Tanya my whole life.

There's no getting away from the fact I only knew Danny for two years. He was everything to me but can I, hand on heart, say I knew him inside out?

'Well, then,' she says. 'Danny had secrets. Niamh had secrets. We all do. But you loved Danny and that's all you need to know.'

Cal arrives dutifully the next morning to drive us to the airport.

I introduce him as an old friend of Danny's.

'What do you work as?' Tanya asks. She's been gently flirting, with that effortless ease of hers, ever since he pulled up outside the apartment in his Jag.

'I'm an unemployed layabout,' he answers.

'You're clearly not police,' Tanya says.

'No.'

'And you drive a Jaguar, you can't be that much of a layabout,' Tanya says.

'Maybe I stole it.' Cal smiles. 'And you're both accessories.'

'You don't look like somebody who needs to steal anything,' Tanya says. 'You're far too wholesome.'

'Wholesome?' Cal says, confused.

'Ignore her,' I say.

He smiles and it's like the beam of a kid who could be used to sell Colgate or breakfast cereal.

Tanya doesn't answer, just laughs at being proven correct.

I go into the terminal with Tanya while Cal waits in the car park.

'Come back soon and see Mam and Dad,' she says.

'If I come over, it's going to be for you.'

I'm too angry at our parents. I've plenty of missed calls from them but their inability to put themselves out for me is unforgivable.

'They're a different generation,' Tanya says.

'They're the generation that understands the importance of funerals.'

'Niamh's death changed them,' Tanya adds.

'It changed us, too,' I retort.

'Please, don't be angry.'

'I'm not angry at you,' I say. 'I love you. And I'm going to be absolutely fine. You're not to worry about me.'

She doesn't look convinced.

'I hate leaving you here,' she says and I swallow.

'You got all the stuff you need?' I ask.

Tanya's suitcase is stuffed with Cheez Whiz for authentic Philly cheesesteaks, Twizzlers, Airheads, Jolly Ranchers, Nutter Butters, Fritos and Lucky Charms. All the unhealthy stuff she's always plaguing me to send over.

'I have everything. And anything I've forgotten I'll mail you a reminder and you can bring it on your next trip.'

'Sure,' I say.

I watch her join the security line and then she's gone.

I rub my bare arms below my T-shirt, suddenly cold, and go outside to where we left Cal.

He's sitting in the car, hands on the wheel, his face creased with worry.

He's told me he's a year or so younger than I am but the concerned expression that seems a constant feature makes him look older.

'What is it?' I ask, once I'm in the car.

'Nothing.'

'It's something.'

'You come from a good family,' he says. 'You seem like good people.'

'Yeah.'

He shakes his head, pain on his face.

'I shouldn't have said anything to you. I shouldn't have come near you. You should just forget everything and move on with your life. I've done enough damage.'

'What if I don't want to? What if I want to know the truth about why Danny killed himself? Whether it's good or bad. I have every right to dwell on it – I can't just move on. Why do people think I can or should?'

He turns and faces me in the passenger seat.

'Are you absolutely positive Danny never said anything to you about me or my sister?'

'I don't ever remember him mentioning a Lauren Hawley.'

'Gregory. She kept her mother's surname.'

I shake my head.

'He never said anything at all, or you're not positive?'

'I honestly don't know. I can tell you he'd been a little quiet for a while. Distant. I knew he was busy but I didn't know what with.'

Every morning when I wake up, every night before I fall asleep, all the waking moments in between, I am going over each and every memory I have of Danny and trying to work out what I missed.

'Look, if he thought this was too dangerous to share with you—' Cal says.

'Dangerous!' I exclaim.

'Yes, dangerous. Danny looking at Lauren's case was dangerous, Erin. You need to understand that. If he protected you from it then maybe I have no right to expose you to it. He's gone now, it's over.'

'No!' I slam my hand on the dashboard and Cal jumps, alarmed.

'That is not how it works,' I say, angrily. 'You don't get to decide for me, any more than he did.'

Cal says nothing.

I fall silent as we take the Southern State Parkway.

Once we've merged into traffic, I glance across at Cal.

'What happened to your sister?' I say.

'I guess,' he says, heavily, 'I don't have a right to decide what you know or don't know about Danny. But I do have the right to decide who I'm going to bring into this mess with Lauren. Honestly, Erin, part of me hates myself for coming to you with this; but I have to admit that as well as wanting to check you were okay, I was desperate to know if Danny had told you anything.'

I set my mouth in a thin line and stare out the front window, watching the tail of the car in front. It's a Chevy, absolutely huge, bigger even than Karla's. It astonished me, when I moved out to the Island, just how big the cars are. Manhattan wasn't a true reflection. People drove cars compatible with the city and most people were happy to use public transport or hail cabs. Long Island is more like the rest of the United States: big cars, big car parks, big roads.

'I will tell you what happened to Lauren,' he says. 'But not yet. No offence, Erin, but I barely know you.'

I promise myself that as soon as I get home, I'm going to Google his sister. You don't work in publishing as long as I have and not learn a thing or two about research. I might even tap David again.

We fall silent.

Not for long. The silence is uncomfortable.

'Is it true what you told Tanya?' I ask, breaking it. 'That you're unemployed?'

'Kinda. I do this and that.'

'You didn't earn this car from a paper route.'

'This car was a birthday present from my father two months after he realised he'd forgotten my birthday.'

Cal's voice is light, but there's an undercurrent and I glance across at him. He's stereotypically good-looking; even with everything I have going on in my head, I can see that. Attractive in a captain-of-the-football-team, Zac Efron kind of way. But his eyes don't match the package. There's no twinkle, no humour there. In fact, he has the saddest eyes of anybody I've ever met.

It makes me wonder what he's seen.

His frankness makes me feel awkward, so, panicking, I make a joke.

'This one time, my parents forgot my birthday and they got me a Fabergé egg to make up for it.'

He says nothing for a moment.

Then he smiles.

The weird moment is dealt with.

'I have a question,' I say.

'Shoot.'

'If you have money, and you're from a family that has a lot of money, well – aren't you the sort of family who can pay for things to get done? In my limited experience, isn't money the answer to everything? Why did you need Danny to help you?'

Cal keeps concentrating on the road, but he inclines his head.

'Because some things can't be bought,' he says. 'I thought the same as you, for a long time. That money could solve everything. That it could protect you. I was wrong.'

I swallow.

'Money never mattered to Danny and me,' I say. 'I mean, we needed more of it but . . . that's what doesn't ring true. If Danny was taking bribes, you'd expect there to be some evidence of that, wouldn't you?'

Cal nods.

'Until they show you evidence,' he says, 'believe nothing, Erin.'

I take a deep breath and unclench my shoulders.

I can do that.

Harvard

MARCH 2019

It was an unusually mild spring at Harvard.

Ally recalled two years previous, when the snow hadn't lifted until it was practically summer and she'd thought she'd never get the feeling of warmth back into her bones.

Of course, she'd had a lot more going on back then to preoccupy her. She'd been failing at her PhD, her job as proctor and, last but not least, contributing to the extreme fucking up of Lauren Gregory's life.

Lauren.

Ally thought of her often but not nearly enough.

Living in New York had been a distraction.

Trying to find a proper job had been a distraction.

Ally could have stayed on at Harvard. She knew that. She was well regarded by most faculty members and if she'd applied for an assistant lecturer position, she reckoned she'd have been in with a shot. At the very least, she could have earned a few dollars as a tutor.

She had a doctorate in English, after all.

But Ally had wanted to get far away from Harvard.

New York wasn't a stretch, geographically, but it was easy to be anonymous there, become one of the millions, where nobody knew you or your business.

Two years of part-time work and freelance writing had taken its toll, however, and when the invite came in from Lucy Müller to attend a networking event at her alma mater, Ally didn't have to be asked twice.

As she walked through the Yard now, the trees in full leaf and the freshly cut grass soft beneath her feet, she realised that, despite her feelings when she left Harvard, she had been very happy here for a good many years. Her final year had been tainted but, before that, Harvard had been a second home to her. Maybe even a first home, considering how little time she'd ever had for her parents' house in Providence. She'd only been back to Rhode Island once since she'd moved. The second time she saw any of her family was when she'd invited her mother up to Manhattan for a Broadway show and cocktails. Her mother didn't know exactly what Ally worked as these days but assumed she was earning proper money now she'd finally left college. It had cost Ally most of her savings and all of her mental strength to spoil her mother for twenty-four hours and keep the illusion alive.

The sense that she had handled everything wrong had been growing in Ally's mind for months now.

She hadn't stayed in touch with anybody from the university, least of all Lauren, whom she should have been looking out for.

It was something that filled Ally with deep regret.

This trip provided her with two opportunities.

One, to keep her ear out for a job that allowed her to finally start realising her earning potential and do what she loved – work in education.

And two, to apologise wholeheartedly to Lauren for her role in letting her down so badly.

Lucy had inquired on Ally's behalf and found out that Lauren was a resident in Eliot House.

When she'd passed the information on via a phone call before the trip, Lucy had expressed some curiosity as to why Ally wanted to catch up with Lauren in particular.

'She's somebody I felt I should have done more for, is all,' Ally said honestly, but trying not to give anything away.

Lucy's curiosity was evidently piqued, however.

'Is she the student that you tried to get counselling for back in 2017?' Lucy asked.

Ally hesitated.

'Why do you ask?' she answered the question with a question.

It was Lucy who grew hesitant, then.

'I snooped around a little,' she said. 'Don't blame me, Ally. You were so off before you left, I was wondering what was on your mind but I didn't want to press you. When you said you were coming back and you asked after Lauren Gregory, it wasn't hard to make the connection.'

'You're wasted as a professor. You should be working in the Attorney General's office.'

'And miss all these wine soirées and holidays!'

Ally laughed, then grew quiet.

'It was related to Lauren,' Ally said. 'To be honest, I'm relieved to hear she's still there. I worried she'd drop out.'

'She's barely here,' Lucy said, her voice sombre. 'According to her tutors, she's hanging in by a thread. Academically and . . . well, they're worried about her. She's in mandated counselling.'

A half hour after the networking event ended, Ally found herself pacing along the banks of the Charles River, almost hypnotised by the swirling currents of the powerful body of water in the high tide.

In the distance, Ally could see the bell tower of Eliot House, lit up bright white in the evening sky.

She was procrastinating.

Ally's own cowardice had got the better of her two years ago.

It had taken only one threat – and it wasn't even to Ally's physical safety, just a hint that something private might be exposed – for Ally to run from the Lauren situation with her tail between her legs.

For the past two years, Ally had been in hiding. From Lauren, from life, from herself.

It had to stop. Lauren's secret was doing to Ally exactly what Ally had feared it would do to Lauren. It was eating away at her.

At the intersection of Memorial Drive and John F. Kennedy Street, Ally turned towards the entrance to Eliot House.

The courtyard was deserted on the dark night and Ally shivered a little. She was tense; after living in the city for so long, she had become accustomed to having people around her.

Knowing her imagination was getting the better of her, she walked on.

She was still trying to think of what she'd say to Lauren when her elbow was brushed roughly by somebody running past.

Ally's heart skipped a beat and her hand flew to her chest.

It took a few seconds to realise it was only a late-night jogger and less than that to realise the long curls in the ponytail of the woman running past were familiar.

'Lauren?'

The woman kept running and Ally noticed the AirPods in her ears.

She yelled.

'Lauren!'

Ahead, the jogger stopped, turned.

It *was* her, but Ally had never seen anybody look so different in two short years.

She was down ten pounds, at least, weight Lauren didn't have to lose. Her face was pinched, drawn; her brow furrowed with lines; her mouth turned down at the sides.

Plus, she looked like she'd seen a ghost.

It's me, Ally realised. She looks terrified of *me*.

And suddenly, Ally realised she'd fucked up again.

She'd come to see Lauren to make herself feel better.

But Ally was the last person Lauren wanted to see.

Ally stood there with her mouth hanging open, trying desperately to find the words to say something, anything that could fix this.

'How are you?' was all she could choke out when her mouth started to move again.

Lauren stared at her.

Then she turned and began to run again.

Ally stood there, in shock.

Was that it?

But Lauren stopped.

She spun on her heel and jogged back.

'You told me to trust you,' she spat at Ally. 'You and your boyfriend. You were meant to be looking out for me.'

'I . . .'

Lauren shook her head, her face awash with pain and disappointment.

'They threatened me. They threatened my family. Do you know that? These people, they don't give a shit. They get whatever they want – they get away with whatever they want. They *own* the system.'

'I didn't know!' Ally gasped. 'I'm sorry.'

'You're sorry!' Lauren took a step towards Ally. She was so close, Ally could smell the sweat on the other woman's body, see the wet sheen on her eyes. She thought for a moment that Lauren was going to hit her. Instead, Lauren just whispered.

'Sometimes I think it would have been better if he'd killed me.'

This time, when she ran, she didn't look back.

If she had, she'd have seen Ally paralysed on the spot, her head hanging in shame.

Erin

THEN

I have Cal drop me outside my apartment. Under pressure from me, he's relented and says he'll meet me for coffee tomorrow, when he'll tell me more about what happened to Lauren. I put a reminder in my phone and wave until he drives off, then I kick my heels on the pavement for a bit, trying to summon the courage to go inside.

I'm going to be on my own in the apartment now until I can move.

Alone, with only my memories of Danny.

I'm thirty years of age and I'm a widow.

Two kids sail by on bikes, heading for Main Street, laughing about something one of them has said.

Maybe now's a good time for that run. I can sweat out my worries, feel the wind in my hair and on my face, just pound out a few miles until I'm too tired to do anything other than shower and sleep.

I don't notice the Lexus pull up and it's only when I hear the car door shut and see Ben approach that I realise I've company.

That car.

It strikes me that if anybody I know appears to have money they shouldn't have, it's Ben Mitchell.

'Your sister gone?' he asks.

I stare at him.

'Are you watching me?' I ask.

'I'm looking out for you,' he says. 'It's a different thing.'

'Were you looking out for Danny?' I ask.

He looks abashed.

'It doesn't feel like you were, Ben. They couldn't have sent somebody else to arrest him, no?'

'Erin, listen to me.'

'Why?'

'You remember me and Danny were the lead on the arrest of that guy over in Blue Point, the one who'd taken out those two gang-bangers in Brooklyn?'

'What does that have to do with anything?'

Ben takes a step or so back from me. He holds out his hands, non-threatening, his face imploring me to hear him out.

I stand there, willing myself to come up with the words that will make him go away but my mouth is dry and my feet are stuck to the pavement.

'That guy from Blue Point came out of his house, yelling murder and threatening to kill every one of us sons of bitches, our wives and children, too.'

I shrug. I remember it perfectly – or how it was relayed to me afterwards, anyhow.

'He was a huge motherfucker,' Ben says. 'Before the uniforms could get him into the back of the patrol car, he managed to break free and he made a lunge at me. Danny jumped in between us, so he took the guy's full body weight and dislocated his shoulder.'

'Yes,' I say, meeting Ben's eye. I'm glad he remembers it exactly as it happened and this isn't something else he's trying to tell me wasn't true.

'That guy's body, a bullet, Danny would have done the same thing. And I'd have done it for him. He knew that. There are only four people I loved more than Danny. My wife and my kids. Push comes to shove, maybe just my kids, but don't ever tell Christina. I have to take care of my family, Erin. My real family.'

He opens the door of the Lexus and takes something from the passenger seat.

He hands me a large envelope.

'What's this?' I ask.

'Proof. You need proof to let all this drop? Fine. Have it.'

Ben's already walking back to his car.

I hold the envelope between my fingers like it contains anthrax.

Upstairs, I open it to find a bank statement.

My hand shakes as I dial Karla's number.

When she answers I have to breathe deeply before I can speak.

'Karla, I know Danny's estate is going to take a while but, I was wondering, can you tell me now what it says in his will?'

She hesitates for only a few seconds.

'In general terms, yes. I was going to call you today, anyway. I've . . . well, I'll tell you about that in a moment. You're the sole beneficiary, with some allowances made for his mother and brother, who get cash bequests and some items of personal value.'

'The money,' I say. 'In his bank account. Have you found out how much there is?'

There's a pause.

'Which account do you want to know about?' she says.

'Danny's account,' I say. 'His personal one. I've access to our joint one.'

Our joint account covered all our bills, savings, etc., and we put most of our salaries in it every month. Our private accounts were for gifts, mainly for each other, for our families. We agreed to keep back one sixth of each of our salaries just to make sure we had some spending independence.

Also, Danny insisted I had my own account.

'I've seen too many women stuck in relationships because they didn't have the financial ability to get out,' he'd said.

'Danny – are you planning to physically, mentally or emotionally abuse me?' I'd laughed.

'You're getting a good spanking if you don't keep that account.'

I close my eyes. When I open them, his ghost has gone.

'Danny's private account was with Chase,' I say.

There's more silence down the line before Karla speaks again.

'Danny also had an account with First National,' she says. 'And one with Bank of America.'

The heat flushes into my cheeks.

'How much?'

'That's what I was going to contact you about. There's one hundred thousand dollars in each. Exactly. But, Erin, listen. I spoke to both banks today and a freeze order has been placed on his Bank of America account by Newport PD.'

'Why?'

A sigh.

'I suspect they're alleging the money in that account is the result of criminal activity.'

My stomach does flips.

'Erin?'

'I'm here.'

'The paperwork came through for Danny's pension. As he hadn't actually been arrested and they hadn't officially suspended him before he died, they can't refuse to pay it, thank God. It's likely that Bank of America account will stay frozen for a long time, and in all likelihood, it will be seized. They either don't know about the other account yet or can't get an order for it. I'd advise you don't mention that account. Let them do their jobs but don't spend anything from it, either. I can help you fill out the pension paperwork and we can get that backdated for you.'

I barely hear her.

I look at the sheaf of paper that Ben has given me.

It's the Bank of America account statement.

On our last date night, Danny had made a run to King Kullen supermarket to pick up the weekly special from the deli counter. We'd sat in with Rueben sandwiches and beers, watching an old black-and-white movie on cable.

'Erin, you want to call by the office, or will I come out to you?'

'What?'

'Tell you what, why don't I swing by tomorrow?'

'Sure,' I say and hang up.

I'm still in a daze when the phone rings.

I don't know what part of my brain is functioning when I answer it – some sort of auto response has kicked in.

'Have you looked at it?'

It's Ben.

I swallow a sob.

'I'm sorry, Erin,' he says. 'Look, here's what happened. He organised paperless statements to his work email. IT said they were buried in his computer. They were still on the hard drive. The bosses wouldn't have even looked at his computer, except they got a tip-off. There was more. He had a whole correspondence with the financial investment officer at the bank about offshore accounts. So fucking stupid. He was doing it on a secret email account but from his desk computer. I can't fathom why he didn't do it at home, unless he was worried you'd spot something. And Erin, nobody can access our computers externally, it's not a mistake. Sully knew somebody in our department was taking bribes; he just . . . none of us would have thought. None of us. If Danny had denied it, maybe, but the fact he did what he did, it . . .'

I can't even summon the energy to say anything.

The evidence is there, in my hand, and Karla has just confirmed it.

Not to mention – there's even more money that the police don't know about.

'I was his partner, Erin. Nobody ever thinks the partner can be innocent. I had to distance myself. I had to be the one who went to arrest him.'

I hang up.

The hours that follow are dark.

I register the text from Tanya to say she's landed safely after the seven-hour flight.

I hear comings and goings in the apartment building.

I forget all about looking up Cal's sister.

Danny had two hundred thousand dollars in secret bank accounts.

He was trying to open offshore accounts.

He was seeing a psychiatrist.

He suffered with depression.

He killed himself in front of me.

My beautiful, loved and loving husband.

Who was he?

Where do the lies begin and end?

I don't realise I left the front door of the apartment unlocked until the next morning, when I wake to find Karla standing over the couch.

I'm lucky to live in such a safe, law-abiding community.

Anybody could have walked in.

I've barely slept. My hair is matted, I reek of body sweat and my neck feels like somebody has hit me with a bat.

Karla suggests, though it sounds like an order, that I take a shower.

I do what I'm told.

I sit in the basin behind the glass, my knees tucked into my body, the hot water cascading on to my shoulders.

I spend long enough in there for my brain to kick back into gear.

I think of the period after Niamh died and how hard it felt to get up every morning, knowing my little sister was dead.

I'd done it anyway.

I think of how much she wanted to live, how, in those final moments, she wouldn't have just been thinking about her own life but about what the loss of it would do to us.

She was that sort of person.

Danny didn't fight.

Danny wanted to die.

I don't know what Danny did to get all that money but the fact he had it has shaken me.

What I'm really angry at is that he's robbed me of the chance to get answers.

That's the least forgivable bit.

Karla has the coffee machine going. She's opened the window in the living area – significance be damned – and the place seems fresher.

'Sit,' she tells me, when I join her.

She serves up the coffee and half a toasted bagel and makes me eat and drink.

'Okay, Erin. You either talk to me or we say prayers together. You choose.'

A Hobbesian choice.

'It's simple, Karla. My husband wasn't the man I thought he was.' She shakes her head.

'It's true. I didn't know him. I thought I did. I didn't.'

'This Cal says—'

'Cal Hawley is a stranger,' I interrupt. 'Maybe Danny was helping him or maybe Danny just told Cal he was. Anyway, the point is, I have to start coming to terms with this. I've dealt with worse, to be fair.'

'Really?' Karla is incredulous. 'You've dealt with worse than this?'

I start to cry.

Karla shakes her head.

'You poor thing,' she says.

I shrug off her pity. I don't want it. I don't want people seeing me as a victim. Or worse – when it came to my husband – as a fool.

'Let's go for a walk,' she says. 'Fresh air.'

I go into the bedroom to get my sandals.

I might be imagining her putting my phone back on the counter when I return to the living area, but I say nothing.

'Let's go to the beach,' she says.

'You know this neighbourhood?' I ask.

'Long Island, chica. Sixteen hundred miles of coastline.'

The beach is packed with summer visitors and locals. Barbecues sizzle and a gang of beautiful people are playing volleyball on the soft sand.

We cut through the dunes and walk towards the boardwalk.

'When I worked in Manhattan, the amount of fucked-up police cases I dealt with,' Karla says. 'Hell, you couldn't throw a popsicle without hitting a bad cop.'

'I'm starting to think I couldn't find a husband without hitting one,' I say.

Karla doesn't smile.

'I knew when you asked me to help you, this one stunk,' she says. 'I've had nothing but hostility from the ninth precinct concerning Danny.'

'Well, we can understand it now.'

'You probably don't appreciate how bad police corruption is over here, Erin. I can't imagine it's like this where you come from.'

'Karla, they could have filmed Serpico in Ireland.'

'Ah. Well, then, maybe you do know. Erin, it's never just one bad apple. It always runs through a department, I find. And it is not tinfoil-hat talk to suggest a police department is capable of framing somebody. I've seen it. God knows I have.'

My stomach clenches. I know where she's going with this. I resist it.

Danny let me down.

He let me down.

But . . . that last morning, in bed, the look in his eyes that told me he loved me as much as I loved him.

Our wedding day, when he held my gaze and I forgot that there was a single other person in the registrar's office.

'I'll be better,' he'd whispered to me, after our first wedding kiss.

Oh, Danny.

'Sometimes they need a fall guy,' Karla says. 'It's not always black and white. I didn't know Danny but I know you, Erin.'

'We've only just met!' I half laugh, mirthlessly.

'I told you. I read people well. If you loved Danny, then Danny had something good about him.'

I so badly want to agree with her.

I see it, the glint of hope, just within touching distance.

And then I think of those goddamn bank accounts.

'Love is blind,' I say.

Karla sighs.

'Do you want a cone?' Karla asks.

'What?'

'I'm getting us one. Sprinkles?'

She walks over to the ice cream shack.

I watch her, bemused, then turn and look at the kids running in and out of the waves, lugging buckets filled with water back up the beach for sandcastles.

I don't see the ambush coming until Cal Hawley is standing beside me.

He's wearing a suit, and even though he has casually slung the jacket over his shoulder and his tie is loose, he looks completely out of place, like he's been teleported from an office to this beach.

At first, I think he's showed up here because we'd a coffee date. Then I realise he couldn't have known I'd be on the beach.

'Did Karla ring you?'

'No. But she answered my call to you. She suggested I call over.'

Jesus Christ. In the face of all the evidence; in the knowledge that she never even met Danny – Karla is determined to fight for his good name.

'Erin, how many of us need to tell you?' Cal says, peering over sunglasses. 'He was a good man.'

As is this guy.

I clench my fists, trying to relieve the tension.

'I want you to be honest with me,' I say. 'Were you paying Danny to help your sister?'

'No,' Cal says, confused, but he keeps my gaze until I blink.

God, why couldn't it have been a yes?

Karla has returned.

'You actually got me an ice cream cone,' I say, astonished.

'You need the sugar. You're wasting away. And before you say anything about Cal here – I just told him you weren't going to make your coffee date.'

I stand between these two people, both of whom I've only

recently met, and wonder why they are more concerned about my welfare than I am.

A weird thought lands in my head.

Danny sent them to look over me.

I brush it aside as soon as it forms.

I'm angry at him and I want to stay that way.

It's the first stage of grief that I feel I can live with.

If I'm angry at Danny, I don't have to miss him so much.

'Do you want to come for a drive?' Cal asks.

'Sure,' I say. 'I'll just eat my ice cream first.'

There's a part in *Alice in Wonderland* where she just starts going along with it.

'You ever been along the Gold Coast?' Cal asks, as we cruise down the Long Island Expressway.

'Got a little pad up there?' I ask. 'My pal Bud told me you Hawleys have quite a few residences.'

Cal smiles, the first time he's relaxed since we embarked on this odd road trip.

'We don't have a patch on your bar friend's family fortunes. Think Vanderbilt old wealth. He's probably related to Whitman, too.'

'And there he is now, dyeing Irish coffees green with some chemical that should be banned.'

Cal smiles, then his face grows serious again.

'Did Bud like Danny?' he asks.

I stare out at the mansions we're passing.

'Bud loved Danny.'

'Seems a lot of people cared for him.'

'Yup.'

'Not too many people care for me,' Cal says.

I glance sideways at his profile. His face is placid; the statement matter-of-fact.

'I'm sure that's not true,' I say, dutifully.

'Sure it is. They care for my money. They don't care about me. You can judge somebody by the friends around them, you know.'

'I guess it's different when you have money,' I say. 'You can't help how people act towards you.'

'I'll give you that. But it does say something about Danny, doesn't it? That so many good people loved him.'

'It says he was great at getting people to like him,' I say. 'It doesn't mean he didn't have secrets. It doesn't mean he could be trusted.'

Cal looks at me oddly, then concentrates on the road again.

We pass by gated estates and I amuse myself by remembering that their drives are probably longer than the main road outside.

The Gold Coast is home to America's wealthiest wealthy people. The one per cent of the one per cent.

I've never been up there, primarily because Danny and I stuck to exploring the south shore, but also because I always suspected just buying a coffee along the Gold Coast would cost the equivalent of a small nation's GDP.

I did have an author once who came from out this way. US publishing is like publishing the world over. The moneyed classes find their way in far easier.

Authors. I must get back to them. My boss has been ultra-supportive, but publishing in New York is a competitive business and I can't expect to be carried forever.

To do: go to work. Find new home. Get a haircut. Remove all traces of dead husband from current apartment.

'I'm sorry for taking up your day,' I say.

'You're not. I planned to go for a swim, meet friends for lunch, have a bottle of Merlot, then obsessively mull over Lauren's case and think about what Danny Ryan might have deliberately or inadvertently told his wife that could help me.'

He's honest, I'll give him that.

We drive for a little while longer, then turn up Middle Neck Road and pull into Sands Point Preserve.

'This is one of my favourite spots on the North Shore,' Cal says, as we enter the vast acreage.

I nod, like this is all totally familiar to me, when actually I'm already pretty gobsmacked at some of the places we've passed on the way up here. I've a notion now of where we're going – everybody's heard of the Gould-Guggenheim historic mansions.

Danny wanted to visit them with me. I'd told him I didn't have a huge interest in the big, old houses of the rich and famous. He was surprised at that, considering I come from Europe.

It's because I'm from Europe, I told him. Before I'd turned eighteen I'd been on school trips to Versailles and Schloß Schönbrunn. What I knew of the Gold Coast was that the titans of American industry had built houses in the style of these great European models, so they could spend their summers in cultured luxury.

Old money in America is still not quite the same as old money where I come from.

'Do you know the history of this place?' Cal asks.

I shrug.

'Castle Gould is my favourite of the three,' he says. 'Guggen-heim, you see, bought it from Howard Gould. Gould had built it for his wife but neither of them liked it much. A 100,000-square-foot castle modelled after Ireland's Kilkenny Castle. So he built a second house, Hempstead, but they never spent a single night in it together. She left him. She must have really had it in for him, right?'

'Maybe he lied to her.'

Cal smiles thinly.

'When Daniel Guggenheim's son Harry married Caroline Morton, his father gifted Harry ninety acres so he could build his own little place. He built Falaise, on the bluffs overlooking the Sound. You've heard of Falaise?'

'Can't say I have.'

'The Lindberghs stayed there to escape the media circus after their baby was kidnapped. Or you might be aware of a little-known gangster movie starring Al Pacino and Marlon Brando. They filmed the scene there from *The Godfather*, the one with the horse's head in the bed.'

Even the view on approach is impressive. We cross a bridge that looks as though it was built centuries ago and pass along a tree-lined avenue, landscaped gardens to either side. My first view of the Sands Point Preserve includes Castle Gould, Hempstead House, and the Long Island Sound from a distance. My jaw drops.

We pull up in the car park near Hempstead House. It's beautiful, Tudor in style, granite and limestone exterior.

I feel like I've stepped out of the car and into an English manor country garden.

'I've only ever seen places like this in *The Great Gatsby*,' I say.

'Tours are meant to be scheduled but I can organise one now, if you like,' Cal tells me. 'It's even more impressive inside.'

'Can we look around the grounds?' I ask.

I'd very much like to see inside that house but, for now, I just want to breathe and feel the sun on my face.

'I was hoping you'd say that,' Cal says.

I pause, looking up at the house.

'Why did you bring me here?' I ask.

He takes a deep breath.

'Lauren always wanted to come,' he says. 'But she never did.'

I say nothing for a few moments.

Then, tentatively:

'This connection with Danny – I need to know what he was doing. Can you understand that?'

He looks away from me, up towards the roses that fill the beds in the garden near the house.

'I get it,' he says. 'Look.' A pause. 'Something happened to Lauren. And it . . . it changed her. She used to be so full of life. Funny. Clever. Charming. The sort of person you want to be around. We got on, even though she was nearly a decade younger than me and my mother didn't want me near her. It didn't matter. Lauren followed me around. I went to Harvard. Then she went to Harvard. If she hadn't gone there, if she hadn't been . . .' His face contorts and I think he's going to cry. 'Anyway. We were close, up until she was, uh, attacked.'

I wince. I can see every word of this is painful for him. He can't even look at me.

The heat rises from my toes right up to my face.

'She never felt like she got justice, afterwards, and Danny, not long before he died, tried to help her. That's how I know he was a good guy, whatever else he did.'

Lauren had been attacked. Now it's starting to make sense.

'I'm sorry,' I say.

He shrugs.

'I'll always be grateful to him,' he says. 'For helping me when he did. Look, nobody's perfect . . .'

'Did he ever tell you why we got married?' I gulp.

Cal frowns.

'We got married because I only had a work visa and it was a nightmare, getting renewals,' I say. 'It was Danny's idea. He proposed so I could stay in the country. So I could cheat the visa system. We had only been together for six months but nobody asked any questions because he was a cop.'

Cal purses his lips and muses on this.

Nobody's perfect, but Danny bent the law when it suited him.

Cal spreads his arms.

'I don't know what to say,' he says. 'That doesn't make him sound like a bad person to me. Just a man who'll help somebody, especially if he loves them. We all break rules. You should see what they do in the world of finance.'

I'm taken aback. I thought my confession would give Cal pause for thought.

'Let's go.' I sigh.

We walk away from the house, down towards the Long Island Sound, and find a spot facing the sea. There are picnic benches but Cal has brought a chequered blanket from the car and he shakes it out, letting it billow in the breeze until it's flat on the grass.

We sit there, staring out at the sea.

'How is Lauren now?' I ask.

I watch the Adam's apple in Cal's throat as he swallows.

He shakes his head, unable to even speak.

I stare at my bare knees, and at the grass to the side of the blanket. Unconsciously, I start to pick at it, using long strands to tickle my knees. Like when we were kids.

'I had two sisters,' I say. 'One of them died.'

Cal whips his head around to stare at me.

'I'm sorry.'

'Just over five years ago. I moved to New York, not long after. Her name was Niamh.'

'What happened to her?'

I swallow.

'She was attacked, too. A total stranger.'

Cal's face pales.

'He raped her, then he strangled her and dumped her body.'

'Erin,' Cal says, softly.

'Yup.' I hesitate. 'Is Lauren dead?'

'Yes. I . . . I'm sorry, Erin. I really can't talk about her. I just – I just can't. It's still too raw. It only happened recently. It's barely months . . .'

When the corners of his eyes start to glisten, I realise that Cal Hawley is a kindred spirit.

And it's at that point I realise he's telling the truth about Danny. Or about Danny helping him, at least.

Danny knew every detail of Niamh's death.

If Lauren had died in a similar way – of course he would have tried to help her family.

That's the Danny I knew.

A good man.

So why did he keep so much from me?

Harvard

MAY 2019

The same day Ally got the call, she drove up to Harvard.

A visibly concerned Lucy met her outside Eliot House.

Two tables had been set up in the front courtyard: one to organise volunteers for the search party, the other to provide refreshments and sustenance for those returning.

Lucy spotted Ally walking across the grass and headed in her direction.

'I didn't think you'd come,' she said.

Ally shook her head. She'd had no choice. She was just grateful Lucy had thought to contact her.

'How did they not notice for three days that she was missing?' was all Ally could say.

Lucy shrugged, helplessly.

'Lauren had a private room. Apparently, she was so hard to live with nobody would share, so they left her to it. She'd missed lectures and stopped going to the counselling sessions, but it was only when her mother and brother drove up and started asking where she was . . . I'm sorry, Ally. I've been keeping an ear out for her because I know she matters to you but with summer exams coming, everybody is busy.'

Ally shook her head. The only person who had anything to apologise for when it came to Lauren was Ally herself.

'Are they sure she went off by herself? Could somebody have taken her?'

Lucy shook her head.

'There were sightings,' she said.

'Where?' This was new. Lucy hadn't told Ally this on the phone.

Lucy hesitated.

'At the river,' she said.

Ally felt the bottom drop out of her stomach.

Please God.

Not that.

'Did she say anything to you?' Lucy asked. 'When you saw her that time you came up? You did see her, didn't you?'

Ally thought back to the night in this very courtyard where she'd seen Lauren running.

To the exchange they had.

And to the email she'd received only weeks ago.

Her face coloured as she shook her head.

'No,' Ally said. 'She didn't tell me anything significant.'

PART II

The Truth

Then

In the months that follow Danny's death, I vacillate between anger that my husband must have been a corrupt cop and absolute certainty that somebody, somewhere, must have got it wrong and Danny was being framed.

No matter what I'm feeling on any given day there are always absolutes.

Danny is dead. Danny took his own life. Danny kept secrets from me.

When you love someone as strongly and as deeply as I did, it's hard to switch it off completely.

But, yes, I've tried flicking that switch a few times. In my lowest moments.

The investigation into his alleged bribe-taking doesn't go anywhere, but the freeze order remains on his Bank of America account.

His First National account stays untouched. Guided by Karla, I haven't disclosed its existence to the police. Her advice is let the cops find it and freeze it if they want to – but she's pretty certain they want everything Danny Ryan-related to go away at this stage.

Why go through the ordeal of bad publicity if the scapegoat is not even there to take the heat?

She doesn't want us opening a can of worms by pointing them in the direction of more potential evidence. I think we're walking a thin line but I'm so angry with Newport PD, I'm happy to do so.

Life goes on. The day-to-day stuff.

Sleeping, waking, eating, drinking.

I decide working from home is not healthy any longer and go back, four days a week, to the office in Manhattan.

I find myself establishing a routine of what can only be described as normal – normal being a relative term these days.

Rather than sinking into the depths of despair, I cope. I keep going. And it's the strange network of newcomers and old friends in my life that help me with that.

Karla, Cal, Bud, my work colleagues.

I know I'm on the road to recovery when, three months after Danny's death, Karla tells me she has a friend who is subletting an apartment in Downtown Manhattan while she goes home for a few months to nurse her ailing mother. The friend is willing to let me have the apartment for far less than current rents.

Despite the fact I'm now commuting into work Tuesday to Friday, when it comes to it, I don't want to leave my apartment.

Yes, what Danny did there was horrific but it also contains my happiest memories.

My feelings about the apartment are as conflicted as my feelings about Danny.

I can even look out the apartment window again without feeling like I'm falling, or that I, too, have the urge to jump.

In my stronger moments, I only want to believe good about

Danny. It helps that I have Cal, Karla and Bud in my ear reminding me what sort of man my husband was.

Karla likes to remind me often how badly the police have behaved. Towards Danny – who must have been under horrendous stress – and towards me.

I want to believe Danny was being set up. It sounds far-fetched. It sounds like something from a film.

But Cal insists Danny was digging around in a case that the police wanted to stay closed. He insists powerful forces were at play. And he's come up with the theory that they planted money in a bank account in Danny's name in order to cast aspersions on his character and provide evidence he was in receipt of bribes.

Karla is still trying to help me get to the bottom of it, but she's aware of her limitations. When she moved to Long Island, she deliberately avoided police-related cases, for an easy life. Manhattan burned her, she says. So she has very few cop contacts here.

At her suggestion, I've asked our mutual friend David to help. One of David's former journalism specialities was financial crime and I've asked him if he could look into Danny's bank account and trace the contents.

He's not having any luck so far, but it helps me sleep at night knowing there are people out there asking questions.

In the meantime, I keep going.

Every morning and evening, I get the Long Island Rail to and from Jamaica and Penn Station and power-walk into my office on Park Avenue, where I've thrown myself back into work. Then on the long weekends I hang out with Karla or Cal, who take turns making sure I'm not on my own.

The Karla Saturdays are always funny. She's started treating me as an intern – bringing me to meet clients, getting me to write up notes on cases, paying me in beer – all under the pretext of me healing. It's useful – I'm currently editing a couple of legal thrillers and I'm starting to feel more familiar with the lexicon than half my authors are.

Karla seems to have a fiery, on-off relationship with a woman she only refers to as a 'pain in my frickin' neck'. I never meet pain-in-the-neck but I get that she is hot as hell, very exciting and extremely jealous. Karla appears quite content with the insanity of their coupling; I keep asking if she worries she'll wake up one night to find her beloved leaning over her with a knife.

Time with Cal is more relaxed. We've formed a friendship, and like all relationships carved in the most unusual of circumstances, it feels tighter than it probably merits. He's lost a sister, I've lost a sister – we don't talk about them much but they were people we loved and our respective losses have given us a unique bond.

Cal has admitted that Lauren's death earlier in the year took a lot out of him and he's still not recovered. I appreciate that. It took years after Niamh's death before I could talk about her.

Danny was one of the first people outside our family to whom I confided.

What's worse for Cal is that, as he tells it, Lauren never got justice for what happened to her. Nobody was prosecuted.

And he's convinced, with Danny dead, she never will. That it's over.

Sometimes I don't know how he can bear to keep going carrying all that pain and then . . . well, then I catch my reflection and realise everybody I know thinks the same about me.

Summer becomes autumn and then, before I know it, it's the

run-up to Christmas, my first festive season alone since Danny died.

I'm not sure who suggests the idea of meeting in the Irish pub Downtown on Christmas week. Bud says it was his idea because he wants to check out the Irish bar competition and steal their ideas, but I'm fairly certain the three of them concocted it as a way to make me acknowledge the season.

So, here we all are, Cal, Karla, Bud and I, all ignoring the dead elephant in the room.

'How do your family feel about you not going home for Christmas?' Karla asks.

'Don't mention the war,' I say.

'Why aren't you going home?' Bud asks. 'Your sister is a nice lady.'

'She is. It's my parents who are schmucks.'

'When they're gone, they're gone,' Bud says.

'You get that from a fortune cookie or a calendar?'

'I'm just saying.'

'If you want me to have Christmas dinner in McNally's, stop trying to send me home.'

Cal nearly chokes on his Guinness.

'You got a problem with McNally's for dinner?' Bud asks him.

'What are you serving?' Cal inquires.

'A traditional Christmas roast.'

'And pray tell,' I butt in, 'what does that entail, Bud?'

'You got your turkey, your ham, your mash, your root vegetables, your gravy. And something called stuffing.'

Many a Christmas dinner has fallen on its stuffing. I suspect McNally's version will become local lore before December is out.

'You know you're extremely welcome at mine,' Karla says.

It's possibly the tenth time she's made me this offer. Poor Bud.

'I know,' I say. 'What about you, Cal? What are you doing?'

In our conversations over the last few months, it has become increasingly obvious that Cal and his relatives aren't close. He's an only child now, so it's just him and his parents. I'm not entirely sure they're on speaking terms. His father, Henry – even though he's had two wives since he split with Cal's mother – spends the bulk of his time at the Hawley mansion but Cal resides in the mansion's pool house. Who knows how long he and his parents go without even seeing each other? They've the typical wealthy WASP-ish approach to family – keep them near enough to make sure you're in the will, not so close that you end up out of the will.

As someone once said, it's hard to feel sorry for the rich man sipping champagne in his pool house, but as I've got to know him, Cal strikes me as having possibly been done a disservice by the stork. I kinda feel he was destined for a normal family, somewhere in the Midwest, maybe. He's sensible with his money, even though I know he has a lot of it. And while plenty of women throw themselves at him, he doesn't appear to take advantage of it.

There's a serious, intense side to him and I have a feeling he's relaxed in our company in a way he isn't with his natural class peers.

Especially with me.

Cal shrugs, and for the first time, I get the sense that while they're all here to distract me from this being my first Christmas without Danny – he's also approaching the holiday season without his sister.

'I'm going to tick all the politically correct boxes and sit down with the great and the good who've been invited to Chez Hawley,' he says, and he couldn't sound less enthusiastic if he told us he was going in for ECT. 'If we can get to the end of the day without my father screwing the maid, my mother passing out on Valium, my father's latest mistress arriving and smashing an irreplaceable crystal ornament in a rage and my grandmother shutting down my trust fund, an angel will get its wings.'

None of us say anything for a few seconds.

'You should come to McNally's,' Bud says.

'I didn't say it would be that bad,' Cal quips.

We all laugh.

Weirdly, I feel marginally better about my Christmas.

I have these guys. I have my sister, even if there's distance between us.

And clearly some memo went around the office because I left work this evening with two giant Santa bags filled with gifts, currently resting under our table.

I'd been congratulating myself for remembering to bring in cards this morning. My work colleagues care for me, and I love them for it.

'Same again?' I ask, jumping up from my stool. Everyone nods, even Cal, who is sipping his Guinness with all the enthusiasm of somebody enduring a thousand paper cuts.

I wait patiently at the bar while the barman, who will never get a job in Ireland if he can't handle this simple crowd, tries to take the creamy head off a badly poured pint.

'He needs to start again.'

I recognise the voice before I see who it is.

Dr Leslie Klein is standing beside me. We're indoors and the place is heaving and airless, but she's wearing a huge pashmina scarf over her wool-knit sweater and still looks unflappably cool. Her grey hair is loose tonight, framing her flawless face, and more than one man in this place is checking her out.

'Hi,' I say.

'Hello.'

She smiles warmly. She seems surprised but happy to find me here.

'What are you doing over here?' I ask.

'Downtown? I've a Christmas party with some peers.'

'Don't you guys have those in hallowed halls somewhere?'

'Usually, but the pints are never as good.'

I smile.

'I saw you at your table but I didn't want to intrude.'

'Oh.' I look over at our gang, laughing at something Bud has just said. He's probably told them what he's planning to put in the Christmas stuffing.

'How are you doing?' she asks.

People ask me this all the time and I've become expert in the shrug-smile that ensures they're not worried and I'm not lying, but they're off the hook for asking.

Professionals, though, have a way of inquiring after your mental health that is a little more probing.

'I'm as well as can be expected,' I say. Good answer, I think.

But the doctor's not won over.

'I've been thinking about you a lot,' she says.

'Have you?'

I've thought about her, too. I've wondered what my husband revealed to her and what secrets of his she has in that big brain of hers.

But I hadn't tried to approach her again. I knew I'd get the confidentiality brick wall and I couldn't cope with the frustration of it.

I did contemplate breaking into her office and stealing her files, but that's another story and one that involved me being pretty blasted and walking the streets at 2 a.m.

Now she's here, though, and she's approached me.

I'd have thought she'd run a mile if she ever saw me again, rather than take the risk of me peppering her with questions.

'Yes,' she says. 'I think about you all the time. I feel I should have handled things better that day, when you came to see me. You'd had such a shock. I should have got in contact with you afterwards, to offer you an ear. I mean, I should have reached out as a friend. I'm not sure it would be a good idea for me to be your doctor. But I can recommend somebody, if you'd like. Have you had any grief counselling?'

I point at the hard-liquor optics on the far side of the bar.

'Nature's comfort,' I say. 'It's cheaper than a billed hour.'

She smiles.

'Jack Daniel's and I are great friends,' she says, 'even if we do only meet up once or twice a year.'

Interesting. I wasn't expecting humour.

She studies me a few seconds longer, then cocks her head.

'You don't have to feel guilty, you know.'

'Excuse me?'

'For living your life.'

'I don't.'

'I'm happy to hear it. You deserve it. He'd have told you that. Merry Christmas, Erin.'

She walks away, disappearing into the crowd of revellers as I turn back to the bar.

That's what I mean about professionals.

Even when I bury it, I feel guilty every second of every day.

For being alive when Danny is not.

I cannot stop thinking about Danny in the run-up to Christmas day.

This year would only have been our third.

Every minute I'm in the apartment, which is achingly free of holiday decorations, I think of last year and of Danny.

So, in need of a distraction, and unable to get my husband out of my head, I decide to dig some more into Lauren Gregory's case. It oddly makes me feel closer to Danny. He might have been keeping it from me, but he was looking into this when he died and, I imagine, for all the right reasons. Five minutes with Cal Hawley and Danny would have recognised in him that pain he saw in me all the time.

The easy way of doing this is to bite the bullet and ask Cal more about his sister, but I've already promised myself I'll respect his right to grieve in peace.

Christmas Eve and I've literally only just sat down with my laptop to start researching when there's a knock on my door.

It could be anybody. One of my neighbours. The building supervisor. Girl Scouts selling cookies.

Our building's front door is a safety hazard.

This time it's Cal, which is less of a hazard and more of an inconvenience, as I was about to start Googling his sister.

I've never seen Cal's house, or anywhere inside of the Hawley estate. He lives in a world I'm not entirely comfortable mixing in and I've seen enough as a New York editor and a Long Island resident to summon up images of the sort of home Cal has. It helps that he seems more comfortable in my world than I would be in his. But I still feel a little embarrassed every time he comes near my place, almost as if I have to apologise for its tiny squalor.

'You haven't got a tree,' is all Cal says when I open the door.

'Did you drive over here to tell me that?'

'I came over to give you your gift.'

I frown. I've sent Tanya gift vouchers, shit even by my standards. I haven't bothered with my folks, though I know my sister wrapped something and put it under the tree from me. I know this because I got a text from my mother this morning telling me she took possession of it from the postman and was hoping my gift had arrived.

'I know you're not doing presents,' Cal says. 'And I was going to get you a copy of *The Grinch* – to be ironic, you know. But, given the weird circumstances in which we met, I wanted to do something entirely normal.'

He hands me a bag.

'Don't open it until tomorrow morning,' he says. 'I gotta run.'

'Oh – you sure? I was planning to get some work done but . . .'

'No, I have plans. You're not the only lady I'm calling on with a gift tonight. The car has a sled attached.'

He winks, an effort at looking like a playboy. He's far too clean-cut, Episcopalian and all-round decent to carry it off.

'Have fun,' I say. He hesitates before he leaves.

'Erin, were you planning to . . . are you going to the cemetery at all over Christmas?'

It's a moment before I can shake my head.

Danny was cremated and I sent Gloria his ashes, but there's a wall in the cemetery where his name has been inscribed. I know people go to places like that and leave flowers.

I can't, though.

'Okay,' Cal says. 'If you change your mind and you want somebody to bring you, just give me a shout. I'll be . . . I'll be going to Lauren's.'

'Drive safe,' I say, unable to think of anything else. 'It's getting icy out there.'

He nods and leaves.

I place his gift – which is wrapped in a way that tells me A. he didn't do it, and B. it probably cost more than all the gifts I have stacked in the corner altogether – over with the rest.

I glance at it for a moment.

A tiny part of me feels a momentary pang of something.

I bury it before it even surfaces. My husband is not even six months dead.

I put myself on research duty so I can keep my thoughts honest.

Not asking Cal about Lauren means I've set myself a Herculean task.

There are tonnes of Lauren Gregorys.

I try to narrow it down to Long Island Lauren Gregorys and get twenty-odd.

They're all still alive.

Then I realise Cal's father works on Wall Street so his second wife, Lauren's mother, could easily have been a New Yorker. Henry's new wife, according to Cal, is from California.

Lauren Gregory, New York, turns up far too many hits.

Lauren Gregory, deceased, turns up too many hits.

It was a big fuck-up to not at least ask Cal exactly when Lauren died, which could have helped me slim the pickings.

I'm hit with a brainwave. Cal and Lauren both went to Harvard. I work out from Cal's age when he would have started and graduated and put in Lauren's name, nine years later, the rough period she would have attended college. I add 'deceased', then hit search.

I find her.

Lauren Gregory — in memory of.

May 2019.

My heart beats faster.

I knew her death had been earlier in the year, but for it to be only two months before Danny died . . .

I click open and read the death notice.

Lauren, taken from us at the tender age of twenty. Family flowers only. Church of St. Paul, Cambridge.

So, her mother must have been from Massachusetts.

There's nothing about the cause of her death but then, it's just a notice.

I have her general location, though.

I find a local newspaper online and purchase access to the archives for a starter rate of ninety-nine cents.

It takes me a while of scrolling through entirely unrelated news articles to discover a small piece on her death.

BODY OF YOUNG WOMAN
FOUND IN SUSPECTED SUICIDE

Police are seeking witnesses after the body of a young woman, who went missing from her Harvard House a week ago, was found. Lauren Gregory, aged twenty at time of death, was discovered washed up on the shores of the Charles River.

No foul play is suspected, but police wish to establish a timeline of her movements prior to her death.

Members of the public can contact . . .

I stare at the computer screen, trying to read between the lines.

Death by suicide?

Is that not cut and dried?

My mind is racing.

Cal said Lauren was attacked. He said she never got justice and that's what Danny was helping with. So it looks as though she might have killed herself – maybe that's what prompted Cal to act and seek Danny's help.

Or did he think that it wasn't suicide; that Lauren might have been killed?

I type in more search words. Lauren Gregory + death + Charles River.

That's when I find a later article. This one is about her funeral and it mentions the follow-through on the earlier appeal made by the police.

The article tells me that, not long after the initial appeal, two witnesses came forward – a cab driver and a man who'd been walking his dog the night Lauren died.

The cab driver had seen Lauren climbing on to a bridge but he'd been on the opposite side of the freeway when he'd spotted her and couldn't stop.

The dog walker had been walking through woods by the river when he saw her jump.

Both had gone to the police at the time, alerting them to what had been witnessed but, in the usual way these things are messed up, the police sent a car out to the bridge, saw nothing, and nobody thought any more of it. Lauren's body travelled along the river and it was only when her mother and brother hadn't heard from her for a few days that she was finally reported missing.

Friends told the police she'd had suicidal inclinations.

Nobody had connected the missing girl with the reported jumper.

So, a definite suicide.

I reread the articles, looking for clues behind the bare facts, in case there was something more to her death or something referring to the attack on her. I can't find anything.

I'm still thinking about it when I stand in front of the mirror, brushing my teeth before bed.

I lean over the sink and spit out the paste.

My head shoots up so fast, I'm shocked at my own reflection.

Lauren jumped and killed herself.

Danny jumped and killed himself.

There's no way that can be coincidence.

Now

The third day of my trial sees a string of witnesses brought forward by Prosecutor Roberts: other neighbours who'd heard shouting in the apartment, the people who saw me driving out of Newport that night, the divers who searched nearby lakes and woods.

Karla handles them all professionally but I feel, in my gut, that this is all adding up to a compelling case against me.

The fact I didn't go to the police first makes it sound like I was running from something.

There was no way I could go into Danny's precinct. The jury don't realise that, yet.

But I did go to the police.

One of them.

I keep a watchful eye on the jury. Several of them, mainly women, keep staring over at me, with countenances already full of judgement, and I haven't even opened my mouth yet.

It's meant to be a jury of my peers but the nature of jury duty means most of these twelve are either retired citizens or young and unemployed. I project on to them what I'd think if I were in their shoes. The older ones are unable to understand a woman who'd murder her husband. The younger ones are unable to understand why somebody like me, who has everything, would blow it all.

When we break that evening, Karla tells me she's still trying to get the next day's witness pulled from giving testimony.

'It's outrageous,' she says. 'Calling him for the prosecution.'

'He's doing what he has to,' I say.

That night, Karla breaks protocol and wraps her arms around me before I'm put in the transfer van and brought back to county. The guard raps on the cell bars at this unorthodox display of humanity. She's the same guard who yesterday accidentally tipped my Jell-O dessert down the front of my clean blouse.

They don't like it in here when you bring their own into disrepute.

Let alone what I did.

The next day, the prosecution calls Ben Mitchell to the stand.

Despite knowing this was coming, despite absolutely everything I have come to expect – or not expect – from this trial, I still panic when I see Ben climb into the witness box.

How many times did he tell me to move on from Danny? To remember him as I thought he was?

How many times did he warn me?

Ben glances at me, only for a second, but a shiver runs down my back.

What is he going to say?

Prosecutor Roberts runs through the preliminaries with Ben quickly – how long he'd known Danny, how long he's known me, and while every other witness statement has dragged, before I know it we're already talking about that night five months ago.

Ben fidgets in his chair, his hands clasped tightly in front of him.

He's tense. Even from here I can see the little sheen of sweat over his brow.

'Detective Mitchell, do you recall what you were doing the night Erin Kennedy arrived at your home – the night she has been accused of murdering her husband?'

'Yes.'

Prosecutor Roberts waits for more but Ben knows how to play this game.

'Would you care to elaborate?'

'I was home alone,' Ben says. 'My wife was staying out of town with our children.'

'But you went and answered the door, even though it was late.'

'It was late but the knock on the door was – insistent.'

Prosecutor Roberts pauses.

'You were already concerned?'

'Yes.'

'What did you see when you opened the door?'

Ben takes a deep breath.

'I saw Erin Kennedy.'

'And how did she appear?'

'She appeared to have been attacked.'

'Attacked?'

'Yes. Her face had sustained bruising.'

'Were there other features about her appearance that stood out?'

Another deep breath.

'She was covered in blood.'

'Her own?'

'It did not appear to be her blood.'

Ben's voice is lower now.

'What did Erin Kennedy say to you?'

'She asked me to go back to her apartment with her.'

'Why did she ask you that?'

'She said something terrible had happened and that she was frightened.'

'What did you say to that?'

'I asked her whose blood was on her.'

'Did she answer that?'

'Yes. She said it was her husband's.'

'Were you surprised by that?'

Ben shakes his head.

'No. I'd learned what the man was capable of.'

I stare straight at Ben.

I want to make eye contact again. He won't look at me.

As Dr Klein said to me once:

So many people let me down.

It's funny. At times like this, I wish so badly I was still talking to Cal.

Ironically, I could also have done with his money. Who knows? With that backing behind me, I might not even be sitting here.

Right now, I feel totally and completely alone.

Then

I want to ask Cal more about Lauren. About her suicide.

But it's apparent Cal doesn't want to talk about Lauren on an ordinary day. I'm going to guess he wouldn't be happy with me pressing him for information on his first Christmas with her gone, either.

All that matters today, anyway, is taking care of myself.

The first thing I do when I wake up is take a Skype call from Tanya.

Ireland is five hours ahead and she's already tipsy, while I'm sitting up in bed, hair tousled and sleepy.

'You don't look like you've even got out of bed today,' Tanya says, distressed. 'Oh, God, tell me you're not spending all Christmas day alone and in bed. I can't cope with the idea of it, Erin!'

'It's 7 a.m.' I say.

Tanya's face goes blank and then she laughs.

'Oh! Sorry. Started drinking at breakfast. But – you are going somewhere today?'

'Tanya, Bud told me you phoned three times yesterday. I'm still going there for dinner.'

'I'm not entirely happy about that,' Tanya says. She's wearing a jumper with red baubles all over it. It's so un-Tanya, it's hilarious. A parental gift, no doubt.

'It's a public bar,' she continues. 'I can't believe they're even open.'

'Thanksgiving is the big one here, Tan. And Bud is only opening for locals, I've told you that. He's told you that. The phone operator can probably tell you that. Where are you, anyway?'

I don't recognise the room she's in. Tanya's apartment is white-walled and minimalist.

Oh.

My mother does up her house every year for Christmas so, of course, the wallpaper is different to last year's.

'She just wants to say hi,' Tanya says.

'You said you weren't going over there until after lunch!' I protest.

'Here they are now.'

Forced family reunions. What fun. At least I have a story to match Cal's when I see him next.

Both my parents appear on the computer screen, staring everywhere but the camera because they can't quite believe technology can work such wonders.

'There she is, John. Look at her.'

My father peers into my picture on his screen. I wave and he sits back.

'There you are,' he says.

'Here I am,' I say.

This is going swimmingly. We've established that I do, in fact, exist inside the computer.

'Happy Christmas,' he says.

'Happy Christmas,' I repeat.

'You, eh, having a good day?'

'It's five past seven in the morning.'

'Grand stuff. I'm going to check the turkey.'

'Great.'

He leaves and I'm alone with my mother.

She doesn't look too good.

'I really thought you'd be over,' she says. 'What with every-thing . . .'

I don't flinch the way I normally do when she turns on the passive-aggressive guilt switch.

Before Niamh was killed, John and Maura Kennedy had fundamentally believed in the goodness of humankind.

When that man took my sister's life, he also took away my parents' trust in other people.

Tanya and I, grown adults, got it in the neck relentlessly. Where are you going, who are you with, what time will you get home, what are you doing? I had it the worst because I was living at home at the time.

It was hard to breathe around Maura's grief, let alone have our own.

'I really thought you'd be over,' I say back. 'What with everything . . .'

She purses her lips.

'You know how your father and I feel about flying.'

'I did ask would they send Danny's body over for a blessing from your local priest but when I found out I'd have to pay for him as extra baggage, it was a no-go.'

'That's not funny, Erin.'

She blinks. Here come the tears. She's wronged me, but I'm the one who's supposed to apologise.

Not today, Maura. Not today.

'I'm sorry,' she says.

I think I've misheard.

'We should have made the effort.'

Now I don't know what to say.

I wipe the tears from my eyes with the corner of the bedspread. It's got reindeer on it. Danny bought it in Walmart and it became our Christmas blanket.

'Please don't cry, sweetheart,' my mother says, so I cry some more. It feels cathartic. I've been carrying a lot these past months. I didn't realise being angry and disappointed with my parents was weighing so heavily until now.

'We'll come over next month,' she says, and she's crying now.

'No, I'll come over next month,' I say.

'We can get flights.'

'I'll get a flight.'

'Well, if you think that's best.'

Too late, I'm bested and she doesn't even realise she's done it.

But at least some of the hatchet has been buried. The tip of the blade.

After another half hour of small-talk nothingness, I'm liberated from the shackles of Skype.

A half hour after that, I'm running along a blissfully deserted beach, fine, salty sea spray on my face, and by the time I hit the shower, I'm actually looking forward to dinner and a few drinks.

First, I sit down with my bags of presents. Cross-legged on

the floor, in one of Danny's T-shirts and fluffy socks, I begin the unwrapping. And suddenly, I regret the decision not to get a tree.

I have an idea. I stand up, find tea lights and fire up a load of them on the coffee table. Then I stick on the TV and find a music channel playing Christmas songs. Finally, I get a bottle of tequila. There you go, the festive season sorted out in five minutes flat.

Tanya has sent over an array of delights from Bath & Body Works. Mam and Dad have put two hundred dollars in a card, with a note telling me to buy myself something nice. They actually stuck two hundred dollars in the post. No faith in humanity but complete trust in the United States Postal Service.

Mike has sent me a postcard from Syria, where he's still waiting to be redeployed. It's a picture of camels and a reminder, from him, that he's there for me no matter what.

I open Gloria's present, knowing what it is before the wrapping is even undone.

It's a framed photograph of Danny and me in her garden in Florida, the palm trees behind us reaching up into a beautiful pink sunset. I'm resting against Danny's chest as we sit on a blanket on the grass, my head turned shyly to the camera. I look happy.

Oh, Gloria.

I know she's hurt that I haven't been down to see her since the funeral.

I'm ashamed of myself for that but Gloria is the sort of person who can see through bullshit and I don't want her knowing what they've said about Danny. I don't want her knowing the evidence that was found. I've told her, on the phone, that it was all a mix-up. In person, she'd know I was lying.

It's almost better that she presumes Danny killed himself because he was depressed.

I put the photo down and move on.

My workmates have stuck to the tried and tested – perfumes and PJs, candles and jewellery, Victoria's Secret scents galore.

I rummage through the pile and find Cal's present. It's wrapped so beautifully, it's almost a shame to open it.

When I do, it takes me by surprise.

Because I work in publishing, nobody who knows me ever buys me books.

They know I can get pretty much every book I want for free.

It's a shame, because the reason I got into this business was because I love books. My favourite part of Christmas when I was younger was opening up new reads, smelling the pages and running my fingers along the smooth spines.

Cal has found me a very old, very precious edition of *The Great Gatsby*.

It's not my favourite book. But real thought went into this gift.

He's placed a card inside: For sharing Falaise with me.

I really should have got him something.

I send him a picture of the book and a message on WhatsApp.

Love it. Hope today isn't too awful. Don't forget McNally's if you can escape.

I get back a series of emojis which indicate he's surrounded by people he wants to murder, and he's probably going to vomit later.

I smile and start to gather up the wrapping paper, putting aside the last few gifts.

One of them catches my eye.

It's wrapped in shimmering gold paper embossed with Christmas trees. There's no name tag or card stuck to it.

For a moment I think it's detached itself from another present that must have had a gift sticker attached.

I hold it in my hands and it feels heavier with every passing second.

I realise what's unsettled me.

This is the paper Danny used to wrap my presents last year.

It's nothing, I tell myself, as I tear it open.

Inside is a box and inside that is a gold chain from which dangle two intertwined hearts.

And underneath, a small card that reads:

You and me forever.

In Danny's handwriting.

I try to process what I'm seeing.

My brain makes giant leaps.

It is a present from last year and somehow it was in this corner, the corner where we placed the tree last year, and it got jumbled up with this year's presents.

Rubbish. If I hadn't opened this last year, Danny would have gone looking for it. We'd have played hunt the parcel.

I don't want to crack up.

I can't have another panic attack.

So, I look at the facts.

Danny is dead.

Danny has sent me a Christmas present.

No, not sent.

It's in my apartment.

My dead husband has deposited a Christmas present in my apartment.

I'm having a panic attack.

It takes twenty missed calls and multiple missed texts before the knocking starts on my apartment door.

'Erin! You in there?'

It's Cal, wearing a three-piece Calvin Klein suit and red scarf, looking like he's stepped off the set of a Christmas movie.

My creepy neighbour Mr Novak is out on the landing, having a nose, and Cal pointedly wishes him a Merry Christmas.

Then he places his phone to his ear.

'I have her. Yes, she's at home. No, I don't think she wants her dinner zapped. Ring her sister, will you, Bud? And Karla.'

He comes in, cautiously, and closes the door.

'If you want me to go, I will,' he says. 'But, first, let me say, thank you from the bottom of my heart for rescuing me from Hawley hell today.'

I blink, slowly, as I try to figure out what he's on about.

'You're welcome,' I say.

'I'm going to suggest water, coffee and some Tylenol,' Cal says.

'I'd prefer more tequila.'

'You sure you're not blue blood? You sound like my mom.'

I sit obediently while he prepares the rescue remedy, then drink and swallow everything I'm told to.

'Just couldn't do it?' he asks. 'The dinner? Nobody blames you. They were just worried, is all. I knew when Bud rang. He couldn't leave the bar, it's hopping. Mine was awful, too. I was going to drive up and visit Lauren's mom as soon as I could get away . . .'

I can barely keep up with his babbling. The box with the necklace is on the table in front of me and it's a struggle to take my eyes off it.

'I was fine,' I say. 'I was about to get dressed and go down to Bud's, once I'd opened all my gifts. Thanks, by the way.'

'You've already said.'

He sits gingerly on the couch beside me.

'What happened?'

'I got a present from Danny.'

Cal frowns.

'There,' I say, pointing at the box.

He picks it up like it's poison, opens it and looks inside.

'It's his handwriting,' I say. 'His wrapping paper. The kind of present he'd give me. And it had no name or stamp on it – it was here, in the apartment.'

Cal stares at the box, his face confused and concerned.

'It's a prank,' he says.

'It's not.'

'It can't be what you think it is. Where was it? Maybe it was meant for you last year but—'

'It's from this year,' I say.

'But . . .'

Cal doesn't state the obvious.

He stares at me, real concern in his eyes, like he's worried I've lost it – but then he looks at the box. Its very presence is testament to the fact I'm not making this shit up.

He starts to pace.

I swallow; say what's been haunting me all afternoon.

'You know – I never saw Danny's body.'

Cal stops, shakes his head, incredulous. He runs a hand through his hair.

'It can't be that,' he says. 'It just can't be.'

'Then what?' I say. 'I can't think of anybody who would play such a sick joke on me, Cal. I've spent the past five months trying to get my head around what happened to Danny and accepting that the one fact I do have is that he's dead. He's gone. But what if . . . ?'

'Does anybody have access to your apartment?' Cal asks.

'Nobody has a key except Bud and I doubt he even knows where it is.'

'Where was this box? Exactly?'

'Over there. With the rest.'

'And how did the rest of the gifts get here? Were they delivered? By mail or by a delivery company?'

He's going so fast I can barely keep up.

'No, I had a few bags leaving work that day, remember? When we all met for Christmas drinks. I put them over there. I emptied them all out on the floor.'

'Could it have been on your desk in work?' he asks. 'Maybe it was sent up from the mail room? It doesn't say Merry Christmas; it might have been an old gift.'

'No,' I say. 'The bags were given to me. And anyway, Danny never sent anything to my office. I worked from home nearly all the time when he was alive. Plus – it's got Christmas trees on the wrapping paper.'

Cal looks me straight in the eye.

'Somebody put it in your bag of gifts,' he says.

Ta-dah. He's solved the mystery. He looks satisfied.

Danny really is dead.

This isn't from him.

For just a moment . . .

It feels like the rug has been pulled out from under me, again.

'Who?' I say, angrily. 'Who would have put that in there? You? Karla? Bud?'

He shakes his head.

'Bud would have told you. I would have told you. And Karla didn't know Danny. Somebody who knew Danny before he died must have had this gift for you. Somebody in your job or something.'

Then I realise. It wasn't anybody at work. They'd have been straight with me.

I met somebody else the night of our informal Christmas party.

I ran into Danny's psychiatrist.

The next time I speak to Dr Klein, it's on her own turf.

The day after Christmas, I visit her at her home address, which Cal secures for me. I don't ask how he manages to track down her private, unlisted address. Even I know money removes a lot of obstacles when it comes to bypassing the usual procedures.

Dr Klein lives in a beachfront property in Quogue, between the Hamptons. I drive along Dune Road, following Cal's instructions, and park up just as I see the tips of the shingle roof come into view.

It's cold today; an icy wind whips in from the ocean and blasts sand on to my face. It's barely mid-morning but already dull; rain clouds threaten and I can feel a smattering of droplets.

I run towards the beach house, taking shelter on the porch. I hope to God the lights are a signal the doctor is at home and that they are not on timer while she's off on a holiday sojourn. I want to get this conversation over with now and am also reluctant to drive home in the storm I know is approaching.

Dr Klein is in and shows no surprise when she opens her door and sees me standing there, staring up at the sky anxiously.

'Erin,' she says. 'Come in.'

No 'How did you get my address?' or 'This is inappropriate'.

She knew I was coming.

If she knows I'm smart enough to figure out the gift was from her, then what's with the games, I wonder?

But I'm biding my time. I step inside and try not to react to how beautiful the house is.

Being a shrink in a nation full of narcissists really pays, it would seem. Everywhere I look, my eyes land on ornate period pieces, a writing desk any of my authors would kill for, bookshelves heaving with expensive hardbacks and classics. White muslin curtains frame the windows and the sills are filled with candles flickering in large glass jars. An L-shaped couch runs around the edges of the living room, dotted with cashmere throws and plush pillows. Beside me, a huge display of white winter roses pervades the open space with a light floral musk. And the Christmas tree is a ceiling-scraping affair, but extraordinarily tasteful in its decoration.

I follow her through to the kitchen. She motions at the breakfast counter and I take a stool. Even though I want to stay angry and confrontational, there's a visitor etiquette part of me that I just can't switch off.

Dr Klein turns to a bubbling coffee pot, but then pivots and opens the refrigerator. She takes out a chilled bottle of white wine and cocks her head in my direction.

'I'm driving,' I say.

'You mind if I do?' she asks.

You take what you need to tell the truth, Dr Klein.

I shrug.

She pours herself a large glass and I accept a glass of sparkling San Pellegrino. I take a sip to wet the inside of my mouth, which has turned completely dry.

'You got the gift,' she says.

I love a woman who eschews small talk.

'I got the gift,' I say. 'And I came here to ask you, why would you play such an awful mind game?'

'He . . . Danny asked me to give it to you.'

Thank God I'm already sitting down.

'When?'

She swallows a gulp of wine.

'When I was treating him. Before he died.'

Every time I start to think the impossible might be true . . . it's like a cold shower of disappointment.

'I don't understand. Why would you do that to me? To let me open a gift from my dead husband on Christmas morning? It's . . . it's heartless.'

She blinks rapidly; the colour rushes up her neck and into her cheeks.

'I thought – I thought there'd be a letter in the box. Explaining everything.'

'There wasn't.'

Now she looks properly remorseful.

'Oh, God, Erin. He made me swear to get it to you but he didn't want you to know he was seeing me.'

'Why did you wait so long? He's been dead for months!'

Dr Klein rubs her temples with her fingers. I could tell her that her headache is nothing compared to the pounding behind my forehead.

'I didn't know where you lived,' she said. 'Danny gave me his work address when he signed up for treatment. I think he was paranoid about correspondence coming to your home. I've been carrying it around in my bag for months, trying to decide if I should mail it to his work, care of you, or if I . . . well, I figured if I waited I might see you again. But you never came. Then I saw you that night before Christmas. I just assumed there'd be something in it to help you understand. You're right: when you came to the office, I should have handed it to you and told you what it was. I wasn't thinking straight.'

'Go back,' I say. 'Isn't there some protocol – some medical thing that means if somebody is going to take their own life, you have to tell somebody? He gave you that gift to give me after he died. How could you sit with him every week and listen to him, knowing he was at risk, and not do something about it?'

I'm trying to keep the hurt and anger out of my voice, but I'm failing.

'It wasn't like that,' Dr Klein protests. 'I didn't think he was at risk of suicide.'

'But he was,' I say, weakly. 'And he killed himself.'

Dr Klein looks inconsolable.

'Danny didn't ever indicate that he might be considering taking his life,' she says, her voice shaking. 'Even when he asked me to hold that gift for you.'

'Why would he give it to you, then?' I say. 'What possible explanation could there have been?'

'He . . . he was worried something might happen to him.'

My heart beats faster.

'Like what?'

'I don't know. But he believed he was in danger. When he gave me the box, all wrapped up, he said: "I think I can fix this, but if I can't, will you make sure she gets it?"' Dr Klein scrunches up her features as she remembers the exact words. 'And then he said: "Just get it to her. But be discreet. I don't want her knowing I came here."'

Time stops.

'But it was wrapped in Christmas paper,' I say.

'Erin, I think he just wrapped it in whatever paper he had to hand.'

I close my eyes and breathe. There's still some of that roll at the bottom of our wardrobe. And it's exactly the kind of thing Danny would do.

'Danny thought he was in danger?' I say. 'From whom?'

'He never said. And thinking back now, I fear it may have been just paranoia.'

Dr Klein hesitates. She drinks more wine.

'Danny was depressed,' she says. 'For many reasons, some that we could put our finger on and others . . . perhaps more relating to a genetic disposition. You know his father suffered from depression? He only discovered that later, after his father died. His brother, too, I think. I'm not entirely sure what the balance was for Danny – I just know that some of the events that occurred in Danny's life wouldn't have had the same resonance if he hadn't had a predisposition to depression. You shouldn't feel bad that you didn't notice it. People who live with this illness are often expert at carrying on like they don't have a care in the world. But – even though he went through bad periods, I did not have Danny marked as a suicide risk. He spoke so convincingly about finding a solution to his problems. When he stopped coming in, I should have pursued it. It's my greatest regret, and that's not a word of a lie.'

'Wait,' I say. I can't keep up. Either my head is spinning or the room is. 'You say he stopped attending your clinic?'

'Yes. A couple of months before he died. I kept the appointments open for him as long as I could. That's my practice because, you never know. And he was still paying for the sessions, just not coming in. It's entirely possible that an event occurred during that time – in fact, something must have, to have triggered what he did – but I swear on my life, Erin, I didn't see it coming. He was frightened, but not of himself. Of others. That's what he told me and I was convinced. At the time.'

Danny wasn't paranoid. I'm sure of it. But who could he have been so afraid of that he thought he needed to leave a gift with Dr Klein for me? And why a gift? Why not, as she says, a letter explaining everything? I've turned the necklace over and over, I've emptied the box of its soft satin cushion – there's no secret message or compartment.

I place my head in my hands. For every step forward, it feels like two back.

'So, he was scared something might happen to him, but then he took his own life,' I mumble. I look up. 'It doesn't make sense. Why didn't he keep talking to you? Why didn't he talk to me?'

She takes a deep breath.

'That's not the way it goes,' she says. 'When somebody has decided to take their own life – I mean, are absolutely determined to do so – they very consciously don't talk to people. Once the decision is made, they don't put themselves at risk of being talked out of it. That's what I mean when I say something triggered Danny and it must have happened after the last time he spoke to me. He sensed something bad was on the horizon.'

'You know, his gun was in a safe in our bedroom,' I say. 'I've never been able to understand why he didn't just go in there and shoot himself; why he went to the window, in front of me. But then I think of what his partner told me – he was there to arrest Danny. And I think maybe Danny hadn't made his final decision, but when he saw Ben's face, he knew it was all over.'

Dr Klein cocks her head.

'That sounds entirely plausible,' she says. 'It's often spontaneous. A person can be having suicidal inclinations but the bomb has to detonate.'

Dr Klein reaches across the counter and places her hand on mine.

'I'm so sorry,' she says, yet another apology. 'For how I handled everything. I haven't stopped thinking about it and I've been chastising myself all Christmas for not approaching you directly with that gift.'

'I don't understand why there wasn't a letter, like you thought.'

'Maybe he couldn't put it into words. Maybe he just wanted you to know what was in his heart.'

I swallow the lump in my throat.

She stares into her wine. When she looks up, she's thought of something.

'This trouble he was in at work,' she asks. 'Was it of his own making?'

I hesitate.

'I . . . I don't know. I was told, by somebody I've come to trust, that he might have been targeted because of a case he was investigating. But, they have evidence that makes it look like Danny was up to something. I've asked some friends to help me get to the bottom of it but it's difficult when it involves cops.'

Dr Klein places her wine glass down on the counter.

'Danny was not perfect,' she says. 'He was a flawed human being and he had done things he regretted. I figured that out, straight away. He wouldn't tell me what those things were, even after all our sessions. But I know he felt guilt and he wanted to atone. I am absolutely positive, however, that he wasn't capable of true badness.'

I meet her eye.

'Can I tell you something, something you have to keep to yourself?'

She considers this, then nods for me to proceed.

'Danny was trying to help a family get to the bottom of a case where a girl had killed herself,' I say. 'She jumped from a bridge, a couple of months before Danny died. Danny jumped from our window. And it must have been shortly after she died that he stopped seeing you. I mean, there has to be something in that, doesn't there?'

Dr Klein frowns.

'It's a pretty fat coincidence,' she says.

'That's what I thought.'

'Why did the girl kill herself?'

'She had been attacked, prior to that, and I'm thinking, maybe she couldn't get over it? Or maybe somebody was threatening her about still looking for justice. But I don't know. After what you've said, I suppose anything could have been going on in her head, so how can I ever find out why she took her own life?'

Dr Klein shakes her head.

'It's not the same in every case,' she says. 'Can you talk to anyone in the girl's family?'

'It's complicated. I only know about her because it was her brother who asked Danny to look into her case. He's dealing with his own grief and he also feels responsible for getting Danny involved. We don't talk about her. I don't know the rest of the family.'

'I see. What about her friends?'

'I don't know how to track them down.'

'What do you know about her life?'

I tell her the few small facts I've managed to garner about Lauren Gregory, including her attendance at Harvard.

'Hmm,' Dr Klein murmurs. 'Harvard is my alma mater. I could try to find one of her old professors and access the class registers?'

'Would you do that for me?'

Dr Klein studies me.

'More than a few of us let Danny down, Erin. I would like to help you any way I can. I have some making up to do, for how I handled that gift alone.'

'I . . . thank you.'

She bows her head.

'Can I ask how long you were treating him?'

There's a moment's silence. Then:

'My sessions with Danny started just after you met.'

Jesus Christ.

I take a deep breath.

'If he was alive now, I think I'd fucking kill him.'

There's nothing else to say.

Now

From the outset, Beverly Ford is a convincing and damaging witness.

Perfectly turned-out in a Diane von Furstenberg wool and cashmere blend wrap sweater and black tailored trousers, Beverly's answers are short, to the point, and very effective.

I know Karla has an effective plan of attack but, for the moment, Beverly's testimony is making me sick with nerves.

Prosecutor Roberts has slipped into efficiency mode also, to match his witness. Two experts impressing the jury with their prowess.

'Enlighten us a little about the crime scene when you arrived,' Roberts says.

Beverly nods, once. There isn't a hair loose in the little French chignon she's knotted at the nape of her neck. This woman leaves nothing to chance.

'When I arrived,' she begins, in a soft Alabama accent, 'the CSI had already performed an inward spiral search.'

'Can you elaborate on what that means, for us laypeople?'

'Of course. The crime scene investigators had started at the perimeter of the room and worked towards the centre. The necessary fingerprinting and evidence photography had been performed.'

'And what was your role in the apartment that night?'

'I am a bloodstain pattern analyst.'

'Which is?'

'My job is to analyse blood at a scene and establish facts around how that blood was drawn.'

'Fascinating.'

Prosecutor Roberts says this like none of us have ever encountered a true crime show on Netflix.

'This is an important part of the forensics examination at the scene, is it not?' he says.

'It is,' Beverly answers. 'Bloodstain patterns can reveal the type of weapon that was used. Let me explain. A high-energy pattern is usually made up of many tiny droplets and that pattern can indicate a gunshot. A cast-off pattern remains when something like, for example, a wine bottle, contacts a blood source and then swings back. Those droplets are often larger and somewhat teardrop shaped.'

'Were you able to analyse the bloodstains in Erin Kennedy's apartment?'

'Yes. There was quite a lot of blood to work with.'

'What did you discern from the blood? Perhaps, Your Honour, at this point we will use the photographic slides for the jury's benefit?'

The judge raises an eyebrow at the prosecutor and the notion that it's the court's decision when those photos will be shown.

The lights are dimmed and the projector screen that's been wheeled in for Beverly Ford's evidence becomes the only illuminated item in the room.

I look away when the first image of my apartment is shown; a blown-up still of the carnage the police found there five months ago.

When I look back, the jury's eyes are, to a man and woman, glued to the screen.

The bloodstains have been ringed where they were found on the floor, coffee table, breakfast counter, walls and ceiling.

Beverly has been given an interactive clicker, which allows her to move through the images and pause as she speaks.

'My analysis of these bloodstains indicated a cast-off pattern. You see here the tear-shaped spatters I referred to?'

Beverly finds an indicative shot and pauses. Everybody at the front of the court, bar Karla and me, nods.

'The cast-off pattern can indicate multiple blows from a blunt object.'

'Why is that?' Prosecutor Roberts asks.

'Usually because the first blow does not cause any blood release. A person has to be hit repeatedly with a blunt object to draw blood.'

'A blunt object like a wine bottle?' Prosecutor Roberts says.

'Yes.'

Prosecutor Roberts takes Beverly's clicker and goes to the last photograph.

There, zoomed in, is a photograph of a smashed wine bottle, its shards still glistening with blood.

'How hard would you have to hit somebody with a full bottle of wine before it smashed?' Prosecutor Roberts asks.

'Objection!' Karla shouts. 'Is the witness an expert on blood-stains or wine bottles?'

'I'll allow it.'

Beverly nods warmly at the judge.

'You would have to hit somebody repeatedly and very hard. In our demonstrations in the laboratory, it takes six to seven blows to crack the glass.'

The tension thickens in the courtroom as that fact hangs in the air.

'One of the things you also examine is trajectory of blood spatter, is it not?' Prosecutor Roberts says, after a few seconds have passed. 'The angle at which blood is drawn.'

'That's correct.'

'How does that help in a crime scene investigation?'

'We look at where the blood spray has landed and we are able to estimate from the trajectory where the victim would have been when the blood first met the air.'

'What were you able to tell from this crime scene?'

'There was a lot of blood around the main living space of the apartment, which indicates that the victim was in motion when he was first struck. However, most noteworthy was the blood we found along the side of the breakfast counter.'

'What did that tell you?'

'That the victim had been struck while he lay on the ground.'

Inside, I'm dying.

I try to catch Karla's eye, but she won't look at me. So, instead, I stare at the images that are still projected on the screen – now showing the side of my breakfast counter.

'Was the volume of blood found at this scene,' Prosecutor Roberts says, 'consistent with a scene where somebody drew blood in self-defence?'

'Well, that depends,' Beverly says. 'If a homeowner shot

somebody in self-defence, I would expect to see a large volume of blood.'

'But there were no gunshots in this apartment?'

'No. There were no traces of a gun fired in the apartment and, as I said, the blood spatter is not compatible with a gunshot.'

'And from the defendant's own statement we know no gun was used, but she has stated she defended herself against her husband. Is the volume of blood compatible with self-defence while not using a gun?'

Beverly inclines her head, measuring her answer.

'The blood found in Erin Kennedy's apartment was of an unusually high volume,' she says. 'I have worked fifty-seven crime scenes this year alone. Fifteen of those have been self-defence in domestic violence and breaking-and-entering scenarios. In one of the latter cases, a man hit the intruder who had entered his home twice with a baseball bat. The two blows were enough to incapacitate the intruder, though of course he was a strong adult male inflicting the blows.'

'How much blood did you find at that scene?'

'Only the blood left by the intruder after he'd broken glass to enter the home and cut his hand.'

'Was the blood found in Erin Kennedy's home more compatible with the scenes you've examined where a murder was committed?'

'Objection!'

Karla's body is humming with rage.

'And, Your Honour, are we done with those images?' Karla says.

The judge raises his hand to indicate the lights should be turned back on.

'Beverly Ford is a bloodstain pattern analyst,' Karla continues. 'She's not a doctor and she's not a pathologist, Your Honour.'

'But she is somebody familiar with the blood deposited at a crime scene,' Prosecutor Roberts interjects.

The judge muses on this.

'I will allow it, Counsellor,' he says. 'You will have your opportunity to question the witness and scrutinise her credentials. Overruled. Answer the question, Ms Ford.'

'Yes,' Beverly Ford says. 'There was enough blood at the scene to convince me, and the detectives, that a murder had taken place. That's why Erin Kennedy was arrested and taken into custody.'

Karla has a bit of a cold today, so her voice sounds a little rough and her face is already slightly red when she stands up to face the cool-as-a-cucumber Beverly Ford.

Downstairs, Karla was mainlining Burt's Bees and Vicks Vapo-Drops. Here, she takes a sip of water before she turns to confront the witness.

'Blood spatter analysis is a contested science, isn't it?' Karla says.

Beverly doesn't blink.

'It has its detractors,' she says. 'Like all crime scene analysis, it can only add to the picture of what has happened. When the police know a witness is lying or withholding evidence, we have to use various scientific methods to establish what actually happened at a crime scene.'

'Isn't it true, though,' Karla says, 'that bloodstain analysis depends on the analyst's interpretation?'

'Not always. Determining between cast-off and high-energy spatter is not ambiguous, it's clear-cut.'

'But if a scene has been contaminated prior to your arrival, you don't know if what you are looking at is the original blood spatter.

Say, for example, two people fight on an already bloodied floor; the scene has been altered, has it not?'

'As I said, we use various methods, an amalgamation of forensic science used by the authorities, to establish what has taken place at a crime scene. We can discern when somebody has moved within a crime scene, or has tried to clean up.'

'And there's the question of bias,' Karla continues, as though Beverly hasn't spoken. 'If you attend a crime scene and you've already been more or less told what has happened there, you are affected by confirmation bias, are you not? Let me give you the definition of that. It's the tendency to search for or interpret information in a way that confirms one's preconceptions or favoured theory and to steer clear of the information that may contradict those preconceptions.'

'I do not bring confirmation bias to my work. My job is to objectively analyse.'

'You told us that when you arrived at the scene, CSI had already done an evidence search.'

'Yes.'

'Were there detectives present?'

'Yes.'

'Was the captain of the ninth precinct present?'

'Yes.'

'Did anybody say anything to you before you entered the apartment?'

There's a battle on Beverly's face. The problem with having an excellent witness who is good and professional is that, darn it, she's good and professional. Beverly is not here to lie, even for the prosecution.

'Yes.'

'What was said?'

'"It looks like she murdered him."'

'Who said that exactly?'

'Captain Sullivan.'

'And you didn't allow that to bias your examination?'

'No.'

'I see. You're a credit to your profession.'

'Thank you.'

Beverly pretends she can't hear the sarcasm.

'You gave evidence two years ago in the case of Reginald Durrell in Texas, did you not?' Karla continues.

'Yes.'

'To clarify for the jury: in that case, Mr Durrell was accused of murdering his wife, correct?'

'Yes.'

'And the prosecution used your evidence to confirm that he had struck Mrs Durrell several times to the head after she fell from the landing banisters above.'

'Yes. He had pushed her over the banisters and while she lay there on the floor of the reception area, he struck her several times on the head. She hadn't died immediately, you see. We found blood patterns on the floor to confirm this.'

Beverly sounds very convincing but she has a tick and I've begun to notice it.

Her little finger is tapping ever so slightly on the bar to her front.

'Mr Durrell was convicted?' Karla asks.

'Yes.'

The jury are sitting up now, wondering where this is going.

Prosecutor Roberts has his eyes fixed straight ahead. He must have prepared Beverly for this. He was hardly hoping we just wouldn't hear about it, once Karla spotted her name in discovery.

Timing, though, is everything.

'But that case is gone to appeal now, am I correct?' Karla says.

'Nearly every case I've seen a conviction in goes to appeal,' Beverly says, her voice light, the hint of a smirk. 'Nobody likes being found guilty and they have a right to contest it as the law allows.'

'Sure,' Karla says. 'But in this instance, one of the cited areas of appeal is your evidence on the blood spatter, correct?'

'I believe there are several areas—'

'Let me read a communication from the defence lawyers in that case, as issued to the national media three weeks ago.'

'Objection!' Prosecutor Roberts calls out. 'Are we twinned with that trial and nobody has told me, Your Honour? What does the defence in that case have to do with this case – unless counsel here is already planning her appeal against a murder conviction?'

'Your Honour!' Karla cries, indignant.

'Hold your horses,' Judge Palmer says. 'I'll allow it. Sit down, for goodness' sake, Mr Roberts. There's no need to get so excited all the time.'

Karla looks smug as she reads from her piece of paper.

'"In the case of the blood spatter forensic evidence presented by the prosecution team's expert, Ms Beverly Ford, it was found by our own analysts, and presented at the time of the original case, that when efforts were made to duplicate the blood pattern found on the walls of the reception area in the Durrells' home, the same pattern could not be established two times in succession. This was clear when we attempted to replicate the prosecution's evidence using a body dummy and a marble floor, as alleged. It was also not consistent with Mr Durrell's evidence that he had tried to move his wife when he found her, in order to save her life, causing contamination of the blood patterns at the scene. Therefore, the expert witness's absolute testimony concerning the blood spray must be called into doubt."'

Beverly Ford looks nonplussed.

'Yes,' she says, 'that evidence was presented at the original trial and Mr Durrell was still found guilty.'

There's a half-smile on Karla's lips.

'Mr Durrell's appeal has, in fact, been successful, as of 18:00 hours yesterday evening. In his ruling, the appeal judge found the blood spatter evidence to be of most concern. His judgement expressed reservations about the fact that the pattern analyst, Ms Ford, had been informed upon her arrival at the scene that the, I quote, *"bastard had murdered her"*, by senior investigating officers.

'He added that he accepted the expert testimony from the defence's forensics team that the victim had tried to move herself after she fell, but in her disoriented state, her head had struck the ground several times during her own efforts.'

'Objection, Your Honour.' Prosecutor Roberts sounds furious but he stays in his seat. 'This is uncalled for – are we assuming the judge and jury in this court cannot make up their own mind without reference to a case in Texas?'

The judge leans forward, his hands joined under his chin.

'Are you still intent on calling your next witness on my call sheet?' he asks.

Prosecutor Roberts baulks.

'Yes,' he says.

'Then, overruled,' the judge says.

The jury watch all this like a tennis match. And now they're dying to know who's up next.

'And therein lies my point,' Karla says. 'You were told what to believe when you entered that apartment and your evidence supports it.'

Karla sits down.

Roberts stands up.

'Redirect, Your Honour. Ms Ford, as my colleague has pointed out, this is a contested science, but, in your long and varied experience, can a blood spatter analyst overestimate the volume of blood at a scene? When you arrived at Erin Kennedy's apartment, there were a number of bloodstains, correct?'

'Yes, that is correct,' Beverly says, trying not to sound as bruised as she must feel. 'You've seen it in the slides. That was the scene I encountered, regardless of what anybody had said or not said to me on my way into that apartment.'

Roberts nods.

It's a strong close, but hopefully not strong enough.

Later, when I stand up to be escorted back downstairs and out to the transport vehicle, Bud leans across the public rail and whispers in my ear.

'I think I've found the car I told you about,' he says. 'The one outside your apartment that night.'

The guard pulls my arm and I don't have the chance to respond but as I'm led off I see the expression on Bud's face.

He's looking at me, and he's worried.

Then

My father had always impressed upon us girls the necessity of attending a good college.

His advice had little to do with education and everything to do with the networking opportunities available if you attended university.

Dad had risen high in public service and one reason for his continued promotions stemmed from the fact that he was seen as a well-connected man, a good team player, one of them. In every society, there's an elite, and more often than not it's not what you know, but who you know.

Harvard is no different to every other university in the world. Once you've attended, you are part of a club and that club's tendrils stretch far.

Dr Klein secures a name for me – Lauren's old proctor – and the day before New Year's Eve, I'm sipping hot chocolate beside the skating rink in Central Park and looking out for a blonde-haired woman wearing a pink woolly hat and white puffer jacket.

Harvard is a decidedly elite club but just because you're a member doesn't automatically mean you're set for life.

Dr Ally Summers, originally of Providence, Rhode Island, holds a PhD in English literature. She's a couple of years younger than I am, but more qualified.

Ally now works on a make-up counter at Sephora and has consented to meet me for a quick fifteen minutes on her lunch break.

And while the chips might not always fall in a graduate's favour, even I can't square that circle.

She's insisted on the location and it hasn't escaped my attention that it's outdoors, very public and very crowded. The ice rink is filled with locals and their kids, and on top of the regulars, New Year's Eve tourists have flocked into the park to enjoy the first light snowfall of the winter season.

A horse-drawn carriage passes by; the two couples inside are huddled under heavy red blankets and chat animatedly in my hometown accent. I smile. I'd done all that when I'd arrived – spending much needed dollars in a rush to get through what I thought were the absolute bucket-list activities in New York City, not realising I'd end up being on this side of the pond for years to come.

After the carriage passes I spot Ally, in the outfit she'd described via text this morning.

I, too, am dressed as promised, in a black wool coat and light blue scarf.

She approaches; even from twenty feet away I can see how nervous she looks. Another carriage cuts in front of her path, the horse whinnying, and she pulls up – a look of absolute terror on her face. When the carriage is gone, I meet her in the middle. I can tell her heart is still pounding.

'Will we walk?' I ask, holding out the second hot chocolate I purchased.

She nods and takes the cup, though she doesn't drink from it. She looks like she weighs seven stone and I really think she could do with the calories but, hey, who'd have thought I'd be having concerns about somebody else's body weight? I still haven't regained the weight I lost after Danny's death. It's been a distressingly positive side effect.

'Thank you for agreeing to meet me,' I say.

'I can't stay long.'

'I know. I work near a Sephora. I don't think you're in that one?'

I give her the avenue and street and she shakes her head, but gives me no more.

So much for girl talk.

'Look, I'll get right to it,' I say. 'You knew Lauren Gregory.'

'Yes,' she says, blinking rapidly.

'I'm sorry for your loss,' I add.

Ally shrugs.

'Were there . . . were there any signs she was going to kill herself?'

'If there were, I'd have done something,' Ally answers, so sharp it sounds defensive. She bites her lip then, colour flushing in her cheeks. 'I guess I wasn't surprised by it. I'd been her freshman year proctor and – well, I could see she needed help. I did try to help her. But . . . Lauren had her demons. I hadn't seen her for a couple of years before she died. Not properly. I guess things got worse.'

Ally looks away from me.

There's something not right about her voice – I think the problem is she's not a natural liar and right now, she's not telling me the whole truth.

Two men skim past on skateboards; their hot breath forms clouds in the frosted air, the wheels crunch over iced leaves. I barely notice them but Ally flinches as they fly by.

'Was she depressed?' I ask.

Ally stops walking and looks at me.

'Who are you?' she asks. 'Why are you asking about Lauren? All my old professor told me was that you were a friend of the family and you wanted some information on her.'

'That's true,' I say, and thank the Lord for the power of old professors to still issue diktats.

'Why do you want information?' Ally asks. 'If you're a friend of the family, why don't you already know all this?'

'I'm a recent friend of the family,' I say. 'And I've been asked to look into Lauren's death.'

By one remove of my dead husband.

I don't add that.

Ally shrugs again. She takes out her smartphone and checks the time. We've walked a little bit away from the rink but we're not too far from the gate at Ninth Avenue. We circle and start to head back in that direction.

'Why was Lauren depressed?' I ask.

Ally hesitates.

'Look,' she says. 'This doesn't make sense to me, that you wouldn't know all this.'

'I know some of it,' I say. 'But I'm deliberately coming at it fresh so I'm not influenced by any preconceptions.'

I'm starting to think I'm wasted in editing.

'And her family asked you to look into this?' Ally says.

'Yes.'

We stop, Ally's decision.

'I didn't know she told her family what had happened,' Ally says. 'She stopped talking to me. She . . . she blamed me for making her . . . try to confront him.'

'Ally—'

'And she couldn't get over it. I should have listened to her at the time. I'm going to give you the advice she gave me. Drop this. It's over. She's dead. It can only cause trouble looking into all this again.'

'Cause trouble how?'

I'm completely lost.

Ally shakes her head.

'And tell her family to let it go,' she says. 'They don't know what they're poking at. They shouldn't be dragging you into this. It's dangerous.'

As if to make her point, her eyes flicker left and right again, like she thinks we're being followed.

And there's that word – dangerous.

There's a recurring theme here.

'She – she sent me an email before she died,' Ally whispers, so low I have to strain to hear her.

'What did she say?'

'She said they were still watching her. That she'd never be free of them. I didn't reply. I thought she was going crazy. She'd made it clear the last time I saw her that she didn't see me as a friend. When she emailed . . . I should have replied. I used her lashing out at me as an excuse. I was a coward.'

Ally's eyes fill with tears.

'Who are they?' I practically shout, I'm so frustrated.

Ally glances around, panicking.

'They threatened me, too, you know. Anonymously.'

'I don't understand. Are you telling me somebody made Lauren kill herself? Who are these people?'

Ally shakes her head.

'I . . . it's better you don't know. I lost a lot, too, you know. You think I want to be where I am in my life right now? I was going to lecture in Harvard. I was going to get married. Now, I just have guilt. So much fucking guilt. I didn't ask for any of this. Everybody who touches this gets hurt.'

'When was she attacked? How long was it before she died?'

'What? Aren't you listening to me?'

'Please?'

She sighs.

'It was two and a half years. She was raped in December 2016. I'll never forget it.'

'Why didn't you go to the police? After – when you were threatened.'

Ally laughs, a harsh, humourless sound.

'The police? You think they're on our side? God, I was you, once.'

I open my mouth but Ally grabs my arm.

'Please,' Ally says. 'Stop asking questions. Don't contact me again.'

'Ally—' I say, but she's already walking away.

I go over everything Ally Summers told me.

It's not much.

But it wasn't her words that replay in my head. It's the way she looked.

I've never seen anybody look more scared.

And I feel a very strange bond with her, even though we've never met before today.

The next day, I meet up with David. I'm well overdue a catch-up with him. For work but also to thank him for his support; for trying to find out stuff about Danny; and, most of all, for Karla.

But now I want more.

David has always been a pleasure to work with and his first thriller sent him straight to the top of *The New York Times* bestsellers. Sadly, David has not yet managed to deliver a follow-up masterpiece but he still insists on expensive lunch dates any time I even hint at our meeting being work-related. And this is why I'm now sitting with David in the Champagne Bar in the Plaza on Central Park, drinking French 75s and eating $140 strips of Wagyu beef.

We discuss his overdue manuscript for a few minutes to justify the expense account.

'You'll get there,' I tell him, when he admits he's still struggling. 'The plot is excellent, David. It's the structure that's bogging you down. Cut down the number of characters. It's paralysing your progress, juggling all those people.'

He sits back, smiles at me in his winning way.

'You are brilliant,' he says.

I make a sound somewhere between denial and dismissiveness.

Quid pro quo.

David gives me an update on his Danny investigation.

'Whoever put money in that account the cops froze, they knew how to do it without being traced,' David says. 'How is Karla getting on with this?'

'Not great. You know she's avoided getting entangled with cops since she left Manhattan so she has no contacts and even if she wanted any – Long Island is a closed shop.'

'Hmm. Well, unlike Karla, I'm popular enough with cops. I know more of them about these parts, obviously, but I can ask around, see if I can find anybody with connections on the Island.' A pause. 'You are doing okay, aren't you?'

I sigh, deeply.

Of course I'm not.

'Let me give you some scandal,' David says. 'Cheer you up.'

This is why I love this guy.

David, in his past life, wasn't just any old investigative journalist. He worked for *The Washington Post*, and when he moved to New York he continued to ensure he knew everything about everyone, even if he allegedly wasn't committing it to print.

I still strongly suspect the political protagonists he created in his debut thriller weren't entirely products of his exceptional imagination, but even the prospect of a large libel payout wasn't sufficient to lure the real-life protagonists into the spotlight.

'Seriously, David,' I say, when he's finished filling me in on the latest affair involving a top gangster and a whiter-than-white mayoral candidate, 'do you let your kids believe in Santa Claus or have you told them Christmas is a CIA conspiracy to support the global expansion of Disney and Mattel?'

He chuckles and we sip our cocktails.

'Enough about my sordid friends,' David says. 'There's something else on your mind, Erin Kennedy.'

He raises his hand and crooks two fingers at the nearest waiter, who reads the signal like an army aide receiving a silent order from a general.

Two more French 75s appear, stat, before I've even finished the first one.

'Talk to me,' he says.

'Do you ever miss it?' I ask. 'Being a journalist?'

David shrugs and looks around us, proving my earlier point. What could replace all of this?

But then his face grows serious.

'The big difference between journalism and this game was that nobody extended my deadline on the paper,' he said. 'I filed, whether I wanted to or not. You guys are too soft.'

'Give me your latest draft.'

'Not a hope.'

We clink glasses.

'I miss the rush of it,' he says. 'It's addictive. The thrill. When I started, at least. We all wanted to be Woodward and Bernstein.'

'You broke some big stories,' I say.

'No Pulitzers,' he says. 'It pisses me off that a group of random people I didn't know couldn't find it in their hearts to tell me I was the absolute best at what I did.'

I turn my head left and right, spot a couple of bankers at the table beside us. They're very spottable.

'Hey,' I say. 'This is David Fox. He wrote Eagle Down.'

'I know,' Banker One says. 'I loved your book.'

'There you go,' I say.

David laughs and goes to shake the man's hand.

'When's your next one out?' Banker Two asks. 'Hasn't it been a while?'

David grimaces.

'You gotta give your public what they want,' I say, when we return to our cocktails.

'Art cannot be ordered to schedule.'

I roll my eyes, theatrically. Then I get serious.

'Would you look into something else for me?' I ask. 'I mean, other than the cops over in Newport?'

'Given I've covered myself in glory trying to help you already?'

'If you can't go at them, you go around them,' I say. 'This might sound entirely separate, but I can assure you it's connected.'

'Hit me.'

'Something happened to this girl up in Harvard,' I say. 'She was attacked, December 2016, and two and a half years later she committed suicide. I wonder if it's possible to find out the details of what happened to her in 2016 and subsequently.'

'What's her name?'

'Lauren Gregory.'

'Okay. Leave it with me.'

'Don't you need more?'

'Erin, if I needed you to tell me more, I wouldn't have been a very good journalist.'

'Well, you never won a Pulitzer.'

A beat later, David orders the most expensive cocktail on the menu.

Now

I lie on the thin mattress and stare up at the fluorescent light on the ceiling overhead.

One of the worst things about being incarcerated, I quickly learned, was being stripped of the freedom to do the simplest things.

Like turn off a light when you want to sleep.

Or make everything quiet.

County jail is never quiet.

After months of this, I've become accustomed to the sensory stimulation and have learned to sleep through it, albeit restlessly.

But tonight, thoughts fling themselves back and forth in my brain like ping-pong balls.

It amazes me now, thinking back over the events in the months following Danny's death, how quick I was to believe everything I was told by the police.

What went in their favour was that Danny wasn't perfect to begin with and I knew that.

I'd seen little things. Like him telling me not to worry about speeding tickets, he'd sort it with a cop he knew. Like him laughing with Bud about his laissez-faire attitude to the licensing laws. Like him proposing to me when we were nowhere near the marriage stakes.

You get to stay. I get to keep sleeping with you. It's win-win.

Be serious, Danny. Technically, we're breaking the law. What if, six months down the line, you hate my guts and tell immigration it was a false marriage?

What if, six months down the line, I realise I can't live without you and we wind up spending the rest of our lives together?

What went in their favour was how he died.

What ultimately went in their favour was that I never saw my husband's body. It was never really over for me.

Prosecutor Roberts is thrilled with his last witness.

He's positively humming with excitement.

Professor Gene Whitman is one of the State's – no, the country's – leading expert witnesses, renowned for his persuasive ability to help secure a conviction when the prosecution case is, let's say, missing a vital piece of evidence.

Karla almost cracked a mug in her hand when she learned Whitman was taking the stand.

'Has this guy got superpowers?' I asked.

'In a manner of speaking,' she said. 'Judges love him. Juries love him. He has been cited in the successful convictions of I don't know how many defendants. What I do know is he has the Midas touch for prosecutors and he's so good he can charge a zillion dollars a consultation.'

'But doesn't that mean they're desperate, if they're shelling out this much money to get me convicted on the say-so of an expert?' I asked.

'Honey, *we* are desperate. They're just playing the game.'

When Whitman takes the stand, a hush goes around the court, the sort that comes when you know you're in the presence of a real celebrity.

Gene Whitman – hold on to your hat – has been on network talk shows.

Prosecutor Roberts does the lawyerly equivalent of a happy dance as he lists the professor's numerous qualifications. Professor Whitman is a guest lecturer at Yale – of course he is – but in true snobbish north-east style, what really impresses the masses is the fact that he is an esteemed fellow of Oxford University, England.

The professor is too much of a professional to react to the prosecutor's heaping of praise and credentials. He sits calmly, chin resting on steepled hands, eyes slightly closed behind large, horn-rimmed glasses. His humble receipt of the many compliments only lends itself to the notion we are in the presence of a true gentleman.

When the prosecutor finishes, he moves on to the reason for Professor Whitman gracing us with his presence.

'You specialise, as I have pointed out, in homicide cases where there is the absence of a body,' Prosecutor Roberts says.

'I do,' Whitman answers.

'There may be members of the jury, even members of the public, who would struggle to convict a defendant when a body is absent from a crime scene,' Prosecutor Roberts continues.

'This is correct,' Whitman agrees. 'But not always the case.'

'I see. Can you tell us why this seemingly massive missing piece is not actually an impediment to deciding a person's guilt or innocence?'

'Indeed.'

Whitman considers for a moment.

He's working hard for every one of his zillion bucks.

'Some might argue that the absence of a body is the *least* concerning piece of evidence about a crime scene,' he says.

Prosecutor Roberts frowns.

'Really? How so?'

'Well, any successful crime scene *should* be missing the body. When a body is left at a crime scene, it is a much harder ask for a perpetrator to dispose of any and all incriminating evidence. A corpse can, shall we say, *speak* to a good investigator, no matter how well the killer tries to rid it of evidence. Even if the dead body is soaked in bleach – the detective can ascertain the type of bleach, where the bleach was sourced, when the bleach was applied. If a body is burned, the detective can find the accelerant used, where it was bought, what injuries the body sustained before it was immolated. To truly dispose of incriminating evidence, a killer will dispose of the body.'

Prosecutor Roberts nods wisely, like he and we are already aware of this and in agreement.

'I see,' he says. 'But an intelligent detective – indeed an intelligent jury – will often see beyond this tactic, correct?'

'Of course. And they have done. There are tonnes of cases worldwide, and right here in the United States. Only a few years ago, in New York, Marc Simpson was convicted of the murder of wealthy widower Ira Goldstein. Goldstein's body was never found and Simpson was found to have robbed him of hundreds of thousands of dollars while he was both alive and dead.'

'I remember,' Prosecutor Roberts says. 'But didn't Marc Simpson, like Maud Parker, admit during the trial to disposing of Goldstein's body?'

'Yes,' Whitman nods, sagely. 'That did help matters. Perhaps a better case to cite is the murder of Jessie Smythe by her husband. Several of her teeth and a bone fragment were found in the ashes of a bonfire in his garden but the rest of her mortal remains were never discovered. Her husband received the death sentence.'

'That is a relevant example,' Prosecutor Roberts agrees. 'We are all aware, following the testimonies of our forensics experts, that a substantial amount of blood was found in Erin Kennedy's apartment on the night in question – far more blood than is consistent with her version of events, in which she claims she only drew blood in self-defence.'

'Objection!' Karla cries. 'That fact was disputed in cross-examination and our own forensics expert will be stating that he did not find the volume of blood at the scene to be inconsistent with the continuance of life.'

'Sustained,' Judge Palmer says.

It goes on like this. At one point, Karla reaches over and squeezes my hand.

I know her cross-examination will be good.

She'll do all she can to put a dent in Whitman's expertise.

But it won't be good enough.

When it comes to the absence of a body, I, for one, know that people believe what they're told.

Then

My short, guilt-inspired trip home in January 2020 goes pretty much as I expect it to.

My parents fuss over me in the usual restrained way.

My mother makes afternoon tea and takes out the nice china, and my father invites me for a walk in the Strawberry Beds beside Dublin's main river, the Liffey. It's their way of falling on their swords and apologising for failing me in my hour of need.

Friday night is spent at home, watching movies while eating sushi takeout. On Saturday afternoon, Tanya and I stroll down Grafton Street in Dublin city centre, window-shopping the January sales in Brown Thomas before stopping into a heaving Bruxelles pub for steaming bowls of Irish stew.

Mildly inebriated, she mocks my 'American' accent and calls me a traitor to my nation.

'I don't have an American accent,' I protest.

'Say it again, this time without the twang,' Tanya says.

She pulls at the sleeve of a complete stranger standing beside us, who also happens to look like Michael Fassbender.

'Do you want to meet my American sister?' she says.

'Fuck off,' I say.

Tanya asks about Cal.

I don't tell her I haven't spent that much time with Cal lately because I've been running a covert investigation into the covert investigation my husband was running on his sister.

Instead, I tell her that he's been down in the dumps lately. I know this from a brief chat we had around New Year's, when he told me a girl he'd been dating had dropped him for somebody with more money. When he told me, I had to swallow back every joke because he seemed genuinely astonished and distressed that this gold-digger had gone to dig gold elsewhere.

'Poor guy,' she says.

'He'll get over it,' I say. 'He's a good-looking man.'

'But he was Danny's friend?' Tanya asks.

I hear, immediately, the suspicion in her voice.

I hesitate.

'You're entitled to see people, you know,' Tanya says. 'It's not like you and Danny were together for decades. But – it's just . . . well, you and Cal did meet in odd circumstances. It might be better to make a clean break.'

'I'm not coming home if that's what you're—'

'That's not what I said.'

'Well, I'm not interested in Cal and he's not interested in me,' I say. 'Men and women can be just friends, you know.'

Tanya says nothing.

Before I leave for home, Tanya and I visit somewhere we can only go by ourselves.

The park where Niamh was attacked.

She'd been coming home from art college.

It had been raining heavily and continued to do so all the next day, which caused havoc with forensics.

Niamh had walked through the park for a shortcut. She did it all the time, especially when the weather was bad and she was in a rush. The fields with the main path through were in the open – they were used for football during the day and in full view of a number of houses. Had it not been raining so hard, somebody might have seen something just by looking out their window.

He'd been waiting there for somebody to come through, hanging around by a wall on the way in, just out of sight of anybody walking fast, head down, in a hurry.

Any woman, he'd told the police. It had been a completely random attack.

The devil was talking to him, he later told the court; his legal team was trying for a psychiatric defence.

As the case proceeded it quickly became apparent that he'd had a couple of these unique psychotic episodes before. Despite what his adoring family, including his wife, had said in his character references, he'd raped two ex-girlfriends, both of whom had been too scared to go to the police until Niamh's court case was well underway.

He'd decided, the day he saw Niamh, to take it one step further.

From what the detectives had gathered, he'd grabbed my sister from behind and pulled her into the bushes. She had resisted with every fibre of her being.

But Niamh was tiny and the man who took her life was almost twice her weight.

He'd given her a horrible death.

I only told Danny Niamh's story once, a couple of months after we got together. I didn't need to tell it again. He understood it, every bit. His face took on this devastated blank look as I factually stated the details and eventually he just put his arms around me and wept.

Niamh was only nineteen. She'd never see her twenties, never finish college, never get married or be bridesmaid to one of us, or have children and nieces and nephews.

He'd taken her and he'd left us, her family, scarred for the rest of our lives.

We sit on the wall on the far side of the field, the side Niamh never made it to. We started doing this a few weeks after she died, just coming here and sitting together, thinking – if there's a heaven she should know that we're here, waiting for her to cross that field, and we'll always be here. We'll never stop wishing for her homecoming. It was here that I told Tanya I was going to the States. She'd assumed I meant for a year. I hoped it was forever, but I didn't say that at the time. My mam knew, though. She said, you'll never come back. I said, this isn't *Brooklyn*, Mam. I'm not going on a boat.

My parents, though, were of the generation of people who left and never came back and it's true – before I met Danny, when my visa situation started to become more awkward, I was worried I wouldn't be able to travel back and forth.

Then he offered to marry me.

I sit beside Tanya, both of us kicking our legs against the wall, sharing a cigarette even though neither of us smoke, because that's what we once did – the three of us, in this field, when we were young and innocent and thought the worst thing that could ever happen would be to get caught smoking.

'When Danny died,' I say, 'I think what made me the angriest is that he chose it, when Niamh had no choice. It seemed like such a selfish act, especially because he knew what I'd been through. But, now, I don't know. I think maybe he didn't have a choice.'

I sigh and I feel something unclench in me as I do.

'I think you're right,' Tanya says. 'I don't think suicide is ever a choice. It's a last resort, isn't it?'

I squeeze her hand.

'I need you to know I would never do that,' I say. 'I know you worry about me being over there and not somewhere you can keep an eye on me, but I'm doing okay. I promise. And even if I wasn't, I wouldn't do that.'

'Good,' Tanya says. 'Because if you did, I'd fucking kill you.'

I smile thinly.

My phone trills in my pocket and I fish it out.

I don't recognise the number for a moment, then I realise it's upstate New York and it's the international prefix that's throwing me off.

'Gimme a sec,' I say.

I jump off the wall and walk a few feet away, into the field, near the goalposts.

'Hello?' I say.

'Erin, I swung by your apartment but you're not in.'

It's David Fox.

'I'm in Dublin,' I say.

'Ah.'

Why was David at my apartment? It's so unlike him to not demand a five-star meeting venue.

'I found out about your girl, Lauren Gregory,' he says.

I freeze. I glance back at Tanya, who's staring into the distance, then turn away again.

Somebody has tied a ribbon to one of the goalposts and I start to play with it nervously. It reminds me of the ribbons on the bouquets that were left here after Niamh died. The flowers were pretty at the start, then they began to rot and eventually the council had to clear them away.

'Are you okay to talk?' David asks.

'Yes,' I say. 'Tell me what you found out.'

David gives me a brief run-down on the people he managed to talk to and, as he speaks, I realise David is wasted as an author. He should be back in the field, chasing his Pulitzer.

'Anyhow,' he says, when he's laid the groundwork for his reveal, 'it sounds very much like Lauren suffered a pretty big miscarriage of justice. And it might have led to her subsequent suicide.'

This is something I'd already suspected. I wait for David to fill in the dots but he seems a little hesitant.

'Can I ask how this girl's case relates?' he says.

'I, um, I'll tell you when I see you,' I say.

There's a pause on the other end of the line.

'Okay, well, here's what I discovered,' David says. 'Lauren reported a rape in December 2016. Apparently, it happened on a night out in Manhattan and a friend accompanied her to a police station in the city. A file was opened. For a time.'

My heart is beating like a racehorse's. I clutch at the goalpost, to steady myself as I taste bile in the back of my throat.

'Whatever happened then is where it gets muddy. My source is police and posted in that station so his knowledge is good. He says the file was closed because she refused to name her attacker and then dropped the complaint. Allegedly.'

'Allegedly?'

David sighs.

'Everything was hushed up, Erin, very quickly. It's not unusual for a woman to report a rape and then withdraw when she realises what's ahead of her. But it is unusual for a file to be opened and closed the same day. That has all my antennae wiggling.'

I swallow and close my eyes, so I can't see the bushes at the other side of the field, the ones my sister had been raped in.

'What do you think happened?' I ask.

Silence.

I panic for a minute that the connection has gone.

Then David speaks again.

'It's like somebody leaned on her,' David says.

'Can your source find out anything more?'

'Honestly? Yes. Will he? No. He's not taking my calls. That's worrying.'

I wait for David to tell me what's really bugging him but I'm already there in my head.

'I've seen it before,' he says. 'Lauren might have been attacked by somebody with a lot of power. She might have been attacked by a cop.'

The pain behind my eyes is blinding.

Raped by a cop.

The question is:

Which cop?

An awful, hideous thought creeps into my head.

The man who killed my sister.

Specifically, what his wife said in her character witness statement when she took the stand.

He's such a good man.

He's never so much as raised a hand.

He's not capable of doing something like that.

She believed everything she was saying. At least, that's what it sounded like.

Cal picks me up at JFK.

He's wearing a baseball cap and Adidas sweater, an incognito millionaire.

I'm not expecting him and I can't rearrange my face fast enough when I see him in the arrivals hall.

'I know your family is far nicer than mine,' he says. 'But I reckoned, it's your first trip home since Danny and after that long flight, you might like a ride home.'

The consideration behind this thoughtful gesture almost makes me weep.

'That's really kind of you,' I say.

He shrugs.

'I'm sure Bud or Karla would have come too,' he says, and he almost seems shy.

But neither Bud nor Karla offered. If I'd called, they'd have been there in a shot. But it's not the same as somebody knowing you might like to be collected. It's not the same as somebody thinking about you, even when you're not thinking about them.

I feign tiredness as we drive along the freeway and Cal doesn't push; instead he talks about a ski trip he took in Aspen while I was away and how he'd almost broken his leg on the slopes because his competitive streak far exceeds his actual skiing ability.

'It's like my father keeps reminding me,' Cal says, 'I have no concept of my own limitations. 'Course, it's difficult to take life advice on limitations from a man who has several women on the go at any one time.'

I grunt in response.

His chatter gets less enthusiastic as we drive. He senses I've something on my mind but it's not until we pull on to the road for Newport that he raises it.

'Is everything okay?' he asks.

'Cal,' I blurt out. 'I know what happened to Lauren.'

We're driving up the coast road slowly because the snow is heavy on the ground, and even though the car is four-wheel drive, Cal's taking it easy.

He pulls on to the hard shoulder, indicating and then parking up, blinkers on.

He stares out the windscreen, red spots on both his cheeks, which have otherwise turned pale.

'What do you know?' he asks, his fingers gripped tight on the steering wheel.

'I've been trying not to talk to you about it because I know you want to let it go,' I say. 'And I wasn't lying. Danny never told me anything about her case. I think I know why, now.'

'Then how do you know?'

'I found out. Myself.'

Cal's breathing has become uneven; his lower jaw twitches.

He's angry at me. Lauren's brother is properly angry at me and I feel instantly remorseful.

'Cal, I'm sorry, I shouldn't have just come out with it. I know how upsetting this is for you. With Niamh, we got justice. But for it to have happened to your family and to end up the way it did . . .'

I place my hand on his arm, gently, but just to let him know I get it.

He looks at it and then at me, and his breathing slows to a more regular pace.

'I'm just shocked,' he says. 'I'd no idea you were . . . I don't want you exposed to anything dangerous, Erin, I told you that. I can't have somebody on my conscience again. I just can't.'

'I know but I'm still trying to get to the bottom of what happened with Danny. I realised I couldn't do that without finding out what he was investigating about Lauren.'

He sets his mouth in a thin line.

'I know she was raped,' I say, softly. 'And that she tried to report it. It's so similar to what happened to Niamh – why didn't you want to tell me the details? We could have talked this through.'

Cal flinches.

'When you told me what happened to your sister, I realised I could never talk to you about Lauren. I don't want us to form some goddamned victims group. I can barely talk about this with people it hasn't happened to. I'd no idea, I swear. I'd no idea when I started dealing with Danny that you'd been through the same thing.'

I feel tears bubble in the corners of my eyes. I press them hard with my fingers.

'Cal, I think I know why Lauren's case fell apart.'

He stares at me, waiting.

'I think she was attacked by a cop,' I say. 'Is that what you think, too?'

Cal gazes at me for another few seconds, then he nods, once. He turns away then, blinking rapidly.

I suck in a deep breath and try to stop my hands from shaking by clasping them together.

'Cal – why did you go to Danny with this? Why him?'

Cal shakes his head and sets his lips in a thin line.

He doesn't want to tell me.

'Please,' I plead. 'I'm panicking here.'

'What? Why?'

I clasp my breast.

'I . . . Was Danny involved in what happened to Lauren? His psychiatrist said she started seeing him not long after he and I met. Lauren's attack was just nine months before he went to Dr Klein. Did he . . . was it . . . ?'

I trail off. Since David Fox told me what he'd discovered, I haven't been able to stop thinking about why Danny went to Leslie Klein.

'Jesus, Erin. It wasn't Danny who attacked her. Is that what you think? You think I'd go to him . . .'

'I don't know what to think!'

'I didn't want to tell you this,' Cal says, his voice so low and serious, I'm terrified. 'You've been through enough.'

'There's nothing you can tell me that's worse than what I'm imagining.'

Cal nods, curtly.

'Danny was helping me because he was the cop that Lauren reported the rape to. He was the first detective on her case. Lauren's proctor was his girlfriend.'

The colour drains from my face.

Ally? Does he mean Ally?

Cal pauses. He struggles to get the next sentences out.

'Lauren didn't want to go to the police but her proctor convinced her she knew somebody who could be trusted. She brought her to Danny. And . . . and Danny was part of the cover-up.'

I shake my head.

No. No, it can't be.

'Erin, he wanted to make things right. When Lauren died, I didn't go to Danny. Danny came to me. He couldn't live with the guilt of her suicide. He wanted to reveal what he knew. He was going against his own, Erin. That's why they were out to get him.'

'Who?' I choke out. 'Who was he protecting? When Lauren came in first, who did she accuse?'

'Erin, cops watch out for each other.'

David was right.

She'd accused a cop.

Cal can't look at me.

The nauseous feeling that's been sitting in my stomach ever since I took the call from David bursts the dam.

I throw open the car door and step out into the snow. The vomit leaves an orange-coloured patch on the gleaming white ground.

Cal gets out of the driver's side – I can hear the warning beeps for the doors being opened while the lights are still on. He has his hand on my back, then he lifts my hair from my face as the rest of my stomach contents come up.

Eventually, I'm just dry-heaving. He turns me around to face him and I bury my wet face in his jacket.

'It's not your fault,' he says. 'None of this has anything to do with you.'

He's right.

This is on Danny.

Ally Summers has changed her number.

And while I'm trying to track her down, Gloria is trying to get hold of me.

She's started to take my self-imposed distance personally.

To make her point, she's brought in the big guns.

The connection from Syria, where he's still stationed, is patchy, but I don't need a clear line to get the general gist from Mike.

He's not happy with me.

'You know Christmas was hard on Mom,' he says. 'Danny might have died but you were part of the family, too. She's on her own over there.'

'Mike—'

'Nobody is expecting you to become her crutch. Hell, no. You're gonna move on with your life. You're young, Erin. Sure, you'll meet somebody else. And maybe Mom will meet him, too, and she'll be happy for you. But this was the first Christmas, you know.'

'It's not that simple.'

'Ain't nothing simple about someone you love dying, Erin. But we still have to get up every morning.'

'Mike, I learned something about Danny.'

'Yeah. I know. He wasn't pure as the driven snow. He got up to some shit in work.'

I swallow.

'Who was Ally Summers?' I say.

A pause.

'How do you . . . ?'

'It doesn't matter.'

Mike sighs.

'She was his girlfriend.'

'Before he met me.'

'Yeah.'

'That was his serious relationship.'

'They were together a while.'

I take a deep breath.

'Did he tell you why they broke up?'

'He just said they grew apart. What does this—?'

'Mike, this is important. Did you believe him? When he said they just grew apart?'

'I . . .' Mike hesitates. 'Look, what has this got to do with anything?'

'He never told me about her, Mike.'

'He was cut up about it at the time, Erin. But then, that following summer, he met you and we could all see he was head over heels for you.'

'From the start?'

'What do you mean, from the start?'

'I – I told him about Niamh a couple of months after we met. I think it affected him. I think it's why he married me. Because he felt he had to do something.'

'What is this?' Mike asks. 'Danny married you because he was in love with you. Not because your sister was dead. This is crazy talk, Erin.'

'And he and Ally didn't just grow apart. From what I can gather, she dumped him. She dumped him because he failed her and some-body close to her.'

'Erin—'

'Danny let me down,' I say. 'He let you all down. But more than all of that, he let himself down. Mike, I can't forgive him.'

'What did my mom do to you, Erin?'

'Nothing.'

'You think you're punishing Danny? Danny is dead. My mother is still alive. It's her you're punishing.'

'I'm not trying to,' I say.

'Well, you sure as hell are,' Mike snaps and it's as angry as I've heard him.

'Mike, I can't look her in the face knowing what I know about Danny. I can't look at any of you.'

There's silence across the line, not even a crackling. I think Mike has hung up, but then I hear a sharp intake of breath.

'What does that mean?' he says. 'Is that it? Are you out of our lives now?'

Tears roll down my cheeks.

At our wedding, Mike had given a best man's speech and then a sort of father of the bride speech, because mine wasn't there.

I've only known Erin a short time. But when I met her, it was the first time I felt envious of my bro. I mean, I might have the looks. The brains. The talent. But he has Erin. No wonder he moved so quick. I'm proud of the two of them and today, we take her into our hearts, the way she's taken us into hers. Erin, you're my sis, today and forever.

'Yes,' I answer Mike. 'I think that's best.'

I wait for the dial tone.

It doesn't come.

299

Just the sound of Mike crying.

When I can't bear it any longer, I put the phone down.

After Cal tells me what Danny did, I draw into myself.

January becomes February and I'm finding every day harder.

I push Karla away. She was my lawyer, but now she's my friend; I can tell she's worried, maybe even a little irritated, but she seems to have a lot of cases on at the moment and is letting me get my way.

Leslie Klein calls every now and again and we've met for coffee once or twice. She likes me and I'm growing to like her, now I know she's human and not just a psychiatrist. But she has that way of asking me questions that makes a polite I'm fine sound like a cop-out, so for the last few weeks I've cried off meeting up.

Bud calls up to the apartment with plates of food wrapped in tinfoil and endless invitations to join the regulars in the bar for happy hour. I tell him work is crazy and it's not a total lie. I'm taking on submission after submission, anything to block out the truth about Danny.

Cal.

I can't bear to be in his company.

I can't believe that Danny could have married me, could have been in my life every single day, and not told me what he'd done to Lauren Gregory.

Sure, what happened to her wasn't exactly what happened to Niamh. Lauren's attacker hadn't killed her. But it didn't take a genius to figure out that she died as a direct result of her rape and subsequent denial of justice.

I can't let it go. I need to know who Danny was covering up for. I have my suspicions.

Eventually, I get hold of Ally Summers, basically by visiting every Sephora in New York City until I spot her.

She ushers me over to the side of the shop, to a counter filled with lip glosses, and starts picking them up and showing them to me, one by one.

I stare at her as she's doing this. She's an attractive girl. A little fragile-looking, but who am I to judge?

If she'd never met Lauren Gregory, would she have been married to Danny?

Would Danny still be alive?

'I know what Danny Ryan did,' I say.

The colour drains from her face.

'I know he let Lauren down. And that you were his girlfriend.'

She's trembling. She glances around the shop, which is packed with young women all caught up in shopping, all of them ignoring us.

'Just tell me the truth, Ally,' I say. 'You want to hide out here, fine. But I'm not leaving until I know what you know.'

Ally ponders on this for a few seconds. Then, the decision is made.

'Lauren didn't want to tell anybody,' she says, quietly. 'But I could see it was getting to her and my response was . . . well, something between compassion and what I thought was feminism. I told her she had to be brave. What if he attacked somebody else? There was a police station in Cambridge. I wanted to bring her there. But she was adamant. No police. Then, I realised – there's a roundabout way of doing this. I could ask Danny. He'd just started in homicide and I was busy so we weren't seeing a lot of each other, but I thought, he'll do this for me. And Lauren had been attacked in Manhattan, so it made sense to go to a police station there. His station. I talked her into it; I convinced her Danny would be discreet, and it still took every ounce of courage she had. He took her seriously, at first, as I knew he would. Even though he was homicide, he promised her he'd look into it. Then, within hours, he told her she didn't have a case. Within hours. I . . . I saw him, coming out of her dorm that afternoon. He'd driven up to tell her. He told her not to bother coming back to the station.'

'Did you ask him why?'

'Eventually. He gave me the usual shit – that she'd been seen with the man, that she'd gone willingly with him, that she'd no case. It was the sort of crap you hear all the time and think, what a load of bullshit. I cut him out of my life straightaway.'

'Did she tell you who attacked her?' I ask.

Ally hesitates and in that pause I wonder if she knows, or at least suspects.

'No,' she says.

'Did you . . . did you think Danny was holding something back?'

Ally hesitates.

'He was . . . protecting somebody,' she says. 'He didn't think that about rape victims. Not normally. He fucked Lauren over to protect somebody else.'

'Somebody you knew, too?'

'No. Please, will you promise me you'll let this drop, now? How did you find out all this, anyway?'

'Painfully,' I say.

I don't tell her that I married Danny Ryan less than a year after she must have broken up with him.

I just promise her I won't bother her again.

That will turn out to be a lie.

As I leave the store, all I can think is that there are only two men I can imagine Danny sacrificing so much for.

Mike is one.

But Mike is not a cop, so the Newport PD wouldn't bother protecting Mike's reputation if they found out Danny was going to reveal an unpleasant truth and wanted him to stop.

Then there's Ben Mitchell.

As I travel back to Long Island that day, I notice two missed calls on my phone from Cal.

I ignore him.

And I keep ignoring him.

I regret it. Resent it, even. But it has to be done.

Cal, though, isn't happy to let me go.

I'm running on the beach in late February when I hear the sound of somebody catching up with me.

There's snow still on the ground but it never sticks by the sea. It's deathly cold, though; I've been out for a while and have yet to warm up.

I decide to turn off beyond the next dune, go home and stand under a hot shower for ten minutes, when I hear somebody running up to my shoulder.

'What's going on?'

The sound of Cal's voice almost makes me jump through my skin.

'Are you stalking me again?' I ask, as we pull up.

Cal is in full training gear, his cheeks puffy and red in the cold.

'Can't I just be running along the beach?' he says.

'You got here from East Hampton? That's quite a distance.'

He doesn't smile.

'Why are you cutting me out?'

'I'm not,' I say and then realise denial isn't the way to handle this situation. 'I mean, I am, but it's not personal.'

'Erin, don't do this,' he says. 'I thought we were friends.'

I throw my hands out, exasperated.

'God, Cal. It's a bit awkward, don't you think?'

Cal says nothing for a moment.

'After Lauren died, I felt nothing but shame,' Cal says. 'I'd failed her. It took me a long time to come back from that. But then I realised, nobody is responsible for other people's decisions. Even if you screw up, what other people choose to do with their lives is up to them. Danny was your husband; you weren't responsible for his mistakes.'

'I know. I just don't know how you can be so charitable about him.'

'Because he was young and he was under pressure and he fucked up, but he was trying to fix it. And he was right. He was the only one who could.'

'That doesn't excuse him not telling me the truth.'

'Haven't you ever lied?' Cal asks.

'Not when it mattered. Have you?'

Cal says nothing.

'You do what you have to, sometimes,' he says. 'I come from a background where that's practically the life motto. How do you think rich people get rich and stay rich?'

'That's different.'

Cal shrugs.

'What I don't understand is why you don't want to be around

me,' he says. 'Don't I get a say in it? Haven't we been through enough to stay friends?'

'Cal, are we friends? I've never even seen your house.'

'I don't want you meeting my family or the people I grew up with. I hate those people.'

'You don't hate them.'

'I do. You're better than them. I want to keep you separate. You and Karla and Bud.'

My cheeks are red and not just from the exertion.

Cal is saying something more to me here. I know it and he knows it.

Maybe. In another life. In different circumstances.

'I'm moving, anyway,' he says.

'Where?'

He looks around.

'I like it down here,' he says. 'Might get myself a little pad.'

I smile, despite myself.

'Where would you keep all your money?'

'I'll get two apartments and I can knock through. It'll get me away from my father. And you won't be able to avoid me if I'm bar-flying at McNally's.'

'You're really determined to bully me into staying your friend, aren't you?' I say.

He cocks his head, sheepishly.

I sigh.

It's not that anything he's said doesn't make sense.

Cal starts to jog backwards, still facing me.

'Erin, just so you know, at the start this might have been about Danny and finding out what he told you about Lauren.'

He turns, faces forward, but calls over his shoulder as he does, 'But now it's about you. I like you, Erin.'

I'm speechless for a moment. Then, 'Bar-flying is not a verb,' I call out.

As I walk back to my apartment from the beach, I'm distracted by what Cal has said and the prospect of continuing to have him in my life.

I'm not stupid. I know our relationship is more intense because of what we've both experienced and that it might be a false intensity. Sure, we didn't spend all those months last year talking about people we've lost, but they've certainly featured in our most important discussions.

Does anything remain when you take out what connects us?

Or is Cal right? What connects us is what makes the friendship special.

I'm so caught up in these internal gymnastics that I don't hear the car driving slowly alongside until I can see its hood.

The Lexus purrs to a stop and Ben winds down the window.

'Erin, get in,' he says.

I frown and look up at my apartment, which is within running distance.

'No, thanks,' I say.

While I'm pretty sure I've aged in the last seven months, I haven't changed much physically beyond losing weight and bagging a few grey hairs.

Ben, though, is a different person and I'm shocked at how he looks. His suit is crumpled-looking and he hasn't shaved. His eyes are creased in wrinkles that weren't there before and his hair, always fair, is turning white.

Good.

'I've been keeping an eye on you,' he says.

Something in his tone chills me.

'Good for you,' I say, as though I'm not bothered. 'For Newport PD or on your own behalf?'

'Danny would have wanted—'

'No. No, don't even say it.'

Ben grips the steering wheel, his jaw clenched.

'What are you playing at, hanging around with that guy?'

'Who?' It takes me a second to realise what he's saying. 'Cal?'

Ben nods, once.

'Do you know who he is?' I ask. 'Do you know who he was to Danny?'

'Erin, whatever he's told you about Danny, it has nothing to do with you.'

'We're friends.'

Ben snorts.

'Right,' he says. 'Because you have so much in common.'

'We do,' I say, my voice small.

'Your husband is not even a year dead.'

It's like a snake slithering from my insides and coiling around my gut.

Danny had told me about this. How, in the 'police family', colleagues looked after dead cops' spouses. Until that spouse moved on with somebody else. Then they were cut off.

Thing is – we're skipping a step.

Nobody in Danny's precinct has been looking out for me. Nobody even looked out for him.

But here's Ben, trying to make me feel judged for being in the company of another man.

The red hot shame burns through me for a few seconds before it's replaced with a similar heat, this time one of fury.

'How dare you,' I say, my voice low and distressed. 'How fucking dare you.'

'Danny loved you,' he says.

'He loved you, too,' I snap.

Ben flinches.

'Tell me something,' I say, leaning towards the open window, bringing my face close to Ben's. 'You ever spend time with a girl called Lauren Gregory?'

Ben recoils.

I see it. I see the guilt on his face.

Bastard.

The absolute bastard.

'You did this,' I hiss. 'You hurt her and you killed Danny.'

Ben reaches out to grab my wrist. I'm shocked but I still manage to jump back, away from him.

I pull my phone out of my running pack and hold it up.

Cars are passing up and down the road.

Along the street, somebody emerges from the diner.

If Ben's going to attack me, it will be in public and I'll have dialled Cal before he can get out of the car.

Ben knows he can't do anything.

'You don't know what you're talking about,' he snaps.

'I think I do,' I say. 'And let me tell you this, Ben Mitchell. If anything happens to me, you can be sure I'll have left enough dirt on you that everybody will know who and what you are.'

I march away, head held high, every bit of me trembling.

I had planned to cut Cal off.

But there's always been a little seed of anarchy in me.

Tell me I can't do something and that's what I'll do, and right now, I need as many people in my life as I can get.

I type a WhatsApp message on my phone as I take the stairs to my apartment.

Okay, it says. Let's do dinner later.

I send it to Cal.

Now

Karla meets me this morning in the holding cell underneath the court. She's brought breakfast: a carton of pancakes smothered in syrup and a cup of coffee.

I'm feeling totally fatigued and I've never been so grateful to see a quick-buy breakfast.

Technically, she's not supposed to bring me anything liquid and hot (which I could use to scald a guard before launching my daring prison escape). But she is allowed to bring me food when I'm at the court and she's struck lucky with this guard; a Merry Christmas before she arrives at my door and then the lock is turned, nothing's said about the cups.

'I recognise this coffee,' I tell her, taking a sip.

'I made up with Boy,' she says.

'He needed your legal help again?'

'Yep. Him and the wife are divorcing and, as it turns out, the deeds for the coffee shop are in his name. He's a *pendejo*, but it's right next door to my office, you know?'

'You can't fall out with good coffee,' I say.

We sip in silence for a while.

'So, today's the day,' Karla says.

She's referring to the fact the prosecution has rested and we can now start calling our witnesses.

'Today's the day,' I agree.

'You don't sound too hopeful.'

'The prosecution sounded pretty convincing.'

'Sure they did. They've had all the control. Now we take the reins.'

'You said we were desperate.'

'We were. Desperate for Roberts to shut the hell up. Their case is thin, Erin. And we have a great line-up to knock down every one of their points.'

'But it's my word against theirs.'

Karla pauses.

'Remember what this case is about, Erin. You wanted everybody to hear what happened with Danny, didn't you?'

I stare at the lid of the coffee cup, from which steam has been rising since I opened the flap. If I lose this case, I'm going to be drinking shit, lukewarm coffee for the rest of my life.

It's such a little thing.

'Yes,' I say.

'And we're still working on trying to track him down. You know that. Bud is close. We're getting there.'

I say nothing.

Karla squeezes my shoulder.

'Chin up, chica. I got this.'

I want to believe her.

Over the past seventeen months, I've learned a lot about Karla. Like how she'd been more than just a good lawyer in her previous practice. She'd been shit-hot. How, before she was even thirty, she'd tried and won cases that involved working around the clock and earning suitcases full of money. Trials that involved bringing down bad guys and nailing them to the cross while she was at it.

Karla was on the cusp of a different kind of life – one where she made partner in a big firm, charging millions in billable hours and owning an apartment in the city and a beach house. Instead, she chose a quieter life. Karla took her savings, moved to Patchogue and opened a tiny practice.

Karla says she's going to get me off, whatever she has to do.

And we both know that when it's over, she's going back to that quiet life.

When I sit in my seat at the defence table, this time it feels different. Like the earth has shifted a little.

We're into the home straight. The witnesses Karla calls over the next few days are going to decide my fate.

'Is the defence ready to call its first witness?' Judge Palmer asks.

'We are.' Karla nods. 'The defence calls Ally Summers.'

We have a strategy and we are going to use it.

My husband might be missing but by the time we're finished telling the truth about what he did – nobody on that jury will be left thinking he didn't get what he deserved.

Ally comes up from the back of the court.

She glances at Gloria and Mike before she takes the stand.

Then she looks at me.

I nod.

She's still scared but she knows she has to talk.

For me. For Lauren. For Lauren's mother.

For Lauren's brother.

In the end, while Karla appealed to Ally's sense of duty and honour, it was Ally's guilt that won. That, and her absolute desperation to move on with her own life.

And when Karla explained she'd never move on until we'd crucified my husband and everybody who'd helped him, Ally bought in.

She's exhausted. We all are. But she has this last fight in her.

She takes the stand and when she does, Ally reveals her own worst, most hideous moment.

She tells Karla about Lauren's email, sent just weeks before her death, and how Lauren was actually in fear not just for her own life, but for her family's lives, too.

Because, obviously, the police weren't on her side.

Then, Ally tells us who Lauren had accused of attacking her.

I'd suspected she knew his identity way back earlier in the year, when I cornered her in the Sephora she worked in.

As Ally confesses everything, I listen and I'm full of admiration.

It takes a lot to be that honest.

I know, because I'm still keeping secrets.

'I think back now, and I realise that I was young and I didn't know any better,' Ally says. 'I could have handled everything differently. But I was also frightened. That's what he did to me.'

'Your Honour.' Prosecutor Roberts sighs. 'Can we confirm who's actually on trial here? This trial is not about what the police did or didn't do in an incident entirely unrelated to Erin Kennedy—'

'Oh, it's all related,' Karla says.

As the lawyers argue, Ally's gaze travels to the public benches again and back to Gloria.

I turn, and it's then I see my own family, all of them, sitting behind me.

My mother and father look ashen but determined.

They're flanked by Tanya and Bud.

I almost cry with relief. Something about just having them here makes me believe that there's hope. Like, if Maura and John could get on a plane and cross the Atlantic then maybe, just maybe – I can get away with murder.

The tide has turned.

PART III

The Whole Truth

Then

Did the altercation with Ben make me grow closer to Cal in the months that followed?

Certainly.

Would it have happened anyway?

Probably.

After that run on the beach, we pick up where we'd left off. Meeting for lunches and drinks. Spending days out on the Island and around Manhattan.

Cal finds a house a little up the coast in Bellport, right by the beach. His 'little' pad looks like my dream home – a Tudor-style villa with real oak beams on its facade and ceilings, and mullioned windows in every room. His deck runs right down to the sea and at night, he lights thick candles in glass lanterns along its length, like a welcoming walkway to a party that's always on.

I can tell that whatever rift he has with his family has deepened, especially after his decision to leave the mansion in East Hampton. He barely mentions them at all now.

We drive past his old home one day – a giant sprawling estate, only the tips of the roof visible from the road.

'I can't believe you aren't able to keep living there and never have to bump into your relatives,' I say.

'Well, I did, in a manner, but my father has an uncanny way of always finding me,' he says, his mouth turned down.

We say no more about it.

Sometimes Cal, with all his money and the currency his name carries, strikes me as the loneliest person in the world.

Which is probably what draws me to him.

There's nothing to make you feel less alone than being in the company of somebody who thinks they have nobody at all.

Nobody bar Cal, Ally Summers and I know the full truth of what Danny did but my family and friends do know that something has shifted in me.

They know that I no longer grieve for Danny in quite the same way; and it's not just because time has passed.

They might not be saying it, but I guess they suspect I now believe what Newport PD were saying about Danny.

Karla still raises it every now and again but it's difficult for her to maintain her enthusiasm in the face of my utter lack of it.

I still believe somebody was framing Danny. It's like Cal says – someone among Danny's colleagues didn't want him bringing up what had happened to Lauren and revealing the truth of it.

And I suspect that someone is Ben Mitchell.

But it's hard for me to see beyond Danny's complicity in what happened to Lauren.

Especially if it was Ben he'd chosen to protect all that time.

The people around me like Cal and they can see my spending time with him is no bad thing.

The only one who's not entirely enamoured of Cal is Leslie, but I think I know why.

We meet for lunch one March afternoon near her office in Bellport. It's not quite warm enough to sit outside, but we do, still bundled in our coats, knotting our scarves around us and laughing as Leslie tells me about her nephew and niece's obsession with Pennywise from *It* and how they've been begging her to download the new movie and she's torn because she's trying to be the cool aunty.

'Is this on you, somehow, that they're fixated on a serial killer monster clown?' I ask.

'I'm sure Trump's to blame,' Leslie says and we both laugh because she's a card-carrying Republican.

I tell her then about the upcoming housewarming party Cal has planned and she pauses just long enough for me to read her feelings.

'You don't like him,' I say.

'I don't not like him,' she answers. 'It's just – I can't put my finger on it.'

'Far be it for me to doctor the doctor,' I say, 'but is it possible you've never stopped feeling guilty over Danny?'

'Of course, I've never stopped feeling guilty,' she says. 'And I do think you should move on, Erin, I really do. I guess it might be because of how you met Cal. The fact he has trauma of his own. It's like they tell people who attend AA. You shouldn't be with somebody else from the group – each of you needs too much.'

'You know, my sister said something similar,' I say. 'But Cal doesn't ask very much of me.'

Leslie hesitates. Her long, slender fingers smooth the creases of her silk scarf as she ponders what she's about to say.

'You were worried that Danny might have wanted to be with

you because he felt he needed to atone for his failings with Lauren,' Leslie says.

My stomach clenches in dread at where she's going with this.

'Aren't you worried that Cal might feel the same way?'

I shrug nonchalantly, even though I'm irritated.

'Cal and I aren't together,' I say. 'That's a big difference.'

'If you say so,' Leslie says.

She drops it then. The look on my face has probably warned her off.

Cal's housewarming party takes place on a warm April's evening.

It's small, mainly our mutual friends. Karla, Bud, some regulars from McNally's, neighbours from along the beach.

As the evening wears on, we four friends gather on the deck among the array of candles flickering in the breeze. And I realise that I am so comfortable with these people, I am relaxed. Not pretending to be relaxed, actually at ease.

I listen lazily as Bud tells us about his former life – which sounds as drink- and drug-fuelled as I always suspected it to be.

'Highlights?' Bud says. 'I can't say I actually remember any. There were a lot of disco balls.'

'Studio 54 in its heyday,' I say.

'Pretty much,' Bud says.

'I wish I'd seen it,' I say and Bud pops open another beer for me.

'I'm surprised you remember anything at all,' Cal says, seriously, and he sounds like a schoolteacher.

'Don't mind him,' I say. 'Cal is a one-man anti-drugs squad. What about you, Karla? Any crazy stories from your youth?'

'Well, there was that one time we all had to run past the border guards with the big guns and climb the barbed-wire fence.'

'Karla?' I gasp, all seriousness.

She laughs.

'We came on a plane, honey, I'm kidding. Yeah, I've got my fair share of nutty stories. Mainly relating to my pain-in-the-frickin'-neck goddess.'

As Karla regales us, I can tell Cal is uncomfortable. I've learned to read him well and if I have one criticism of Cal it's that he's very clean-living. It's not like I'm some kind of hedonistic princess but I have noticed that Cal tends to stick to a couple of beers when we're drinking, and that he never seems to get too wild, even when we're all out enjoying ourselves. There's a reserve there, and I'm never quite sure if it's because he doesn't want to act like some one-dimensional playboy or if he's not as comfortable in our company as he claims.

I hang back after the house party that evening, which winds up despite Bud's efforts to keep it going.

'I thought we'd be up until the sunrise,' Bud says.

Only Bud could campaign for an all-nighter while drinking orange juice.

I wave him off in his car then return to the house.

Cal is standing in the centre of the kitchen, looking genuinely puzzled.

'How can so few people make such a mess?' he says.

I search through his cupboards for black sacks.

'It's like you've never been at a party before,' I say. 'Cal, where are your refuse sacks?'

'I don't know.'

'Don't you have any?'

'I don't think so.'

'How do we clean up, then?'

He starts to laugh.

I watch him, bemused.

'What's so funny?'

'I'm used to the cleaners coming in after the caterers. I forgot to book cleaners.'

For such a smart guy he can be guileless at times.

'I guess we can do it tomorrow,' I say. 'Can you call me an Uber?'

He hesitates.

'Yes,' he says. 'Or . . . you could stay.'

I freeze.

I knew this was coming.

'I don't mean . . .' He trails off, nervously. 'I mean, I've a lot of guest rooms.'

'I've seen them.'

'No pressure,' he says. He's standing so close to me, I can smell the musk of his body, the scent of beer on his breath. His hair is tousled and he looks tired, but he's still . . .

'I don't feel any pressure,' I say.

And I don't. I feel comfortable.

I should feel guilty. I should feel numb.

I guess I would, if I felt that staying here meant leaving Danny behind.

The truth is, Danny left me behind and that's what makes this easier than it should be.

I haven't been with another man in almost a year.

And the man I was with wasn't even really there, it turns out.

So, it begins.

We sleep together that night, but all we do is sleep.

Not even a chaste kiss.

We lie on the bed facing each other and hold hands. Two sad, lonely people who've found something in each other and are hanging on to it for dear life.

I feel at peace for the first time in a long time.

I've no idea what's coming.

Danny broke my heart once.

I didn't think he could do it twice.

'When is your birthday?' Cal asks.

'My birthday?'

We're walking through the farmers' market where I first met Cal. The season has well and truly turned for the better, the warm spring sliding into a hot June, and the market is awash with vibrant colours and smells.

Cal is picking up everything and examining each item like he's an alien trying to wrap his head around all these exotic, edible things. He's just about learned how to make toast without burning it. I mock him for being a walking rich boy cliché and he replies with sentences like, yeah, but can you play water polo?

'My birthday's in August,' I say.

'Ah.' Cal places mushrooms he's never going to include in a recipe in his basket. 'I guess that's why you didn't mention it last year.'

I raise my eyebrows over my sunglasses.

'I was wondering because I've known you almost a year and you haven't had a birthday,' he says.

It has been almost a year.

So much can change in twelve months and so much stays the same. This market is as welcoming as it always was. The sun still feels warm on my face. The smell of the salt air is familiar in my nose.

Cal has become one of those familiars.

We spend most of our spare time together.

We both know we're moving in a certain direction but neither of us are rushing it.

'I'd figured your birthday was this month,' he says.

'I don't really do birthdays,' I say. 'I stopped getting excited about them when I turned twenty-one. Cal, put that back.'

I take the wildly expensive vial of saffron he's put in his basket and return it to the chequered table he sourced it from. He wouldn't know what to do with it.

'You're not exactly party central yourself,' I say.

'It's not my birthday, though, is it? Let me make a fuss of you this year.'

'What do you have in mind?'

He hesitates. He's nervous about this, whatever it is.

'Can you get a few days off in July? I know it's not your actual birthday but I have to go somewhere for business and it feels like the perfect place to kill two birds.'

'You have business?' I say wryly.

We both laugh, Cal's mouth crinkling up at the sides in that good-natured way he has. He doesn't show it as much as he should, but I love that smile.

'Sometimes I do actual work, you know. I'm meeting the owner of a company who is looking for investors. It seems like a good start-up.'

He tells me what dates he has in mind.

I'm picking up jars of fruit preserve as he talks and I almost drop the one I'm holding.

Of course I can get the days off. I'd already planned to.

I wasn't sure how I'd be spending Danny's anniversary but I knew it wouldn't be commuting to work and sitting in the office.

'I know,' Cal says, and I realise he hasn't forgotten. 'I thought you might like to get away for a few days. And, instead of making a big thing about it being that date, we can just say we're heading off for your birthday.'

I gingerly place the glass jar back on the table, lest it fall from my hand and I end up wearing strawberry jam.

'Where are we going?' I ask.

We fly out on a Sunday.

'I never asked, have you ever been to Las Vegas?' he says, as we recline on our American Airlines flight, me with a JD and Coke in hand, Cal sipping a sparkling water.

'Actually, no,' I say. 'I don't like gambling.'

Cal starts to laugh.

'You don't think you should have mentioned that prior to boarding?'

'Well, it's not just casinos in Vegas, is it? There are shows and bars and I hear the fountains are great.'

'You're hilarious. What's wrong with gambling?'

'I worked in a bookies when I was in college.'

'A what now?'

'A betting shop? Where punters come in and bet on horses and dogs and other sports?'

'At the track?'

'No. There are just shops, all over the place. Usually next to bars.'

'Right.'

He hasn't a clue what I'm talking about.

'And I guess it's like being a sober barman,' I say, 'serving alcohol to incredibly drunk people who keep ordering. It kind of turns you off. I saw people lose their marriages and homes because of gambling.'

'I don't plan on losing while we're here,' Cal says.

'Spoken like a true gambler,' I say.

'No, my plan is to find Robert Redford and sell you for a million dollars.'

'I'm happy to go for less,' I say.

He shakes his head and nods to the flight attendant.

'Another one of these for the scarlet woman,' he says, pointing at my glass.

'Coming up.' She beams.

Nobody says no to Cal. I've noticed that.

'It's not gambling you have a problem with,' Cal says. 'It's addiction.'

'Yeah,' I say. 'I guess. You get it, don't you? I mean, you have the thing about drugs.'

He doesn't say anything.

'Where does that come from?' I ask. 'Normally, when somebody is anti-something, it's for a reason.'

'I think you're spending too much time with the psychiatrist,' Cal says, then he sighs and it's loaded.

'What is it?' I ask. 'Does somebody in your family have a problem with drugs?'

'Mommy dearest is prone to pill-popping but it's not that.'

He hesitates.

'I used to abuse drugs,' he says.

I'm so surprised, I nearly snort my drink. Clean-living Cal?

'It wasn't too bad,' he adds, quickly. 'I wasn't like an addict or anything. It's just, a lot of those parties I went to, the people in my circle, it's right there in front of you, you know? I saw people fuck up their heads and I didn't like what it did to mine. I don't like that feeling of not being in control. And my father, he . . . he has a big thing about being in control.'

Cal is saying all this lightly, like it's just something from his past that doesn't really matter any more, but I can see how much it has affected him. I put my drink down on the little seat table and reach over to take his hand.

'When Lauren was . . . when everything happened to Lauren, I wasn't there for her. I was off my face. I'd taken cocaine that night and . . .'

He trails off, his voice funny.

'I let her down,' he says.

I continue to hold his hand; it's all I can do. I know how ineffective words are in this scenario.

'That's why you don't blame Danny,' I say eventually. 'You've been blaming yourself.'

He nods. Then he reaches over, asks me silently with his eyes if it's okay, and lifts my JD and Coke. He knocks it back.

'Sorry,' he says.

'You've nothing to be sorry for,' I say.

He looks so devastated that I want to lean over and kiss him.

But I don't. Not now, not like this.

Instead, I rest my head on his shoulder and that's where it stays for the rest of the flight.

Eventually, I feel him relax.

And as he does, I'm filled with guilt.

Cal has gone out of his way to help me deal with Danny's anniversary, all the while not mentioning his own loss.

Lauren's anniversary passed in May and Cal never even mentioned it.

I never mentioned it.

I feel like the most selfish person in the world.

There and then, I promise myself to enjoy the next few days and be grateful for having this man in my life.

We have a deal. Once he's had his business meeting, Cal is allowed to treat me to one nice evening. Outside of that, we've split the costs of everything. I don't want him to ever think I'm one of those women who only sees his money.

But I'm not exactly flush. I've been covering my rent and bills with one wage for the past year. Danny's pension doesn't amount to a whole lot and I haven't touched the money in his bank account – the one the police never seem to have discovered. I'm terrified that they might be waiting for me to go near it; I have no idea where that money came from, maybe I can be charged with using the profits of criminality or something. Karla has a more laid-back attitude. She's convinced they've no interest in pursuing the facts of what Danny did or didn't do and are only holding on to his other account because the city is greedy for its contents.

I'm not convinced. They never returned Danny's laptop or cell phone. If that doesn't say open investigation, I don't know what does.

I budget for some gambling money – two hundred dollars per day – and I insist we eat regular food in grills and burger joints. Cal says he likes my normality. Well, it doesn't get more normal than this.

As we walk down the Strip on the second day, nursing our hangovers with large cups of iced Coke, I ask him what he has planned for that evening – his designated evening.

'Ah, I have put a lot of thought into this,' he says.

'Is it a helicopter ride? I gotta tell you, if it is, I might pee myself.'

'Definitely not a helicopter ride.'

'Should I wear a nice dress?'

'You look good in everything.'

'Thank you, but should I?'

'Think nightclub,' he says.

'Okay. But I can't imagine how you'll top that hotel. Unless you've managed to get Elvis reincarnated for a one-time show.'

'Would that make you happy?'

'I'm already happy.'

It's only a white lie.

I'm not happy, despite trying my best.

Even with the colours, the lights, the absolute decadence and me allegedly having nothing to worry about, as the hours have ticked by, I've felt more and more in turmoil.

Tomorrow marks a year to the day that Danny died and try as I might, the memory will not let me be.

I'm grateful I'm not home – Cal was right to suggest this. But I'd actually really like to get smashed and just see out the next two days in a blur. Cal's not quite the right company for that. Maybe we should have brought Karla and Bud.

'You're not happy,' he says, and I realise this man really knows me now. 'You can't stop remembering. But I have a plan to take your mind off things. Trust me.'

He kisses the top of my nose and takes my hand.

We're doing a lot of that lately. Holding hands like two teenagers on a permanent first date.

I like the way mine feels in his. His hands are large but they're smooth, well cared for. Not like Danny's; different, but nice.

I feel protected when I'm with Cal, and it's not that I need a man looking after me, but it does give me a warm glow knowing he wants to. A little bit of me knows it's because he still feels guilty about Danny. And after what he told me on the plane, I know he feels guilty about Lauren, too. But that's not all it is. Cal really cares for me and I've started to really care for him.

If this was any other time, if we were any other people, I know in my heart tonight would end with me and Cal throwing caution to the wind, screwing in that big hotel bed and probably getting married in a tunnel of love.

But we can't because, in my head, I'm still married. I'm still expecting to see Danny; I'm waiting for him to just walk up beside me and whisper my name.

Every time a tall man with Danny's build walks past, I think it's him.

When somebody nearby is wearing his scent, I sniff the air.

I hear him, in the deep laughs of other men.

I've had over thirty years on this earth and only two of those contained Danny, yet he filled my life.

Even though I've discovered something so absolutely awful about him, I can't get over him.

But if I could, it would be with Cal.

We while away the afternoon gambling in one of the smaller hotel casinos.

I can't lose my money, putting paid to any notions I had about gambling being for schmucks.

We play twenty-one, a nod to the last birthday I properly celebrated, and I take the house – in a modest way.

Cal watches with sheer incredulity as I amass my fortune.

'Yes,' he says, wryly. 'This is an awful way to spend an afternoon. Gambling should be banned.'

'Go get some shrimp from the buffet.' I laugh. 'I'm going to be here a while.'

We leave the casino, me $5K richer.

Later, we head into the Bellagio for our night out.

A man, who I'm pretty sure might be the manager of the hotel, approaches us.

'Mr Hawley, the private viewing room is all set up for you.'

Cal smiles at me enigmatically, and guides me gently into the elevator that takes us up to the Hyde Bellagio nightclub.

We pass through the nightclub and enter our own private room. I stop on the threshold and gawp at the magnificent view of the Vegas Strip through the floor-to-ceiling glass windows. The casino's famed fountains haven't started for the evening yet but I know when they do, the velvet couches in this place will have the best view.

'Holy cow, Cal,' I say. 'You have thought of a way to distract me.'

'Look,' he says. 'I might not be into having crazy nights all the time these days, but I sure as hell picked up a few tricks back when I was.'

I laugh.

My heart might want to dwell on Danny tonight. He might even manage to creep in.

But Cal is the one who's here.

'We need to pick some music,' Cal says, handing me a book of songs.

I assume he means for our private room and I pick a joke song to make us both smile. And then they bring us a giant red button and I realise that we are actually in control of the fountains for the evening.

So, instead of the Vegas lights blowing up to the tune of an Elvis classic, the crowds outside are treated to 'Baby's Got Back'.

I'm still trying to catch my breath when the security team arrives with the three-foot-tall gold bottle of champagne.

I stare at Cal, gobsmacked.

'How many bottles are in that?' I ask.

'I think it's forty,' he says.

'Cal.' I swallow. 'Are you even going to help with this? Hand on heart, I reckon two bottles is my limit and I will vomit after.'

He laughs.

'For one night only, my dear, I am yours to go mad with. Maybe not that mad. That comes with the room but we can drink what we're able and then I'll have it sent into the nightclub.'

I feel a momentary unease. I can't even imagine what this night is costing but I know it's beyond my wildest dreams.

And then I bury the unease and take my first glass of champagne.

'Bottoms up,' I say.

'What?'

'Skull it.'

'You're speaking in tongues.'

I clink his glass.

'Cheers.'

'Cheers.'

That's how the night begins.

Four hours later, Cal is still enjoying himself. He is, in fact, standing on the plush red couch in his socks, his shirt hanging out of his trousers, dancing like Tom Cruise in Risky Business to 'Old Time Rock and Roll'. He looks pretty much as I imagine seventeen-year-old Cal would have looked; his face lit up with joy and abandonment, the worry he normally carries in his features smoothed away.

I, on the other hand, have become drunk and maudlin. Best-laid plans.

At some point, he realises I'm drinking quietly and with intent, while he's dancing like a jock at a frat party.

'Let's get you home, Irish,' he says, sobering up.

I flinch. Danny used to call me Irish.

As we walk back to the hotel – him insisting on air and lots of water – Cal wraps his arm around my waist to both prop me up and comfort me.

'I don't know why I'm like this.' I hiccup. 'That was the best night of my life.'

'It's today,' Cal says.

He's right, of course. It's after midnight, which officially makes this Danny's one-year anniversary.

This day last year, I woke up to what I thought would be an ordinary day.

I was somebody's wife. I was loved. I was happy.

Twelve months on, I've just been sitting in the Bellagio controlling the fountains – and all I've had to sacrifice in the interim is my heart and everything I believed in the world.

'I wanted to try my hardest to make you forget,' Cal says.

'I want to,' I say. 'And then I don't want to.'

We sit on the perimeter wall of the fountains we've just been looking down on.

'I hate it,' I continue. 'It's like I'll never move on from Danny. Do you feel like that about Lauren?'

He lets out a deep sigh.

'Yes,' he says. 'I do.'

'You get it,' I say. 'It's been a whole year and I can close my eyes and still see him, clear as day. I see him walking to the window and jumping. For months, I had these one-sided conversations with him. Why'd you do it, Danny? I had no choice, Erin, sorry. No, not good enough, Danny. On and on, Cal. It's like he's more alive in my head than he was in real life.'

Cal takes my hand. He strokes my palm, then turns it over and places his thumb on my wedding band.

'You're still wearing this,' he says. 'Do you think, maybe, it might be time to take it off?'

I look down at my wedding ring. I've taken it off and put it back on plenty in the last year.

I haven't been able to leave it off for good. I don't know why or what that means.

'My hand will look empty without it,' I say, not even realising that's what I've been thinking. 'When it's on my finger, I can pretend, even for a few minutes, that everything is normal. I think if it was gone, I'd look at that space and remember what caused it. Does that make any sense?'

Cal nods, but it's half-hearted.

He seems angry with me, and I'm not sure what I've said to annoy him.

Then he meets my eye.

I stare back and I know in a heartbeat he's fallen for me.

'It doesn't have to be empty,' he says. 'I could put a ring there.'

I half laugh, half sob.

'Cal, we haven't even had sex and you want to marry me?'

Cal turns and grabs both my hands now. He's gazing at me earnestly, looking far more sober than he has a right to be.

'I want to take care of you,' he says. 'There's more to us than I've ever had with any of the women who've passed through my life. I've wanted to marry you for about nine months, Erin, but I couldn't tell you. I want to marry you because you're unlike anybody I know or am ever likely to know. Even in the pits of despair, you can make a joke. No matter what happens to you, you're still standing. You're the strongest person I've ever known and just being around you makes me feel better about the world.'

I catch my breath while he pauses to take one.

'Cal – just because you don't know people like me, doesn't mean I'm special. It just means you've been living in a bubble.' I laugh, like this isn't one of the most serious conversations I've ever had.

'You are special,' he says. 'Have you any idea how dull and mundane most people are? With their little problems and all their whining about the most inane things? I know people who have everything and they still don't light up a room the way you do. I want to be with you. I can't bear to think of you with anybody else. Even Danny. He didn't deserve you, Erin.'

Danny. Cal was Danny's greatest defender. But all I can sense from him now is irritation.

Cal wants to be with me and he's angry that Danny had me and let me go.

I close my eyes.

I thought I couldn't live without my husband, yet I never even knew him.

In my darkest moments, I think of him with Ally Summers. I imagine how they'd still be together if things hadn't gone so wrong.

I was the compensation prize.

But I'm not Cal's Plan B.

When Cal leans closer to kiss me, I don't pull back. I lean into it.

Everything about it seems natural.

He's not a replacement Danny. He's just Cal – the man who has helped me through the worst moments of my life, who came into my life despite the fact I must have been as much a source of pain for him as he was for me.

We kiss. And then we go back to the hotel and deal with what's been building for months.

And at 5 a.m. that morning, drunk on what we think is love but is definitely alcohol, we get married in a Vegas chapel.

They keep putting it in movies because it keeps happening in real life.

I've done the walk of shame before.

I've done it in clothes smelling of alcohol and cigarette smoke and a headache that could blind you. I've done it giggling about the night before and I've done it asking myself, on loop, what the fuck I was thinking.

I've never done it with a marriage license.

The regrets set in with the hangover and the flight back to New York.

I don't regret sleeping with Cal.

But getting married – in Vegas of all places – the mortifying cliché of it all.

I can't bear the thought of telling my family. Of telling anybody.

I'm going to say it, even if Cal is too embarrassed to bring it up. He's sitting in the plane seat beside me, staring out the little window, his Adam's apple bobbing with every nervous swallow.

'All so I wouldn't have an empty ring finger,' I say.

I can't even look down at my hand.

Danny's ring is still there. In the early hours, I agreed we could buy a new one when we returned to New York and, hey, a ring was a ring.

Cal hangs his head.

'It's not that I don't want to be married to you,' he groans.

'God, you don't even have to say that, Cal. I really care for you, too. We're both still dealing with so much; it's only been a year since Danny and Lauren. And, sure, it's not what defines us but neither of us could claim to be completely on top of things. I don't think we should go too hard on ourselves. It was just a drunken mistake.'

'Getting married to you is not what I'm worried about,' he says. 'It's my family. There are things . . .'

Oh. Fuck.

The realisation dawns on me.

Cal got married without a prenup.

Now I get it.

This, for wealthy Long Island families, is a far greater sin than deciding to get hitched in Las Vegas to a woman you've only known a year, a woman your folks haven't even met.

'We can file for a quickie divorce the second we land,' I say. 'Karla can help. Or maybe you have somebody?'

Cal looks up at me.

'We can't do that,' he says. 'You have to meet my folks and help smooth things over. Erin, stuff happens when I get married. There's a domino effect.'

I open and close my mouth.

I want to get divorced. I don't want to be married again. I want to leave what happened in Vegas in Vegas and for it to be a bad joke in years to come. Hell, maybe I will marry Cal in the future but it will be for the right reasons. This can be a story for a speech at our proper wedding dinner.

But Cal looks so anxious that I'm lost for words.

'I'll bring you to dinner tonight,' he says. 'My father will bring in his legal team, but at least we can deal with it together. Just, when you meet them, don't mention Danny. Or the reason why we did it. Let's just . . . let's just pretend we planned it.'

'Cal!' I exclaim. 'This is ridiculous. We can't be married. We can fix this.'

'We can't just fix it,' he says. 'Erin, there's a clause in my trust. When I get married—'

He stares at me, eyes wide, mouth opening and closing like he can't figure out how to phrase the next bit.

'What?' I say.

'I inherit all my money.'

'What money?'

'All the money in the trust. It's how my grandparents set it up. I get all of it.'

I blink.

'What's all?'

'One hundred million.'

My eyes almost bug out of my head.

And, seconds later, a thought.

'Cal – you didn't . . . ?'

I can't even say it.

He stares at me.

'Erin, really? You really think I'd get married just to get my inheritance? I've had women throwing themselves at me for years. I could have got married at any point. And you think if I was that calculating I wouldn't have thought of the prenup first?'

It sounds a little stupid when he puts it like that.

'I'm sorry,' I say, contrite. 'I'm not thinking straight.'

'We just – we just need to meet my parents and explain,' Cal says.

Then he summons the flight attendant and orders a whiskey.

He looks like he's going to vomit.

I open my mouth to protest but say nothing.

He's panicking. I, of all people, know the signs.

Whatever we have to do – we are going to get divorced or annulled and wipe the slate clean.

Cal might have family problems, but they're not mine.

Not yet, anyhow.

What I've failed to absorb about Cal is that he's used to getting his own way.

Like when I tried to break off contact with him earlier in the year and he refused to let me.

Or when he insisted Lauren's case shouldn't have been closed and tried to get to the bottom of it.

Once Cal is determined to take care of something, he takes care of it.

When we get back to my apartment in Newport, he starts to talk about me moving into the Bellport house.

'Cal, we can talk about that, but let's not rush it. We need to deal with this mistake first.'

He pauses in the act of hauling my bag into the apartment and looks at me, hurt.

'It wasn't a mistake,' he says. 'I mean – it was a mistake, how we did it. But I do want to be married to you, Erin. We spend every minute together as it is. I love being with you. I told you all this.'

I close the apartment door and usher him inside, lest prying ears across the hall are listening. Cal, unlike Danny, finds Mr Novak amusing and he's chatted to him a few times. We're at the stage now that when my neighbour hears Cal's voice, he makes a point of coming out to say hello.

'Cal, we said generic vows in front of a complete stranger with two more strangers as witnesses. "Baby Got Back" is now our song. We've only known each other a year. This is a mistake.'

'You only knew Danny six months.'

'That was different!'

Cal shakes his head, his expression distant.

He's barely listening to me. He's in complete denial.

'We can do it again,' he says, 'in a nicer, better place, planned this time.'

340

Like that's the problem.

'Cal!'

'Why are you yelling at me?'

He looks genuinely shocked, but I've realised I have to shout at him to make it sink in.

'I can't meet your parents tonight and tell them I married their son in Vegas when I haven't met them in the whole year I've known you.'

'You can't not meet them,' he says, gravely. 'The sooner we sort this out legally, the better. Erin, I'm worth a fortune now. Whatever about before, I have to introduce you to them now. Just once, and then we never have to see them again. If we can just get through tonight and sign the papers, it will all be over. Otherwise, my father will never back off. Please. You don't have to say anything. And after – look, if you're really determined to divorce and do it again properly, we can.'

I'm shaking my head now. This isn't happening. It's like a bad dream.

He crosses the room and places his hands on my lower back, pulling me into him. It's like the pause button has been hit; that he realises how upset I am and how this is all moving too fast.

I whimper into the collar of his polo shirt, smelling his aftershave and the scent of the sun on his neck.

'Erin,' he whispers, 'they'll know about the marriage already. I guarantee they will. I don't want them thinking I'm more of a fuck-up than they already do. Can you help me? Please? I'm begging you, Erin.'

'I . . .' I'm lost for words.

He's being manipulative. I know it and he knows it.

341

But he's right.

'Okay.' It comes out like a sigh. 'But once we meet them and you do what you have to do legally, we need to sort this out.'

'Fine,' he says, nodding, but I can tell his head is no longer in the room. 'I'm going to go up there now and smooth the path. I'll send a car for you at seven. Erin, just remember: don't mention Danny. I promised I wouldn't pursue the Lauren thing and you must realise they hate Danny for what he did. They cannot find out you were his wife. Swear to me.'

'Okay,' I say.

'No, swear.'

He's gazing at me, sheer desperation in his eyes.

'I swear,' I say, utterly confused. 'I won't mention Danny.'

'Or Lauren. My mother does not like any talk of Lauren. She wasn't part of our family . . . in her eyes.'

'I don't understand, Cal—'

He inhales deeply.

'Erin, I went . . . I went funny in the head after Lauren. There was talk of a . . .' He hesitates. 'A clinic. I don't want them to think . . . You know I'm not back on drugs. We didn't take anything last night.'

His breathing is becoming panicked.

It's me who puts my arms around him now.

'Cal, it's okay. I get it. I won't say anything.'

Cal stares at me, nodding. He's trembling. I've never seen him like this.

'I promise, we'll fix this,' he says.

I nod, dumbly.

Cal leaves and I collapse on my couch.

I look across at the window.

It's still Danny's anniversary.

Oh my God. I got married on Danny's anniversary.

My phone, off since last night, has not stopped buzzing with texts since I returned. Voice messages and missed calls from my family and from Danny's. Checking in, to make sure I'm handling today okay.

I curl up in a ball of shame and remorse.

What have I done?

Entering the Hawley estate is like driving on to the set of Dynasty.

We pass a gatehouse that's bigger than the home I grew up in.

Then we drive past the man-made lake and curl around the bend towards the palatial residence fronted with Corinthian columns.

And to think, the devil on my shoulder whispers, this could all be yours one day.

But I don't want it. What attracted me to Cal was how he's eschewed all of this. The way he's acted in the last twelve hours has reminded me that he's very much part of it. One hundred million, he said. I knew he was wealthy but I'd no idea what was waiting in the wings. And no matter what he says, I imagine that kind of money, combined with family, is a lot harder to get away from than he lets on.

Cal greets me in the entrance hall, flanked by an older man and woman, both of whom he resembles. He has his father's stature and colouring, his mother's eyes, mouth and kink in the hair.

I tense, and have to restrain myself from running out the door and down the driveway, all the way home to what I know as normal.

These people smell of money and I'm expecting a full frontal attack for luring their eligible bachelor son up the aisle to get my claws into the family fortune.

I'm taking in everything around me, including the security cameras all over the place.

I've worn my best cashmere twinset and tailored trousers, but I feel like the scruffiest person alive. Like those cameras are pointed at me, waiting to see if I'll try to steal something – more than their son, that is.

I'm actually quaking in my slingbacks, desperately wondering if Karla could expedite something over the phone that would convince these people I'm not the money-grabber they must think I am.

'So,' his father says, his voice low and deep. 'You're the woman we have to thank for bringing our son back into our lives.'

Come again?

'I . . .'

Can't even get the words out.

'Cal has told us what happened,' his mother says. 'I can't say we're pleased with the, let's say, rather unorthodox way you both proceeded with this, but from what he's told us, he is very much in love with you. It's just like Cal to go running at something head first and think later. I'm sorry you didn't get the occasion you wanted. We can fix that.'

I look from one to the other of Cal's parents. He's in the middle, his face twisted in half a smile, half panic. He's fallen on his sword, it seems, exonerating me of blame for what happened. But his parents don't appear to be angry with him. They seem proud.

'You look absolutely terrified,' his father says. 'Cal, get the girl

– sorry, get your wife – a drink. We have a little while before dinner. We can talk about the other stuff after.'

Ah. The lawyers.

'Oh, Henry, don't bring that up now,' Cal's mother says. 'I can't imagine for a moment Erin is that sort of girl. We've met plenty of those over the years, believe me.'

Cal's mother laughs. There's no mirth in it.

Just minutes into meeting this family, I can see why Cal has so little to do with them.

He might wear the uniform. He might look and smell like them. But this is not his tribe. Not naturally.

'The lawyers are just a formality,' Mr Hawley says. 'Cal says you completely understand. Now his trust is open, it's important we retrospectively date that prenup.'

'I do understand,' I say, seizing my chance. 'In fact, I think we should just get an annulment.'

Cal's parents smile at me, smile at him, smile at each other.

'I told them you'd say that,' Cal says. 'She doesn't want a cent from me. That's why I love her.'

His parents pat him on the back, benignly, and I know they're both thinking – you poor, happy, lovestruck fool, she probably wants a payout for the annulment.

I'm having the most surreal experience of my life since this time last year.

'Of course, it will be a generous prenup,' Mr Hawley says. 'Nobody could ever accuse Cal of being miserly. I suppose he's told you, Erin, that I've been married a few times. Lana here taught me everything I needed to know about not getting screwed after she well and truly screwed me the first time.'

Cal's parents laugh again.

I am dying inside.

Floating on a cloud of disbelief, I let myself be ushered into what I think they call the receiving room and then accept a glass of amber liquid from Mr Hawley.

Maybe it's my destiny. To spend this day every year in a dream-like state, not really knowing what the fuck is going on or how I can make it better.

The Hawleys make polite small talk while I come across as the village idiot, with monosyllabic answers and a vague, daft look on my face.

I imagine they're thinking – she's not pretty enough to be that dumb, what the hell does he see in her?

But they are so very polite and Cal makes up for my confused silence by enthusiastically filling them in on my job and my family.

He's selling me, I realise.

I guess I don't come across as the worst. These people know what a proper gold-digger looks like. Once I sign all the relevant forms I might even be welcomed with open arms. After all, I'm educated, I'm presentable – sort of. I'm exotic. You sidestep the class thing – who's who in your family – when you're from outside the circle and a foreigner. I could tell them I'm loosely related to an old European aristocratic family and they'd be in raptures.

Lana is going to check on the table and she demands Cal join her, as though the positioning of the place settings is a special expertise of his.

I'm being left with the boss, Henry, who I presume is going to sniff me out properly when we're alone. Divide and conquer.

Cal doesn't want to go with his mother. He doesn't want me left alone with his father.

I get that.

But his mother is insistent.

'You'll be okay?' He pulls me to one side, his whisper low and urgent.

'I'll be fine,' I say. 'I can make small talk until you come back.'

Cal still looks unsure but he follows his mother.

'So, editing,' Henry says, pouring more bourbon from a crystal decanter. He offers me some, but I decline. I don't need to impress him. I don't want to drink, I won't drink. Walking away from his son's fortune will impress him more than anything.

He smiles.

'I like a woman who knows her own mind,' he says.

I can't take it any more.

'I'm really sorry to be meeting you like this,' I blurt out. 'It's absolutely insane.'

'It is a little. I've met a fair few of Cal's girls over the years but none in quite such exciting fashion. He did say you were different, though. I'm rather intrigued as to what about you attracted my son so strongly.'

'I wasn't trying to attract him. We've been growing close but this wasn't meant to happen. At least, not this way.'

Henry studies me over his bourbon, lips pursed, a hint of a smile at their corners.

I think, even in a few short minutes, he's already gauged I'm not a threat.

Now he's just playing with me.

'You shouldn't entirely blame yourself,' he says. 'Perhaps if Cal and I had been on better speaking terms we'd have met you earlier. And Lana would never have let you both take that flight to Vegas. We all know what happens in Vegas when people get drunk and stupid. Cal's spontaneity has backfired on us before.'

I don't know what he means by that but I'm stung at how little value he places on Cal's choices. We might have gone about this all wrong but Cal hasn't been duped by me and he's chased me a lot more than I've chased him.

'I am sorry,' I say. I'm no match for somebody like Henry Hawley, who probably chews and spits out people cleverer than me most days of the week.

'I genuinely do want to make it so it never happened,' I say. 'You don't need to worry about protecting Cal. I don't want anything from him, bar his companionship. We're fond of each other but everything this year has been so intense. I'm not ready for this, especially after . . .'

I trail off. I've sworn not to mention Danny or how Cal and I met.

Henry, though, isn't one for letting details go.

'After what?' he asks, his head cocked.

I struggle for something. I look around the room, every piece worthy of a case in a museum, and spot a family portrait on the wall. Henry and Lana, with Cal between them. All their mouths are set in straight lines.

A small, unhappy family.

'My sister died a few years ago,' I say. 'This year was tough for a few reasons but it helped meeting somebody who'd . . .' I gulp. Should I mention Lauren at all?

'Who'd what?'

Too late now.

My polite grief etiquette gets the better of me.

'I am so sorry about what happened to your daughter,' I say.

'Who?'

I blink.

'Your daughter? Cal's stepsister.'

He stares at me, genuine confusion on his face.

'I'm sorry, I—' I stop, unsure how to proceed.

'I don't know who you're talking about,' he says.

Henry is staring at me like I'm insane.

I feel insane.

'I don't have any daughters,' he says, harshly.

I try to speak but my tongue is fat and heavy in my mouth.

I swallow and try again.

'His stepsister, Lauren?'

Henry frowns, then his face fills with realisation, followed quickly by something more . . . sinister.

'Cal doesn't have any siblings, step or otherwise,' he says.

I back away from Henry and find myself out in the entrance hall.

I presume somebody is going to stop me, but there's nobody there.

So I open the huge front door and run down the steps. By the side of the house, the car that brought me here this evening is parked up, its driver resting against the bonnet, smoking a cigarette. He sees me running towards him and drops the butt.

'Please,' I cry. 'Get me out of here.'

The front door of the house behind me is flung open.

I hear Cal yelling my name.

'Erin!'

The driver looks at me. He's opened the car door for me, a look of hesitation on his face.

'I'm begging you,' I plead, and it's an effort because I'm almost hyperventilating.

He nods.

He's just closed his own door when Cal starts banging on my window.

'Erin,' he shouts.

I smack the window with such force, I'm surprised it doesn't break.

'You lied to me!' I scream. Then, to the driver, 'Go!'

I don't hear what Cal yells before the wheels spin on the gravel and we're driving away.

I have no idea who the fuck I'm dealing with.

Again.

I'm not sure why I have the car drive me to Ben Mitchell's house.

My head is telling me to go to Karla or Bud, but instinct takes over.

As we zip up Sunrise Highway I learn from the driver that he's not an employee of the Hawleys, which is good. He might get into trouble with his agency but he's not answerable to Cal.

'Hey, I'm only doing this to pay my tuition,' he says.

He doesn't want to take any money off me, but I give him fifty when we pull up outside Ben's house and ask him to let me wait in the car for a little while.

It's Wednesday night and, to the best of my recollection, Christina has book club with the girls midweek. When I first moved here, she tried to convince me to go with her. I had no interest in spending time with her, let alone talking about books, which would have been a busman's holiday for me.

Sure enough, shortly before 21:00 on the dashboard clock, the garage door opens in the Mitchells' home. Christina pulls out in her SUV. I lower myself in the back seat as she drives past. This is the kind of neighbourhood where a strange vehicle is noticed, but thankfully, Christina shows no interest in the black sedan.

When the coast is clear, I hop out.

'You want me to wait?' the driver asks.

I hesitate.

'I think I'm okay,' I say.

I'm still shaking. Even I'm not convinced.

He hands me a card through the driver's window.

'Call, if you need me,' he says. 'If I'm on a job, I'll send one of the guys out to you.'

I'm so touched by this random act of kindness from a stranger that I almost sob.

Then I think – what if he wants to keep tabs on me because Cal asked him to?

My trust in people is decimated.

I take the card anyway, scrunching it in my hand.

The porch light comes on as I run up the steps to Ben's front door.

I ring the bell. From inside, I hear Ben coming down the stairs, yelling to his kids to get back into bed at the same time.

He opens the door and stares at me.

I guess I look a fright because his face pales. He steps out, peers up and down the street and then steps back in, beckoning me to do the same. He closes the door quickly behind me.

'Why are you here?' he asks.

'Who the fuck is Cal Hawley?' I sob.

Ben's face hardens into a grimace.

'You need to stay away from him.'

'I can't stay away from him,' I almost yell. 'I'm married to him!'

Ben's jaw drops at the same time as one of his kids appears on the top step.

'Daddy?'

'Go to bed!' Ben roars. Then he pivots, immediately contrite.

'I'm so sorry, honey,' he says. 'Daddy just got some bad news. Jump into bed and I'll be up soon with some warm milk.'

The child, still stunned, runs off into his room.

'What the hell were you thinking?' Ben says.

He storms into the kitchen. I trail in his wake.

'It was a mistake,' I say, as he throws open drawers and cupboards, finds a pot and bangs it on to the stovetop.

'I thought he was just after you to see what you knew. That's what he said.'

Ben's talking about me, but it's like I'm not even there, not even a real person.

Still, the room spins as these words leave Ben's mouth and register with me.

'I didn't know you were . . .' Ben smacks his hands against the counter, hard, making a thumping sound. 'Jesus Christ, Erin. Do you know what you've done?'

I panic. Ben wouldn't hurt me with his kids in the house, would he?

'No,' I whisper. 'I don't. I don't know who he is. I don't know what's going on. You need to tell me.'

Ben squeezes his eyes shut.

He's shaking.

And suddenly, I realise he's not angry.

He's scared.

'That man is dangerous,' Ben says.

I can barely process the words.

Cal. The man who's never so much as raised his voice since I've known him.

'Dangerous how?'

I'm shaking now.

There's a stool behind me, thank God, and I come to sit on it without even being aware I've stepped back.

'What did he tell you?' Ben said.

'He told me . . . he told me his stepsister Lauren had been raped. He said Danny had handled the case and let her down and Danny had approached him after she died to try to fix things. But—'

I don't even know how to say it.

How do I put into words what Cal had lied about?

It sounds nuts.

'Lauren wasn't Cal's sister,' Ben says.

This day last year, I fainted just feet away from Ben.

The last thing I see now is a carton of milk as my head hits the breakfast island.

When I come round, it takes me a few minutes to realise where I am.

The room is dimly lit – I'm lying on a comfortable couch but I don't recognise the bookshelves on the walls or the toys strewn across the floor.

Ben is holding an ice-pack against my forehead.

'It's just a cut,' he says. 'I've applied a Band-Aid; I don't think you need stitches. It'll hurt, though.'

I sit up, gingerly, because my head is banging and my neck feels funny.

'You knew,' I choke out, the words thick on my tongue.

'I know what he's capable of,' Ben said. 'I was there when Ally brought Lauren in.'

The spots in front of my eyes are dancing. I blink and my eyes fill with tears.

'What did Cal do?' I ask Ben.

Ben shudders.

He shudders.

'You have to get away from him,' Ben says.

'How? Ben, tell me what he did.'

Ben hangs his head.

'I should have protected you,' he says.

'Ben, I don't care what you did or didn't do. Are you going to help me now?'

Ben raises his head.

'Yes,' he says.

I nod, even though my head is aching.

'You'll help me,' I say.

He nods back.

'Tell me everything I need to know,' I say.

'I've lied to you,' he says. 'But it was only to protect you. Mainly, though – and I'm so sorry about this, Erin – it was to protect myself.'

Now

I only met Henry J. Hawley once.

And our meeting lasted for less than a half hour.

He's been subpoenaed to appear by the defence.

He doesn't want to be here at all. If he did, he'd have been called by the prosecution and come willingly.

According to Karla, his very-well-paid attorneys tried everything to prevent him being called. Then they decided it was in his best interests to comply; at least this way it doesn't look like he's trying to be obstructive.

He is what they call 'a hostile witness'.

His body language tells me he's going to play very hard to the jury's sense of the grieving father. Lana Hawley, the grieving mother, has been sitting in the court since the trial started, aiming daggers at the back of my head.

The judge, Prosecutor Roberts, the jury and pretty much everybody in the court is probably wondering why on earth we've called him to the stand if not to bury my defence.

But we had to call him. He's one of only a few people who know the truth.

Karla is wearing her best blue suit with the white blouse that I know has a little rip at the seam, so she won't be taking that jacket off.

It works – because the heating is flaring again, we're all sweating, and Karla looks too cool for school.

'Mr Hawley, I appreciate your coming here today,' she says, as she stands.

'I had no choice,' Henry says.

'Indeed.'

'And I would have preferred to appear for the prosecution.'

'Understandable. You know my client, Erin Kennedy?'

'Yes.'

'But not very well.'

'I know *of* her very well. She's ruined our lives.'

'Erin contends she has done nothing wrong,' Karla says. Before Henry can offer any further opinion, she speaks again.

'You only met her briefly, did you not?'

'Yes.'

Henry shifts uncomfortably.

'She came to your home after she and Cal, your son, got married in Las Vegas.'

'She did.'

'And on that night—'

'She came and she left in a hurry,' Henry butts in. This is a man used to speaking when he wants, not when he's allowed.

'Why don't you tell us what happened that night,' Karla says.

'That woman.' He glares at me. If looks could kill. 'That woman talked my son into marrying her. He was incapacitated. I have multiple witnesses at the hotel and wedding chapel that night who say Erin Kennedy practically held a bottle of alcohol to Cal's lips to get him up the aisle.'

Baloney. I was drunker than Cal.

'When they arrived at our house, supposedly to celebrate their nuptials, she got the shock of her life. I had my legal team there. As soon as she realised a prenuptial agreement could be retrospectively applied, she skedaddled. I didn't even have time to bring the suits into the room.'

Some head shaking from some of the jurors. I don't know if that's because they believe him, or if they know what's coming. They heard Ally's testimony, after all. They now know Lauren Gregory existed and what happened to her. They know what Danny did and didn't do. And they know that Ally believed Lauren was raped by somebody with a lot of money to cover his tracks.

Now we're going to tell them who raped her.

I haven't met them yet, but I know that Lauren's mother, Belinda, and her brother, George, are sitting in court today. I know because David Fox found them and made sure they knew what was coming. He's brought them here today, just to hear Henry tell his lies.

'You claim Erin left because you wanted her to sign a prenup?' Karla continues.

'That's true, yes.'

'But didn't she put in a call to her lawyer – that's me – the next day, initiating the annulment process for the sham marriage? I have the emails we exchanged with your son, cc'd to you, right here. Shall I read these emails to you?'

'I know what's in the emails.'

'There's no reference to money at all in these exchanges. Erin doesn't ask Cal for a cent. She asks him to stay away from her. Does that sound like the action of a woman who married your son for money? Surely, even with a prenup, she would still be living in the lap of luxury?'

'It sounds like a woman who knows she was found out.'

Karla frowns.

'You have heard of Lauren Gregory, have you not?' Karla asks.

'No.'

So much for the oath.

'I remind you, Mr Hawley, you have sworn to tell the whole truth—'

'I know what I swore.'

'Did Erin Kennedy not tell you on the night she came to your house that she believed Lauren Gregory to be Cal's stepsister? That she had been told this by Cal?'

'I didn't know what she was talking about. She might have been rabbiting about a girl of that name. She was saying anything and everything to try to get around the fact she would later that evening be meeting my lawyers. And, I might add, while she's repeated that claim that my son told her he had a sister, she hasn't been able to bring forward any single other person to whom he made these wild claims.'

That's true. Cal never spoke about Lauren to anybody but me. Always so clever.

'So, you have categorically never heard of Lauren Gregory?' Karla says.

'No.'

'Have you heard of Danny Ryan?'

'Yes.'

'You know that Erin Kennedy was married to Danny?'

'Yes.'

'Are you aware that Danny Ryan was paid a large sum of money, we believe to cover up what had happened to Lauren Gregory?'

'I am not.'

'You dispute that your son paid Danny Ryan to cover up Cal's role in the rape of Lauren Gregory?'

'Objection!' This from the prosecutor.

Judge Palmer, listening as raptly as the rest of us, sits up.

'Sustained. Counsellor, neither Cal nor Henry Hawley are on trial here.'

'I withdraw it, Your Honour. Mr Hawley, did anybody in your family ever pay a sum of money to Danny Ryan?'

'Not that I'm aware of.'

'Are you aware that Lauren Gregory made an accusation of rape against your son and subsequently, inexplicably, dropped the charges? I have her original statement here, made to Detectives Danny Ryan and Ben Mitchell, as provided to me by Ben Mitchell.'

'I believe nobody is named in that statement as her attacker.'

'That is correct,' Karla says. 'But we do have the email that Lauren sent to her proctor, Ally Summers. She names Cal as her rapist and tells Ally that, while she'd stopped short of naming him in her police interview, she did, in fact, tell Danny Ryan his name before she left the police station.'

That's why we needed Henry on the stand. To put all this to him and have him deny it.

So when we connect that money in Danny's account to a foundation under the Hawley family's business umbrella, Henry will have perjured himself in court.

'It seems to me that the words of a dead girl concerning a dead man are irrelevant to whether or not Erin Kennedy murdered my son,' Henry says.

Then he meets my eye.

He'll talk his way around all this but he knows and I know what the Hawleys did.

Then

Karla issues Cal with an immediate warning letter. It's not a restraining order – for that, he needs to have harmed me in some way – but she words it in such a way that says, 'Come near my client, motherfucker, and you'll regret it for the rest of your life.'

In legalese.

Then she puts the annulment in process.

I find Bud pacing outside my apartment block the next night.

He's packing a Glock.

'Bud. What on earth?'

I've come downstairs to meet Ben.

Last night, Ben stopped short of telling me everything. He said he needed to sort out somewhere for Christina and his kids to go. The way he acted – like he was absolutely terrified – it scared even me, and I got a glimpse, just for a moment, of why he'd acted like an absolute coward for the last year. When it comes to family, there's little you won't do to keep them safe.

Tonight, Ben is going to tell me everything.

I have a new phone, a new number, a new email address. Everyone who needs to know how to contact me, knows.

'I'm going to shoot him in the head if he comes here,' Bud says.

I take a deep breath. I don't want Bud knowing I'm frightened. So, I turn on the sarcasm.

'I thought you liked him?'

'I did,' Bud says, and for a moment he looks so lost, my heart goes out to him.

'It just goes to show,' he adds. 'You cannot trust people with money.'

Ben pulls up as I'm remonstrating with Bud to go back to the bar and put the gun somewhere safe.

'I'm going in with her,' Ben says.

'Am I supposed to be glad about that?' Bud asks.

Ben says nothing.

Bud checks with me. I nod, grimly.

He shrugs and slopes off back towards the bar, still toting his gun.

'What do you expect?' I say to Ben.

'Nothing,' he says.

We go inside.

I take care to check the main door is locked behind us.

'I keep expecting him to just turn up,' I say.

'The first thing you need to know about Cal Hawley is that he has other people do his dirty work for him,' Ben says, as we wait for the elevator.

I stare at him. For a moment, a horrifying thought crosses my mind.

Could Ben have been sent by Cal?

'Has he ever hurt somebody that way?' I say. 'I mean, is he capable of killing me?'

'He killed Danny,' Ben says.

In the hall outside the apartment, I'm stopped by my neighbour, Mr Novak.

'I was talking to your, eh, new husband,' he says. 'Congratulations.'

I freeze, before realising that he must have seen Cal yesterday, after we got back from Vegas.

'He won't be coming around here again,' I snap.

Mr Novak raises his eyebrows.

'Sorry,' I say. 'We're not together any more. If you see him, will you let me know? He shouldn't be in here.'

Mr Novak nods and retreats into his own apartment.

Inside mine, I don't put on coffee or offer Ben a beer. We sit facing each other at the kitchen table: him nervously picking at the cuffs of his shirt, me trying to keep my breathing even.

'Tell me from the start,' I begin.

Ben nods. He takes a deep breath.

'Cal Hawley met Lauren Gregory at a Harvard drinks party, in her first term. He was back for an alumni event; she was serving cocktails. According to her initial statement, at first she found him charming, kind, very attractive. She didn't name him in that interview. After, when she was leaving, and the tape recorder was off, she told us then. In the interviews, she said he was older. He had money. He brought her out on a few nights in New York and spoiled her. Didn't push for too much. He seemed laid-back. Sensitive, was how she described him.'

I shudder.

Didn't I think the exact same?

'They had a few dates but Lauren was trying to concentrate on her studies. She wanted to keep her head down, graduate and get a good job. Cal was easy-going to start but he was a man used to getting his own way.

'She went out with him that night in Manhattan, thinking they were just going to have dinner. He'd booked a fancy hotel, a five-star restaurant, and she thought it was a little over the top, but she was enjoying herself. He was enjoying himself, too. A bit too much. He came back from the restroom at one point and it was obvious, she said, that he'd taken something. But she didn't want to complain and she found herself going along with it . . . you know how this story goes, Erin.'

He looks up at me.

I do. Except I wasn't as clever as Lauren. I went along with it right up to and including jumping off the cliff.

'When they went up to the hotel room, she started to have second thoughts. He was acting odd, she said. Complaining about his father running his life, getting agitated. He was drinking heavily and didn't seem in control of himself. She tried to blow him off gently. She said she was tired and wanted to go home. He got pushy, she got defensive. They argued. She reminded him she was only eighteen, she'd just started college, she didn't want to get into anything too intense. He got upset, said she was a gold-digger. She was alarmed by that, by how quickly he turned. She decided to just leave. He wouldn't let her.'

Ben takes another breath.

'She never saw it coming. He punched her in the face to disable her. Then he raped her. She said she found the aftermath the most terrifying bit. He seemed torn between what looked like genuine remorse and protecting himself. He told her it was just sex; they'd done it before. Then he said if she reported him, nobody would believe her. He came from money, she came from nothing, etc., etc. He could ruin her life. Then he started to cry, told her his father would kill him. She said she almost felt sorry for him.'

'But she reported him anyway.'

'It took a lot of strength and courage. Ally talked her into it and only because she thought Danny could be trusted.'

Ben hangs his head.

I'm pretty sure I've stopped breathing.

'We took her statement. It was going to be a tough one. Her injuries had faded; she had no witnesses. But we knew she wasn't lying. We called out to Cal's Manhattan apartment to pick him up. That's when we met his daddy and his lawyers. Cal had already been moved – probably home, but we didn't know.'

I shake my head. Ben fiddles with the ends of his shirtsleeves. This is painful for him. Not as much as it is for me, but he's uncomfortable.

'Erin, you have to understand something. Neither Danny nor I had much by way of evidence. The conviction rates for prosecuting rape in NYC at the time were appalling. Still are. Hawley Sr. promised the girl would be taken care of. That Cal would be taken care of in quite a different manner. He implied we'd also be looked after but he was very careful not to mention money. Then we were sent details of bank accounts that had been opened in our names, anonymously. That's the money in one of Danny's accounts – the one the department doesn't know about. I got the same. He never spent a cent of his.'

'What the hell, Ben?'

'I've lived with this every day since it happened, Erin. I can't offer an excuse or a reason other than we were greedy, stupid, scared motherfuckers and Hawley was smarter than us. He offered the carrot and the stick. Walk away and be wealthy and untouched, or keep going and find ourselves fucked over seven which ways. He already knew about us, Erin. He knew my folks had problems with the IRS. He knew Danny had buried a DUI and an assault charge for Mike so Mike wouldn't have a record when he applied for the army. He also told us Lauren's mother was working off the books, so her income hadn't affected Lauren's grant aid when she secured her place at Harvard. He'd managed to gather all this information in a few hours. A few hours. We were scared shitless, Erin.'

I'd met Henry J. Hawley last night. I didn't doubt what Ben was saying. He'd do whatever he had to to protect his son.

What was shocking was other people going along with it.

'We let the case go,' Ben says. 'Danny went to visit Lauren and explained the evidence just didn't meet the standard required to convict. She'd been seen at dinner with Cal. She'd gone up to his hotel room. She'd been out with him plenty of times before. Lauren already had doubts anybody would believe her. We cemented those doubts.'

'Why didn't anybody stop you? In your station? The other officers who'd seen her come in?'

'We were in charge of the case. Lauren dropped the complaint. Eyebrows were raised, a few soft questions. We saw it through. Then we put in for transfers. Me first. I wanted a quiet life for my family and couldn't have that in Manhattan. I moved out here with Christina. A month or so later, once I was settled, I suggested Danny for a job. He applied and he got it. Ally dumped him, straight away. It should have been all over. Then you happened.'

'Me?'

'Once you told Danny what happened to your sister, it started to eat away at him. First, he started going to the shrink. Every week. I'd drive him there. He needed to talk to somebody. He never told her what happened, just that he had demons, and I think she tried to help, but how could she when she didn't know everything? It seemed to keep him going, though. But then Lauren committed suicide. When Danny found out, he couldn't hack it any longer. He wanted to confess. He made the ultimate fucking mistake. He confronted Cal Hawley, told him he was going to bring it to our bosses and fall on his sword. He'd leave me out of it, take the blame himself. He offered Cal the option of coming forward with him, of letting Lauren's family know he was sorry and making amends.'

I moan, softly. All of this had been going on and I'd had no idea. No idea.

'You should know, it wasn't all just Cal. His father has a lot of power. But Cal didn't fall that far from the tree. They started to mind-fuck Danny. Danny got emails about you – how you'd been about to lose your visa when he married you. Next thing, Danny's cases are being reopened. Any dodgy step he ever took and even hints at things where he was straight down the line. You know what it's like, Erin. Throw mud. And it would have been difficult for him to out the Hawleys with his name already tarnished. The Hawley family are solid supporters of the police benevolent fund, Erin. Sully has been to fundraisers in their mansion.'

I swallow.

'What did he do?' I ask.

'Danny knew what was happening, so he confronted Cal again. Cal told him it was just the start. He kept increasing the pressure and Danny kept coming back saying he wouldn't back off. But

Danny was starting to crack. He stopped going to the shrink. Erin – that is something I'll never forgive myself for. I should have talked him into sticking with her. I think Danny had real issues at that point. He loved you more than anything but you were this constant reminder of Lauren and what we did to her. He wasn't acting rationally. He'd gone all weird on me – he pulled his gun on me once. And he was a loose cannon with suspects. I had to pull him off a guy in an interview, and even I started to think they were telling the truth about the Dwayne Miller case. Danny was ready to snap and nothing I or anybody could say could fix it.'

'He was never like that at home!' I say. 'I never saw him be violent, not once. I don't recognise this man you're telling me about.'

'Why do you think he snapped, Erin? Can you imagine what it was like keeping all that separate from you? All that stress?'

My eyes fill with tears.

'And then they found out he'd all that money,' Ben says.

He stares at the table.

I sit, perfectly still, waiting.

'Danny was in a bind. That account wasn't his. He hadn't set it up. But he did have a secret account, we both did. I'd spent mine but Danny still had the full $100K in his. The Hawleys didn't know that, though – I guess they'd have just alerted our bosses to the original bribe account if they did, save themselves the money. But setting up the new account in his name was their way of reminding Danny how easily they could plant evidence; a little twisted reminder that they'd already paid him $100K and could stitch him up with that amount. Cal told him it would get worse. He'd destroy Danny, he'd destroy me, he'd destroy you and Christina and everyone we loved. Whatever about Danny admitting to you what he'd done, he couldn't risk anything bad happening to you. And at the same time, he couldn't go on.

'Then, I was summoned by the captain and told about the arrest. I warned Danny, Erin. I told him to take you and get out of the State. I stalled the arrest. It was meant to happen the night before. You know what Danny said? He said, You won't come for me. Not you, Ben. But I had to. I had to. Do you understand? It was Danny or me. When I came to the door that morning – I think he knew it was over. If I wasn't going to back him up . . .'

I stand and walk around the table, coolly.

Then I take all my rage and fury out on Ben Mitchell.

I slap and I hit and I even try to get my hands on his neck so I can squeeze the life out of him.

Ben defends himself, half-heartedly.

'You should have told me,' I choke out. 'You should have told me!'

'He made me swear!' Ben says. He takes my hands, firmly, which is easy for him because he's so much stronger than me.

Even though he has me under control, he's the one who looks shattered.

'He made me swear never to tell you,' Ben says. 'He said if any-thing ever happened to him, if he couldn't tell you himself, he never wanted you to know. He might have lost his mind but that was the one thing he was adamant about. I didn't know he was going to kill himself. It broke my heart, Erin. It broke me.'

'You saw Cal getting close to me,' I moan.

'I tried to warn you. I have three kids. I had to protect them. I told you, didn't I? I loved Danny. The only people I love more are my kids. If the Hawley family come after me and Christina, who'll take care of my kids?'

'Why did he come after me?' I whisper. 'What did Cal Hawley want with me?'

'He wanted to know what you knew,' Ben says. 'Everything else – Erin, he's fucking insane.'

I bury my head in my knees.

I slept with that *man*, I think.

'I'm going to kill him,' I say.

I know Cal is coming.

I'm sure he's watching me and I spend the day after Ben tells me everything in a state of anxiety mixed with anticipation.

I want him to come.

Ben doesn't know yet if I'm going to ask him to admit everything but he says he'll do whatever I want of him; that he owes me and Danny that.

I don't know what I want.

Karla and Bud, who know enough now to be extremely worried, check in. She doesn't want me staying in the apartment. I tell her I'm fine. Bud is outside with his gun again and I tell him to go home, that I need some space.

Leslie rings and offers to come over.

I give her the same line.

'You knew there was something off with him,' I say.

'Yes,' she says. 'But not that he was capable of that sort of lying. I never, ever would have suspected this, Erin.'

I believe her. Who would have?

She reluctantly lets me go.

I sound like I'm handling everything.

I am. Just not the way they think.

The minutes tick by until dark.

I go for a run.

I shower.

I drink coffee.

And I wait.

It's not long after the sun sets that Cal's key turns in the door.

I hear him jiggle it. When I gave him the key a few weeks ago, I explained the problem with the lock.

You practically have to whisper to it, I said.

He opens it.

I'm sitting at the kitchen table, the same place I sat with Ben.

Cal is wearing a cap, a dark hoodie and running bottoms.

He's as handsome as the first day I met him.

His face has that honest, sincere expression I had grown to love.

And I thought Danny was a good actor.

'Erin,' he says, his voice breaking on my name.

'Cal.'

'Can I come in?'

'You've let yourself in.'

He stares at me. He doesn't know what to expect but it's probably not this.

He turns, shuts the door then comes towards me.

He hovers over me, then plants a kiss on my head.

I wince.

He notices and takes the seat across from me, not beside me.

'I won't hurt you,' he says. 'I'd never harm you.'

'You already have,' I say.

'I didn't mean to. Once I got to know you – you have to believe me – I regretted so much that you got caught up in this.'

'I was collateral damage, huh?'

Cal hangs his head.

'Erin, I made one stupid mistake. I'm not even going to pretend I didn't do something wrong. All I'll ask you to understand is that I was brought up with a sense of entitlement. It screws up your head. I expected people to give me what I wanted. She – Lauren – didn't. I wasn't in my right mind. I'd taken drugs and she was my girlfriend and I . . . fuck, there's no excuse. I should have suffered the consequences, but my father stepped in. That's what he does. It's what he's always done. You can see now why I'm practically estranged from them.'

'I don't care what you did or how you dealt with it, then,' I say. 'You told me she was your stepsister. You inveigled your way into my life after your actions resulted in my husband killing himself. You shattered my world then made yourself part of it. You're a psychopath.'

He shakes his head.

'I was only trying to protect myself. If Danny hadn't given in to my father back then, I would have had to deal with my shit. But he left me to get my act together and then he comes back two years later and says he's going to blow up my life? That he's even going to blow up his own? Whether he was alive or dead, Erin, you were going to suffer. If he'd sat across from you and told you what he'd done to Lauren, would you have accepted that? After what happened to Niamh?'

The pain I feel is physical.

Cal is right.

Danny was not the man I thought he was.

'But why, why did you say you were related to Lauren?' I ask, but before he can answer, I tell him. 'Because you knew how my sister had died. You knew how to manipulate me. It was the perfect lie.'

He hangs his head.

'I didn't know how else to—'

'You could have established I knew nothing and then walked out of my life,' I interrupt. 'I tried to push you away. You were the one who insisted on us getting close.'

'Because I wanted you! I could see exactly what Danny could. A person can change. I changed. Nobody's all good or all bad. Look at Danny!'

I swallow back the bile in my throat.

Cal puts his head in his hands and rubs his hair, roughly. When he looks up at me, his expression is so desperate, I feel the tug. I hate myself for it, but I feel the tug.

'What do you want to do?' he says. 'How can I make this better? It doesn't need to end this way. We can stay together. You don't even need to sign the prenup. We can put all this behind us. You'll be a wealthy woman. I love you. That isn't a lie. I know I hurt that girl and I have to live with it but does that mean being punished for the rest of my life? I will never, ever hurt you.'

Ha! Somebody else told me that, once.

'Why did you let me meet your parents?' I ask. 'You must have known I'd find out about Lauren.'

'It was just one night. I thought we could get through one night and then we wouldn't need to see them again. I had to have you there to sign the legal documents or they would never have left us alone. We could have moved. Used my money and just got away. You'd never have known.'

I push my chair out and stand up. Cal jumps at the screech of the legs on the wooden floor.

'There's something wrong with you,' I say. 'I don't believe you. I think you knew I'd find out, somehow. You just figured you could talk me round. You were playing sick games with me.'

'No.'

'I want you to give me a divorce.'

Silence. Cal stares at the floor. Then:

'If that's what you want.'

'Then I want you to come to the police with me.'

'I'm not going to the police, Erin.'

'You need to come to the police with me and tell them what you did.'

'No.'

'Yes!'

I've shouted. I didn't mean to shout.

It's just so hard to keep it together in the face of this . . . monster.

'If you are remorseful,' I say, quietly, 'if you really feel sorry for what you've done, then you'll fix this. Show me that you're not the person I think you are. Show me.'

I stare at him, pleading silently.

I want to see something in him, anything, some sign of repentance. Not so I can forgive him. So I can forgive myself for being taken in by him.

He stares back and I see it – something I haven't noticed before. When he's not wearing that pained expression, his eyes are blank. Completely blank.

'I'm not going to the police, Erin, and you're not going to the police. I know you have your little pal Ben filling you in but he's not going to back you up. He doesn't want to end up like Danny, do you understand? And think of Danny's mother. Do you want her to know what he was capable of? Or his brother?'

I feel rage coursing through me.

He is so fucking calm.

Cal is prepared for every outcome. Me willing to be complicit. Me standing up to him. Whatever way I come at him, he's not going to flinch.

So I pick up the vase from the breakfast counter and throw that at him, just to get a reaction.

He ducks. The vase smashes on the floor.

'You motherfucker,' I say. 'You might have had something over Ben and Danny but you've nothing on me. You've nothing on my family.'

'Erin, my family don't need anything on you. We can just make something up.'

There it is.

The mask has slipped.

That's my Cal standing there, and yet it's like another person has walked into the room.

I fly at him. I don't reach him. He stops me with a single punch to my face.

I fall flat on the floor, my head slams against the wood; I feel the ghost of the pain from two days ago when I fainted in Ben's kitchen.

'Erin!'

He's by my side instantly.

'God damn it,' he moans. 'I didn't mean to hit you.'

I gaze at the ceiling in a daze. I feel his hands on me, cradling my neck, holding me gently.

I shove him away with all my strength.

He slams into the breakfast counter and gasps.

I flip on to my front and push myself up on to all fours.

'I'm phoning the police,' I say, through a mouthful of blood.

I'm crawling away when my leg is pulled out from underneath me.

He flips me back over and pins me to the ground.

'You are not phoning the fucking police,' Cal hisses.

A couple of days ago, I was lying under this man and he was making love to me and I wanted to be there. I wanted to be with him.

I think of how he must have pinned Lauren down like this. How astonished she must have been at the sudden turn.

I think of how my sister had been pinned down like this.

It is not going to end like that for me.

I spit in his face.

He frowns and lifts his hand to wipe it from his eye.

It's all I need. I reach for the broken piece of glass lying near my right shoulder, a shard from the vase. I thrust it into his back.

He screams and falls off me.

'You fucking . . .'

I scramble to my feet.

That's when I see the wine bottle.

I'll tell them later that when I left my apartment Cal Hawley was still there and still alive.

Ben takes one look at me and grabs his car keys.

'I'm taking you to the hospital,' he says.

'No,' I say. 'We need to go back.'

'Back where?'

'I've locked him in my apartment.'

Ben turns and stares at me.

'What have you done?'

'I defended myself,' I say. 'I did what you and Danny couldn't. I stood up to him.'

We drive in silence and at speed.

When I left the apartment, I locked it from the outside.

When Ben and I arrive the door is unlocked.

'Shit,' I moan. 'I forgot he had a key.'

My apartment is like an abattoir. There's blood everywhere. Far more blood than when I left, to my eye.

It looks like the scene of a crime.

But Cal is nowhere to be seen.

'Fuck!' Ben cries. 'What have you done?'

I place my hand calmly on his arm.

'Ben,' I say. 'You need to phone this in.'

He hesitates. He's actually thinking of helping me clean this up.

I shake my head.

I want everybody to know what Cal Hawley did.

What Danny did.

Ben can live with his own conscience.

'Ben, I'm going to leave you out of it,' I say. 'All of it. You can say you didn't know what Danny did to Lauren. I need you, on the force, helping me. I need to prove what Cal did. He'll come for me again, otherwise.'

He stares at me, then he nods.

When the cops come – that's when it starts to turn.

Cal can't be located.

Forensics arrive at the apartment.

Ben is taken off somewhere to give a statement.

She's a friend of mine, he tells them. But he doesn't know what happened here.

I tell the police my story. I tell them about the fight and how I defended myself, how I'd stabbed Cal with a shard of glass and then fled.

'You stabbed him?' the detective repeats to me.

'Yes,' I say. 'And I hit him with that bottle when he came at me again. But he was fine. When I left, he was fine.'

I'm advised to phone my lawyer.

Karla answers on the second ring.

'You know when I met you, you said you specialised in criminal law,' I say.

She inhales, sharply.

'Where are you, Erin?'

'I'm standing in my apartment. I'm about to be brought to the ninth precinct. I think I'm going to be arrested.'

'For what?'

I hesitate.

Across from me, I see a detective studying the blood on the breakfast counter. I've been made to stand perfectly still. They won't let me move in case I contaminate any more evidence.

'For murder,' I tell Karla.

Now

There's been a delay in proceedings this morning.

Karla sent the message down to the cells but I haven't seen her. I don't know what she's doing.

She's organised a surprise for me, though.

It's ten days until Christmas. I guess this is her gift.

The friendly guard who takes care of me in the holding cell brings her down.

Gloria.

She's aged terribly in the last year and a half. Her hair is fully grey and her face is tired and worn.

She can't take any more.

But she takes one look at me and puts her arms around me.

'I'm sorry,' I say.

She pulls back.

'I told you once before and I'm telling you again, *you* have nothing to apologise for.'

'If I'd left it alone, you would never have had to know what Danny did.'

'I needed to know,' Gloria protests, weakly. This is hard for her.

As hard as it was for me. 'He did a bad thing. I didn't raise him to lie. I did not raise him to help hurt people. I'm ashamed of what he did.'

I swallow.

I've gone through all this in my own head.

And made peace with it.

Danny did wrong.

It wasn't all his fault. His greatest sin was cowardice; there was no malicious intent. It's like Leslie said. He was capable of mistakes but not of true badness.

And he was trying to make things right.

How do you weigh a marriage?

If I keep an account of our relationship, the good column far outweighs the bad. His failings happened before he met me. And I keep repeating to myself the words Ben left me with. He wanted to be a better man because of me.

A few months after we met, a week after Danny proposed, we were at a carnival together. We walked through it, eating cotton candy and drinking beers, going on thrill rides he claimed made him nauseous but that I couldn't get enough of.

Later, we walked past the small kids' section and a little girl tripped over my foot in her excitement to get to the merry-go-round. Danny picked her up with such gentle strength my heart skipped a beat.

He'd taken my hand then and whispered, *one day*.

Maybe one day we'd have had our own little baby.

The truly awful result of all this coming out is that the case the All-Sides Project took up looks set to see Dwayne Miller freed. Ben told me he believed Danny *had* lost his shit with Miller, but he's also absolutely convinced that man did murder the college student. Ben reckoned Danny couldn't bear the thought of another man walking away from a crime he'd committed, so he'd beaten the confession out of him. Danny had beaten Miller to salve his own guilty conscience.

But who'll believe Danny's convictions can be trusted now?

Because of me, everybody who's been in court for the last couple of weeks knows exactly what my husband did for Cal Hawley.

'I wish I could go to the cemetery to see his name inscribed,' I tell Gloria. 'You know, I never went.'

This makes me cry, for some reason.

For a long time, I thought I'd spend my whole life with Danny Ryan.

And when he died, I never even laid a flower for him.

'Danny is up in heaven, right now, because good people like you loved him,' Gloria says, and I think of the inner strength it must take for her to say that.

We sit quietly, holding hands, and wait for as long as the guard will let us.

'What are they doing upstairs?' I ask.

Gloria shrugs.

'I don't know, child. I saw a lot of running around. With that *man*.' She's referring to Ben. Gloria has heaped a disproportionate amount of blame on Ben's shoulders because – well, I guess because he's not her son and he's still alive – but also because she believes Ben knows more and isn't saying. She's right – she just doesn't know it's because I'm shielding him.

Ben was attempting to protect his family, sure, but he was also trying to protect me, as fucked up as it sounds. We've all suffered enough. He lost his best friend. And he has been trying to make it up to me ever since my arrest.

I know, if I had asked him to help me hide Cal's body, he would have agreed in a heartbeat.

It was that willingness to come to my aid, even so late in the day, that made up my mind for me.

'He came to the court with your pal Bud and met your attorney and there's been some hullabaloo,' Gloria says. 'She asked for one of them – what did Mike call it? – a sidebar or something. They've gone into the judge's chambers.'

I feel a sizzle of excitement in the pit of my stomach and I try to bury it.

Everything that could go wrong has gone wrong in the last few months – starting with Cal being able to get out of my apartment and go into hiding.

Even I've started to think it's easier for the justice system to convict you without a body than with one. If I'd killed Cal and claimed self-defence in my own home, I would have stood a chance of walking or receiving a bye on a manslaughter charge.

But they say I killed him and then disposed of his body and that's where the problem lies.

That's premeditation and wilful obstruction of justice.

Karla appears as though summoned.

Her face is flushed.

Her eyes are sparkling.

Ben and Bud made me one promise, all those months ago.

They would find Cal Hawley.

You can't be charged with murder if the person you killed is found alive.

'They have him?' I ask Karla.

She shakes her head, and I panic.

'No,' she says. 'But what they have is good enough.'

I try to figure out what they have.

I know for a fact Cal hasn't used credit cards or been caught on public CCTV. Ben and Bud have searched extensively for all of those things over the last few months.

'Bud traced the car that was outside your apartment,' Karla says, 'and found the driver. I don't know how he got him to talk, but he did. The car was one of Henry Hawley's.'

'And?'

'Ben got a warrant issued for the Hawley estate,' Karla says.

'How?'

'Drugs. Lana Hawley has been buying illegal batches of prescription drugs.'

'What?'

Karla nods.

'It was such a left-field move, Hawley Sr. didn't see it coming. He threw a fit but couldn't react fast enough. Ben seized the security cameras. Before they could be claimed back, he spotted Cal on them. They should have been wiped but I guess Hawley Sr. figured his private estate was safe.'

'Tell me he hasn't been hiding out there the whole time?' My face drains of colour at the thought that, while I've been in jail, Cal has been holed up in East Hampton.

'No,' she says. 'But he went there the night you fought with him. He's caught on camera, his father treating his wounds. The footage is time-stamped and dated. And now we have the driver willing to go on record to say he drove Cal to the Hawleys that night. He'd been paid off – but he's got more to lose if he doesn't give a statement on your behalf.'

Gloria gets to her feet slowly beside me.

'What does this mean?' I say, too scared to breathe.

'It means the judge has to declare a mistrial,' Karla says. 'Cal was alive when he left your apartment.'

This time, when my legs buckle, I've two strong women to hold me up.

I'd already made the decision before I was arrested.

I love Long Island. I love New York. My job, my friends.

But I swore, if I got through all this, I'd go home.

I've no work lined up in Ireland. I don't even have anywhere to live, so I'll be staying with Tanya.

I never spoke in person with Lauren's family but I got a short note from her mother, thanking me for exposing what happened and expressing her appreciation for how hard all this must have been for me, particularly after what happened to my own sister. I got something similar from Ally Summers, who has returned to Harvard and intends to resume her life after what must have felt like a very long hiatus.

I'm sitting at the gate in JFK terminal, waiting for my flight to be called.

I had planned to kill Cal Hawley in my apartment that night.

That's the truth.

I never told Ben, but after I got Cal off me and I reached for the nearest item I could find – which happened to be an unopened bottle of wine – I hit him far more than once.

I hit Cal on the head.

I kept hitting him, even when he was unconscious.

He *should* have died.

Nobody was more shocked than I was when we returned to the apartment that night and Cal was gone.

I think about him sometimes; wonder where he is now.

I imagine he's moved out west somewhere. He liked Vegas; maybe he's in Nevada. He's probably grown a beard. Perhaps he doesn't wear expensive suits so much now. He might dress down, so as not to draw attention. Maybe he goes into the casinos some nights and thinks about me.

His father has been charged with perjury, but he'll buy his way out of it. Henry Hawley dines with the most powerful politicians in New York.

Cal's mother was charged with purchasing illegal prescription drugs, but that was dealt with before a summons was even issued.

There's a warrant out for Cal's arrest in relation to an alleged attack on Lauren Gregory in December 2016.

It'll never be executed, even if he could be found.

All I know is, if I ever encounter him again, I won't leave until I know for sure he's finished.

Bud sits down beside me and hands me a cup of coffee.

He claims he's only accompanying me because he wants to see Ireland once and for all, that he needs to lend greater authenticity to his Irish bar and silence the naysayers.

In reality, Bud is making sure I get home safe.

'I tried to get them to make an Irish one but they've no vodka in Starbucks,' he says.

'Bud.' I sigh. 'They don't put vodka in Irish coffees. They use whiskey.'

He frowns.

'I'm not sure you're right about that,' he says.

I can't help it.

I laugh.

Then my expression turns serious again.

'What's on your mind?' he asks.

I shrug.

'Not much.'

There's lots on my mind.

Including the goodbye I said to Ben this morning.

Before I left, I asked Ben how Cal had managed to plant details of the bank statements and email exchanges on Danny's computer – especially as Ben told me nobody could access the servers from outside the department and nobody had used the computer bar Danny.

Ben said he had no idea.

I have an idea.

I think Cal used somebody within the department to do it.

I think he used somebody who would have known Danny's password and had access to the computer.

I think he used Ben.

I'd gone to get Ben that night because I knew he'd help me dispose of that body.

He owed me.

He'll never know that.

But I've stopped judging Ben for what he did to Danny.

Now that I know what I'm capable of myself.

Acknowledgments

As always, my deepest thanks to my editor Stef, my teams at Quercus and Hachette Ireland, and my agent Nicola.

Absolute gratitude to the maker of tea, the sounding board for messy plots, the proposer of ideas (including the worst titles) and the finder of proofing errors, my husband Martin. In fact, he wrote that last sentence himself. Or at least tried to.

This book was edited and prepped over the first coronavirus lockdown, when my four children were home from school and with us every day in our tiny house, so a massive thank you to WiFi, Xbox, TikTok, Fortnite and Roblox (and my darlings for coping admirably with the whole thing).

Finally, my humble appreciation to you, the reader, for finding and reading my books.

Something inspired this novel outside my usual plot and character thought process. I wrote it before Covid but even then, I couldn't get out of my head how difficult it must be to live abroad when tragedy strikes. While I know many people happily make their home in other lands, so many Irish have had no choice in that regard. In almost every generation, economic and social crises have resulted in the empty chair at the dinner table, half a team on the GAA pitch, scenes of tearful reunions in Dublin airport at Christmas time, and the recent phenomenon of Skype calls where grandparents meet grandchildren for the first time. And during Covid, the inability to travel compounded that distance.

So, this book, which features a young woman who must cope with the worst thing while living abroad, is dedicated to all those, but especially the Irish diaspora, who were far from home when Covid entered our lives.

Author's Note

While many of the locations referenced in this novel are real places, the town and geography of Newport is a product of my imagination. Likewise, the division of the police force I've created on Long Island does not exist. Harvard is described using some actual references, but the course mentioned and all references to teaching staff and students are fictional.